3-8/22

Acclaim for

WOLF SOLDIER

"*Wolf Soldier* does not disappoint! Hannibal delivers an action-packed quest through a world of fantastical creatures and unexpected friendships. A journey of faith and freedom from start to finish and an epic beginning to the Lightraider Academy series!"

— LAUREN H. BRANDENBURG, award-winning author of *The Death of Mungo Blackwell*

"From the gorgeous world-building to the delightful characters and surprising plot twists, *Wolf Soldier* thoroughly captivated me. James R. Hannibal has crafted a remarkable adventure that is sure to sweep readers away."

— LINDSAY A. FRANKLIN, award-winning author of *The Story Peddler*

"James R. Hannibal creates superb stories. His imagination and creativity are literally out of this world . . . Exciting and suspenseful reading!"

— DICK WULF, creator of *DragonRaid*

Wolf Soldier

WOLF SOLDIER

LIGHTRAIDER ACADEMY | BOOK ONE

JAMES R. HANNIBAL

Wolf Soldier

Published by Enclave Publishing, an imprint of Third Day Books, LLC

Phoenix, Arizona, USA.
www.enclavepublishing.com

ISBN: 978-1-62184-195-1 (printed hardback)
ISBN: 978-1-62184-197-5 (printed softcover)
ISBN: 978-1-62184-196-8 (ebook)

Cover design by Emilie Haney, www.EAHCreative.com
Typesetting by Jamie Foley, www.JamieFoley.com

Printed in the United States of America.

For Dick Wulf.

From all of us who fell in love with the world you created.

From all those whose lives you touched for His glory.

Thank you.

Ras Telesar
Forest of Believing
Mer Nimbar
The Gathering
Watchman's Gate
Ravencrest
DAYSPRING FOREST
Red Willow Hill
The Anamturus
Stonyvale
Pleasanton
Keledev

Tanelethar
Fortress of Vorax
HIGHLAND FOREST
The Southland Road
Trader's Knoll
The Southland Road
Maiderwood Grove
Ashbarrow
Spider Rock

FOREWORD

THERE IS A LOT OF EVIL IN THIS WORLD AND WE NEED to fight it. What you are about to read is a fantastic story. But, if you understand the deeper truths hidden in *Wolf Soldier,* you can become a lightraider in the real world–complete with the real supernatural spiritual power of the Holy Spirit.

For example, in *Wolf Soldier,* the characters are protected by a supernatural shield when fighting goblins and orcs. In this real world, I have been protected by such a shield of faith. One example of many was when I was trapped in a room with no way of escape by eight of the most dangerous prisoners in the maximum security prison at Fort Leavenworth, Kansas discussing how they might kill me and get away with it. But God saw me through with His protection. I could give you many more real-life examples, and I am sure that James R. Hannibal could also. So, ask yourself to look for the secret to this protection from evil when you read *Wolf Soldier.* From where or whom does real power and protection come?

The lightraider world is also about togetherness and teamwork. So much in our culture tells us to pursue being a hero alone. Learn in this story how very wrong that can be. So much more can be done to battle evil by small groups of people working together as a team. Note how each character in *Wolf Soldier* needs the others. Then, determine to face life with others to deal with trouble and evil.

In 1983 when I invented the game *DragonRaid,* upon which

the world of this story is based, I wanted to develop strong, brave, and courageous soldiers to fight evil. In addition to reading this story, you might want to gather a few friends and play that game or new games from Lightraider Academy. Over the years *DragonRaid* has transformed many players into soldiers of the cross in one way or the other. It would take pages and pages for me to tell you all of those stories.

I am thrilled to have given *DragonRaid* and its world and allegorical ideas to James R. Hannibal. He will carry Lightraider Academy forward and see that more and more people are becoming lightraiders in real life.

Read *Wolf Soldier* and then join us in making this world a better place by facing down and defeating evil.

Dick Wulf

PROLOGUE

A JAGGED BLOCK SHEERED FROM THE GRANITE WALL and split in two at Malid's feet, inches from his claws. He paused in his work to hiss at the underling beside him, flecks of spittle escaping between yellowed fangs. "If we should delve deep enough to reach the white core, Cousin Gorid, take care not to touch it. Yes, take care. Take care." The goblin mine boss set his pickaxe down and thrust a gray-green hand into the lantern's glow, showing off a mottled scar. "It burns."

Malid's crew hauled away debris behind him and shored up the passage. They'd channeled a good deal south from the northern foot of the monstrous peaks. Most feared to tunnel there, afraid the unnatural mountains might come crashing down on them. But Malid's crew feared his wrath more than cave-ins.

Seeing his chief resting, Gorid upended his pickaxe and leaned a pair of wiry forearms on the handle. "The dragons will be pleased with us, Cousin. Yes. Pleased. Pleased, indeed. No one has come this far before. No one."

Weak, Gorid was, and lazy–a sniveling toadstool-kisser.

"Who told you to stop working?" Malid kicked the axe handle and sent his cousin tumbling to the ground. "Now pick yourself up and get to it. Get to it!" He added a second kick for good measure, letting his claws stab into the smaller goblin's fungal flesh.

The others laughed.

Gorid recovered his pickaxe and swung with new fervor at the solid black granite. Each strike bounced off with a disappointing *clink*.

"Useless cur!" Malid let the rage, the black fire of his people, surge. He spun Gorid by the shoulders and shoved him against the wall. "Useless, useless!"

The cackles of his crew fed his frenzy, and Malid pounded Gorid's skull against the rock. "Perhaps . . . if you used . . . your head . . . cousin."

With a *crunch* of brittleknit bone and a *crack* of granite, a chunk of wall broke loose and slipped away. White stone glistened behind.

A thunderclap sounded within the mountain.

A crewman snorted. "It worked. Using his head worked."

"Shut up, you. Shut up. Be quiet." Malid let Gorid slump to the floor and stared at the exposed face.

The core.

He crept forward, stepping upon his groaning relative to get a closer look. The white stone had always been as smooth as polished glass. No tool of goblin or dragon design could ever mar it. Yet a web of spidery cracks sparkled in the lantern's flicker. This little patch of the Southern Overlord's impossible barrier looked as fragile as eggshells.

He swung his pickaxe. The fragile shell chipped. Malid swung again, and then again and again. Sparks flew. White dust surrounded him. The tough, fibrous skin of his face and arms sizzled. Gorid screamed at his feet. Then fragments exploded from the patch in a sudden torrent of cold air.

Pain.

Agony, yet not from the burning. Malid feared his head might burst. He dropped his axe and doubled over, clawing at his temples.

"Boss?"

"I'm fine." His voice. Not his voice.

"But boss, your skin is burning–burning still."

Malid struck the worried crewman across the mouth with

the back of his hand. "I'm fine. Fine, I say." The pain in his flesh was welcome fuel for his rage, and the pain within his skull had fled as quickly as it came, leaving him stronger than ever before. Stronger. Yes. Wiser. Malid knew things. Ages of understanding poured into his mind. He couldn't shut it out. He didn't want to.

All settled to silence, save for Gorid's dying moans. Malid's attack had hewn a hole the size of an oak mocktree's knobby head through the white core, joining his mine to some ancient tunnel dug from the other side. The torrent of wind had dropped to a mere breeze, and the air carried with it a foul smell that hadn't affronted Malid's nostrils for decades. No. Not Malid's nostrils. The memory was not his. It belonged to the ancient spirit filling his mind, and the ancient spirit knew that stink–the unmistakable stench of the Keledan.

PART ONE

BREACH

"Pay careful attention, then, to how you walk–not as unwise people but as wise–making the best use of the time, because the days are evil."

Ephesians 5:15–16

1

"SEVENTEEN, EIGHTEEN." CONNOR ENARIAN SAT ON the low stone wall of a hillside pasture, letting his tehpa's sheep brush against his crook as they passed through the gate, out into the road for the drive home. The hunters of the southern forests and the farmers of the central plains counted sheep as a cure for wakefulness, or so he'd heard. Yet the Enarians and the other hill folk had managed to make a living of it. Connor counted forty-eight sheep four times a day, give or take.

"Twenty-five, twenty-six." He didn't bother watching. He merely felt the bump of each ewe waddling by. They knew the routine. Nor did he watch the flock waiting in the road, baaing and bleating in a mindless chorus he'd long since learned to ignore. Connor kept his gaze fixed north. The winds were picking up high in the Celestial Peaks, and he didn't want to miss the spectacle.

Evening. The best part of Connor's day, and not only because the scent of a dozen dinners wafted up from the village. More than the scent of bread and pork, he loved the view.

Icy swirls blew among the countless summits of the Celestial Peaks, colored red by a sun about to fade. Before the next tick of Stonyvale's fountain clock, the perpetual storm hanging to the Western Sea would hide its fire. Together, the peaks and the Storm Mists formed the Rescuer's barrier, a giant wall defining the edges of Connor's world. There were points beyond. But the Keledan no longer ventured there. The Assembly had forbidden it.

Connor's tehpa–his *father* in the high-mannered diction of the coastal cities–agreed with them. Often, Tehpa had warned Connor about the horrors north of the barrier, evils no Keledan need ever face. His stories were enough to wither all but the lightest fantasies of daring adventure a shepherd boy might harbor in his heart.

"Forty-seven, forty . . . *eight*." Connor's crook clacked against the stone wall. He poked around with the butt of it, still mesmerized by the mountain swirls. "Forty . . . *eight*," he said again, as if repeating the number would make a ewe magically appear. The crook stabbed empty air. He blinked and glanced down. No ewe.

Connor looked to the flock waiting in the road. They stared at him, bleating out a collective *I told you so*. He counted them again. Forty-seven.

Not once in the eight years since his tehpa first bestowed on him the dubious honor of grazing the flock had he lost a sheep. How could this happen? The sheep weren't clever enough to breach the trees at the top of the pasture. More than one wolf pack lived in Dayspring Forest, and autumn was their season, but they rarely ventured into the light to disturb the flocks. Connor swallowed. *Rarely*.

"Stay." He pointed his crook at the flock as he hopped down and closed the gate. "All of you." He raced up the hill and blew a shrill note on the reed whistle hanging from his neck. No ewe came running. Down below, the rams bucked at the gate, trying to obey the call. Using the whistle again risked putting them into a frenzy, but Connor couldn't go home to Tehpa shorthanded. He drew another breath.

A wilting cry from the boulders at the forest's edge stopped him. Connor knew the boulders well. He often passed the long ticks of the day running up their sides to reach the tops or leaping from one to the other. There were no drops or sharp edges between them to hurt a ewe—no narrow gaps where she might get stuck. He slipped a stone into his sling and shielded his eyes against the setting sun. "Ho!" he shouted, as Tehpa had taught him, lest he catch a feeding wolf unaware. "Ho!"

He felt ridiculous.

A second cry led him to a shadowed hollow in the largest boulder. Before his eyes adjusted, his head smacked against a low-hanging shelf.

The ewe bleated at him.

"You think this is funny?"

He said it to calm his own nerves. Far from laughing, the ewe cowered in the hollow, trembling. Connor rubbed his aching head and frowned. Sheep had no imagination. They didn't conjure up predators where none existed. Something real—wolf or otherwise—had terrified this ewe. With a troubled sigh, he gathered her into his arms and carried her out into the failing light.

"Oi! Connor Enarian!" A booming voice rolled up the hill. Barnabas Botloff waved to him from the thickly padded seat of a wagon filled with bundles and burlap bags, a half-eaten loaf in his hand, his reins in the other. "Are you plannin' to move this flock along, or shall I return to Pleasanton to spend the night?" The parcelman showed no real sign of impatience. His horse, however, gave Connor and the ewe a look that could peel the paint off a barn door.

"Something spooked her." Connor set the ewe down and nudged her through the gate.

"Wolf?"

"Don't think so. No tracks."

"Hawk, then. Owl?" Barnabas squeezed each question out around a mouthful of bread. "Owls're mean. Ask our ravens. They'll tell you."

The ewe took her place among the flock, and Connor worked his crook to press his rearguard into a loose formation. He wanted no stragglers during the drive home. "That'd have to be one big owl to go after a full-grown ewe."

"'Tis possible." Barnabas patted his round belly. "I m'self have tackled a good many giant birds in my day."

"Those were geese, Barnabas."

"*And* a few turkeys."

The horse turned its great head and gave them both a wet, pointed snort.

"What?" Barnabas leaned out and patted the horse's rump. "You in a hurry, Clarence?"

A pair of big brown horse eyes shifted dolefully to the loaf of bread.

Barnabas winked at Connor. "We'd better get his majesty to the inn for some oats, or I'll never hear the end of it. He's haulin' quite a load–wood and apples from Dayspring Forest and smelted iron from the mines at Huckleheim." He set the reins in his lap and struck a flame to his lantern. The warm yellow light grew between them. "Thank the High One I only bring the iron downhill and not up, or Clarence'd quit me for sure. He'd plop down in his stall at Ravencrest and ne'er get up again."

With a short blast from Connor's whistle, the rams started forward. Clarence ambled behind the flock, wagon wheels creaking under the weight of his load. Connor fell in step beside the cart. "Speaking of Ravencrest . . ."

He let the name hang in the air. The mountain outpost might have dwindled in recent years, but messenger birds from the south still flew to its towers, to Glimwick the ravenmaster. At times, those messages found their way to the parcelman's ear. Connor pressed him. "I haven't seen you in weeks. You must have a story to tell."

"Oh, but I do. *You* are the story, my young friend."

A lagging sheep bumped into Connor's knees. He stumbled and caught himself with his crook. "Me?"

"Sure." Barnabas twisted over his big belly to reach into the cart. "Every wool waver and egg pusher in the five vales wants to know what it's all about. But the old man's not sayin' a word." He drew a rolled parchment from within his vest, sealed with blue wax. A scrawl of black ink–Connor's own name–caught the lantern light and gleamed in burnt orange.

The star seal pressed into the wax told him little. Many in Keledev used the Rescuer's birthmark for seals and signatures–either that or a blacksmith's hammer. The letter could be from anyone. He took it with an unsteady hand. "But who would send a letter to me?"

"Who would–" Bread flew from the parcelman's mouth in an explosive guffaw. Clarence shook the half-chewed pieces from his mane and glowered at Connor as if the indignity were his fault. "The proper question," Barnabas said once he'd recovered, "is why haven't you answered any of the *other* letters?"

2

CONNOR SAT ON A SPLIT-LOG BENCH IN THE HEARTH room of his family's cottage. The unbelievable letter lay open beside him. *Cottage* was Mehma's word. *Grotto, cave,* or *hole* fit better. The dwellings of Stonyvale had been dug from the valley walls—caverns of refuge, centuries old and dressed with homey facades by families who'd never moved on after the dragon war ended.

He rested his chin on his knees and lifted his eyes upward to the painting over the fire. Faelin Enarian, the patehpa Connor never knew, stood defiant on the canvas, a young man in dark blue steel etched with gold scrollwork, a great silver wolf at his hip. Connor had never fully worked out the wolf's tameness or wildness. At times, he detected a smile in the curl of its lip. At others, he saw the beginnings of a snarl.

Faelin's hand rested lightly on a tall sword slung at his side, partially covering the deep purple jewel in its pommel—a starlot, forged in a crucible of ice and dragon fire on the day the Celestial Peaks came to be. Starlots were the tokens of those who had crossed the barrier. They were the tokens of the Lightraider Order. Or so Connor had heard. The Lightraider Order, like his patehpa, was no more.

Over the last two generations, the Keledan had huddled down in the peace and safety of their land, none daring to defy the Assembly's command—until now.

Biting his lip, Connor raised the letter to read it once more.

Connor Enarian of Stonyvale,
Greetings and Blessings to You,

Four birds have I sent since high summer, and four birds have returned to Glimwick the ravenmaster bringing no reply. I must admit I am aghast at your rudeness. Yet I hold out hope for some justification, as you are Faelin Enarian's grandson.

At worst, you are dead, and so this rudeness might be forgiven. At best, my letters have gone astray. This is what the Helper has pressed upon my heart. Thus, I am sending this final notice in the care of our parcelman Barnabas. After this, I am afraid there can be no further letters. There is no time. The harvest is nearly upon us.

As stated in the other messages, I am pleased to inform you that Lightraider Academy is opening its gates after remaining empty these many years. The Order will be restored. You, as one among twenty potentials, have been chosen for the inaugural class, should you pass the entry trial. The Order once called it the Initiate's Quest, but that was long ago. For now, let us just say you will be tested.

Look for me at Ravencrest on the first night of the harvest moons. At dawn on the morning after, we begin our climb to the fortress. Pray do not be late. Once the company departs for Ras Telesar, no potentials may join us. Doors do not remain open forever. That is the way of things.

In the Rescuer's Mighty Name,

Avner Jairun
Last and Latest Headmaster
Lightraider Academy

Connor dropped the letter onto the bench and returned his gaze to the painting. Faelin would have raced off to Ravencrest. Connor could easily do the same. Tehpa and Mehma were in the birthing stall catching a new lamb. That very moment, he could steal a bite from the cupboards, take the family mare, and slip away. The letter spurred his dreams for a life beyond counting sheep.

The letter also dredged up nightmares born of Tehpa's dark stories, and the nightmares overpowered the dreams. So, Connor sat there, unable to move.

The cottage door swung open. A breeze tousled Connor's brown hair as Mehma hurried past with her water pail. Behind her, Tehpa lingered at the threshold. He tossed his birthing apron in the corner. "You didn't stay for the birthing, boy. I feared we might come in and find you ill." He forced a laugh. "And here I find you reading, of all things."

Connor did not have patience for Tehpa's roundabout manner—not this evening. "Why, Father?" he asked, using the formal diction to show him the graveness of his mood. "Why would you hide this from me? What right did you have?"

"I had every right." Tehpa stepped between Connor and the hearth. "My sehna, *my son*, far from having a house of his own, is receiving ravens? I am your tehpa who loves you. Those letters rightfully came to me first, and I disposed of them for your protection."

"Do you mean protection from ravens or from a life beyond these caves?"

"A life?" Tehpa let out a sharp laugh. "Where? In Tanelethar? The Dragon Lands? The Assembly closed the academy for good reason. The Order's raids brought death to their knights and pain to our people—our family. Faelin, your patehpa, gave up his life for folly. And the headmaster at Ras Telesar sped him on his way."

"Avner Jairun is a great man."

"Avner Jairun is a senile old crackpot hiding in the hills." Tehpa snatched the letter from Connor's hand and shook it at him. "Are you so eager to face the darkness, boy?"

Connor glared at him for another heartbeat, then dropped his gaze to the rushes lining the floor.

"I didn't think so."

A loud *thock* interrupted their argument. Two halves of a lettuce head fell apart, split by Mehma's cleaver. "Calm yourself, Edwin," she said with a stern look he'd never have suffered from anyone else. "Connor only wants to–"

"This is a fool's quest, Mara." He turned to the hearth, crumpling the letter in his fist. "Even if Avner had license from the Assembly to open those gates, I'd not let Connor go. I gave my father for the Order's cause. I will not give my son!" He cast the parchment into the fire and stormed away.

Connor watched the letter burn and blacken. The wax seal lingered. For an instant, the star shined bright blue, then melted away.

3

CONNOR SAT STRAIGHT UP IN BED, ROUSED BY A CRY. HE saw nothing in the black of his windowless room, another consequence of making a home from a cave. As the fog of sleep lifted, he realized the cry might have been his own—a scream within a nightmare. Sweat drenched his nightshirt, now cold and clinging to his skin. He gathered his wool blanket about his shoulders and tried to recall his dreams.

Supper had been silent, and Tehpa's evening prayers short. Connor had drifted off to sleep listening to harsh whispers in the other room. Listening had given way to dreaming, and dreaming sent him back to the night's argument. In the dream Tehpa yelled at him before a blazing hearth twice its usual size, with Patehpa's wolf glowering down from the painting.

For the second time, Connor watched the letter burn.

For the second time, he felt an unsettling sense of relief.

In the dream, it had not been the star seal that shamed him, but Patehpa's wolf, snarling with disappointment. Connor's voiceless thoughts pleaded with the beast. He wanted to go, but the letter had made the shadows of terrifying creatures from half-remembered stories real. And as the crumpled parchment unfurled in the fire, ribbons of red snaking along the edges, those shadows poured out like smoke. Fangs and claws threatened to claim him as they'd claimed his patehpa. Monsters surged from the hearth. The wolf howled, diving into the fray.

Connor shuddered. That must have been the moment he cried out and woke.

He settled back, but before his head touched the sack of straw serving as his pillow, he heard a desperate bleating. A ewe was in pain.

It hadn't been Connor's own voice that woke him from the nightmare after all. He'd better deal with the wounded animals before Tehpa woke. What had those sheep done to themselves this time?

Outside, a stiff wind blew down the vale, wet with dew, chilling him to the bone. Connor hurried barefoot across the sheep pen–still dark in the night's first watch. The bright moons Phanos and Tsapha had not yet risen, and the shadow moon Molunos was little more than an empty void among the stars.

Across the pen, the door to the cave serving as the family barn creaked open and banged shut again. Tehpa must have forgotten to drop the latch after the birthing. Perhaps a ewe had wandered halfway out and been caught by its swing.

Connor ducked into the barn and dragged the door closed behind him, wind whistling through its slats. He pulled an iron lantern down from the wall and struck a light. No wool on the door. No blood. If a ewe had been hit, it got away clean. He straightened, turning to face the flock, and had to stifle a dismayed cry.

The sheep pressed themselves against the backs of their stalls, trembling the way the ewe had trembled when he found her in the hollow. At the barn's center, at the edge of the scattered light shining through the star holes punched in the lamp's shielded walls, lay a pair of sheep, side by side. A pool of blood soaked the straw beneath them, seeping from many wounds.

This was no wolf or bear attack. The cuts were long and straight, and widely spread. Connor knew the slice of a knife when he saw one. The sheep were still bleeding out. The killer had slit their throats last, cutting on the bodies while they were still alive.

The door banged. Connor whipped around. "Who's there?"

No one answered. Slowly, he lifted his crook from the wall and held its curved end to his chest like a shield. He'd left his sling by his bed. No good to him there. The door creaked open again with the wind. Hadn't he latched it?

The cottage door stood open too. He heard Mehma scream.

4

THE FLAME IN THE OLD IRON LANTERN GUTTERED TO barely a spark as Connor raced toward the cottage. He burst through the door. "Mehma?"

"I'm here, Connor. Stay back!"

The fire was dead, the hearth room all but black. As the flame in the lantern recovered, Connor saw her. He saw them both.

Mehma cowered in the corner next to her shelves of cookware, holding an iron pot like a sword. Before her stood a foul creature–short and hunched with fungus ulcers growing like cave mushrooms from its hide. It wielded a curved knife as long as its arm. The creature turned halfway round and glared at him with yellow eyes, disproportionately large for its skull. "Hello, shaggycap," it said in a squeaky voice. "Come to play, did you? Did you, now? One more step and I'll gut her."

Connor remembered the old stories well enough to know what stood before him. The ulcers, the loose-woven hide like stinkhorn net. This was a goblin.

Impossible.

Or had Connor's nightmare been real? Had a monster truly climbed out of the burning letter?

Mehma advanced from her corner, pot held high. Without taking its eyes off Connor, the goblin lowered the knife to her midsection to back her away. "M'lady is so impatient. Yes, she is. But don't worry, shaggycap. Don't worry. I'll see to you next, to be sure, to be sure." With a tittering laugh, the goblin turned and prepared to disembowel its victim.

Connor raised his crook, ready to swing.

"Leave her alone!" Tehpa barreled in from the hall, nightshirt flying behind him, wielding a sword Connor thought had been lost forever–a sword with a deep purple starlot in its pommel. The goblin hissed and raised its knife to deflect the strike. Tehpa slammed into its body and the two rolled to the floor.

Whether by accident or skill, the goblin wound up on top, still in command of the knife. It swung the weapon down in a vicious arc.

"Tehpa!" Connor started toward them, expecting to see the knife slice into the arm Tehpa had raised to defend himself. A white flash knocked the blade off its mark. The ghostly form of a warrior's shield lingered, then vanished.

Connor stopped in mid-step. "Tehpa?"

"Stay back, boy. You don't know how to fight a dragon corruption!"

Enraged by the resistance, the creature swung its knife again. Once more, the shield flashed, but this time Tehpa grunted in pain. The goblin cackled and rained down blow after blow, each one getting closer and closer to bare skin, until, in desperation, Tehpa made a weakened counterblow with his sword.

A sweep of the goblin's long knife sent the sword skittering across the floor. The creature raised its blade high for a killing blow.

"No!" Connor lurched in to thrust his crook at the goblin's head.

The creature merely jerked its face back. The crook sailed past its nostrils and stayed there, awkwardly extended. The goblin cocked its head and sneered. "I told you to wait your turn, shaggycap. Wait your turn, I said." It didn't seem to notice the ram's-horn hook hanging just below its knife hand.

Connor twisted the crook to catch the wrist and yanked with

all his might. The goblin yelped. The blade flew from its grasp. It bared its claws and charged.

A wild swing of the lantern connected full force with the goblin's head, and the iron crumpled. The light went out. The creature shrieked with rage.

"Run, Connor!" Tehpa shouted from the shadows. Connor could hear him scrambling to his feet. "Take your mehma and run!"

There was a scuffle.

An angry hiss.

A pained shout from Tehpa.

In the midst of it all, Connor ran to get Mehma, but he tripped and fell. When he rolled over beside her, he saw the faint glow of two yellow eyes. He heard Tehpa, distant, much weaker than before. "Run, Connor."

The eyes inched closer. "Do you feel the fear, young Keledan? Do you? Do you? Is it all that you dreamed?"

Connor raised one arm to protect Mehma as he scrambled back against the wall. His other hand came to rest on cold steel. He had no doubt as to what he'd found. But when he tried to pick up his patehpa's sword, the edge bit into his hand. Connor gasped and let it drop to the rushes. Blood trickled down his palm.

A hideous laugh.

Fangs flying toward him.

He fumbled to find the hilt, hampered by the slipperiness of his own blood, and snatched it up to brace the jeweled pommel against his stomach. The blade slid into the goblin's throat.

5

ALL REMAINED DARK AND SILENT FOR SEVERAL heartbeats. Connor felt Mehma's arms about his shoulders. He felt the tremor of her sobs. Sword and goblin fell to the side as one. "Mehma?"

"I'm all right. The corruption didn't touch me."

They helped one another to their feet, and Connor found a candle on the shelves. As he struck the light, he heard a groan. Tehpa was sitting against the wall, one hand gripping his shoulder. Blood soaked his nightshirt.

Connor rushed to his side.

"It hurts." Tehpa gritted his teeth as Connor eased his hand away from the wound. "It hurts like a hundred wasp stings." The flesh above his collarbone was torn and ragged, black with blood. "You'd think a creature made of fungus would have softer teeth."

Mehma appeared beside them, apron on, moving with purpose. She set the night's water pail and a bowl of herbs next to her husband and dabbed at the wound.

With each touch of the rag, Tehpa winced. He fixed his eyes on Connor. "I told you to get her out of here. But you wanted to play the hero. You wanted to be Faelin."

"No, I–"

"Ignore him." Mehma cut off Connor's reply. "Get me another light."

He nodded and retreated to the cupboard to find a lantern.

Tehpa's voice chased after him. "They hunt in packs, you

know. This isn't ov–" He sucked in a sharp breath as Mehma pressed the rag into his wound.

"Quiet, you," she said. "Let us work."

By the time Connor returned with the light, Mehma had cleared away most of the excess blood. Holding the lantern close, he saw the deep puncture wounds from the creature's fangs, oozing blood. Veins visible through the skin darkened and spidered outward. "Infection is setting in. I should wake the physician."

"Stay." Mehma caught his wrist with a wet hand. "Rash action will do us little good here."

"But, Mehma–"

Tehpa's hand flopped at him. "Hush, boy. Your mehma told you to hush. He never was an intelligent child, was he, Mara?"

Mehma slapped a fresh rag, covered in herbs, over the wound. "I told *you* to hush, as well. Now hold that in place while I go make a proper dressing."

Connor followed her to the bedchamber and watched her throw her favorite dress across the bed. "What are you doing?"

"Making a proper dressing, as I said."

"That's a dress, Mehma, not a dressing. Let me ride to Pleasanton. Tehpa needs the physician. I can have him here before the next watch, less than two ticks."

She cut the hem with a kitchen knife and tore away a strip of linen to wrap the cut on Connor's hand. He'd quite forgotten about it. "Mehma, the doctor."

"Put your clothes on–your cloak too. Then go hitch the horse to the cart. Pack food and water for two days' journey." She tied off the bandage and returned to tearing her dress into narrow strips of pink and blue flowers. "The broken flesh must wait. There is deeper damage done."

Connor began to wonder if panic had stolen her good sense. "I won't need the cart or food. The ride to Pleasanton is short."

"Pleasanton is not your goal. You must ride all the way to Ravencrest, fast as you can. Get your tehpa to Avner Jairun before he heads up into the mountains."

"Master Jairun?" Connor lowered his voice to a whisper and glanced down the hall. "The man Tehpa called a senile old crackpot? He'll never–"

"Give him no choice. Senile or not, Avner is a guardian and a renewer, trained in the healing arts."

They were going in circles while the infection set in. Connor had seen the same spidering veins on a ewe that caught her leg on a rusty nail. They'd found her too late, and Tehpa had put her down to end her suffering.

He tried being firm. "We have a healer *here,* Mehma, in the hill country. *Let me get him.*"

"Good. Excellent. You'll have to be just as confident and strong on the road." Mehma raked her hands across the bed, gathering up her flowered strips, then looked her son in the eye. "A village healer's herbs and bloodletting will not rid your tehpa of this poison. He needs a renewer, a man who has walked the world beyond the peaks–one who has waded through the black effluence of a thousand dragon corruptions and survived." She stepped around Connor and headed for the hall. "Your tehpa needs a lightraider."

6

CONNOR CRINGED AT EVERY BUMP IN THE ROAD AND every grunt and moan from the wool-covered heap in his cart. He had the mare up to a trot, the fastest he dared. Tehpa lay in the back, grumbling in delirium, thanks to Mehma's sleeping draught.

Lifting Tehpa into the cart had been a trial, but they'd managed it. Mehma had covered him with blankets then disappeared into the house for a moment and returned with the sword, wiped clean and sheathed in an ornate scabbard of black leather.

"This is Faelin's sword," Connor had said as she helped him strap it to his belt. "Isn't it? Why did Tehpa keep it hidden?"

"You know why. Now go. Every moment counts."

Connor hesitated when he passed the physician's house at Pleasanton, on the River Anamturas, beneath the largest clock tower in the five vales. The big waterwheel had filled all the smaller vessels in the tower's face–the twelve ticks of the day. And it had filled the first of the four larger vessels representing the four night watches. Each of those ticks and watches would be filled once more and half again before Connor's journey brought him to Ravencrest and Master Jairun. Could Tehpa wait that long?

He drove on–only because he'd promised Mehma–and turned north onto the river bridge to join the Rising Road. The trees of Dayspring Forest loomed ahead, with ragged clouds gathering above them in the foothills. The air smelled like rain.

"Perfect."

The first large drops spattered on the gravel mere seconds

before Dayspring swallowed the cart. Broad-limbed trees spread their canopies over the edges of road. Connor shifted the cart to take cover beneath them, crunching chestnuts under hoof and wheel. He patted the mare's neck. "See, girl? Nothing to worry about."

Thunder cracked in the foothills. An acrid, metallic taste filled the air.

The mare whinnied her disagreement.

"It's just a little lightning. Far away. Be thankful the rain is light."

Within minutes, the patter became a pound and stirred the gravel to a slurry of mud. The gutters became rivers. The overhanging branches offered no protection at all. The horse whinnied in earnest, calling him a liar outright.

"Sorry, girl," he said, reining her to a stop. "Take a rest. I need to check on Tehpa."

The wool blankets would not stay dry for long. As Connor added the few waxed skins he'd brought, Tehpa sputtered against the rain. "I'm all wet, boy. All wet. What's happening?"

"I'm taking you to a healer." Connor withheld the name. Better to save that argument for the journey's end. He pressed Tehpa's hand down to hold a skin in place. His fingers were hot. Fever was setting in. "Melima says rest slows an infection. Go—"

A rustling came from the trees, loud enough to be heard over the rain. A rabbit burrowing under the brush to escape the rain? Connor swallowed. "Go back to sleep, Tehpa."

"But . . . the goblins . . ."

"The goblin is dead. Sleep. Please. We need to drive on. The storm is moving south. The faster we head north, the faster it'll pass."

"No, boy." Tehpa's eyes popped open, and he grabbed Connor's wrist. "Remember what I told you. Remember." Lightning flashed, revealing two silhouettes on the road behind. Connor heard cackles within the fading thunder. Tehpa's grip went slack. "They hunt in packs."

7

MUD FLEW BEHIND THE MARE'S GALLOPING HOOVES, thudding against the cart bench. The hill ahead was more waterfall than road, but Connor cracked the reins to drive her harder. She dug into the slope, steady and strong, then faltered.

The mare's legs buckled. The hitch splintered and cracked, throwing Connor to the wash at the road's center. His whole world became grit and the taste of mud as he crawled, clawing and slipping through the flow, unable to gain a foothold. The mare suffered the same problem, thrashing against the broken hitch.

Giving up on trying to stand, he crawled on hands and knees to the cart's wreckage and dragged his tehpa free, still asleep thanks to the herbal draught. He saw no wounds other than the goblin bite. Connor propped him against a knoll that peeked above the underbrush. "Stay put," he said, as if Tehpa might run off. "I have to get the mare up soon or we're done for."

Using the brush and trees for support, he made it to his feet, then crossed the wash to the horse.

She was no help at all.

When Connor tried to lift the hitch pole from her side, the mare kicked the crossbar and sent him flying to land with a *splat* onto his ruined pack and blankets. He let out a frustrated shout and rolled over in the mud. As he pressed himself to his knees, a shadow fell across his vision.

Steel rang. By the High One's grace, Connor found his feet. He leapt up with Faelin's sword leveled.

A hooded form reeled back, splashing. "Hey. Watch it!"

Not a goblin. A girl.

The rain had settled, and in the moonlight breaking through the waning clouds, Connor saw a young woman about his own age, red hair tucked into the hood of her traveling cloak. She stared cross-eyed at the blade. "I try to help you, and this is your thanks?"

Connor let the tip slap down between his feet. "I thought you were a goblin."

A second traveler came up beside the girl, towing two geldings by their bridles. "A *goblin*. He's mad, Teegs. Leave him be, or we'll never reach Ravencrest in time."

The girl glared at the speaker and introduced herself as Teegan. She helped Connor with the mare and in gathering the muddy remains of his supplies. They transferred what they could to the saddlebags of the two geldings.

The young man turned out to be her twin, Tiran, who did nothing to help, but interrupted often while Teegan explained their purpose on the road. "We left four days past, not three, Shessa. If you're going to tell him our business, get it right."

"Four days since we left, Brehna. But only three *on the road*."

"What sort of measure is that? Do you only count the ticks by the time you spend on a horse's back?"

"I measure ticks by the time I must spend listening to your prattle."

They went on and on.

The twins, Connor gleaned from their bickering, had traveled from Sil Tymest, a forest village on the southern coast, as potentials for Lightraider Academy. They had spent an extra night in Pleasanton, and so they'd risked traveling in the storm to keep their pace. During the deluge, they'd watched Connor take off at a mad pace and wreck his cart. His subsequent proclamation that Teegan might be a goblin solidified the appearance of lunacy.

"A wolf attacked your tehpa," Teegan said in a tone usually reserved for little children and very old men. She eyed Tehpa, who still slept against the knoll. "Yes. A wolf. Not a goblin. Autumn is season of the packs, after all. And they'll eat the rest of him if we leave him there bleeding too long. We must find the road." She pushed a final, dirty sausage into the mare's saddlebags, picked up her lantern, and wandered off into the forest.

"But . . . we're standing on the road," Connor said to Tiran, who didn't bother to respond.

Soon, all he could see of Teegan was her lantern, bobbing up and down. "The marker must be here somewhere."

"What marker? What road?"

Tiran left Connor's side to fuss with the horses' tackle. "One that'd offer us a shorter path, but one she'll never find." He finished tightening a billet strap, then cupped a hand to his mouth and shouted. "Mehma told us those stories years ago, Teegs. Face it. The Old Road is gone, claimed by the trees."

The light continued bobbing, ignoring him. Tiran let out a breath through his nose. "We wouldn't be in this mess if you hadn't insisted on delaying in Pleasanton."

"Aethia wasn't well." The light drew close to the road again, and the girl poked her head out through a curtain of vines, holding the lantern close to her freckled face. "She needed the rest."

"And she got it. Now we're late."

Aethia? Connor didn't ask. "We should be on our way."

"Worried about the wolves?" Tiran answered him with a smirk. "Or is it your goblins?"

"Believe what you will. I heard something in the forest. Either way, I must get my tehpa to Ravencrest before dawn on the morrow next."

"The morrow next? Either you've underestimated your road or overestimated your horse. By the Rising Road, Ravencrest is still two days' ride. My shessa, in her folly, has been counting on a more direct route." He raised his voice again. "Give it up, Teegs. The Old Road is lost, either to myth or forest."

"How strange, then"–Teegan waved the lantern–"that I should be standing at its gate."

Getting to the small clearing she'd found was no easy task. When Connor finally emerged from the brush, pulling the mare and supporting his wounded tehpa, he found Tiran squatting with Teegan's lantern, running his hand through the leaves.

"I don't scc these markers of yours, Shessa."

"Because you're searching in the wrong place, Brehna. Look up, not down."

He straightened. "You could have told me."

"You didn't ask."

"I just did."

"And I just told you. See how that works?"

"Hey!" Connor faltered for an instant, struggling to keep Tehpa upright. "Could we?"

Tiran shot him a glare, then nodded to his twin. "All right. I'm looking up, but I don't–" His light fell upon an aging tree, catching a swirling lattice of blue jewels embedded in the trunk. Higher up, each thread of jewels followed a branch and spread apart into sparkling droplets of sapphire–a living sculpture of a fountain.

Teegan turned Tiran by the shoulders. "Over there, as well."

The jewels set into the second tree were amber, set in the shape of licking flames. Dozens more shined down from the branches like embers rising from a fire.

"The fountain and the flame," Connor said.

Teegan gave him a surprised look. "That's right–the oldest symbols of the Maker, from before the dragon scourge. Few Keledan remember them. These once marked the southern edge of Dayspring. A small corps of lightraiders called the Knights of the Way maintained the forest for years until the Assembly disbanded the Order."

Tiran touched one of the blue jewels. “Lightraiders made these?”

“Did I say that?” She swatted his hand away. “These jewels were set by more ancient hands, those with the deep understanding of creation only endless life can bring.”

Tiran dropped the lantern to his side. “Gems pounded into wood are not proof the Elder Folk walked here. Nor are they proof the Old Road still exists. I see no path, only a wall of ivy and brush.”

“Hmm. A wall of ivy.” Teegan cocked her head, sending a red braid flouncing to one side. “And there you are with a sword on your hip. What *should* you do with it?”

Between his sword and her knife, the two cleared the ivy in minutes. The remnants hung from slender trees, wound together into columns and bent so their leafy branches intertwined. Beyond these, a long hallway of similar arches stretched away into the dark.

8

CONNOR SAT BEHIND THE SADDLE OF TEEGAN'S gelding, trying to hold Tehpa upright. She'd traded mounts with him, remarking that she doubted the mare could handle two riders after the fall. After steadying Connor, she mounted the mare in one effortless swing and let out a hard, shrill whistle. A falcon, snow white and flecked with silver, alighted on a leather guard strapped to her forearm. It rotated its head nearly all the way round and regarded Connor with black eyes.

The shock of the whistle had nearly unseated him. "Aethia, I presume," Connor said, shifting once more into a stable position.

Tiran laughed. He urged his gelding into the arch of trees. "You should have seen your face, Goblin Slayer."

Teegan coaxed her mare onto the path behind her twin. "I'm sorry I startled you with my call, Connor. Aethia likes to move about in the treetops, and sometimes she roams far away to keep an eye on things."

Things? From what Connor saw, the falcon was keeping an eye on *him*, and nothing else. Her backward head remained oddly level despite the mare's sway. He did his best to look anywhere but at the bird directly in front of him. He found her steady black-eyed gaze unsettling.

The overgrowth had not encroached upon the hall beneath the tree arches. It did, however, close the passage off to the surrounding forest. The air smelled stale. The only light came from the lantern hitched to Teegan's saddle, illuminating long steps of soil and rock carrying them ever upward into the highlands. "In the elder days, green grass carpeted the whole forest," she said, turning in her seat to look back at him. "The trees were well spaced for hunting and travel. In daylight, you could see the stretch of this hall from miles away. And at night . . ." She gave him a wistful smile. "Well, in the Elder Tongue they called it *Vy Asterlas*."

"The Path of Starlight." Connor knew small pieces of the founders' language, mostly from memorizing sacred verses for Resteram but also from the tales and poems Mehma favored. His translation earned a pleasant nod from the girl. He looked up at the arches. "But there is no starlight here. Even in those days, without the ivy, the branches would have blocked out the sky."

"The sky had nothing to do with it." Teegan thrust her arm in front of her, and the falcon shot away, curving nimbly past Tiran's shoulder and sailing up the tunnel of trees. A ripple of blue-green raced after her–twinkling stars hanging from vines and hovering in the air.

"Star beetles." Connor reached for the closest light. It zipped away. "There are none at the forest's edge where our pastures lie."

"Too bad. Sil Tymest is filled with them. They like the mist." Teegan whistled her shrill tone, and the falcon returned to its perch, taking a sliver of dried meat from her fingers. It swallowed the morsel whole before swiveling its head to chuff and chortle at the lights.

Teegan stroked her feathers. "Aethia doesn't approve of star beetles. They flash at the first sign of a predator, giving her away to the rabbits and field mice. Mehma used to say star beetles were one of many counterweights the Maker built into creation, to keep the falcons from getting fat and the rabbits from becoming scarce."

"Your mehma sounds wise."

"She was." Teegan's smile faded, and she lapsed into silence.

The star beetles soon faded as well. The watches passed, and night gave way to the gray of dawn, and the hall broke into fragments of dead tree stumps and half columns. The long, rocky steps climbed ever northward, interrupted on occasion by the Rising Road as it meandered slowly east and west.

Tehpa woke on occasion, but not fully. He mumbled and groaned, but the fever kept his mind from breaking the surface of consciousness. At times, he kicked at Connor's shins. At others, he shook with tittering giggles. This kept up until night fell again. Connor's legs burned from holding his bareback position. "How long, Teegan?"

"We'll see Ravencrest soon. Before dawn, I assure you."

Dawn. Four watches away. Connor sighed, twisting left and right in a futile attempt to stretch one leg at a time. A good distance behind, he saw the star beetles were at it again, the ripple of their blue light racing to catch up. What had Teegan said about Aethia's contempt for the bugs?

They flash at the first sign of a predator.

"Teegan. The star beetles. Something's coming."

9

"FASTER, TIRAN." TEEGAN SLAPPED THE TWO GELDINGS to force them into a gallop and spurred the mare to follow. "We *must* go faster." The three horses broke through a curtain of vines onto an open hilltop with a giant willow at the center. Its leaves were blood red, nearly black in the starlight.

Tiran reached the tree first and wheeled his horse to face the others, jerking a vine from its mane. "Enough. This is pointless. There are no goblins south of the peaks, and no Dayspring wolves would dare attack three riders at once. Anyway, we've reached Red Willow Hill, the last rise before the cliffs. We're almost there."

"Cliffs?" asked Connor, catching up. "What cliffs?"

Tiran merely pointed over his shoulder.

Clouds broke, allowing the two bright moons to spread their light over a sheer rock wall, a jagged break in the landscape. The Anamturas poured over the cliffs and plummeted down into the forest beyond the hill. Short towers held a three-story inn suspended over the falls. Connor had never laid eyes on the outpost before, but he knew it by sight from the parcelman's tales. "Ravencrest."

"Built in the days after the barrier rose." Teegan nodded to the northwest. "The Rising Road approaches there–a gentle slope. But our road takes us straight north to the cliff stairs. Before this watch is ended, we'll reach the top."

"And safety, I hope," Connor added. "From whatever pursues us."

Tiran gave him a look of pure distain. "Oh, please. Haven't

we–" A thin black shape sailed past, inches from his nose. Another struck the ground short of his horse. The gelding reared.

"Arrows!" Teegan yelled, snapping her reins. The falcon launched itself from her arm, and she turned in the saddle. "Aethia, no!"

Tiran recovered control and spurred his gelding. "Leave her!"

With the added weight of his tehpa, it took Connor a moment longer than the others to get his horse moving. But the gelding still had more power than his little farm mare. He grabbed the mare's bridle as he passed, pulling Teegan along. "Your brehna's right. Leave the bird!"

The two horses surged forward together. The falcon let out a shrill cry behind, diving out of the heights. Something answered with an angry shriek.

Teegan glanced back. "She's fighting them."

"Then we owe her a debt but not aid. Keep going."

They hit the trees on the hill's downslope with Tiran in the lead. In seconds, the trail narrowed. Connor reined the gelding to force Teegan ahead. She frowned, parting her lips as if to complain, and let out a startled cry instead. The mare went down.

Tiran's gelding went down too, and Connor tried desperately to keep his own mount from running them over. He needn't have worried. An arrow sank into the gelding's shoulder, and it crumbled. Both Connor and Tehpa tumbled into space. Connor hit the ground and skidded through mud and rock, pain jarring his torso. The horses lay all around, whinnying in pain.

Teegan appeared, half crawling, cradling her arm. Blood glistened from a gash on her forehead. "Are you wounded?"

"No more than you." That might not have been true. Connor's side screamed with every breath, and his neck burned. "Tehpa, where are you?"

An answering groan rose from the brush. Connor and Teegan found their patient behind the dying horses. His eyes were open, a touch of yellow in the irises. "They have us. And now they'll want to play."

Tiran came running down the trail at a crouch. "That thing *wanted* us to run. It drove us into an ambush."

A light *twang* sounded from the forest.

Teegan yanked him down, and an arrow split his red hair. A second missile struck the gelding she lay behind with a sickening *thump*. The horse, drained of its fight, let out a pitiful whine. "Stop it!" she cried, pounding the mud with her fist.

The goblins tittered in the shadows.

Connor gripped his patehpa's sword and looked to Tiran, who laid his own sword across his chest. Tiran might not be the best of company on the road, but Connor was glad to have him there for a fight. He clearly knew how to handle a blade–far better than a shepherd.

He pushed up to an elbow.

Teegan held him fast. "Wait. Listen."

The laughing stopped. The goblins shouted to one another in some shrill distortion of the Common Tongue. Hooves thundered on the path ahead. Connor peered over the dying mare and saw a massive charger barreling down the trail, a cart bouncing behind it. A hood shrouded the driver's face.

Arrows flew. The driver steered his horse and let the cart skip sideways to take the missiles broadside. It rocked to a stop, and he slapped the wood. "What are you waiting for? Get in!"

Needing no further prompting, Connor and the twins dragged Tehpa into the cart and scrunched down on either side of him. The driver cracked the reins. He showed no fear. Much to the contrary, he muttered to himself the whole time, as if a pack of goblins were merely an annoyance. One arrow arced directly toward the man, then veered off to the trees in a flash of ghostly red. As the last of the arrows fell behind, a pair of unseen creatures crashed and cracked through the underbrush, heading toward the threat.

Soon the charger slowed to a canter. The pounding of its hooves on dirt became the clopping of horseshoes on stone, and the cart went up and over a bridge. The cliffs and the roaring falls came into view above the cart's wooden walls. They stopped. An elderly face appeared above Connor–steel-gray eyes and a weathered but cleanshaven face. "Having a lie down are we? A little rest? Get up! Move!"

Once they had Connor's tehpa on his feet, the driver led them past the stairs to a railed wooden platform, suspended by ropes from a series of pulleys. He waved an impatient hand at Tiran and Connor. "Pull away, boys. A lift won't lift itself."

Both boys obediently grabbed the main rope and tugged, hand over hand, pulling the rig up the cliff face. "What about Connor's goblins?" Tiran asked between heavy breaths. "Won't we be exposed to their arrows once we're above the trees?"

As if in answer to his question, a series of shrieks erupted from the trail. The driver shook his head. "Those particular goblins will never trouble another soul."

Raising the lift was no easy task, made harder by the wet rope. Or was it some sort of grease? Connor quit pulling long enough for a look at a hand and found it deep red in the moonlight.

Blood. Where had it all come from? The red fingers blurred together, turned sideways. "I . . . I think . . ." He couldn't complete the thought. He saw the weathered face, the moons, the falls, then nothing more.

10

CONNOR WOKE COUGHING, CHOKED BY A TONGUE AS thick and dry as wool. Daylight shined through linen curtains. He was lying on a bed, unable to remember how he got there, wearing nothing but his wool britches and a linen wrapping at his midsection.

Struggling to a sitting position, he saw Tehpa on a bed across the room, rolled on his side to protect the bad shoulder.

"Don't wake him," a voice said. "He needs his rest."

An elderly man sat on a stool in the corner, long legs crossed at the ankle, hands behind his head. Connor pulled the wool blanket to his waist. "You're . . . the driver."

The old man bobbled his head side to side, sitting up. "Among other things. I keep the inn here with Glimwick–the Black Feather, it's called. I saw your lanterns on Red Willow Hill, and so I was halfway down the cliffs to meet you when I heard the horses scream." He leaned against a staff, grunting with the effort of standing. "By the Rescuer's grace, I had already prepared a cart for your coming, else I might not have reached you in time."

"You prepared for our coming?"

"Well, of course I did. I summoned you, didn't I? Besides, your mother sent me a raven."

Connor's eyes widened. "You're Master Jairun. But you said you were an innkeeper."

"An aging schoolmaster must do *something* with his final years. Although, now the Rescuer has called me from retirement,

I'll have to pass those duties on to someone else." He raised a pair of bushy eyebrows. "How do you feel about young Barnabas? He'll do, I think, although I'm not sure his horse is up to the challenge." He crossed the room with surprising quickness, hardly using the staff, and pushed Connor's head down to fuss with his neck.

"Ow! What's wrong with you!"

Connor snapped his mouth shut. How had such harsh and disrespectful words escaped his lips? He cleared his throat and tried again. "I mean, what happened to my neck?"

"You don't know? I see. That would explain why you kept pulling on the lift hoist despite your wound. You failed to grasp its severity." Master Jairun finished unraveling blood-soaked strips of linen and laid them on the bed. "I mistook this ignorance for bravery. Happens all the time in battle."

"What wound?"

"A goblin arrow sliced your neck. A deep cut. You lost a lot of blood. I let you sleep for a day and a half so the flesh might begin to mend. Now hush a moment. Let a man work."

Pain shot down Connor's spine as Master Jairun laid a hand directly on the cut. "*Ond mecheth mi pesha'enu, ond brueth ma av'enu. Ala ethmod kecastig shalomenu, po bulcothrod medicethi'anu.*"

A few of his words, spoken in the founders' language, appeared unbidden in Connor's mind. *Crushed. Wounded. Healed.* A coolness seeped into the wound. "You cast a spell?"

"A spell?" Master Jairun began wrapping the wound with fresh linens. "What kind of nonsense are the vale clerics teaching these days?"

"But Mehma said you were a–"

"A guardian, yes. A renewer of some skill too, I don't mind saying. But not a sorcerer." He crinkled his nose in distaste. "What I spoke was a prayer, child–a sacred verse–the very words of the High One spoken back to him in supplication." Master Jairun folded his hands in his lap, leaning left and right to appraise his handiwork. "Unlike foolish spells, prayer depends upon the High One's will and power, not our own."

"Yes. Fine. Right. But that . . . connection . . . is why Mehma sent us to you, isn't it?"

"Yes and no. Mara hoped I could deal with the poison in your father's blood." He poured steaming water from a kettle into a stoneware cup, looking at Connor sideways. "The same poison that has now infected you."

"Poison?" The sting in Connor's neck sharpened. The arrow. A goblin arrow.

"Yes. Now you see. And seeing makes all the difference. Now. I assume your cleric taught you the two greatest commandments. I'd like you to recite them for me."

Connor paled. A dark arrow had poisoned him, and this old man wanted him to recite from the Scrolls? "Why should–"

"Recite them!"

The command reverberated in Connor's chest. He dropped the defiance from his expression. "You shall love–"

"In the Elder Tongue, please, my boy. It forces you to think harder about what you're saying."

Connor had to reach deep into memories of Resteram evenings with Mehma to pull up the words. *Love. Heart. Soul. Neighbor.* As soon as he recognized the verse, he understood what he'd done. "*Rumosh* . . . um . . . *avah'iov bi* . . . *koth lavechovu ba koth anverovu bo koth se* . . . *cherovu. Po pelorovu avah'iov ovuneh.*"

"Good. Mostly. And you know what those verses mean, do you?"

"Yes." Connor lowered his eyes. "I do."

"These are not mere words, child–phrases to memorize and recite. Loving the High One. Loving our neighbor. We are to live that out as citizens of this kingdom. Do you understand?"

"I understand the commands. I understand my harsh words just now were wrong, and I'm sorry for them. But"–Connor lifted his eyes again–"I don't see how speaking or understanding an ancient verse will cure me."

Master Jairun returned to his work, adding a spoonful of green powder to the steaming cup he'd poured. "You and I are part body and part spirit. Goblin fungus corrupts both. Herbs heal the body, but the infection of your spirit demanded a deeper treatment."

"And this deeper treatment is counsel?" Connor found the idea difficult to swallow.

"Spiritual battle has much in common with physical battle. No one should face either alone. We are to carry one another's burdens. With counsel, we have laid bare the attack. Now you must allow the Helper within to join the fight. A regimen of prayer"–he tapped the spoon on the edge of the cup and set it aside–"and reconciliation should do the trick."

Connor allowed himself an embarrassed smile. "I'm sorry for the way I spoke to you."

"There you go. An excellent start." Master Jairun pressed the mug into Connor's hands and raised it to his lips to make him drink. "And don't worry about your father. I'll have him right as rain before you say your goodbyes on the last leg to the academy."

The academy? The bitter fluid pouring down his throat prevented Connor from protesting. He hadn't come as an academy potential. The herbs went to work quickly. Connor's head swam, and he had no choice but to lay back, letting Master Jairun draw the covers about his shoulders. *I only came for Tehpa's sake,* he tried to say. But the words never left his lips, drifting instead across his fading consciousness as the sunlit room dissolved into a white haze.

11

THE HAZE PARTED. THE PATCH OF LIGHT FROM THE window had shifted a good deal across the floor, and there was a long shadow within it. Someone stood behind Connor, having turned him on his side to get at the bandage on his neck.

"Master Jairun?"

"No."

Connor flipped over and came nose to nose with a young man his own age with deep-set eyes and jet-black hair, spiked with a fragrant red paste in the tradition of the western boatmasters. "You're a . . . a fisherman."

"Of course. All people from Lin Kelan are fishermen. Every single person." His visitor frowned at him. "I was a scribe, actually, in the Second Hall. My father gave me to the clerics as an apprentice a year before I reached the age of reckoning." The boy twisted a cobalt ring around a finger for a long moment, as if lost in thought, then met his eyes. "I am Lee Trang. Call me Lee."

Connor sat up, wincing. "And now you work here, for Master Jairun and Glimwick?"

"Don't be absurd." Lee turned him by the shoulders and tugged at the edges of the dressing. "Headmaster Jairun is letting me help with your care. I never dreamed I'd see battle wounds so soon, not to mention a goblin bite. The spacing between the fangs, the flesh torn by the forward teeth, it's all very intriguing."

"Headmaster Jairun." The formality of it stuck in Connor's foggy mind. Here was a fisher-scribe talking like an Assembly clerkmaster and performing medicine at a mountain outpost. "So, you're a potential. You got a letter too."

"Same as yours. I arrived a day early." The scribe finished his work and released him. "We're going to be lightraiders, you and I–brothers of the Order. Exciting, right?"

The longer Connor stayed at Ravencrest, the more he'd have to make excuses. He needed to get out of there, back to Stonyvale and his sheep. He wrung the blanket in his hands. "I can't go. Tehpa is injured. Mehma will need me."

"Oh." The air left the fisher-scribe's chest like water from a burst flask. "So few have come. And now we've lost our only goblin slayer?"

Connor had expected disdain, not disappointment. It had never occurred to him that the other potentials might be counting on him to answer the call. Who needed a shepherd in an order of warriors?

"Your clothes are on the chair," Lee said, turning for the door. "Supper's in one tick."

Supper. Connor felt the gnawing hunger left by a day and a half of starvation. But he had no desire to face the others over a meal. "I'd rather eat up here. Could you bring me something?"

"I told you. I don't work here. Headmaster Jairun says you eat downstairs or you don't eat at all." Lee walked out and slammed the door.

NEAR THE FIRST WATCH OF EVENING, CONNOR descended a mahogany stair, pausing halfway down to peer through the balusters. How many potentials would he have to face just to settle his growling stomach?

A steady, rhythmic ring filled the Black Feather's great room, accompanied by the crackling fire and the drone of the river passing under the floorboards. Tiran sat by the hearth, running a whetting stone down his blade. Lee sat across from him along with another potential, twice as big, with thick arms of deep brown and the tall boots of a Huckleheim miner. The miner had his nose buried in a leather-bound text. The scribe stared into the flames, twisting his cobalt ring.

Tehpa was also in the great room, arranging supplies for the journey home. But Connor had no desire to talk with him. Connor walked, or rather crept, to the nearest of the tall windows lining the southern wall. From there, he could see the great red willow on its hill, long delicate threads brushing the grass. The old tree bore an air of sadness.

"Our mehma told us the story." Teegan was gazing out another window not far away, as somber and solitary as the tree below. She'd been so still, Connor hadn't noticed her. "Of the red willow, I mean. Willows mostly grow in the lowlands, near water. But this one is special. You see, the land had to be broken before the Celestial Peaks could rise, like the Rescuer's body. It started here, forming the cliffs of Ravencrest. The High One wept to see it all, and the red willow bloomed where his tears fell."

Connor said nothing. His eyes dropped to the bandage peeking out beneath her sleeve, and the sight drew the pitiful whinnies of Teegan's gelding from his memory.

"Aethia would have adored that willow," she said.

The falcon. Aethia must not have survived. He'd never thought to ask.

"She would have made us wait half the night while she explored its branches, if not for . . ." Her voice faltered, and she dabbed her eyes.

Teegan's falcon. Her gelding. Both lost. Connor felt compelled to finish the accusation for her. "If not for the goblins following in my wake."

The dinner bell's discordant *clang* sounded behind them. Teegan walked away. Not once while they spoke had she looked at him.

12

A SILENT DINNER PROVED TOO MUCH TO HOPE FOR. Tiran saw to that. The mulled cider had not made it halfway round the table before he raised his voice above the clatter of stoneware. "What of Connor's goblins, Master Jairun? Are you certain they're dead?"

Connor flinched. Why must they be *his* goblins?

Master Jairun seemed to sense his discomfort. "They were not Connor's goblins any more than they were yours, Tiran Yar. Connor did not bring them through the barrier."

"But someone did." Lee sat at the far end, opposite the headmaster, pouring cider into his mug. "There are no passes over the peaks. No creature has ever successfully tunneled through. And cave goblins do not travel over water, even if they could pass the Storm Mists. So, did they stumble through a fold in the fabric of creation? Like one of the Passage Lakes? Would the Rescuer allow such a thing?"

The headmaster quieted him with a wave. "Such questions must wait. For now, we must be sure the woods harbor no more goblins, and we must send word to the vales."

"And who will clear the woods?" Connor asked as he reached for a platter of cheese. His fingers touched bare stone. Empty. All the remaining wedges had found their way to the miner's plate. Connor cast a sidelong glance at him and withdrew his hand. "Glimwick? Barnabas?"

"Despite what you may have heard, the Order still has knights posted at Ravencrest—older knights, but capable. I sent two to clear the forest and a third to warn the vales. And Glimwick sent ravens to the Seven Councils." Master Jairun set his mug down, dabbing cider from his upper lip and returning his gaze to Lee. "Investigating this breach is the Assembly's task, not ours."

The guardian glanced around at the others seated at the table. "Our task is more urgent. If dark creatures can cross the barrier, then the fires of Ras Telesar must be rekindled, and quickly. Our company has tested Glimwick's hospitality too long. We make for the fortress at first light."

"Our *company*?" Tiran banged his cup down, sloshing cider over the rim. "What company? How can we rebuild the Lightraider Order with only five?"

"Four." Master Jairun slapped a helping of bread pudding onto his plate. "Connor has refused the call, or so his father informs me. And a count of four presumes I'll allow the rest of you to stay after your trial at Ras Telesar. You are potentials, not initiates. Don't forget that in the days ahead."

Connor shot a hard look at Tehpa, who scowled at his own plate, refusing to meet his eyes. Connor had planned to refuse Master Jairun's invitation and had tried to do so before the medicine took him, but that did not give Tehpa the right to do it for him.

The headmaster's rebuke had silenced Tiran, but Lee took up the argument. "Four, then. Hardly a company. Shouldn't we wait here in hopes more will come?"

The old man sighed. "Many are called to the harvest, Mister Lee, but the laborers are few. Ever has it been so. We shall head out into the fields as the Rescuer commands and pray he sends others." He returned his eyes to his plate, though Connor caught him glancing his way.

Tehpa pushed back from the table. "I'll say goodnight, then. And thank you for your care. Like you, Connor and I will leave at first light."

"Of course you will. You're coming with us."

A spoonful of bread pudding hovered at Connor's lips. He looked from the old schoolmaster to his tehpa, waiting for the inevitable blast of anger.

Master Jairun took a bite of apple and spoke through the corner of his mouth. "Your treatment is incomplete, my boy. Did you think I would send you home half healed? Mara would never forgive me."

"She would. As is her duty. And she needs both me and Connor at home."

"Mara will keep. The fortress is only two days' ride."

"A day and a half," Lee said. "I studied Glimwick's map book all morning, and I–" The two older men glowered at him, and the scribe buried his eyes in his plate. "Never mind."

Master Jairun cleared his throat. "Edwin, if I'm satisfied with your healing by the time we reach Ras Telesar, I'll send you on your way."

"And if you're not satisfied?"

"Then you'll stay at my side until I am."

Tehpa let out a long breath and headed for the stairs. "We shall see what the morning brings."

No shouting. Not even a glare from the steps. How could Master Jairun hold such sway over his temperament?

When Connor lifted his plate and followed, the headmaster barred his way with his staff. "Stay. Your father needs rest, but you've slept long enough. Join the potentials in the eastern courtyard after the meal. Some fresh air would serve you well."

"The courtyard?" The big miner finally spoke, in a voice as deep as the fattest chapel bells, though he and Connor might be a year apart in age at most. He pushed his empty plate away and rested heavy elbows on the table. "What is it you have for us in the courtyard, Headmaster?"

"As I said, Dagram Kaivos, our task is urgent. We leave for the academy in the morning"–Master Jairun leaned on his staff to push himself up from his chair–"but your training begins tonight."

13

LODGE-HOUSES SURROUNDED THE COURTYARD ON three sides, with the roaring flow of the Anamturas bordering the fourth, held at bay by a stone wall. In the outpost's heyday, these might have housed twenty families or more, each connected in some way to the Order. That night, not one light burned in their windows.

Tiran and Dag–as the miner preferred to be called–had built a raging fire in the central pit. They warmed their hands with the others as Glimwick the ravenmaster tottered among them, balancing a platter of sweet biscuits. Dag downed a handful. Lee took only one, but a raven swooped in and snatched it from his hand before he could toss it into his mouth. A cacophony of crowing erupted from the eastern tower, drowning out his protest.

The ravenmaster bowed. "That's my cue. Dinnertime for my darlings." He set the biscuits down on a stone bench.

Lee reached for a second, but Master Jairun bopped his hand with the knot of his staff. "Train now. Sweets later." He pointed the staff at a pile of wooden swords called wasters not far from the fire. "Take one and line up."

Connor had seen other boys and girls spar with wasters in the square at Stonyvale on many cool evenings, but Tehpa never let him join in. He sat beside the biscuits and watched the potentials take their places.

"In time, we'll learn what weapons suit each of you," the headmaster said, standing between the potentials and the fire. "But the sword makes a good foundation for all. Now, up. Like this."

He showed them a proper grip and how to balance their weight as they moved. Teegan and Tiran looked well acquainted with it all. Dag and Lee did not. The miner held his sword like a pickaxe, and swung it just as heavily, while Lee held his weapon at arm's length, as if the rounded wooden edge might cut him.

After some time, Master Jairun seemed satisfied that all four had grasped enough of the basics to spar. He led Teegan over to the bench and sat her down with Connor. "The goblin fight left your wrist in no shape for sparring, my dear. You'll have to watch for now."

She still wouldn't look at Connor. He tried offering a smile, but his efforts were cut short when the headmaster yanked him to his feet–no comfort to his bruised ribs. The old man half guided, half pushed Connor to the others. "We need a fourth. You don't mind, do you?"

He set Connor before Lee and pressed a waster into his hands, then positioned Dag to face Tiran. "There is no substitute for sparring when quick learning is needed. We'll make a tournament of it. Disarm your opponent, convince him to yield, or bring him down. Those are the conditions for victory. Winners move to the second round." He raised his staff and dropped it between the two pairs. "Fight!"

Lee struck with surprising eagerness, hacking, stabbing, and glowering at Connor. "We'll see if you're truly the goblin slayer you claim to be."

Connor never claimed to be anything. He retreated in a flailing defense until the two wasters met. The impact knocked Lee's from his grasp. It spun to the stones and broke in two. The scribe couldn't have looked more betrayed if Connor had stabbed him in the back with a real sword.

Connor offered him his own waster hilt first. "Fight the next round with mine. I'm not even supposed to be here."

"You're right. You're not. You didn't deserve a letter." Lee strode off to join Teegan on the bench, tossing his broken pieces into the fire.

The match between Dag and Tiran lasted longer. Dag seemed loath to swing at the smaller boy, as if a single blow might split Tiran's head in two—as Connor imagined it would. The match became an undeserved punishment, with the miner rocking side to side while Tiran swatted him about the legs and shoulders. Dag finally raised his waster in surrender and withdrew.

"Connor," Master Jairun said, "you're up. Stand here with Tiran."

"But I'm not—"

"Nonsense, my boy. You're here. We might as well get some use out of you." The headmaster shoved him into place before Tiran and dropped his staff between them. "Fight!"

Connor felt the strike before he saw it, right in his sore ribs. Tiran had lunged, stabbing with enough force to drop him to his knees.

Tiran gave a shout of victory.

Master Jairun grumbled under his breath.

The match was over.

14

MASTER JAIRUN'S IDEA OF FIRST LIGHT DID NOT AGREE with Connor's—or the sun's. The old guardian had his troops up and on the road before the sun first colored the misty sea at the barrier's eastern extent. The company stretched out along the Anamturas in a column of twos. Lee rode at the front with the headmaster, with the twins behind them, and Dag took up the whole road behind those two.

Connor drifted to the rear with his tehpa where he belonged, behind the pack mules carrying the stores. He could not bear riding with the others. His ribs still carried the sting of Tiran's strike, reminding him his victory over the goblin had been a stroke of providence and nothing more. Connor had no place among the potentials. They, at least, had not quailed in the face of the call.

The Anamturas wound away from the road at times, but always returned, ever climbing toward its source high in the Celestial Peaks. When the morning haze burned away, the mountains appeared so close and so impossibly high Connor had to strain against the tightness of his neck's bandage to look up at them. The groves of red elms and yellow chestnuts thinned where the road steepened, relinquishing the higher ground to their evergreen cousins.

There had been no breakfast, and there was no stop for lunch. Dag mentioned this oversight to Master Jairun—the first words he'd spoken since Ravencrest.

"Yes," Tiran agreed, letting his horse lag along the gutter toward the mules and their bundles of bread and pork. "Shall we lighten the load for poor Amos and Berta?"

Without looking, the headmaster hooked the reins of Tiran's mount with the knot of his staff. "Those stores are not for the road. What do you suppose we'll find in the cupboards at Ras Telesar after two generations? Naught but a few humble spiders and the webs of their ancestors. Preserve what food we've brought–unless you're partial to eight-legged soup." Master Jairun patted a saddlebag at his knee. "Glimwick packed you each a pouch of dried fruits and oats. His family's special way rations have sustained many a lightraider on longer and darker roads than this. I daresay they're good enough for all of you."

Connor saw Dag's great shoulders slump and heard the miner's stomach growling over the crunch of hooves. The counsel Master Jairun had given him rose to his mind. *These are not mere words, child . . . Loving the High One. Loving our neighbor. We are to live that out as citizens of this kingdom*. He withdrew a narrow stick of sausage from his pack–one Tehpa had packed for the road south–and spurred his horse.

Tehpa grabbed Connor's saddle, but Connor inclined his head toward the hungry miner. He let Connor go.

The mules parted. Connor tapped Dag on the shoulder with the sausage, whispering, "You need it more than I do."

Dag accepted with a grateful nod, bit off a fifth, and tucked the rest into the saddlebag with his way rations.

The effort of moving up and down the column brought the soreness from Connor's previous ride back to his legs. He returned to his spot next to Tehpa. "He's driving us hard, isn't he?"

"He is. I expected your Master Jairun to shelter at Watchman's Gate tonight, but he's outpacing the sun. We'll reach the towers with far more daylight than we need."

"The towers?"

"A pair at the southern tip of Anvil Ridge, the largest ridge descending from the barrier, separated by perhaps a quarter of a league." Tehpa laid the reins across his lap and let his body sway with the horse. "One tower looks northwest up the Anamturas Valley to the Passage Lakes. The other looks northeast along the other side of Anvil Ridge, up the valley of the River Gathering to Ras Telesar."

"So, Watchman's Gate is a signal post."

"Correct." Tehpa cracked a smile, the first Connor had seen in days. "The towers serve as a link between the fireglasses at the Passage Lakes and Ras Telesar–one flash for raiders coming through the barrier, two if the party brought any rescued Aladoth with them." His pleasantness faded. "All too often there was no flash at all."

"But the Order did rescue some?"

"Precious few."

"But some, right?" Connor watched him, gauging how far he could press. "Which means the lightraiders did all those things people spoke of"–he leaned closer and lowered his voice–"things Patehpa showed you."

His efforts earned him a dark glance. "You speak of the shield that saved me from the goblin's knife."

Connor nodded.

Tehpa said nothing for a long while, then took up his reins again and sighed. "Ras Telesar had long been closed when I reached the age of reckoning. The remnant of the Order lived at Ravencrest, and I with them. I picked up a few things."

"But you never joined. What held you back?"

"Common sense, boy. I lived with the Order, but I stood with the Assembly. I said as much before your patehpa left on his last raid, with words harsher than I intended. He handed me that sword you carry and rode away."

Connor knew the ending that followed–like a sad opposite of

happily ever after. "And he never returned."

"No. He didn't. I waited for him. Oh, how I waited. I rode to Watchman's Gate every week–like a pilgrim rides to a tomb, until the Assembly sent the watchmen home and the fireglasses went cold. Afterward, I withdrew to the farm and accepted the truth. The Order's arrogance had robbed me of him."

The Order? In the muttered answers given during Connor's childhood, dark creatures or a dragon had taken Faelin, not the Order. "I don't understand. What arrogance?"

Tehpa lifted his eyes to the mountains. "The Order became mystics, Connor, every one of them. They believed they could discern the Rescuer's will." His tone sharpened. "Imagine believing a man can know his creator's mind. They were obsessed with the idea that the Rescuer needed their help against the dragons. Most paid for this obsession with their lives."

15

THE SUN STILL HUNG ABOVE THE WESTERN SEA WHEN Watchman's Gate came into view. The gray towers breached the pines in the distance. Their faceted crystal spheres, half hidden by copper shields, trapped the last ticks of daylight. One stood on the west slope of Anvil Ridge. The other marked the crossing ahead, where the road split to chase the two rivers–the Anamturas and its tributary, the Gathering.

At the bridge beneath the near tower, Master Jairun called for a dismount, though he gave no orders to make camp. Instead, he took Tehpa aside and set to work on his wound. Connor tried to join them, but the old man shooed him away, commanding Lee to tend to his neck.

"I think Master Jairun means to continue to the fortress," Lee said as he replaced Connor's bandage. "By moonrise, we'll make Ras Telesar, and *you*"–he pulled the wrapping uncomfortably tight–"can go back to your sheep."

Connor had apologized for disarming Lee in the waster tournament, but not for disappointing him. "Lee, I–"

"Get the horses watered," Master Jairun called. "All of you. And be quick about it. As soon as I'm done with my patient, we must be on our way."

The Gathering's rocky bank offered only a few scattered spaces where the horses could bend to the water. Connor soon found himself far upstream from the others, alone with Teegan. He did his best not to look at her, fidgeting with the tackle on the new mare he'd been assigned, until the echoing screech of a falcon drew his eyes skyward.

Teegan glanced up as well, stroking her new mount's flank. "I thought I knew Aethia's voice from all the others in the world. Yet now with each call I hear, I expect to see her."

"She was your mehma's, wasn't she? Before she was yours."

"How could you know that? I never told you–"

"You did." He kept her from speaking of her mehma's death. He didn't want her to say anything if she didn't want to. "Sort of."

The two lapsed into silence. Teegan returned her attention to her horse, checking its tack. After a time, she peered over the saddle. "I'm not angry, you know. I don't blame you."

The timbre of her voice told him neither statement was entirely true. He nodded dumbly and started for the road with his mare.

"Connor, wait." She stepped around her horse and walked straight up to him, coming so close she had to tilt her head to look up into his eyes.

He took an instinctive step back.

She followed, drawing close again.

"What are you doing?"

"Master Jairun will put you against my brehna the next time we train. Count on it. This is how you beat him." As she spoke, she stepped to the side, almost brushing his shoulder.

Connor turned to keep her at his front, taking another step back.

She closed the gap. "Press Tiran. Turn him as I just turned you. Stay inside his reach to spoil his attacks." Before he knew it, she was looking up into his face once more, her nose an inch from his chin. "You understand?"

He swallowed, unwilling to nod for fear of the impropriety that might result. "Yes."

Teegan walked away, taking up her gelding's bridle. "Good."

Teegan and Connor were the last to rejoin the company, and

Tiran gave his shessa a stern look.

No one said much for half a tick. The sun set behind the rising Anvil ridgeline, and the company marched up the valley of the Gathering. Master Jairun turned northwest along a small brook, heading into steeper terrain.

"But that's not the way." Lee lagged behind and pointed north up the broader road. "We should keep to the Gathering. The way to Ras Telesar follows the river."

"I was the headmaster of Lightraider Academy for a decade and a professor for nigh on three. Are you saying I don't know the path to my own school?"

"Respectfully, Headmaster, I saw Glimwick's maps. And if I saw them, I know them. This road will take us out of our way, up to the lake at Mer Nimbar."

Master Jairun urged his horse on up the trail beside the brook. "Glimwick's library is quite old. There is no lake at Mer Nimbar, my boy. Not anymore."

16

THE BROOK DWINDLED TO A TRICKLE AND disappeared into a ruined mine. Boulders and rotting timbers lay strewn about the hole with periwinkle growing in their shadows. Rusty tools lay beneath the burbling flow.

Above the mine, the trail joined a small road winding up from the west, and the climb steepened until Connor thought they might be covering more distance vertically than otherwise. The land this high on the stout legs of the Celestial Peaks was broken, disrupted as it had been at Ravencrest. Cliffs and stairways became the rule. The flattest stretches led them beneath giant rock arches or up long, rocky halls—caves that had sprung from the earth. At the end of one of these halls, Master Jairun called a halt.

Connor gathered with the rest at the tunnel's mouth. The full dark of night had taken hold, and he could see little but the start of a stone bridge over drifting fog. *Mer Nimbar.* He spoke it aloud in the Common Tongue. "The Lake of Clouds."

But, as Master Jairun had told the scribe, there was no lake.

"Single file on the bridge," he said. "I don't trust it as I used to."

Gray vapors drifted through utter darkness below. On the far side, peeking through the wandering gaps in the mist, were windows and doors cut into a high rock face. Those on a level with the road were wide enough to launch one large fishing vessel each, except they opened not to a lake, but oblivion.

Lee craned his neck, squinting at the empty windows.

"Where are the inhabitants?"

"Gone." The high rock walls trapped Master Jairun's soft reply, making it clear as a chime. "All of them, gone. The goat herders. The fishermen. They left when the lake drained. That water was their lifeblood."

"So, the lake drained to nothing when the peaks rose?" Tiran leaned out to peer over the rail. He drew back an instant later, gripping his reins tighter.

"Quite the opposite." Reaching the far end, Master Jairun guided his mount to the side of the bridge to make room for the rest of the column. "Our beloved Blacksmith brought forth new creations when he raised the peaks, like the Passage Lakes and the Storm Mists. Here, he opened a ravine and filled it with runoff. Fish multiplied in the deep water. Families of Keledan settled in, carving homes from the caves and terracing the ridge for their goats."

The mules finished their crossing, then Tehpa. Connor rode off the bridge last. "If our Blacksmith created it, then why did he drain it away?"

Tehpa answered before the headmaster could reply, directing a hard stare at Dag. "It was not our Blacksmith who drained the lake, boy. That achievement belongs to the miners of Huckleheim."

Dag turned his horse about and headed deeper into the fog.

Master Jairun wheeled his horse to follow, steel shoes clopping sharply on the pavers. "No more chatter. Time to set our minds on making camp. Get a fire going. The nights here bring a cold you lowlanders have never felt."

Lee, Connor, and Tiran gathered scrub from pastures north of the village. Each trip took them past a tall, menacing shadow near the courtyard's center, but none strayed closer to investigate. With the fuel they brought, Dag and Teegan built a hasty fire beside a long alcove, once a bay for the village merchants. The company sheltered there for the night.

The fire seemed to do nothing to fight the cold. Mist clung to Connor as he unpacked his bedroll, wet and frigid, soaking into his clothes. When all was set for the night, he huddled down under his blanket and willed the shivering to stop long enough for sleep to take him.

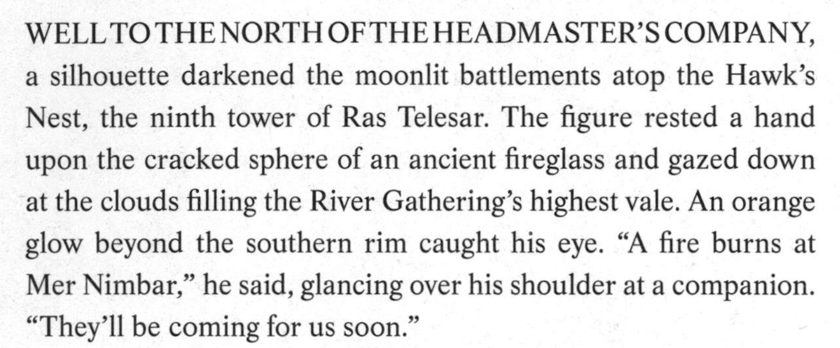

WELL TO THE NORTH OF THE HEADMASTER'S COMPANY, a silhouette darkened the moonlit battlements atop the Hawk's Nest, the ninth tower of Ras Telesar. The figure rested a hand upon the cracked sphere of an ancient fireglass and gazed down at the clouds filling the River Gathering's highest vale. An orange glow beyond the southern rim caught his eye. "A fire burns at Mer Nimbar," he said, glancing over his shoulder at a companion. "They'll be coming for us soon."

The other, larger and stouter than the first, drew a battle-axe from a sheath at his back and brandished its double blade. "Let 'em come, then. We're ready."

17

MORNING CAME LATE TO MER NIMBAR. THE RAVINE'S high walls sheltered it from the rising sun. Connor groaned at the ache in his bones.

Cleared of its nightly fog, the courtyard looked less dreary. The light revealed the menacing shadow from the night before to be a central fountain clock, the sixteen vessels of its ticks and watches empty and crumbling. Within this circle of dry vessels, the statue of an armored warrior spiraled up, transforming into a waterspout, palms raised to the heavens. Connor tilted his head, looking for Master Jairun on the other side.

"Master Jairun is not here." Lee sat glumly in the corner of the merchant bay, playing with his ring. His packed bedroll lay idle beside him. "I woke before dawn to saddle my horse, but he stopped me." The young scribe waved toward the northern gate. "Then he wandered off."

The others stirred. Dag rekindled the fire. Tehpa grumbled about the scarcity of its warmth, tossing a handful of way rations into his mouth. "It seems Avner intends to delay us further. I'd have preferred he held us prisoner at Ravencrest. Better to break our fast with bread and cheese beside Glimwick's hearth than chew cud on this frigid mountainside."

In the afternoon, the potentials practiced their swordplay, and Connor joined in, if only to work the soreness from his limbs. He let Teegan help him with his grip and stance, aware of Tehpa's watchful gaze. Lee dared to spar against Tiran, and Connor was relieved to see the scribe beaten almost as quickly as he. Lee had speed and agility but miserable aim. Tiran dodged his every strike and landed a half dozen blows before the scribe withdrew.

Not long after sunset, the clouds returned, as did Master Jairun. He lined his pupils up before the fire without offering an explanation for his absence. The light and heat of the flames cut the thickening mists, but only a little. Connor, cajoled once again by Master Jairun into training with the others, could barely make out Dag's huge form at the far end of the line.

As Teegan predicted, Master Jairun pitted Connor against her twin in the sparring, and Tiran opened with the same lunge as before. Connor dodged, shooting her a glance. She gave him a nod, and he used the opening to change his angle and step close.

The strategy worked. Tiran backed away. Connor swung twice, meeting defenses more desperate than calculated.

Tehpa stood up. Was there pride in his eyes? Connor couldn't afford a look away from the fight to be sure. His muscles tightened. He pressed harder, backing Tiran toward the bridge.

"Are you afraid of a wooden sword, Mister Yar?" Master Jairun stamped his staff on the pavers. "Stand your ground!"

Anger flashed in Tiran's eyes. He swept Connor's sword aside and shoved him away. A flurry of blows rattled Connor's waster, stinging his hand through the hilt, reversing his advance. Within seconds, Connor felt the fire's heat on his legs.

Lee jumped to his feet. "Look out!"

A fragment of paver gave beneath Connor's heel. He threw his sword arm out for balance. Tiran whacked his wrist, and the waster dropped into the flames.

Master Jairun pulled Connor away from the fire and flicked the waster from the embers with his staff. As he regained his feet, Connor's eyes fell on Tehpa. For a moment, a look of concern lingered. Then Tehpa dropped his hands and walked into the bay.

18

THE COMPANY REMAINED AT MER NIMBAR A SECOND day, and then a third and a fourth. Each morning, Connor woke to find Master Jairun gone and Lee disappointed. The headmaster returned in the afternoons, offering no explanations, walking straight to Connor's tehpa to tend his wounds and whisper counsel. By the third afternoon, Tehpa stopped grumbling, but he still kept mostly to himself.

Each morning and night, Lee tended Connor's cut, which healed nicely, and over the long ticks of waiting, the scribe's coldness faded. The hopeful inquisitiveness that marked their first meeting returned. To fill the time, he and Connor explored the chambers and stairwells leading to the open portals in the ravine wall. They found old pots and tables, a few old texts and journals. Lee read the texts as soon as he found them, but Connor declined. He didn't mind exploring, but he couldn't shake a quiet feeling of trespass.

"Your ring," he said while Lee thumbed through one of these journals. "I've never seen its like." He hadn't risked asking about it before, but now that things between him and Lee were better, curiosity overtook him. "Are such rings the token of a scribe? Did it belong to an ancestor?"

Lee snapped the journal closed, sending up a small cloud of dust. "It was a gift," he said in a sharp tone, and walked away into the next chamber. He said nothing more, and Connor didn't ask again.

Tiran hung close to Dag. He jabbed at the fire's ashes with a waster and told the miner of his exploits with his tehpa, hunting in the southern forests or traveling through the coastal mountains. The miner rarely gave a story in trade. One evening, however, Dag lifted a pot and some spices from the supplies and asked the rest to toss in their night's way rations. Soon the smell of simmering porridge spread across the courtyard, warming the fog. Dag ladled the first portion into Connor's bowl. A few slices of the sausage Connor had given him floated to the top.

As for Teegan, mostly she sat alone on the bridge, feet dangling over the endless drop, but she did spend time each day helping him with his swordplay. He suspected she wanted Tiran to lose more than wanting Connor to win, but he didn't mind. And every night, Master Jairun gave him the chance to practice what she'd taught him.

In the fading light of each day, the headmaster told them stories about the terrors of Tanelethar and the lightraiders who faced them. He spoke of the wild brutality of ore creatures–orcs for short–and the unnatural forms of trolls, of battles with the ice giants that roamed the Frost Islands, and of bat-winged granogs–sniveling, half-dragon creatures given authority to manage the towns and villages.

Connor soaked in every word, despite the monsters. Master Jairun's stories had fire and life. They had hope. But, inevitably, the tales would end, and the freezing mists would come.

"Up!" Master Jairun would shout, rousting the potentials from the fire circle. "Line up with your wasters." Connor didn't mind the drills. His muscles had grown accustomed to the weight and balance of the wooden swords. But the unstoppable approach of the sparring still tied his stomach in knots. Every night, without fail and without mercy, Master Jairun set Tiran against him.

The pressing and advancing strategy no longer worked. The red-haired boy landed dozens of strikes and jabs in every match before catching Connor's wrist or cracking his knuckles, knocking his sword away. Withdraw was no option, not with Tehpa watching. So Connor took his lashings each night, and each morning, he counted his bruises.

On the fifth morning, a *tap, tap, tap* of wood on stone roused him. The mists were gone, but darkness still held the courtyard, perhaps at the last half tick of the fourth watch.

Tap, tap, tap. A hooded figure passed through the gate. Master Jairun was leaving. Nothing new. Connor tried to fall back to sleep, but curiosity grew like an itch up his spine. Where was the old man going each day? He threw aside his covering and followed.

From the gate, he saw Master Jairun taking a steep trail to the terraced pastures, and raced after him. But by the time he reached the lowest pasture, he'd lost sight of his quarry. He hurried on, following the trail higher.

Finally, as the gray dawn colored the sky, he reached the topmost pasture and saw Master Jairun walking northeast, up the ridge. His staff hovered over the grass, touching down only once every three or four paces. Then he dropped out of sight.

Connor blinked. "Where'd you go?" He broke into a run until, without warning, the ground fell away, and he stumbled down a grassy stair. He landed a few yards from a domed portico. Master Jairun sat on a fallen column within, holding a copper tube to his eye.

The old man lowered the tube and wiped the ends of it with his cloak. "Stealth and clumsiness, my boy. The two are not easily mixed. And I heard your wheezing in the upper pasture. We have much work to do to get your lungs into fighting shape. Come and sit. I'm not angry. I never commanded you or the others to stay put."

After a moment's hesitation, Connor climbed the steps and sat with him on the fallen column. "Does that mean you wanted us to follow you?"

"This is a spyglass." Master Jairun wiggled the copper tube

as if he hadn't heard the question. "The invention of a dear friend. Similar to a map glass, except it magnifies faraway places instead of those drawn on hide or parchment."

North, up the rising valley where two massive ridges joined, Connor saw a lighter patch within the mountain's gray–a hint of walls and towers. "Ras Telesar. You've been watching the academy."

Master Jairun held the tube steady and leaned aside. "Have a look."

Connor set his eye to the glass. Ramparts and high walls came into focus, stacked one upon the other above a high, grassy hollow within the crux of the ridges. There were a dozen or more towers at different heights, beset with curtains of vapor.

"I have not delayed our journey for your sake as your father suspects," Master Jairun said as Connor took the spyglass and panned it along the walls. "Not entirely."

"Then why haven't we–" Connor's voice caught in his throat. On the highest tower, he saw a shadow moving. He dropped the tube to his lap, as if looking through it had exposed him to the intruder. "Someone's up there."

"Or some *thing*." Master Jairun retrieved the device and placed it in Connor's hands once more. "Keep watching. Tell me what you see."

It took time for Connor to find the tower again, tracing the narrow circle of magnification up the battlements. When he found it, he saw nothing but stone. "Whatever it was, man or creature, I've lost–" A flash from the tower interrupted him. "Wait." Another flash, and then another. "Three flashes–not from the fireglass, but from the wall of the uppermost tower. Subtle, like a shield or a sword catching the morning light."

"An axe, I'd guess." Master Jairun let out a breath, seeming relieved, and took the spyglass. "Good, Mister Enarian. Very good."

"Is it? What did I just see?"

"The all-clear signal."

19

MASTER JAIRUN HAD BEEN STUDYING THE ROAD ahead, watching from the south while a pair of his professors watched from the walls of Ras Telesar to the north. The guardians feared an ambush might wipe out the potentials before their training began. "The dragons remember Ras Telesar well, and with more and more young folk taking the ships into the Storm Mists each year, you can be sure they know its halls have gone dark. They want to keep it that way. I do not think it a coincidence that these creatures appeared in the same season that a new class of the Lightraider Order rises."

Connor said nothing about their conversation to the others when he returned. Such a revelation was best left to a wiser voice than his.

Master Jairun returned not long after noon, carrying what looked to be a second staff, wrapped in goat cloth.

Lee jumped to his feet. "You're back early. Are we going on, then?"

"Not just yet, child. Right now, I should like to observe your sword work in the light of day. The nightly fog toys with an old man's vision."

Without question, the potentials and Connor lined up for drills.

"No, no. You've drilled enough. Sparring. I want to see your sparring." Master Jairun nodded to Connor. "You and Tiran first. Square off."

Connor narrowed his eyes at the old man. Was this the time for playing at battle with wooden swords? Shouldn't they make haste for the academy fortress while their path remained safe?

"Before you begin, though . . ." Master Jairun pulled a string to release the goat cloth from the second staff–a crook with a black ram's horn for the head and a shaft of ebony, wrapped in a spiral of steel from the spiked foot to the horn's tip. Such a crook was meant for greater foes than sheep. He placed it in Connor's hand. "I found this on the upper terrace. I thought our party's only shepherd should give it a try."

Tiran lowered his waster. "Am I to fight a long stick with a short one? In the Dragon Lands, am I to meet pyranium steel with wood? This is hardly fair."

"You make an excellent point, my boy." From beneath his cloak, Master Jairun drew the blade Tiran had brought with him.

Connor waited for a laugh. It never came.

The headmaster's expression remained grave–impatient. "Go on, Mister Yar, take it. We haven't got all day."

Hesitant after being called on his bluff, Tiran traded wood for steel. He gave Connor a shrug, a question in his eyes.

Connor nodded, consenting to the battle and thinking he must be a fool to do so.

Tehpa seemed to agree. "Avner, do you really think it wise to–"

"Fight!" The old man's staff sliced the air between the boys.

Tiran spun to the left, a move he'd never opened with before. He reached out with a slash at the crook as if intending to chop it in half. Connor answered with a two-handed block. The sword sparked off the steel band, and the two separated, blinking at each other.

With his long arms, Master Jairun nudged them together. "You can't live forever. Not in these frail forms. Fight, I said!"

Tiran lunged. Connor circled out of the way, eyes flaring. That sword could have run him through. And Tiran didn't stop there. Connor dodged a downward slash and blocked a strike at his midsection. The distraction of the resulting sparks gave him room for a swat at Tiran's ribs. The boy staggered sideways with a surprised grunt.

Teegan let out cheer.

Her twin shot her a glare.

The blow to Tiran's side was the best Connor had ever landed, and the shock of it nearly cost him his advantage.

"Don't just stand there gawking, Mister Enarian. Attack!"

He pressed in, striking with both ends of the crook. The agility and footwork he'd gained in his sword training merged with the surety of wielding a farm tool he'd carried since the day he could walk.

He backed Tiran to the fire, then feigned retreat, waiting for an inevitable slash. The moment came. Tiran swung wide a desperate, overreaching attack–and Connor bounced the blade away with the ram's horn. Before Tiran could recover his balance, Connor slipped the spike between his feet and tripped him.

Tiran fell to the ground, sword clattering beside him. The match was over.

Connor's eyes shifted to Tehpa, who stood at the fire circle with his mouth slightly open. A moment later, he came to himself and walked off. "A fluke. A trick. Nothing more."

Teegan, at least, offered congratulations. "Well done. I'm always happy to see Tiran put in his place."

The half-smile this brought to Connor's lips quickly fell away. One day, he'd have to fight Tiran again, and Tiran would be ready. He offered the crook to Master Jairun, holding it across his open palms. "It's a work of art. A treasure. But why show it to me now?"

Master Jairun pushed the weapon back at him. "I am not merely showing this to you, Connor. The crook is yours to keep. You'll need it for what I must ask of you next."

20

"BUT YOU MUST COME." LEE STOOD BETWEEN THE potentials gathered at the fire circle and the old merchant bay where Tehpa had Connor laying out gear for the journey home. "I saw your skill, Connor. We all saw it."

Connor glanced at the crook leaning against the fountain clock. He'd laid it there for good. "A fluke. As Tehpa said, I tripped Tiran with a stick. That's all."

After the match, Master Jairun had confessed to the group his reason for delaying the journey. "But the other guardians and I could watch the road north for a month and still miss a band of enemies. The Assembly's inaction across two generations left Keledev exposed. With too few defenders on the barrier slopes, there are too many gaps to cover–too many places for the shadows to hide. We ride north tonight and guard ourselves as best we may."

"Leave him." Tiran tugged Lee toward the mules. "We have work to do. Connor has made his choice."

Tehpa hoisted his saddlebags over a shoulder. "That he has. Ride north with this old zealot if you wish, but we will make haste for Ravencrest and hope these creatures he fears haven't gathered behind us on the road south." He paused on the way to his horse, shoulder to shoulder with Master Jairun, staring him down. "From there, I'll send word to the Assembly of your actions. I thank you for your healing and your counsel, but I'll not condone this folly any longer, nor let you take my son. I beg you, Avner. Return these other young folk to their families. If you send them into battle, whether here or on the far side of the barrier, their blood will be on your head." He walked on and flopped the bags across his mare's back. "And on your head alone."

Without acknowledging him, the headmaster beckoned his pupils to their horses. "Mount up. Pack mules at the rear. It's not a pretty thought, but Amos and Berta serve as a decent rear shield."

Despite Master Jairun's orders, Teegan let the mules pass, lagging behind as the column rode through the gate. She gazed at Connor in a silent request for him to follow.

He looked down, shifting his feet on the pavers. When he looked up again, she'd gone.

"Every one of them will die," Tehpa said as he and Connor turned their horses south and urged them up the slope of the chasm bridge. "Not tonight. I place little stock in Avner's worries. A single pack of goblins in Keledev is an aberration, not an invading army. But your new friends will die soon enough and long before their time. The path northward leads to a fool's death, fighting a fool's battle in a wasteland of terrors."

His words dropped into the mists, and Connor tried his best to let them fall as he always had. But the storm of umbrage and guilt built inside until he could no longer contain it. He halted his mare at the bridge's end and raised his voice. "You mean the same fool's battle that took Patehpa?"

Tehpa slowed, but he did not reply.

Connor would not be ignored. "Patehpa was no fool. And neither is Master Jairun. The Order was right. The Rescuer wanted them to fight against the tide. Don't you see what's happened? The Keledan hid in their caves, letting evil fester at the gate. And as we speak, that evil now crosses the threshold. The first talons of the dragons clawed at Mehma in our very kitchen. They tore into your flesh. How deep must they cut before we fight back?"

Tehpa's mare clopped on at a steady plod. "You are brash

and young, and you do not know as much as you imagine. Do you truly think the dragons' hordes won't strike you witless with fear? Come, boy. We're going home."

"Stop!"

The shout echoed down the tunnel, finally drawing Tehpa's gaze. He turned his mare, red-faced, with an explosive rebuke visible on his lips.

Connor gave him no chance to speak it. "I *am* afraid!" He pointed behind him at the road beyond the courtyard. "And so are they. I saw it in their faces. Those potentials are afraid of the dark creatures, as they should be. But more than monsters, I'm afraid of my own smallness. For so long, I've suffered from the cowardly delusion that one shepherd–one man–cannot hope to stand against the darkness, because that's what you taught me."

Connor took a breath, letting his words boil. He wiped away a tear. But in the moment he confessed his cowardice, a weight had dropped from his spirit. He sat straighter in the saddle. "Now I see this is your fear, not mine, forged in Faelin's loss and draped about us both like a chain. Well, Tehpa, I am chained no longer."

He wheeled the mare and spurred her across the bridge, reaching a full gallop by the other side. The crook lay ahead, leaning against the fountain, ebony and steel gleaming in the waning sun. Connor snatched it up and barreled through the gate.

21

THE SPEED OF CONNOR'S CHARGE COULD NOT LAST, not on such a long and treacherous road. The trail beyond the upper pasture led north across the steep side of Anvil Ridge. And by the first watch of evening, his mare had slowed to a walk, scraping Connor's left leg against the rock wall to avoid the sheer drop on the other side.

Night fell, and when the fog rolled in, Connor thanked the Maker for the wall against his leg—his only guide. The cold and dark enveloped him, holding him so long that he wondered if he'd ever escape. Not until a dim gray light appeared ahead, did he realize that at some point he'd entered another of the region's strange, aboveground tunnels. He emerged at a switchback trail leading both up and down a sheer rock wall. Connor went up.

"Teegan! Lee?" At each bend, he called for the others. "Tiran? Dag!"

The trail narrowed, and Connor dismounted to lead his mare through the corners. In the stillness, he heard scuffing and scratching, but the rocky terrain toyed with his hearing. The noise could have come from anywhere, even his own boots. "Teegan?"

A hand clapped over his mouth and yanked him into a crevice. "Hush, Mister Enarian. Do you wish to warn the whole mountain of our coming?" The hand came away.

"Master Jairun?"

"You bring me gladness, my boy. Lee, Teegan, and Dag as well, I imagine." Master Jairun squeezed his shoulders. "I'll take you to them. But no more shouting, please."

Connor noticed he said nothing about Tiran.

The mare nuzzled the gap, trying to join them. Connor patted her nose. "What about my horse?"

"Leave her." Master Jairun faded into the black, forcing Connor to follow his voice. "I sent our mounts and mules up the switchbacks to the broad green that stretches to the gates. They know the way well enough, and your mare will follow their scent. Meanwhile, we shall take a safer, more protected path."

"The gates. So, we're close to the academy?"

"Close? My boy, you've been on the academy grounds for more than a league."

Starlight reached Connor's eyes, and the rush and pound of falling water came with it. Spray touched his cheeks–cool, but not cold like the Mer Nimbar mists. In fact, the air seemed warmer than down below. Master Jairun halted at the tunnel's end, where a trio of wooden cranks secured the three strands of a steep rope bridge to the rocks. It crossed the water to another tunnel mouth much higher than theirs.

Master Jairun thrust his staff toward the white foam crashing through the canyon below. "These are the Gathering's upper reaches. The spray wets the ropes, making them slack. They must be tightened for every crossing." He gave each crank a couple of turns, and the cords creaked in protest. "Bound to snap one day. Up you go, then."

The central rope swayed with each step. Halfway up, Connor felt the jiggle of Master Jairun's long stride behind him. He glanced over his shoulder. "Do you think that's wise–both of us on the rope at the same time?"

"Excellent point, my boy. Too late now, though. Best keep going."

A face appeared as the two reached the top. Lee clapped Connor's arm so hard the bridge shivered. "You came!"

"Easy, Mister Lee," Master Jairun said from behind Connor. "It'll do him no good to knock him into the river for his efforts. Nor me."

The scribe pulled Connor off the rope and into an embrace. "I knew you wouldn't let us down."

Tiran leaned against a rock formation not far away. "Yet you've been whining that he did exactly that ever since we left." They were all there, the whole company, gathered in a high grotto with a toothy gap open to the north. Dag and Teegan sat on a bench-like formation. The miner gave him a nod. Teegan offered an almost imperceptible smile.

Master Jairun swept the spray from his cloak. "Do not mock a blessing, Mister Yar. The Rescuer sent us another sword. Be grateful."

Tiran nodded at Connor's crook. "A stick, you mean."

His taunt stirred Teegan from her perch. "You have a short memory, Brehna." She brushed past him and took Connor's arm, guiding him toward the natural window. "Come look. You'll want to see this."

Silver starlight shone down on a vast hollow where two great arms of the mountains joined, and there, on the steep wall of the barrier, stood the former home of Lightraider Academy.

The fortress of Ras Telesar was a study in stone and water, a rising labyrinth of ramparts and towers stacked around a chapel perched on a high outcropping. Hot streams, giving off steam, fell from the chapel's windows–nine by Connor's count–each picking its own path down through the maze. The water poured over ledges and tumbled down staircases, until it gathered out of sight behind the lowest wall.

Connor guessed these same waters filled the great black pool outside the gates. From there, a small river flowed down a grassy glade to become the cataracts they'd crossed on the rope bridge.

"See the many threads of my tapestry," Teegan whispered,

still holding Connor's arm. "Marvel at their unity as I weave them together."

"A verse from the Sacred Scrolls?"

"Poetry." Her cheeks reddened, and she glanced down at her hands. "My poetry."

Master Jairun joined them at the opening. "Any sign of trouble while I was away, retrieving Mister Enarian?"

"None," Tiran said. "All's quiet."

A slow *clip clop* echoed across the hollow as if to counter his assertion. A horse's head came into view at the top of the steps leading up from the switchbacks to the green, swaying with the effort of mounting the last few. Connor's mare. She sniffed the mountain breeze, snorted, then wandered across the grass to join the other horses and the mules at the river for a drink. Connor smiled. "She followed their scent, just as you said. I was nervous leaving her behind. I'm glad she's safe with her friends now."

"Safe." Tiran let out a harsh laugh. "Don't you get it? Master Jairun sent them out there as bait."

22

"IS THAT TRUE?" TEEGAN WALKED AHEAD OF THE rest as they followed Master Jairun deeper into the cave. "Is that why you sent the horses up the switchbacks without us?"

"We needed to travel on foot, and I needed to know if any creatures lay in wait at the edges of the green."

"So it is true. The horses are bait."

"Yes, child."

"That's so cruel."

Master Jairun lit a candle to illuminate their passage–no longer a cave, but a narrow hall of fine masonry. His expression showed no anger when he turned to face the girl. "I understand the loss you suffered below Ravencrest, more than you can know. Sending good animals out into the open where they might be set upon by evil creatures is a hard thing for me as much as you–perhaps more. But horses and mules I can spare. Servants willing to answer the Rescuer's call, I cannot. You are far too few." He turned and continued up the passage.

After that, no one spoke for quite some time. The passage steepened, flattened, then steepened again, narrowing enough to force them into single file. Until then, Connor had walked beside Teegan, intending to comfort her, but he couldn't seem to come up with the right words. And when the passage narrowed, Tiran wedged himself between them in the line, robbing him of the chance.

"We've walked far since the grotto," Lee said, breaking the

silence. “We’ve traveled the length and breadth of the green and then some. By now, we must be inside the western wall.”

“Very good, Mister Lee.” Master Jairun lightly tapped the stones with the knot of his staff. “The original passage ran through the outer ramparts between the towers on the first and second levels. The Order joined the low end to the grotto generations ago.”

“What use had the lightraiders for hidden passages?” Tiran rose on tiptoe to look over Teegan’s shoulder, blocking Connor’s view. “There were no enemies in Keledev during their time. Or was it built for keeping secrets from the Assembly?”

The old man cleared his throat, showing more than a hint of annoyance. “The original intent of this passage is lost to history, Mister Yar. It predates the lightraiders by a thousand years. The Elder Folk built this fortress, not the Order.”

“Ras Telesar.” Lee lowered his voice in reverence. “The Hill of the Fountain–sister to Ras Pyras, the Hill of the Flame in the far north.”

The guardian slowed his pace and held his candle close to the wall, as if looking for something. “The sudden rising of the barrier carried Ras Telesar up to its present perch on this mountainside. But in the elder days, its four ringlets crowned the tallest hill in the south, and the Fountain Chapel *Nevethav* served as the central jewel.” His flame guttered. A moment later it went out altogether. “Ah. Here we are.”

A crack of dim light appeared in the darkness. Master Jairun had pressed a shoulder against the wall, forcing a section to move. The secret door swung noiselessly open.

They filed through into a small tower chamber where starlight shined in through high windows. Master Jairun’s secret door turned out to be the statue of a placid warrior with wings nearly touching the floor–one of the Lisropha, a race of the Elder Folk. “This is the second level’s westernmost tower,” the headmaster told them, heaving the figure into place. "We're well inside the fortress, now. Safe as can be expected." He lit a lantern with his candle and lifted it from the wall, handing it to Connor. "Now to meet up with your other professors, Masters Quintain and Belen."

"And where do we find them?" Dag asked. "The kitchen, I hope."

"They'll be waiting in our great hall, cut into the mountainside behind the chapel outcropping. We call it *Salar Peroth,* the Hall of Manna." Master Jairun crossed the chamber to a spiral stair and walked down a few steps. "So, yes, Mister Kaivos, they'll have supper waiting. Try to find your way there before it gets cold." He blew out his candle and disappeared.

23

CONNOR HURRIED TO THE STAIR WITH HIS LANTERN but saw no sign of the headmaster. "He's gone. What are we to do now?"

"We find the great hall." Dag drew a handful of way rations from a pouch and showed them to Connor before popping them into his mouth. "And supper."

"Perhaps you weren't listening in the passage," Lee said. "This fortress was once a sanctuary, built by the Elder Folk. Four concentric walls with many towers and joining bridges surrounded its hilltop chapel. When the Rescuer raised the great peaks, he jumbled them all together. This fortress is one giant labyrinth. We may never find our way without a guide."

"And I think we have one." Tiran had gone to one of the stairwell windows. He pointed out into the night. "Master Jairun relit his candle. If we hurry, we can follow his light through the maze."

He started down the steps, and Lee, Connor, and Dag followed, but Teegan raced ahead and stopped them with arms held wide. "No. Not yet."

The others exchanged glances. Tiran set his jaw, glaring at his shessa. "This is a test, Teegs. Remember our invitation letters–and Master Jairun's warning at Ravencrest? We are mere potentials; we must pass a trial to become initiates to the Lightraider Order. Don't you see? We're here now. That trial has begun. Do you want to fail on our first night?"

"I don't care. We're not going anywhere until the horses and mules are safely inside these walls."

The horses. Connor understood now. He'd seen Teegan's anguish during the attack in Dayspring Forest. He'd seen her tears over the falcon. Tiran didn't stand a chance of swaying her. None of them did. And an argument would only waste time.

Connor slapped Tiran on the shoulder. "Come on. We're only on the second level, not far from the gates. The sooner we get the animals to safety, the sooner we can start the maze and get Dag to supper."

"I'm all for that," the big miner said with a gentle nod to Teegan.

The journey to the gates proved a simple task, giving credence to Connor's assurances to Tiran–more credence than he'd imagined when he'd spoken them minutes before. An arch from the tower stairwell opened onto the second-level battlements. A curving, natural stairway of rock joined those to the lower ward.

"Look!" Lee hopped down to the courtyard, skipping the last few steps, and bent to touch a tuft of grass where the rock had burst through the pavers long ago. "See how the Rescuer merged the mountain with the sanctuary to make this fortress? Wonderful."

Tiran snorted, walking by without a second look. "It's just a rock formation. It was the lightraiders who cut the steps after they took over Ras Telesar."

The scribe watched him for a moment, then looked to Connor and shrugged. "The Rescuer had to leave them something to do when they moved in, right?"

The potentials had no hope of raising the double portcullis on their own, even if they'd had the key to unlock the winches. Teegan peered through the grates. "I see the horses, not far beyond the bridge. But how do we bring them in?"

"There should be a gatekeeper's passage," Lee said, walking west along the main wall. "Look for a small door, barely wide enough for–"

"What about this one?" The voice was Dag's, from the southeast corner of the courtyard. But the door he'd found was anything but small. It took Tiran's strength and his to lift the bar holding it shut. And when they pushed it open, instead of a cramped tunnel, the potentials found a grand hallway fit for a giant that cut diagonally through the bulwark. Murals of winged warriors flying and tall servers carrying baskets came to life in the wash of Connor's lantern.

Lee laughed. "Built by the Elder Folk to suit the largest of their kind. I should have known."

They opened a second barred door at the far end and were greeted by six horses and two mules. Teegan pressed her forehead to her gelding's and stroked his mane. "You sensed us coming, didn't you? Good boy. I'm sorry we sent you out as bait. It won't happen again."

Their group–especially the mules, Amos and Berta–could not move fast enough for Tiran in their return to the lower ward. "How long do you think they'll wait," he asked, grunting as he and Dag lowered the inner door's bar into place, "before deciding we've failed the first and simplest task of our trial? Without Master Jairun's candle to follow, it will take us till morning to find the great hall."

"I'm not so sure." Dag brushed his hands together and nodded at a turbulent black pool taking up much of the courtyard's eastern half. "A candle isn't the only thing we might follow."

Connor followed the miner's gaze as he looked up from the pool to the chapel. "The streams. They all start at the chapel, within reach of the great hall. And they end here at the pool. All we have to do is pick one and follow it through the maze."

The plan worked well. Mostly. The water poured through windows and down channels at the center of sloping halls. It wet their boots as it trickled down stairwells, growing warmer the higher they climbed. Four times, they lost their chosen stream where it gushed from a culvert through which none of them could fit. But on each occasion, they scaled a rocky wall or passed through a doorway and found it again. Until at last, they doused themselves completely to climb through a window waterfall out onto the ramparts at the base of the chapel outcropping.

"Well done, both of you," Lee said, slapping the wet tunics clinging to Dag's and Connor's backs. "And well done, Teegan. If we hadn't gone backward to rescue the animals, we might never have seen the solution. Right, Tiran?"

Tiran grumbled a reply, but Connor couldn't make out the words.

More natural stairs brought them to the outcropping, shrouded in vapor from the warm streams, and another led up from there to the Hall of Manna, one level above. Looking back, Connor saw the chapel's tall doors rising out of the mist, much larger than the doors they'd faced at the gatekeeper's passage. The Order had been disbanded two generations before, but Nevethav looked as if it had been shut far longer.

The doors to Salar Peroth, however, stood wide open. Lanterns lit up at the potentials' arrival, casting their glow across a broad, wedge shaped chamber pressing deep into the mountainside.

Master Jairun stepped forward from one of the lanterns, along an aisle between the long stone tables. He clapped his hands. "You found your way. I'm so pleased. But of course you did." He gestured to another guardian stirring a big iron pot seated in a circle of coals. "Master Belen and I never doubted you."

"You and I, perhaps." The other guardian scratched at a patch of whiskers and tilted a weathered black forehead toward a hulking figure with a pair of axes strapped to his back. "But Swordmaster Quinton had all but given up on them."

The larger guardian crossed his arms. He looked to be close to Master Jairun in age, but it seemed to Connor his muscles hadn't suffered for the years. "One of us must keep the standards of the Order high," he said in the brogue of the far eastern foothills. "An' it won' be either o' you two mollycoddlers. I can tell ya that."

Tiran stepped forward out of the group. "Meaning we passed the first test of our initiate's quest, right? What's next?"

"Don' know." Master Quinton sniffed Master Belen's pot and sat at one of the nearby tables, on a stone bench so tall his boots barely touched the ground. "In days past we might've sent ya high up on the peaks to pluck a snow flower from the Clefts of Semajin, where yer fingers turn brittle an' blue from cold an' yer breath comes in wee little gasps."

"Or to the Western Vale of the Passage Lakes," Master Belen added, "to fetch a bushel of silver trout from its farthest lake, Mount Challenge. I know it doesn't sound so hard, but keeping them fresh on the journey home is no easy feat."

"Is there something special about those silver trout?" Lee asked.

The two guardians glanced at one another. Master Quinton replied as if the answer should be obvious. "They're delicious."

"Yes, yes." Master Jairun pounded his staff on the floor, gaining their attention. "Be all that as it may, these are not days past. They are new days, and a new start for the Order. And I think we must consider the feats these potentials have accomplished on their road thus far."

The headmaster leaned on his staff, gaze drifting over the group. "Three have already faced dark creatures in battle, an unprecedented test for any lightraider potential." His eyes settled on Connor. "And one dispatched his foe, saving his family."

Masters Belen and Quinton murmured their agreement in low rumbles as Master Jairun continued addressing the potentials one by one. "You treated another's wounds and forgave hurts. You trained night after night in the cold without answers, living on faith. You used the talents the Creator gave you," he said, nodding to Dag, "to brighten a meal and warm your friends' hearts and stomachs."

Last, the headmaster smiled at Teegan and cast a glance out the window toward the lower ward. “And you put the needs of innocents above your own desires, becoming a voice for the voiceless. Such treasures are more valuable than rare flowers or delicious food, and they prove your worth more than any hardships you might have endured in a traditional trial.”

Master Belen let his ladle rest for a moment. “So, what are you saying, Headmaster?”

“I’m saying the trial is complete. These five are no longer potentials.” He took a step back, so that he could capture them all in his gaze. “Welcome, initiates of the Order, to Lightraider Academy.”

PART TWO

A SPARK IN THE SOUTH

"For you are all children of light and children of the day. We do not belong to the night or the darkness. So then, let us not sleep like the rest, but let us stay awake and be self-controlled."

1 Thessalonians 5:5–6

24

KARA ORSO BORE NO ILLUSIONS ABOUT HER SEWING skills. One customer had called her the worst seamstress in all the Highland Forest, perhaps the whole of Talania, both Tanelethar and Keledev. True. She knew it, and so, it seemed, did the pudgy, bearded traveler picking through the fur cloaks and blankets at her market stall.

"Look at these stitches," he said, turning up the seam between a patch of rabbit fur and a patch of beaver. "They're as jagged as the Eastern Crags. A child playing at her mehma's table could have done better." The turn of his meaty paws pulled the hides so taut Kara feared her awful stitches might burst.

She kept her expression stolid. "They'll hold. Three petas for the cloak. Four and I'll throw in a blanket–half my usual price."

"One peta." The man released his hold on the cloak, wriggling his fingers in distaste. Each bore a weighty gold ring like a thick collar choking the life out of a pig. Sorcerer's runes marked their facets, a clear sign of a dragon stooge. One did not gather so much wealth and magic without sucking up to the granogs and their lords. "One peta for the cloak and blanket together, mind you. I'll not pay a copper more."

One silver peta would barely cover a week's worth of the corn Kara's brehnan used to bait their traps. "Four," she said, glancing at a shuttered boutique across the square of Trader's Knoll. "Or you can wait for Charlotte's to open, if she opens today at all. You'll find prettier seams in her shop, but you won't find any fur, I can tell you that."

Morning had broken cold on the hilltop village, and Kara had seen the shiver and the look of shock on this fool's face the moment he stepped out of Bristlecone Lodge. He'd crawled up into Highland Forest from the lowland hills ill-prepared for the season.

To drive her point home, she inclined her head toward the Impossible Peaks to their south, their upper reaches veiled under a curtain of clouds. A dusting of white already covered the pines well below the tree line. "Snow's coming down the mountains. It'll be here by noon, I'll warrant. Think you and your horse can beat the weather to Safety's End?" Kara was no weatherseer. She had no idea how soon the snows would come, but it sounded good.

The pudgy traveler looked to the peaks, and Kara thought she had him. But then he bent his fat nose near to the fur cloak. "Smudged. There's soot all over this. Likely from your charwood stacks." His eyes drifted down her form, gaze lingering in the way too many travelers had let their gazes linger of late. "Or from you. You're covered in the stuff. What sort of fool sells clothing and charwood from the same stall?"

"We all do what we must." Kara pulled her own fur cloak tight over the blue of her tunic–not to cover up the char, but to shield herself from his eyes. The char, she didn't mind. Some of it she'd drawn on her skin on purpose. A few black streaks, combined with soot to dirty the platinum blue of her hair, masked her blood, sparing her from her mehma's fate.

The traveler snorted. "One peta. And you should consider that a gift."

She would not win this battle with her prowess as a trader. No surprise there. Kara's merchant skills matched her sewing ability. Her brehna Keir fared better when he manned the stall, but he and Liam–the eldest of the three–would be off ranging for another two weeks, finishing the season's final hunt. That left her the task of turning furs and charwood into bread.

She swept the menace from her eyes and stepped around her wares to stand beside the traveler. "Mm. Yes. I see the smudges." As if they could not be wiped away with a brush of his hand. "One peta, then. For both. And I do thank you."

The traveler narrowed his eyes. "Settled?"

"Settled." Kara gave a little shiver and glanced up at the gray sky. "And when the snow comes, don't forget to tell others where you found your furs, though I'd take it as a kindness if you failed to mention the price."

The traveler laid down a coin and snatched up his purchases, bumping into Kara in his hurry to move on. "Out of the way, filthy girl."

Kara waited until he'd gone into the stables and then laid four more coins down on the countertop. She might be a terrible haggler and seamstress, but she had skills. She'd only lifted enough silver from his pouch to cover the cost of her goods, plus one more coin as a tax on his rudeness. That was fair, right?

Before Kara could slip the coins into her iron money box, another shadow darkened her counter. "Good morning, young lady. Might I have a moment of your time?" The gravel in the voice made her skin crawl. She found it familiar, nonetheless.

"Dropping by a little early, aren't we, Gaman? And since when do you call me—"

The question caught in her throat as her eyes traveled up the folds of a velvet cloak as black as a void and as broad as a curtain, held in place by a jewel-encrusted clasp. She had to lift her gaze far higher than expected. This was not Gaman, the runtish boss of Trader's Knoll, too fat to make use of his rotting wings. But the visitor was, like Gaman, a granog—a dragon administrator.

Some said the granogs were part dragon themselves, but Kara had never believed it until now. She could nearly stand on a level with Gaman. This granog towered over her. The claws resting on her wooden counter were polished and meticulously shaped. The horns topping the wings tucked behind his shoulders were inlaid with silver and gold and etched with runes.

"My apologies, sir. With who–" Kara coughed and glanced down, trying to remember her manners. A granog could have a peasant like her beheaded or burned at a snap of his scaly fingers. She couldn't afford to provoke him, not with the five coins sitting between them on her counter, four of them stolen. "With whom do I have the pleasure of speaking?"

The creature grinned, showing appreciation for her display of respect and showing off his coal-black fangs. "I am Nesat, the new high regent for the southern highlands. I must set up residence here in this"–his voice flattened as he looked around the square–"place. I require housing for my entourage. Direct me to a fitting establishment."

Surely, this creature saw the inn when he entered Trader's Knoll. What was he playing at? "The lodge. Bristlecone Lodge. Old Wilibrond has many rooms. And he'd be glad of the payment."

"I'm sure he would." Nesat circled one silver coin with a claw, carving a groove. "However, I will be taking Gaman's house. And my retinue are not accustomed to the confinement of lodge rooms. I'm looking for something more . . . open. A barracks, perhaps."

Why would this new granog be taking Gaman's house?

Even as the question struck her, a forest goblin pushed a small cart past her stall, covered by a leather tarp. One wooden wheel bounced over a dislodged paver, and a clawed hand flopped down into view. The goblin shoved it into place beneath the tarp and rolled on.

Kara swallowed hard.

Nesat pressed her, drumming his claws. "Please, young lady. My inquiry? I am in haste. As you can well imagine, there is much here to do."

"Of course." Kara had no desire to anger the creature, but

he'd not been entirely clear. What sort of retinue would not want to stay at the lodge? "The stables, then?" She looked toward a long, thatched roof peeking out behind Bristlecone Lodge. "It is the largest structure in town, set on a flat piece of ground dug into the north side of our hilltop. It is level, dry, and hardly used. Wilibrond owns it. You'll find him at the inn."

Nesat stared at the structure for a long moment, then returned his red eyes to Kara. "My thanks, young lady. You've been most helpful." Each of his five claws rested on a silver coin–Kara's coins–and he dragged them across the counter as he turned to go.

"Wait!" Without thinking, Kara laid two fingers on the nearest peta, then froze, aghast at her own impertinence. Was she trying to lose a hand?

Nesat's gray throat quivered with a growl.

"I mean . . ." Kara curled her fingers back. "I was wondering. Why have you removed Gaman? What changed?"

The granog dragged four coins into his fist, leaving only the one she'd touched behind. "Everything, my dear," he said as he walked away. "Everything."

25

"AWAKE, SLEEPER!"

Connor rolled over amid gruff shouting and the pounding of a fist against a wooden door. He groaned. Daylight streamed in between wool curtains. A thousand flecks of dust hung in the light. Ancient dust.

His eyes popped wide open, and the night's events came rushing back. He had joined Lightraider Academy.

A rustling of straw met Connor's every movement, bits of it poking out from a moth-eaten mattress–a human mattress lying on a stone slab carved for something larger. Several of these giant bed-slabs were lined up, all in a row. Between them, a stone table rose from the floor, overlarge like those in the Hall of Manna. Both he and Tiran had bumped into it when Quinton ushered the boys into the chamber the night before. They were in a barracks. The swordmaster had offered Teegan the women's initiate barracks on the other side of the fortress, but she'd insisted on being closer to the rest of her class, so he'd given her the captain's chambers next door.

The pounding continued. "Awake, sleeper!"

Lee lay on the next slab over, head covered with his hands. "What is his problem?"

Awake, sleeper. Connor shook his head at the archaic call, a derivative of a Resteram prayer song, "The Sleeper's Hope." "Perhaps he's insane. He did suggest sending us on a quest for a flower last night."

Across the room, Tiran sat up, eyes fixed on the huge, shaking door as if a troll stood on the other side, trying to beat its way through. “Of course he’s insane.” He planted both hands on his mattress and shouted, “We’re up already!”

“If you were up and out o’ yer snuggly little beds, this door would be *open*!” Master Quinton pounded all the harder. “Awake, sleeper!”

Dag, for his part, remained flat, two enormous feet poking out from beneath his blanket. Master Quinton’s latest burst of pounding and shouting elicited a loud snort but nothing else.

Connor hauled himself out of bed, padded across the cold stones, and swung the door wide, jumping aside, lest the guardian come barreling through and flatten him.

Master Quinton only stood there, fist raised in mid-pound. “About time, Shepherd Boy. We allowed ya to sleep away the mornin’, since last night’s sport ran deep into the watches.” He thrust a chin at the others. “Get yer flock down to the lower ward–to the courtyard o’ the barbican gate where ya brought the horses in. We’re takin’ ya on a patrol o’ the grounds. Be there in half a tick, or I shall be all kinds o’ cross. The day is half wasted already.”

Stunned, Connor watched the swordmaster saunter off down the passage for a full second before the weight of the task dawned on him–another journey through the maze without a guide. And for this trip, they had a definite time limit. Their initiate’s quest might be over, but it seemed their tests and trials were just beginning. “Wait! Can we have a hint?” His call echoed in the empty hallway. Master Quinton had already rounded the corner.

The initiates burned through the first third of their half tick trying to get Dag out of bed.

“Perhaps he’s ill,” Lee said. “Some sort of sleeping sickness, brought on by the high elevation.”

“I doubt it. His snores sound healthy enough.” Connor lifted a heavy arm and let it fall to the mattress. "This is hopeless. The swordmaster will have our heads, mine especially because I was fool enough to answer the door and receive our task."

"Glad to see you're catching on." Tiran, dressed and ready, leaned against the wall beside the door and watched the other two wrestle with their sleeping comrade. "Now you know why I stayed put."

Lee shot him a frown. "Well, try to be of use now, please. Go and wake your sister."

"She's up."

The scribe's eyes narrowed. "How can you possibly know that? Can you sense Teegan's mind because she's your twin or–"

Before Lee could finish the question, Dag sat up, knocking the scribe off-balance with a great stretch of his arms. He offered Connor a serene smile. "Morning. When's breakfast?"

"Well past. It'll be luncheon time in a few minutes." Connor tossed the miner's britches onto his lap. "Dress now. Food later." He turned to Tiran. "Seriously. Go get Teegan."

Tiran pointed at the window.

Through the break in the curtains, Connor saw a flash of red hair and green cloak. Tiran had not sensed Teegan's wakefulness–he'd seen her, standing out on their shared balcony. Connor rolled his eyes and pushed through the oversize door.

Teegan stood at the balcony rail, in much the same way as she'd stood at the Black Feather's window, gazing out over Red Willow Hill. Except she wore a look of contentment rather than sorrow. She lifted her face to the blue sky and the late morning sun. Beneath her stretched the academy's bottom two levels, glistening gray in the daylight, and the blue spruce and orange oaks in the forest valley below. She seemed to sense his presence "Do you see it, Connor? That forest, high on this mountain, is a miracle fed by the Gathering. Master Jairun says it's just teeming with life."

A screech echoed up to them. Connor watched Teegan's eyes, expecting her contentment to fade at the reminder of her lost falcon. It didn't. His eyes shifted, searching for the source of the sound. There, racing low over the treetops, was the bird.

Teegan let out a shrill whistle, and the falcon answered with another call. It climbed, heading right for them, and Teegan raised her left arm, wrapped once again in her leather guard. The bird settled on the offered perch and accepted a sliver of dried meat. As Teegan stroked its feathers, it turned its head nearly all the way round and fixed Connor with black eyes.

He'd seen that look before. "Acthia?"

Teegan beamed. "Master Belen returned her to me last night. He found her in the red willow on the night we came to Ravencrest." She pulled one of the falcon's wings wide, revealing a linen dressing, hardly visible against her snow-white feathers. "Aethia took an arrow defending us. Glimwick patched her up and sent her ahead with the guardians, along with a couple of ravens for our messenger tower. Master Belen nursed her back to health while we trained at Mer Nimbar."

The falcon dove away to swoop down over the barbican courtyard, where all three masters waited, along with several horses. Master Quinton cupped his hands and shouted up at them. "Oi! Shepherd! Was I unclear as to yer job? Bring 'em down!"

"We'd better do as he says." Teegan raised her arm and whistled for the bird to return. "Have you any idea how to get down there?"

Aethia vanished from sight near the place where the natural steps they'd used the night before joined with the second-level battlements. At first Connor thought she must have landed, worn out by her wound. But a moment later she burst through a jagged break near the eastern edge of the balcony.

While the bird alighted on Teegan's arm. Connor inspected the gap. A set of steep, narrow stairs had been cut into the wall below them, leading to a passage between overlapping ramparts. He grinned at the falcon. "I do now."

DOWN IN THE LOWER WARD, THE STUDENTS FOUND the masters mounted and ready to ride, though the barbican's double portcullis remained closed. The light of day offered a better view of the nine streams gathering in the turbulent pool on the east side of the courtyard. Some entered through their own channels. Others merged before they reached it. "The Gathering," Dag said as the students approached. "Huh. Now I get it."

Quinton looked as cross as he'd promised. "I said a half tick, lad. Ya took closer to a full. Did I not tell ya the day was wastin'?"

"But I found the way down. That's what you wanted."

Quinton shot a glare at Aethia, perched on Teegan's shoulder. "I suspect a wee lit'le bird told ya the secret. T'won't be so easy next time."

As soon as the guardian's gaze moved on, Connor turned to Lee and mouthed, *Next time?*

"If we're in such a hurry"–Tiran strolled along the pool, right up to Quinton's horse–"why haven't you opened the portcullis?"

"We haven't raised the portcullis 'cause we're not sendin' forth an army, lad."

"You don't have the key, do you? I'll bet the Assembly never returned it."

Quinton growled, but Master Jairun raised a quieting hand. "You are correct, Mister Yar. The Assembly withheld the key–a purely symbolic gesture on their part. A way of appeasing certain high clerics. And I did not have the heart to break the lock on the winches, for it is very old. We'll take the gatekeeper's passage, as you did last night. In the meantime, let us make a symbolic gesture of our own."

Master Jairun signaled Belen, and the two guardians rode across the black pavers to the watchtowers on either side of the gate. Each lifted a burning torch from the wall.

"He wants to light braziers," Tiran said with a snort. "As if there's any oil left in the cisterns after all these–" The rump of Quinton's gelding shifted, knocking him into the pool.

Master Jairun gave the swordmaster a hard look.

Quinton shrugged. "Apologies, Headmaster. The horses are a mite fidgety, ya know. Must be the nip in the air."

While Teegan helped her brehna out, sputtering and dripping wet, Master Jairun rode to an archway in the eastern watchtower, and Belen rode to a matching opening to the west. Connor had mistaken these portals for doorways, but now he saw they were more like the mouths of great ovens. The two guardians lowered their torches and touched bronze braziers inside. With a tremendous *foomp*, flames swirled up. The initiates gave a collective gasp. Connor stepped back to take in the crystal collectors atop the towers, shining with golden light.

Quinton used the butt of his axe to gently lift Tiran's chin, closing his mouth. "The oil cisterns at Ras Telesar are always full, lad. Ever has it been so since the dawn o' time. Ever shall it be."

The other two guardians returned to the courtyard center, and Master Jairun raised his voice toward the gate, as if addressing a crowd on the empty green. "The fires of Ras Telesar burn once more. Let all who see them know that today, the Lightraider Order is restored."

26

OUTSIDE, THE PARTY FOLLOWED A PATH BETWEEN the pool and the outer wall, then crossed the bridge to the white gravel road running down the center of the glade.

At night, the outer pool and the glade river had looked the deepest black. Now they were clear blue. The polished rocks beneath the waters reflected the noonday sun like jewels. Connor spurred his mare to ride beside Lee. "This place looked so terrifying in the dark. In the light, it's almost cheery."

"I wouldn't say cheery, my friend. This is, after all, Ras Telesar." Lee turned in his saddle to look back. "I think the word you want is . . ." He trailed off, grabbing for Connor's shoulder. "Connor, look."

The braziers Master Jairun and Belen had lit revealed two giant figures in the barbican watchtowers, carved from translucent stone that now glowed from within thanks to the fires.

The eastern figure held a bowl with pale blue water–an offered drink to welcome travelers. The western figure bore an air of command in the grim set of its deep bronze brow. Feathered wings rose from its shoulders, and in its hands, it clasped the hilt of a downturned sword of pure amber. The swirling glow gave the blade a look of burning flame. Though their aspects were different–one serving and one warlike–each seemed equal to the other, and both wore the faceted collection glasses atop their heads like princely crowns.

"Breathtaking." Lee finally managed to finish his statement.

"The word you want is breathtaking."

"Eyes forward!" Quinton shouted to them both. "Or had ya forgotten we've had dark creatures in the land? The word *I* want from my initiates right now is vigilance."

The company took the ridge road, traversing the wall of Anvil Ridge as Connor had done on his ride to catch the potentials. Without the mist and the dark, the trail looked far less treacherous, though narrow enough to make the horses nervous. Aethia too. The falcon chuffed and squawked until Teegan finally set her free to swoop down over the forest of oaks and spruce below.

The guardians halted their column at a cleft in the mountainside, where an arch of pale green stone marked the head of a trail. A hammer and anvil were cut into the arch's face, and armored horsemen carved into the rock walls beyond. "Where does it lead?" Connor asked.

Master Jairun cast a glance down the trail. "That is the road to the Passage Lakes."

"But only when the pass is clear," Quinton added. "With winter approachin', 'tis wiser to take the long road down to Watchman's Gate and up the valley o' the Anamturas. Ya don' wanna be caught crossin' Anvil Ridge in a snowstorm, lad. Trust me."

Lee dismounted and pressed closer to the green stone, walking with a slow reverence. "I read the story of this trail during my time at the Assembly. It was discovered by a small band of Keledan–the first to venture out of hiding after the peaks rose. They followed it to the highest vale of the Passage Lakes and found our Blacksmith, alive and unharmed beside the water." He touched a small star carved on the anvil, as if etched into its steel. "There, he commissioned them as knights in his service, tasked with spreading the news of his return among the Aladoth and bidding them come rest in Keledev's great sanctuary."

"That is an excellent telling of the history, Mister Lee," Master

Belen said. "That small band of Keledan were the first lightraiders. The Rescuer sent them immediately into the lake, transporting them into Tanelethar to begin their mission."

"What *about* the Passage Lakes?" Tiran urged his mare forward between Lee and his horse to ride closer to the guardians. "If they can transport lightraiders out of Keledev, couldn't Connor's goblins have used them to get in?"

"Tread carefully, lad," Master Quinton said. "Those're the Rescuer's gifts yer slanderin'. Neither the lakes nor the Storm Mists have ever served as a gateway for dark creatures."

Belen raised his thin eyebrows at the swordmaster. "Young Mister Yar has a right to ask such questions, Angus. The goblins got in somehow. What other options are there?"

Dag raised a hand. "Have you considered the lost portals? You know. The hollow hills of the ancient kings?"

The three guardians looked his way, and Master Belen furrowed his brow. "What do you know of the hollow hills?"

Dag shrugged. "A few tales from the old histories. Lee is not the only one of us who likes to read, you know."

"No, of course not," Master Belen said. "My apologies, young sir. And you raise an excellent question. One worth investigating."

Tiran grunted his agreement as he circled back to his place among the initiates, as if he knew exactly what Master Belen and Dag meant by *the hollow hills* and *the lost portals*.

Connor did not. He leaned closer as Tiran reined up beside him. "What's a hollow hill?"

"I . . . uh . . ." Tiran cleared his throat. "You know . . . a hollow hill. It's . . ."

"When the Maker formed our world," Belen said, rescuing him, "he pinched folds into the fabric of creation so his Elder Folk might walk from one end to the other in their service and authority. And when the Elder Folk departed, the ancient kings fought over them for a time. These portals were called hollow hills. There are none here in Keledev, and those in Tanelethar are long forgotten."

Master Jairun gave Belen a sober glance. "Or so we thought." He pointed farther along the ridge road with his staff. "The academy grounds extend another league or so, to the place where this road meets the southern slope of the forest valley. The Assembly set a marker there for us, back when the two institutions were on better terms. But, until I say otherwise, you initiates will not travel any farther south than this arch. And you will not travel farther than the switchbacks below the green without at least two companions. Understood?"

They all nodded, and Master Jairun turned east along a path leading down into the forest valley. "This trail marks the line you are forbidden to cross. It cuts through the valley and then up to the road on the eastern split ridge, which we call Hammer and Tongs. And that road will take us back to the fortress."

Lee took a place at the head of the initiates as the column formed up again. "Are you restricting our movements because you still fear an attack, Headmaster? Was it not a good sign that we saw no enemies on our approach last night?"

Master Jairun sighed. "I am not certain, Mister Lee–an unusual circumstance for me. When young lives are at stake, it is difficult to discern between the whispers of the Helper and the worries of the heart, even for a lightraider guardian."

Connor rested his hands on his saddle horn. "But you think the goblins may have found one of these hollow hills, or something like them?"

"Not the goblins, my boy. A dragon. A wyrm's mind is a powerful force. With the right focal point, a dragon might command a shifting portal to deliver one of its dark creatures almost anywhere."

The headmaster's pronouncement sobered the company's mood, and no one spoke for a while, until Lee quietly asked Belen about the forest valley into which they had descended, nestled between the terraced pastures of Mer Nimbar and the cliff face beneath Ras Telesar's glade. "How can there be a forest this high in the mountains? Isn't the air too cold for trees?"

"True, true." The guardian grinned at the boy. "The Gathering's warm water lends its healing to the soil, making the impossible possible." He gestured at the oaks and spruce around them. "We call this the Forest of Believing, and it is home to some of the most unique flora and fauna in all creation."

The guardian opened his cloak and lifted a journal from a leather vest cluttered with pockets and metal attachments. He flipped through the pages and showed them a sketch of a fat-toed and fat-headed lizard with long flaps of skin stretched between its legs. "I am attempting to catalogue the fauna. I named my favorite the paradragon—as in similar-but-standing-opposed-to dragons. They glide like leaves from the trees, and they are an image of creation over corruption, flying lizards as they were meant to be. Quite scarce, mind you, even for this forest. Incredibly rare."

At the word *scarce,* Connor heard Teegan let out a quiet "Eep!" She yanked a wiggling orange tail from Aethia's beak—only a tail. She tossed the gruesome remains away and folded her hands just as Belen glanced back again.

The guardian misinterpreted the nature of her outburst. He waved the journal. "Don't worry, dear. I'll be happy to share my drawings with the rest of you when we return to the fortress. Plenty of time. Plenty of time."

Teegan forced a smile. "Wonderful. Yes. Thank you."

Connor stifled a laugh, but Dag nearly gave them away. "Will we pause for a late luncheon? If the bird gets to eat, so should we."

For all their work to earn it the night before, their supper had been another disappointing round of way-ration porridge. All the stores had been left in the lower ward with the pack animals. Connor imagined that by now someone Dag's size was in need of something more substantial. He certainly was.

Fortunately for Aethia and her co-conspirators, Belen did not connect Dag's complaint to the now even scarcer paradragon. "You'll eat in due time, young sir. In due time."

"For now," Master Jairun said, "focus on the trees, not your stomach. Stay sharp. If we encounter enemies, look to your swordmaster. He is carrying extra weapons for those who have none."

Quinton pulled his cloak aside to reveal a pair of daggers and a hand axe strapped to his belt and thigh. "An' the other side is equally weighted–but not just for you lot. I always carry extra."

Connor didn't doubt it.

The guardians led them through the warmth of the forest valley then back up the road along the Hammer and Tongs to the fortress. There, they dismounted and walked the sloping perimeter of Ras Telesar on a near-invisible trail through the mountain rocks.

From the blustery cold of the trail's highest point, Connor could see most of the fortress. Viewed from below or within, Ras Telesar had been a confusion of walls and towers. But from the high trail, looking down over the fortress, Connor saw order within the chaos. He saw what Lee seemed to have known from the start, that the Rescuer had planned every rejoined stairway and shifted wall–something new from the old, formed in mere moments as the mountains sprouted from the peninsula.

Despite Dag's request, there was no late luncheon. Supper came in the lower ward–another pouch of way rations and a boiled egg for each of them–placed in their hands as they were sent back to the barracks by the same route they'd used to come down. Belen explained that he and Quinton had traveled light in the race to Ras Telesar after the goblin attack in Dayspring Forest, bringing only a few chickens. "We shall make use of the new stores you brought us soon enough. I promise. But we must make them last."

Dag accepted his ration without the slightest grumble. Tiran did not, though his complaint had nothing to do with the food. "I must confess, I'm disappointed. I expected a greater challenge out of academy life–something more than riding around to look at carvings and trees."

Even in the failing light, Connor could see Master Quinton's face reddening. "Oh, lad. I suggest ya learn to curb that tongue o' yours. Today was an orientation–gettin' the lay of the land, so ta speak. Tonight, ya'd better get yer rest. 'Cause tomorrow yer real training begins."

27

KARA WALKED HER CART DOWN THE STEEP TRAIL ON the south side of Trader's Knoll, listening to the steady squeak of its wheels. The cart carried only furs. Feeling the cold touch of winter, the locals had snatched up her entire pile of charwood. She'd have to visit Halas, the old collier who cooked the wood for her. And she'd have to go this evening, lest she miss a similar opportunity on the morrow.

Charwood sales had been good, but too few travelers had taken an interest in the furs. Kara hadn't dared to lighten any more purses while Nesat haunted the square. Granogs were thieves by nature, but they did not suffer humans to be the same. His presence unnerved her far more than Gaman's. She couldn't wait for her brehnan to return from their hunting trip.

The light had faded by the time Kara turned down the winding trail to the collier's cottage–a long hovel of mud and sod, as much part of the forest as any grassy hummock in the southern highlands. She had no trouble making out the orange glow of his kiln through the trees. The slender mound stood as tall as a bristlecone pine, with smoke pouring from its top.

It took a skilled and patient hand to make charwood. A single misstep could burn a month's supply of wood to gray dust. Kara knew. She and her brehnan had tried to make their own supplies once.

"Hal?"

Someone had lit the kiln. Kara usually found him right

beside it, watching for cracks in the mound. She wheeled the cart to a stop, ending its incessant squeaking. For the first time she felt the evening's deep quiet. The fresh cold had driven the bugs underground and the beasts into their burrows.

"Hal?"

No answer. A breath of wind brushed Kara's neck, followed by a groan of hinges in desperate need of grease. The door to his hovel stood open.

"Hal, it's Kara. I've come for more charwood." She ducked into the hearth room. A low fire burned in the pit, casting dim shadows across what meager furnishings Hal kept–a wicker chair, a square table with legs of gnarled driftwood.

She didn't see him.

The hearth room had but one other door, which Kara presumed led to a bedchamber. She heard an ominous snarl from the other side. A wolf? One of Nesat's goblins?

She burst through and found a much larger room than expected–a second hearth room and a shop. Hand tools and wood shavings covered a long worktable against one wall. The shelves and walls were filled with pots, jars, and drawings. Her drawings.

Hal stood at the opposite door, whole and unharmed, as if conversing with a neighbor. Kara caught a flash of gray beyond the threshold. Then it was gone. "Hal?"

"Well, good evening, child. Welcome. Do come in, please, and don't bother knocking or observing any of the usual traditions of polite society."

Kara blushed. "I did call out to you. I heard an animal. I thought you were in trouble."

A gentle smile lifted his braided beard. "In that case, I thank you, my champion."

"What were you doing?"

"Sharing a meal with a friend." The collier carried a wooden plate with a few cubes of cooked meat. He set it down on the worktable and popped a morsel into his mouth, licking his fingers. "Now, I expect you're here for another half cord? Go on outside. I have a load stacked and ready for you in the shed. I'll catch up in a moment."

"First, I have something for you." Kara cast a quick glance at the drawings on the wall. She'd never known what he did with them, or if he even kept them. She removed a roll of scrap hide from her coat.

"Oh, lovely." Hal took the charcoal sketch with ginger hands and spread it out on the worktable. "The market square, I see. A little darker than your usual fare but nicely drawn."

Kara had started giving him the charcoal sketches almost two years earlier. And Hal, it seemed, had kept every one. She drew on scraps of hide left over from her efforts as a seamstress, sketching the square or the people in it. Quite often her art had turned to the Impossible Peaks. Hal had taken her childish gifts and turned them into real works of art, making frames of bark and stone.

"I've always said you should sell these instead of your furs." The old collier rolled up the drawing and set it aside.

"I don't want the others in Trader's Knoll to see them. But you're . . ." She didn't quite know how to finish. Hal had become a patehpa to Kara, but she wasn't ready to admit such a thing.

"I understand," he said with a kind nod. "And I'm honored. Now. Let's get you sorted."

Kara waited for him outside the hummock. "Winter is nearly here," she called. "Demand for charwood is up. On the morrow I'll raise my price at the market, and I wouldn't fault you if you did the same for our arrangement."

Hal appeared, closing the door behind him. "One peta for the lot will suffice, as usual."

"One peta. I'm stealing from you."

Something between a cough and a laugh shook his beard, and she could have sworn she heard *Not from me* within the sound.

"What was that?"

"Nonsense, I said. One peta is a fair price to spare an old man the trouble of pushing his wares up that dreadful hill." He reached the shed and fiddled with the lock.

To call it a shed was a gross insult. With its stone foundation and walls of stout timber, Kara often wondered how Hal, bent with age, had built it. "Why do you keep your charwood in such a place, this small fortress?"

"Goblins." Hal turned the key. "Vile and destructive creatures, but lazy. Show them a solid wall and strong lock, and they'll move on to easier targets."

Kara handed him the peta and began carrying black logs to her cart. "Do you see many goblins out here?"

"Too many of late. Too many, indeed."

They worked in silence for a few moments before Hal spoke again. "Kara, who is the creature at the center of your market sketch?"

Kara knew which creature he meant. She'd made him even taller in the drawing, working her fear into the broken lines of char. "He calls himself Nesat. Gaman is dead, Hal. Nesat is taking over Trader's Knoll and all the southern highlands."

The collier nodded. "A stronger granog is necessary to govern the forces now spreading into Highland Forest–creatures that haven't ventured this far south in ages. Sprites in the woods. Centaurs guarding the river crossings. I hear a wood troll has moved into the valley near Maidenwood Grove." He dumped an armload of logs into the cart, sending up a cloud of fine black dust. "Have you ever seen a wood troll, my dear?"

Kara shook her head.

"Corky fellows, but dangerous. Mocktrees and oaksquids, they're called in some places, and their recruits are known as barkhides. A wood troll press-gangs men and women into small armies to help a dragon control the locals. Their sorcery lures those who desire power." He regarded her with a penetrating gaze. "But I don't think you suffer that particular malady. A wood troll is no problem for you." He turned and locked the shed, muttering under his breath again. "River trolls, though . . ."

"Why have these creatures come? What does it all mean?"

"It means these woods are no longer safe, child." The old man hung the key around his neck. "It means you should hurry home before the night gets any darker."

28

"AWAKE, SLEEPER!"

Connor's second day at Lightraider Academy began as the first, with shouting and pounding.

"Awake, sleeper!"

"Is he going to do this every morning?" Lee pulled his blanket over his head. "The fourth watch isn't over yet. It's still dark."

Connor rolled off his giant bed slab and hurried through the barracks, slapping at Tiran's ankle as he passed. "I've got the door. Don't bother getting up."

Tiran buried his face in his pillow. "Didn't plan to."

Quinton looked as grumpy as ever. "How long'll you and yer classmates sleep, Shepherd Boy? How long must I wait at the threshold?"

"In our defense," Lee said, "Dag's snoring rivals your pounding and shouting for volume."

Quinton cocked his head and listened to the miner's deep rips and rumbles. "Fair point, lad. Wake him up and end the noise. And you, Shepherd, get yer flock to the western lists fer trainin'. Bring what weapons you have. If the sun is up before ya reach me, I'll take yer payment in sweat."

He sauntered off as before, but this time Connor was ready with a question. "And will you tell me the way? Or at least give me a hint?"

"Follow the way o' the Rapha."

What was that supposed to mean? But something else the

swordmaster had said seemed more important in the moment. *If the sun is up before ya reach me.* Connor shot a glance at the crack between the curtains and saw the gray of dawn coloring the sky. "Up!" He clapped his hands at the others. "We have to get a move on, or we'll all suffer."

"Fine. Let's get to it, then." Tiran threw off his blanket and walked out to the balcony, returning with a stoneware cup brimming with water. "I prepared this last evening upon our return–left it out all night in the frigid mountain air. You can all thank me later." He strolled to the end of Dag's bed and dumped the water on his face.

Dag sat straight up, letting out a roar. "What? Who?" He wiped a hand across his eyes and looked down at the wetness of it. "*Why?*"

Connor tossed the miner a shirt, looking to Tiran. "Well done. Wake your shessa next, though I suggest a gentler method."

"And why can't she wake herself?" Teegan stepped into the room through the balcony doorway, eliciting a gasp from Lee. He held up a shirt to cover his bare chest.

"Oh, stop." She yanked the shirt away. "You come from a long line of fisherman. The men of your town run about all day in nothing but their britches."

She threw the shirt at his face, and Lee hurriedly dragged it on. "Well, I don't, thank you very much."

Connor had them moving in short order, but he still had no idea where to lead them. "*Follow the way of the Rapha*. As if I should know what it means."

Dag raised a thick hand. "The Rapha are an Elder Folk race with hearts for ministering to others."

"He's right." Lee opened the balcony doors wide and nodded to the barbican towers where the two collection glasses still burned bright. "The figure with the water bowl in the eastern tower represents their kind. They were masters of hospitality, renewing body and spirit." His eyes lit up, and he turned to the miner. "I know what Quinton meant. Dag, do you think you could find the kitchen?"

The miner yawned and smacked his lips. "I thought you'd never ask."

The initiates had seen a little more of the fortress after supper the previous evening. Belen had dropped by the barracks and shown them how to find the bathhouses. These diverted a portion of one of the nine warm streams into a line of rooms, creating what amounted to dressing chambers each with their own miniature waterfalls. The runoff watered the academy's lists.

Quinton had met the group there, and before allowing them to use the baths, he'd assigned them chores. Connor and Lee helped the swordmaster lug eight great bags of wasters to a storage room, Teegan and Tiran helped Master Jairun stable the horses and mules, and Belen had recruited Dag–without much convincing–to help him carry the food stores to the kitchen.

"Wait till you see it." The miner led the group up a winding stair. "There's more than a dozen giant ovens and–" He stopped. The stair had ended at a square chamber with a recessed fountain in one wall and three window slits cut into another but no exits. "I . . ." Dag stammered. "I could have sworn Master Belen brought me through this room and down those stairs on the way to the barracks."

"Not likely. And now the sun is almost up." Tiran smacked the miner's arm with the back of his hand and gestured at the windows. "I don't know why we chose this plan. We should be headed for the training fields, not the kitchen." He turned and started down the stairs.

"Wait." Lee sniffed the air. "Do you smell that?"

"I do." Teegan pushed past them, deeper into the room.

"As do I." Connor widened his nostrils to catch a better trace. "Pork. Cooked pork."

Even Tiran could not resist those words. "Did you say cooked pork?"

They followed their noses to the recessed fountain, where a bent stone pipe poured its stream down into a shallow basin.

"Do you think . . ." Lee lowered a cupped hand toward the water, hesitated, and pulled it back again without dipping it in. "Do you think the water tastes of cooked pork?"

The others all frowned at him. Teegan touched the statue of a hooded figure, ankle deep in the basin but beside the spout rather than beneath it, so the bowl in its hands remained empty. "The Rapha are never shown with an empty bowl. I think you did come this way, Dag. You didn't recognize the door because last night you passed through heading the opposite direction. Remember the statue where we first entered the fortress? That was a door too." She cranked the spout over until its stream arced sideways to fill the bowl.

They waited.

The bowl tipped under the water's weight. A click sounded from the stones. The whole fountain rotated out into the room and a wave of warm, pork-scented air rushed over them.

Dag sighed. "Breakfast."

Belen, not Quinton, shambled toward them across a vast space, clapping hands covered by leather mitts. "Excellent, excellent. You found me. Well of course you did, right?"

The chamber's grandeur dwarfed the guardian. At least a dozen giant ovens lined one kitchen wall, each large enough to cook three or four boars. Connor tried to imagine the heat and glow if they'd all been lit instead of just one. Shelves and cupboards filled the walls, cut from their very stone, with ladders to reach the highest.

Most of these cupboards were empty, as Master Jairun had told them, but Belen had made good use of what stores they'd brought. He pulled off his gloves and pushed a steaming tray of pastries across a polished-slate cutting table as high as Connor's shoulders. "Come. Eat."

Dag needed no such invitation. He downed his first pastry in moments, and the guardian pressed another into his hands. "A little pork and a lot of fat, baked with oats and berries into a pastry–everything an initiate needs for combat training."

Connor soaked in the scent and flavor of his two pastries, but it didn't last.

Belen glanced up at a shaft in the canted ceiling. "Oh dear. Look at the light." He shoved Tiran off the stone counter where he'd perched himself. "Your swordmaster awaits, and you know how cross he gets. Head out from the far end of the kitchen, take two rights and a left, then up the stairs. Off you pop."

Lee jogged beside Connor as the whole troop hurried down the hall. "Did he say up the stairs? We've already climbed a good bit. At some point we have to go down–down to the lists."

Yet they didn't. Belen's stair took them up as predicted, out onto a green field bounded by mountain rock, the bulwarks, and a long stone house on the north end. A low mist hung over the grass. Quinton stood next to a great pile of boulders, with the morning sun peeking over the eastern wall to illuminate his scowl. "Late again, Shepherd Boy."

29

AS PROMISED, THE SWORDMASTER TOOK HIS DUE IN sweat for their lateness. He grumbled and bellowed, driving the initiates like cattle as they moved the pile of boulders across the yard. The moment Connor placed the last stone, he bellowed even louder, and they moved the pile back again. None of it seemed fair. The task Quinton had given Connor when he awoke–to get the troop down to the western lists before sunup–had been impossible.

Perhaps that was the point. Impossible tasks meant guaranteed suffering for the initiates.

"So much . . . for the baths . . . we took." Lee collapsed beside the archery targets. He raised a weak arm. "Swordmaster, we need a rest."

Quinton would have none it. "No lounging! Shepherd, get yer flock to the eastern wall. On the way, you and the jackanapes fetch yer weapons."

"Jackanapes?" Connor looked around at the others.

"A jackanapes," Lee said between his heavy breaths, "is an . . . impertinent . . . child."

"He means me." Tiran got up and headed for the grass slope below the northern wall, where he and Connor had left their swords and the crook.

Masters Jairun and Belen had joined Quinton at the eastern wall. Beside them lay a broad canvas tarp, covering lumps with the general shape of wasters.

Tiran slowed as he and Connor approached, strapping on his scabbard. "So, it's to be swords today, is it?"

"Not cxactly," Quinton said, glancing at the lumps. "You'll see in a moment, lad. But first, I'll need ya to give me that blade o' yours. I'll take charge of it fer now."

"What? No. You can't."

Quinton stared him down until Tiran relented, then turned to Connor. "You too, Shepherd Boy. Pass yer burdens to Master Belen."

Connor obeyed, handing over his ebony crook and Faelin's sword, and Belen accepted them with a reverent hand. "We'll take good care of these, young sir. I promise. This sword and its master saved all three of our lives at one time or another."

Once Belen had left with the confiscated weapons, Quinton and Master Jairun peeled back the tarp, revealing the mystery lying beneath.

The rows of lumps turned out to be practice weapons. Not wooden wasters, but real bows and axes, daggers and maces, and weapons Connor could not name. They'd wrapped every tip and blade with leather and twine.

"Today is an important day." Quinton paced down the line of initiates. "'Tis Clunker Day, when ya choose yer practice weapons, which're called–"

"Clunkers," Tiran said.

The swordmaster hit him with a glower, then cleared his throat. "The clunkers ya choose today'll become yer constant companions. You'll carry 'em everywhere–to every meal and class, to bed every night–until ya know them as well as ya know yer own hands. You may choose up to three, but don' . . . er . . . take the added weight lightly, if ya know what I mean."

Tiran knelt and grunted as he tried to hoist a padded battle-axe from the grass. "We're to drag these unwieldy monstrosities everywhere we go?"

Dag picked up a matching axe and flipped it in the air. "Doesn't seem so bad."

"We never said this'd be easy." Quinton pivoted at the end of the line and continued on. "The gatekeeper's passage is always open fer those who wanna leave. But *if* ya choose to stay, you'll do so without any more o' yer *incessant whining*!" He boomed the last two words into Tiran's ear. "Anyone else have somethin' to say?"

No one breathed.

"Good. Then choose, and choose wisely, fer no one can be a master at all arms. You'll focus on these alone fer the rest of yer time here."

The guardians allowed the initiates some space to walk among the padded weapons. Dag, still holding the battle-axe, chose first. He picked up the other axe and a harness to carry the pair at his back. "Perfect."

Tiran declared that the only correct choices for a proper lightraider were a sword, a longbow, and a dagger, noting that an elderly knight of the way had once told him as much. Lee accepted his advice and chose the same, but after walking around a bit with all three weighing him down, he returned the sword to the pile.

Ignoring a good deal of chiding from her twin, Teegan chose a weighted net and a three-pronged spear she called a trident. Connor had not seen such arms before, but Lee had. The scribe clapped his hands. "Three cheers for the fisher queen. You'd fit right in at the docks."

Teegan slung the net around her torso, and the weights locked themselves together. "We hunt with similar tools in the coastal forests. A trident serves well for fish, foul, or beast. I don't see why it won't serve for orcs and goblins too." She hurled the thing at an archery target, and it stuck.

Quinton mumbled in Master Jairun's ear, "Those tip pads

might've suffered a wee bit of dry rot. I prob'ly shoulda checked 'em earlier."

Connor had little trouble with his choices. He'd become accustomed to sword work, and so he picked one about as long as Faelin's. A padded staff made a good stand-in for his confiscated crook. His old sling still hung from his belt. He showed it to Quinton. "What about this? May I choose a sling as my third?"

"Keep it, Shepherd Boy. It suits you."

Quinton set them to sparring with their choices right away. The dry-rotted padding did not make them hurt any less than a waster—more, in fact. A metal blade covered in broken leather carried a remarkable sting.

Tiran suffered for the chiding he gave his twin. She wielded her trident and net simultaneously, locking his sword with her tines and beating him about the head and shoulders with the weights. Again, Connor heard Quinton mumbling in Master Jairun's ear. "Oof. We prob'ly shoulda padded them weights too. Hurts me just watchin' this."

Connor held his own against Dag, though he spent most of his time dodging axes. He even managed to bring the miner down once with a sweep of his staff. But poor Lee could not land a single strike with his dagger, nor hit a single target with his bow and its snub-nosed arrows. Quinton hollered and bellowed at every miss.

When Belen returned, Connor pulled him aside to show him his friend's struggles. "Lee's been hopeless in a fight since the beginning. He's practiced, and he has speed. He just never hits his mark. Is there something you can do?"

"Perhaps." Belen pulled his journal and a narrow stick of black stone from his vest of devices, scratching out a note on a page. He consulted another, filled with script and symbols, and scratched his short beard. "Yes. Indeed, I can. I've seen this problem before."

30

KARA STALKED HER PREY THROUGH BRISTLECONE pines and cottonwoods hung with ivy. She pushed neither branch nor vine aside, but slipped between them, molding each step into root and soil. When she came to a clearing, she paused and listened to the crunching of cold leaves up ahead. Her quarry was fast, but Kara was faster–and deathly silent.

Rock. Tree. Root. Soil. Kara did not belong in the marketplace at Trader's Knoll, and she did not want to, especially after the fortnight she'd endured since her last meeting with Hal. Charwood and fur sales had dropped to almost nil, despite the cold. The people of Trader's Knoll kept to their homes and shops, fearful of the new granog.

Nesat the Menace prowled the market square from dawn to dusk. He'd taken over Gaman's three-story cottage, the butchery, the stables, and the lodge. And no one had seen poor Wilibrond for days. Each morning a troop of goblins carted barrow after barrow of dirt from the stables, snarling at anyone who crossed their path. And each evening Nesat collected his due from the shopkeeps. All told, he'd taken three quarters of Kara's earnings.

She needed her brehnan to come home.

Kara gained sight of her quarry and quickened her pace. A moment later, the man–tall and strong for his age–stopped and knelt to check a fox trap, as she'd known he would. His delay made a gift of the last few steps between them. Kara took these at a run and pounced.

Liam went down with a shout, though his impact with the dirt sheared the last of it into a stilted grunt. He always checked the family's smaller traps on the way home, while Keir pushed a wheeled cart along the main road—carrying the take of furs and meat.

Before Kara could pin him down, her brehna rolled clear. Liam rose to a knee, knife extended. "Stay back or I'll—" He let out a breath. "Shessa. What are you doing? I could have killed you."

"Not likely. You move through the brush like a horse."

Liam eyed her fur cloak. "If I'm a horse, then you're a bear."

"Do you like it?" She refused to take offense and twirled her shoulders to make the misshapen hem flounce. "The stitching is my best work."

"Yes. Sadly, it is." Liam sheathed his knife and inclined his head toward the knoll. "We'd best be going. If Keir reaches the cottage before me, he'll worry. The woods beyond are growing dangerous."

The Orso cottage lay in the knoll's western shadow, a good distance from Liam's final trap. As they walked, Kara told him about Nesat.

He hefted a canvas bag of carcasses up to his shoulder. "So, the troubles have come to Trader's Knoll."

"What troubles? What rumors have you heard?"

"Too many. And Keir and I met enough strangeness in our travels to see the truth in them. Hordes of dark creatures are moving into the southlands. From Spider Rock to Safety's End, the granogs are tightening the reins. Those who were known to be lax are gone." He pushed a thick branch aside and waited for Kara to pass. "What became of Gaman?"

"Dead."

"Of course he is. And there's something else." He hesitated. "Men have gone missing, Kara."

The revelation did not shock her. She had her own piece of the puzzle to share. "A wood troll moved in near Maidenwood Grove. Hal spoke of him gathering men and women for an army."

"So I've heard. Krokwode is his name, and his army grows by the day, spreading west from the great elamwoods. But Krokwode's barkhides are all accounted for. They serve him openly, bossing and bullying the hunters and townsfolk." Liam scowled at the trail beneath their feet. "No. The missing I speak of vanished without a trace, taken from their beds. And . . . they were all of a certain age."

Kara searched his face. Liam was a fighter, not a worrier, yet she saw the strain of fear in the crease of his brow. "What age?"

"Young men, Kara. My age. Younger than Keir, even."

They walked a well-traveled path toward the main road, listening to the forest together. After a time, Kara bumped Liam's arm with a shoulder in an effort to lighten his mood. "So a wood troll has come south. What do we care? What use is Krokwode's enchanted army of barkhides in a lawful woodland? Have the rabbits of Maidenwood Grove gone rogue? Are the beavers turning to bandits?"

Liam remained serious. "People, Kara. They're hunting people. Krokwode's patrols sweep the woods after dark. The granogs are setting curfews." As the path joined the main road, Liam held her back. "But the barkhides are a distraction. The real threat are the platoons."

"Platoons of what?"

He pulled her into the trees and nodded at the road.

Ore creatures. A troop of them marched toward the knoll. So, this was Nesat's mysterious entourage. Each stood a head or more taller than Liam, with hide like the color of iron ore, broken into twisted muscle and etched with wicked silver runes. The same runes adorned their halberds and scimitars–weapons of black pyranium, a dragon-forged alloy harder than steel.

"What language is that?" Kara whispered.

"A corruption of the Elder Tongue. The orcs carve the runes into their young to ignite the flame within. They glow red hot in the rage of battle."

As the orcs marched by, one paused and turned its gargoyle head Kara's way. She held her breath. The pupils were closed to narrow slits against the daylight. If it saw her, it gave no sign. After a time, it turned and followed its comrades.

As the troop disappeared around the bend, Kara stood, snorting to hide the quaking of her shoulders from her brehna. "I refuse to believe orc runes glow in the dark. It's a child's story."

"It's not a story, Kara." Liam remained in his crouch, staring after the dark creatures. "I saw it many years ago. And so did you." He looked up at his shessa. "You just don't remember."

31

"AWAKE, SLEEPER!"

Connor opened the barracks door, squinting through sleep-worn eyes. The sun had not yet risen, but his body had woken him before Quinton's arrival.

"Morning, Shepherd Boy." Quinton seemed disappointed that he'd gotten no chance to pound the door. But he gave Connor a nod. "Better."

The routine of academy life had set in.

For two weeks, every day began the same, with the swordmaster shouting his favorite phrase. After a short battle to wake the miner, the students would hurry through the fortress maze to one of the three lists, lugging their cumbersome clunkers all the way. Their days ended on the fields as well. "Combat day and night," Quinton said. "The only way to train a warrior."

The eastern lists were his favorite, shaped like a rectangular dish, with steep grassy slopes on every side. He made the initiates race up those slopes over and over until their legs refused to carry them.

Each morning, Belen greeted them somewhere along their route and shoved hot pastries into their hands. Each evening, as they trudged back through the castle, he'd do the same. The flavor of oats cooked in pork fat grew old. Connor yearned to start his day with something as simple as an apple or end it with something as nice as a bread pudding.

Lee still struggled and suffered in the sparring and shooting.

When Connor queried Belen regarding his promise to help, the guardian always answered with something cryptic. "Obstacles, young sir. So many obstacles. And variables too. But we must press on, mustn't we?" Occasionally he watched Lee and made notes, and then he would wander off, brow furrowed, muttering to himself or drawing in the air with a finger.

Routine may have marked the beginning and end of each day, but not the middle. Letters and lectures at Lightraider Academy were never dull, because the guardians never used a single chamber more than once. The initiates raced all over the fortress maze, carrying clunkers and solving riddles and puzzles to find their way to the next class, until countless hidden doors and secret passages became second nature.

One morning, Belen gathered the students in the highest tower, in a chamber so cold the floor was slick with frost, and taught them about the frost goblins and ice giants that swept the last of the northern kings from their strongholds. On another day, Master Jairun called them to a cellar beneath the barbican cauldrons, a room filled with flaming pots. They baked in the heat while he told them of a Lisropha warrior named Heleyor, who'd been lord of Ras Pyras and chief of the Elder Folk. He'd rebelled against the High One to become the Great Red Dragon.

The headmaster called these hot and cold extremes endurance training. Tiran called them torture, and Connor agreed.

With the variety of chambers, Connor expected at any moment to push aside a tapestry or slip through a passage and stumble into Nevethav, the Fountain Chapel, and see the source of the nine waterfalls. Every so often, one of the students asked if they could visit the place. Whichever guardian was with them always gave the same answer. "You're not ready, initiates."

On one of these occasions, Lee asked how they would open the chapel's giant doors once the time came. "Surely they are too heavy for human hands, even with the eight of us here."

Quinton, who was with them at the time, had nodded. "True enough, lad. No human hand can part those doors. They've been shut fer ages, an' they'll stay shut till the Rescuer sends one o' the Elder Folk to open them. In yer time, you lot'll enter by a different path."

After combat training on the fifteenth day, burdened as usual with their texts and clunkers, the students weaved their way up to the fourth level and found a hallway they'd not yet seen. Master Jairun waited for them before a set of grand doors four times his height. "Welcome," he said, pushing the doors wide, "to the library."

"Books." Dag's face lit up like a little boy's on the first day of Forge season.

Connor followed the miner in, turning in a circle. Four stories of books filled a domed chamber that might have been carved from a single giant oak, even the wrapping balconies and long winding stair.

Without permission, Lee slid onto the bench of a writing table twice his size and smoothed his hands over the top. "Finally, a proper surface for a scribe's pen." He drew his parchments from a satchel at his hip. "Is this another lesson in the Sacred Scrolls?"

"It is." Master Jairun pushed the boy from the seat with the knot of his staff. "But I've brought you here for recitation, not writing. Follow me and bring to mind the sacred verses I taught you regarding barriers."

"Sacred verses," Connor said, nudging the scribe. They'd become his favorite subject, even though Lee outshined him in their application. The scribe could memorize any scripture at a blink. Like every other text, he picked it up, set it down, and was done. And when he put pen to parchment, he turned each phrase into a work of art.

Still, Connor loved the Elder Tongue. Every new word he learned felt like a cloud parting.

Master Jairun led them up to the second balcony, to a door of iron with no rivets or lever, and not a speck of rust, set into an alcove amid the shelves. Once all five had gathered at the alcove, the guardian knocked on the door with his staff. It rang with a deep, hollow tone. "This is the *Shar Razel,* the Iron Door."

Tiran snickered. "The Elder Folk were never creative when naming things."

That bought him a pointed cough and a grim look. "Every lightraider initiate for generations has stood on this very balcony at this very moment in their training, Mister Yar. Today, you'll employ a sacred verse in dynamic prayer for the first time."

A murmur passed among the students. They had recited a good many sacred verses for memorization, but never for application.

"The Shar Razel marks a pivotal moment in a lightraider's training and faith. Once you cross the threshold, you are no longer an initiate but a full cadet. To that end, our initiates always begin with the No Barriers prayer. Remember, we are asking for the Rescuer's help, not making demands. Who'll be the first to try?"

"I will." Tiran stepped forward, rolling his head and wiggling his arms as if stepping up to a sword fight. After a deep breath, he spread his hands and let the door have it, reciting the verse in the Common Tongue in a loud voice.

Everyone stared at the Shar Razel as Tiran's final, booming word echoed off the iron.

Nothing happened.

"Yes. Well. Thank you, Mister Yar. Thank you for making my point." His gaze passed over the befuddled faces. "*Ask. Receive.* These words sound simple—perhaps a bit selfish. But you must remember, moments before he gave us those words, the Rescuer also admonished us to seek first his kingdom. The High One is not a wishing well. Whatever you ask, ask it according to his will."

His will. What had Tehpa said? *They believed they could*

discern the Rescuer's will. Could Connor do such a thing? Was it right? "But how can we know his will?"

Master Jairun laughed. "Why, the Sacred Scrolls, my boy. They are his guide for us." He looked to Tiran. "When you spoke, child, were you commanding the Shar Razel to open? Or were you asking the Rescuer to open the door for you, that you might step through in servanthood?"

Tiran didn't reply, and Connor didn't blame him.

Teegan seemed confused as well. "But what if the answer isn't in the Scrolls? I haven't memorized them all, but I know I won't find the Shar Razel there. Aren't we presuming too much to think the High One would push open a door for a lowly initiate?"

"We presume nothing, my dear. We make our requests and rely on him to do what is best, which may not be the answer we expect. He's not opening the door for you. He's opening a door in his plan. And you must be ready to walk through to meet his timing, not yours." Master Jairun positioned Connor in front of the door. "Your turn, my boy. Give it a try."

Rely on him. Don't presume. Ask that you might serve. It all seemed harder than Master Jairun made it sound. Connor faced the door. "Um . . . Ask–"

Master Jairun thumped the balcony with his staff. "In the Elder Tongue, please."

Connor swallowed against the straw in his throat, calling the primary words to mind–*ask, seek, knock, receive, find, open*. The rest fell into place as a whisper. "*She'am po naboliov, kavah po mashteliov, doq po keshar felasiov.*"

They all waited.

The Shar Razel didn't budge.

Master Jairun patted Connor's shoulder. "Well, as I said–his timing, my boy, not ours."

32

ON THE FOLLOWING MORNING, CONNOR AND THE others descended a stairway from the Hall of Manna, passing close to the chapel outcropping. He watched the misting streams fall beneath tall, many-colored windows, wondering what lay inside.

Resteram had come–Connor's third since the start of his training. Despite the name, which meant Day of Renewal, each Resteram began with combat training like every other day. Quinton made these sessions lighter and said they were necessary to prevent injuries for the new trainees. Afterward, the guardians would gather the initiates in the Hall of Manna for prayers and readings from the Sacred Scrolls. These were not actual scrolls, but leather-bound books that recorded the sacred verses captured in the original writings.

The initiates had the rest of the day to themselves. Tiran would practice his shooting. Dag usually hung out with Master Belen in the kitchen, but on this day, he planned to get lost in the library. And Teegan spent every Resteram on the switchbacks below the green, flying Aethia over the Forest of Believing. Lee and Connor had agreed to accompany her on this day's hunting trip, since Master Jairun's restrictions allowed three initiates to travel farther into the forest than one, but before they could set out, Master Belen called to them from a window in the Hall of Manna. "Mister Lee. Mister Enarian. I wonder if I could borrow a tick of your time."

The boys followed him up the steps of his tower workshop. Square buckets rose through the middle on a pulley system, animated by a waterwheel in the tower's base. These dumped their burdens into a rickety wooden trough along the inner wall. Through pipes and spigots, the water powered all manner of contraptions.

When they came to the upper chamber, Belen released a flood that flicked lever after lever, striking flint against steel to light a succession of lanterns. A warm glow filled the reaches the daylight couldn't touch. "Do you like it?" he asked. "I call it the *flicker,* for it brings the flicker of flame to many lamps at once."

Strange tools and devices hung from pegs or were strewn about the tables–a hammer small enough for a faerie, pincers suited to the huge hands of a giant, spinning mirrors, a silver orb hovering above a pedestal. Connor counted three different versions of the spyglass Master Jairun had shown him more than two weeks before.

Belen gestured to a stool in the corner. "Have a seat, Mister Lee. I think I have the solution to your troubles with Swordmaster Quinton."

Lee looked stricken. "What troubles?"

The guardian went on as if he hadn't heard. "You can't score against your opponents on the lists or hit the archery targets. You can't hit anything at all, if I'm honest. I've been watching. Tell me, young sir. Does the world look fuzzy to you?"

"No fuzzier than it looks to anyone else."

"Yes. Well. That may not be as true as you think." Belen spun Lee and the stool together to face a workbench, where a single candle stood on a brass stand. He lit the wick. "Within the Lightraider Order, there are spheres, some of which are divided into disciplines. I am a master of the Sphere of Tinkers. You may consider yourself blessed because of it. Tell me. Which of these makes the flame sharper." He held a lens like those in the spyglass before Lee's right eye, then lowered it and held up another.

Lee shrugged. "I guess the second one makes it a little sharper."

"Good. Very good." Belen raised a third lens. "And which is better, that second lens, or this one?"

The process continued through enough lenses to fill a window. Finally, Belen withdrew to another workbench where he donned a leather apron and a half helmet with a tinted glass shield. His foot worked furiously at a pedal beneath the bench. Sparks flew about his shoulders. Connor leaned left and right, trying to see around him. "What are you making, Master Belen?"

Belen blew on his project. "I call them spectacles, for when Mister Lee puts them on, the world will be a spectacle the likes of which he's never seen." He set not one or two but six of his glass lenses into a thick band of leather and bronze. Four were fixed to little arms, so they might flip up and down. The thing looked more like a set of horse blinders than an aid for Lee's sight.

Lee pulled his head away to dodge the apparatus as Belen approached, but the guardian caught him and pushed the apparatus onto his head, securing the leather strap. He stepped away to appraise his efforts, leaving Lee sitting on the stool like a skinny, bug eyed paradragon. "What do you think?"

Lee grumbled about the weight and tugged at the strap, but then he looked up at the other two and caught his breath. He stood, steadying himself against the workbench, and his googly gaze settled on Connor. "Is this how the world looks to you?"

"Sure. I guess."

Lee laughed. "Wonderful."

"Yes. Wonderful," Belen said. "Excellent. You've got the hang of it. And I want to show you something else about these spectacles—a feature of sorts. Features are a specialty of the Tinker's Sphere." The guardian took Lee by the arm and pulled him to a window. He pointed at the next tower over. "Do you see the weathervane?"

"I do see it. The copper is formed in the shape of a running lion."

"Very good. But that's not the point." Belen pressed a beautiful ash longbow into Lee's hands. "The point is to shoot it. Shoot the lion, Mister Lee."

"I can't. The distance is too great."

"Is it?" Belen flipped one of the extra lenses down in front of Lee's right eye.

"Oh."

The guardian flipped down another one.

"*Oh,*" Lee said again, a little louder.

Belen lifted the initiate's elbows to raise the bow and nocked an arrow on the string. "Now you get it. Take the shot."

Lee let the arrow fly, and Connor heard a distant ping. He ran to his friend's side and saw the lion weathervane spinning.

THAT NIGHT, BOTH BOYS SAT BETWEEN THE FOURTH wall parapets, watching the two bright moons rise over the Hammer and Tongs. The spot had become their favorite haunt. Three chapel streams passed nearby and lent the warmth of their waters to the night air.

"You've hardly spoken since the tower." Lee clicked his extra lenses up and down. He'd been doing it all day and showed no signs of stopping. "Celebrate with me. The forest, the mountains, and the moons–they're all new tonight." He flicked a green lens into place. "I can even see the dark moon."

Connor kicked his heels against the bulwark stones. "I know. And I'm happy for you. But I keep thinking about the Shar Razel. It wouldn't open for me."

"The Iron Door hasn't opened for any of us."

"Yes, but–"

"But what, my friend? You're special?"

Connor said nothing. The notion didn't sound good when

Lee spoke it out loud.

Lee continued his clicking, tilting his head to look up at the stars. "Master Belen told me the Shar Razel is less about the initiate and more about the High One. There are a host of reasons he might not open the door. Few have anything to do with us."

"What reasons?"

"Who knows?" Lee clicked another lens down, zeroing in on one particular piece of the heavens. "The High One is infinite. So are his plans. Perhaps he keeps the door closed waiting for some event we can't fathom, a thousand leagues away. None but he can see that far."

"*You* can see a thousand leagues." Connor elbowed his friend. "Well . . . almost."

Lee laughed but then sat forward. "I do see something." He pointed at the grotto near the Gathering cataracts. "I see Master Jairun. And he's talking to something fuzzy."

"Fuzzy? You mean your spectacles aren't working?"

"No. Fuzzy, as in furry. It's big and gray, but the stones of the grotto are hiding its form. Master Jairun is talking to it, and he's holding a sealed parchment." After another moment, Lee shook his head. "They're gone. Both of them." He flipped up his extra lenses. "Did we just catch our headmaster having a secret meeting with a creature of some sort?"

Connor drew a knee to his chest and stared at the spot. He'd seen nothing but shadows, but he didn't doubt Lee's eye. "Perhaps we should find out."

33

"AWAKE, SLEE–"

Connor flung open the barracks door. "Hang on a minute," he said, holding up a finger, then slammed it closed again.

Dag chuckled, which came out as a light rumble. "You'll pay for that."

"We'll all pay for it," Tiran grumbled, buckling his belt.

Lee fastened his new spectacles in place and blinked googly eyes at the others. "Tiran's right. Best not make the swordmaster wait. Someone should go get Tee–"

Lee's voice fell away as a balcony door swung open. Teegan stood in the dawn's pink light, red hair drifting in the morning breeze, trident planted on the stones. "I'm here. Let's go."

The scribe had not yet managed to close his mouth. Connor clapped him on the back. "Yeah. She's always looked like that. You just couldn't see her properly before."

Connor may have had the first laugh of the morning, but Master Quinton got the last. He sent the initiates to the eastern lists and drove them up and down the sloped edges, bellowing about the shepherd boy watering the field with the sweat of his flock. Afterward, they all stood in a half circle, buckled over and breathing hard.

Tiran glared at Connor. "Why are we *your* flock?"

"I don't know. Why were they always my goblins?"

The two quieted as Quinton and Belen strode over. The swordmaster gave Belen a frown. "I doubt those spectacles'll serve Mister Lee in bat'le. He looks . . . unbalanced."

"The swordmaster is right." Tiran straightened, still panting. "He's as top-heavy as a kingfisher." He raised his leather-bound sword to Lee's shoulder as if to tip him over.

In a single, arcing motion, Lee wheeled the blade away with the curve of his longbow, caught Tiran behind the knees with the other end, and sent him crashing to the grass.

Teegan leaned over her twin. "I'd say fighting blind so long has done our scribe some good."

Quinton walked away. "Right. Moving on, then."

The morning's combat lesson involved disarming and binding opponents. "'Tis far more difficult to spare an enemy than kill him," Quinton said as his pupils formed a line for drills. "Each o' ya must learn how, for a lightraider is forbidden to kill the Aladoth."

"Why?" Teegan unslinged her weighted net. "Won't they try to kill us?"

"They will, indeed, lass. But human folk in Tanelethar are not soulless orcs or mocktrees. They're deceived, poisoned against the Maker. Don' forget, we were all Aladoth once, even those born here, until we accepted our Blacksmith's gift. To kill an Aladoth is to deny them the same chance, handin' their soul over to the second death. There're consequences fer such a terrible deed."

Dag raised a fist at the end of the line. "I read of this in the *Talin's Chronicles*. A young lightraider, enraged during a battle with orcs and Aladoth, killed a Scarlet Moon sorcerer. Regret weakened his body and sent him into a depression for months. He left the Order."

Connor had not heard the miner utter so much in one breath in the entire time he'd known him. "Sounds like you're making good use of the library."

Dag shrugged. "I told you I like to read."

The swordmaster showed them a few tricks and techniques—how to catch an arm with the flat of a blade, how to sweep a leg with a heel. After drills, he paired them off for sparring. "One of you'll attempt to score killin' blows. The other must disarm and subdue the attacker without harm. Fight!"

Whether by chance or design, Quinton paired Lee with Tiran for the first round and left Connor as the odd man out. Lee did well as the Keledan defender, using his bow as a staff the way he'd done before, until he finally brought Tiran down.

They swapped roles, making Lee an Aladoth with murderous intent. But as the defending lightraider, Tiran showed little control. His blocks turned to strikes, and with an angry shout, he thrust his leather-wrapped blade into the scribe's gut and knocked Lee's dagger from his hand.

Connor felt the blow to the gut as if he'd taken it himself, which he had—on that cold night at Ravencrest.

In a rage, Tiran advanced, raising his sword above his head.

"Enough!" Quinton rushed in and shoved him away. "Did ya not hear what I said? Defenders aren't to land any killin' blows."

"I . . ." Tiran emerged from his fog. "I was angry. He took me down hard."

"And how much angrier will ya be when an Aladoth tries ta lop yer arm off?" Quinton thrust a finger toward the edge of the field. "Stand over there and think about it." He helped Lee take a seat in the grass and nodded to Connor. "You're up, Shepherd Boy."

The evening session went much the same, though Tiran would barely raise a sword as either attacker or defender, and they all retired to their bread, baths, and beds with little chatter. Exhaustion had set in. But the night's work for Lee and Connor was not finished.

They had plans.

34

KARA STABBED AT A SLIVER OF VENISON ON HER wooden plate, her ration for the night. "How long will our meat last?"

"Not long." Her brehna Keir sat across from her at the family's small table. "The stores from the hunt won't last the month. We were after furs, not food. We should head into town tomorrow, sell a few, and buy bread and pork while we can."

"No." Liam had already finished his ration, which had been markedly smaller than Kara's. He sat by the hearth, brooding. Liam hadn't allowed the other two to go to town since his return from the hunting trip. And he'd made only one trip of his own, long enough to sell the last of the furs and charwood. "We stay clear of Nesat's eye so he'll not miss us when we leave."

"Leave?" Keir stood. "And go where, brehna? Look out the window. There's naught south of us but the Southern Overlord's giant mountains. And winter rolls farther down the slopes by the tick. We ran as far as we could years ago."

"We could go east, all the way to the Stone Hills." Kara swallowed the last meager bite and pushed her plate away. "I hear the villages there are left to themselves."

"And what if they aren't?" Keir said. "I say we wait for–"

"We *cannot* wait." Liam glowered at Keir from the hearth. "The noose will tighten, as it did in the north. First the curfews, then journey writs, always in hand. And then liege runes." He pulled up his sleeve, showing them the brand burned into his arm. "You were too young. But you'll see. And when they begin checking liege runes, they'll find out about Kara."

Keir shook his head. "You don't know that. None of this may come to pass. The wood troll, the orcs–it's all Nesat, a new granog making his mark, nothing more."

"It *is* more. You heard Bartholomew Fowler. He saw a troop of goblins building a castle in a high-mountain vale east of Maidenwood Grove. A *castle,* Keir."

"Barty Fowler is a southlander. He wouldn't know a castle from a cave goblin. For all we know, he saw the makings of Nesat's summer mansion."

Liam paused while stoking the fire. "You're right. What does Barty know? I must see for myself before we make plans."

"That's not what I said."

"But it's no less true"

"Then let me go." Keir knelt beside him. "You stay here and hunt out the last of the deer. You're the better shot."

Kara had been watching the argument in silence, but she could bear it no longer. She raised a hand. "Or I could go."

Both brehnan replied in unison. "No."

"But I–"

Liam shushed her with a wave of his hand. "Keir will go, traveling by day only. Right, Keir? Stay at the inns and keep to yourself."

"Of course."

"When you find what the goblins are building, look for the foundations of four pyranium spires. Look for cogs and chains."

"Yes. Obviously." Keir rose and crossed his arms. "I know the signs of a dragon gate."

35

LEE CLOSED THE BARRACKS DOOR INCH BY AGONIZING inch, until Connor gave an impatient sigh and pulled his hand away, letting the door fall into place with a *thump.*

"Careful. They'll hear."

"Not likely. Dag is dead to the world. Tiran can't hear over his snoring."

Both boys turned and found Teegan right behind them. "Hello. What's this?"

"See." Lee smacked Connor on the arm. "She heard."

"I hear everything. Always have." Teegan dragged them farther down the passage. "Now, tell me what you're up to, or I'll start shouting 'Awake, sleeper!' at the top of my lungs."

"Come on," Connor said. "We'll tell you on the way."

Ras Telesar looked different at night. The moonlight seeping in through the windows brought the fading tapestries to life—ghostly soldiers fighting endless battles. The tall statues of Elder Folk became wraiths hovering in shadowed corners.

As the three climbed a spiral staircase, Lee shuddered. "I feel as if Swordmaster Quinton will jump out and grab me at any turn."

"Ooh." Teegan flicked his shoulder. "Are you afraid he'll make you run up a hill or carry something heavy?"

"Heavier than usual? Yes. Aren't you?"

Connor turned to give them a hard stare. "Quinton will come for all of us, if you two don't pipe down."

His rebuke did not quiet Teegan. She hopped up a step to walk next to him. “You still haven’t told me where we’re headed.”

“The headmaster’s chambers. The creature Lee told you about brought him a parchment, and we’re going to find it. But we must keep quiet. If we wake a guardian, we’re done for.”

“Too late.” Teegan pointed up the steps. A light flickered against the staircase’s curving wall. “Someone’s up already.”

Connor yanked the other two behind the statue of a Lisropha warrior, and they squished together behind its wings, doing their utmost not to breathe.

The headmaster hurried past with his staff and candle, cloak dragging on the steps.

Lee slipped out of hiding. “He’s gone. Now’s our chance to get into his chambers.”

But Connor waited. He peered down the stairwell after Master Jairun. “But we expected to catch him sleeping.” He thought about it a moment longer, then started down the stairs. “He’s up to something. Let’s follow. Quickly, before we lose him.”

They followed the candle’s glow at a distance, scurrying across open ramparts and creeping down long hallways, until the headmaster turned beneath a low archway. His light vanished.

Connor rushed ahead. He grabbed the corner and swung around it only to find an empty alcove. Master Jairun was gone.

Lee and Teegan caught up, and the scribe examined the bare stones. He pressed against one that stuck out from the back wall. “There must be a hidden passage.” But the stone didn’t move.

Connor and Teegan tried other protruding stones with the same result, until Teegan stepped back. “There’s a pattern here, almost like”–her gaze tracked upward–“a ladder. Look.”

Connor saw a hexagonal well in the ceiling above. Without warning, Teegan jumped up, caught a stone high on the wall, and climbed into the well.

“She’s quite skillful,” Lee whispered to Connor, watching her go.

"What'd you expect? She grew up in Sil Tymest, living among the trees."

Lee went next, and Connor followed, but his fingers slipped on the last block. Teegan caught his wrist and hauled him up through the hexagon, falling backward with him into a small nook exposed to the ramparts. He rolled away. "Thanks."

"Don't mention it."

"Hey. Look, you two." Lee showed them a wooden door. Warm yellow light spilled out over the threshold beneath. "Do we go in?"

"Too risky." Connor jerked his head toward the battlements. "I have a better idea."

They crawled along the rampart walkway and crouched beneath two windows, peering over the sills into the lantern-lit chamber.

Master Jairun was there, and so was Quinton, reclining in a chair beside a strange table of glistening green stone. The table had jagged inlets and sweeping curves like the outlines of a map, and ran nearly the whole length of the room.

"And where is our Master Belen?" Master Jairun poured two cups of some steaming concoction from a copper kettle. The scent of cinnamon and cloves filled the room, drawn out by the night breeze.

Quinton took a sip and wiped his sleeve across his whiskers. "Pavel's up in his tower, tinkerin' with some device'er'other. Fer certain, he's forgotten all about us."

Master Jairun brushed Belen's absence aside with a wave of his staff and drew something from his cloak.

"The parchment." Lee clicked a lens down over his eye and leaned over the sill until Connor pulled him back. "That's the one I saw. I'd swear to it."

"I see you've had a visit from Pedrig." Quinton pushed himself up from the chair. "Go on, then. Show me."

"Who is Pedrig?" Teegan whispered.

Master Jairun spread the parchment out upon the table, muttering a prayer. "*Rumosh vynovu howdi'eni; Rumosh calina'ovu luminateni.*"

Connor soaked in the Elder Tongue words. *Exalted One. Your ways, show me. Your paths, teach me.*

The parchment dissolved into the glistening green stone. Mountains rose from the far end, all the way to the ceiling, their peaks hidden by swirls of icy mist. Forests, rivers, hills, and towns spread out across the table from the mountains' roots.

Lee drew an excited breath. "Tanelethar," he said, too loud for Connor's comfort. "We're looking at the known world north of the Celestial Peaks."

So much movement. So much life. Like watching the world from Aethia's eyes on her highest flight. Connor had fixed his gaze on a forest near their window, with trees as black as night. A dark fog hung in the branches, and pale green and yellow lights flashed here and there. He heard an almost imperceptible scream.

"I don't like that place." Connor pulled Lee over to the next window, and the two crammed together with Teegan at its sill.

The new vantage point brought him closer to the guardians and the trees covering the northern foothills of the Celestial Peaks–the southern extent of Tanelethar.

"The migration to the Highland Forest is getting worse." Master Jairun pointed to a hilltop village rising above the pines. "Our spy is here, close to Trader's Knoll, as far south as possible, yet goblins now roam his woods in numbers to rival the Black Forest." As if to emphasize the headmaster's point, dozens of tiny squeaking monsters climbed the village hill.

Master Jairun grimaced and shifted his staff east to a grove of reddish-brown trees, much larger than the forest pines. "And now a mocktree has set up camp near the giant trees of Sil Elamar."

"What o' the goblin laborers?" Quinton thrust his chin at a

mountain vale east of the big trees. "Has Pedrig told ya what they're buildin' yet?"

"I think we can guess. We may be facing dark days, and soon. I've asked our man to seek rumors of hollow hills, to see if what we fear is truly possible." The living map vanished in a puff of white mist, and the parchment reappeared. Master Jairun slid it into his cloak. "And there's something else. Pedrig dispatched four more goblins on his way in from the Passage Lakes."

"In our woods? On this side of the barrier?"

"Precisely. With winter setting in, Pedrig forsook the high pass and took the long road south to Watchman's Gate. As soon as he turned north again toward the academy, he caught their scent. He ran them down at Mer Nimbar."

"Headed here?"

"He wasn't sure."

More goblins in Keledev. Was a larger attack coming? In his effort to hear the discussion, Connor pressed himself against the sill. The loose clasp of his cloak scraped the stone, and the guardians turned. Lee and Teegan yanked him down, out of sight.

Quinton stuck his head out into the night. "What was that?"

"I don't know," Master Jairun said, appearing beside him. "Perhaps an echo from Pavel, still fiddling up in his tower. It's late. Pavel should get some rest, and so should we."

Quinton grunted his agreement and closed the shutters.

36

RESTERAM CAME AND WENT WITH NO SIGN THE guardians knew about their eavesdropping pupils. But Connor had his suspicions. And Quinton seemed to confirm them. On Aram, the day after Resteram, he made their morning training the most brutal yet. In place of stones, the initiates carried each other up and down the lists, all the way up the grassy slopes at each end. It took two to carry Dag one length, and then the miner carried the same two back again.

Master Jairun also acted strange. He watched from the edge, forearms resting on his staff, and his gaze never seemed to leave Connor.

"Do you think . . . they're punishing . . . us?" Teegan asked, jolted about as Dag lumbered down the field with her and Connor tucked under his arms. "Do you think . . . they know?"

Dag glanced down, breathing hard. "Do you think . . . they know what?"

"Nothing," Connor said. "Just keep . . . running."

The less Dag and Tiran knew, the better, for now. No sense in getting them all in trouble.

More goblins had appeared in Keledev. Orcs and trolls were amassing on the barrier's northern slopes. Was it right for the guardians to keep such things to themselves? Connor had lain awake through the night wondering if Master Jairun had planned to be seen in the grotto, and if Belen had given Lee the spectacles on just the right day.

What if all this was a test?

Dag and his burdens collapsed next to the other two, and Lee looked up at Quinton. "What about armor? Many dark creatures wear it. So do the Aladoth. Surely, you don't expect us to fight without armor of our own."

Tiran joined the argument. "He's right. You have us lugging our clunkers all over the fortress, but we've never carried shields, nor worn so much as a breastplate. How are we supposed to defend ourselves?"

"Ya carry a shield ev'ry day, lad. And ya do wear armor, as do all Keledan. Have ya learned nothing from the scriptures?"

The students glanced at one another in confusion.

Quinton knelt beside them. "All Keledan wear the breastplate of his righteousness, gifted by grace. Yer helmet is his salvation, yer belt is truth, yer boots are meant to carry his peace and word to those who've not heard, and yer shield"—the swordmaster raised himself up again—"yer shield is the faith by which ya serve. All these ya carry at all times. How could ya not know?"

Dag leaned back on his elbows and cocked his great head. "We've never seen this armor."

"Oh," Master Jairun said, looking straight at Connor, "I think one of you has."

Connor picked at the grass between his knees. He knew what the headmaster meant—the white shield Tehpa had used against the goblin, the shield that had broken.

Master Jairun released him from the stare and turned to Dag. "Our armor is meant for battle, Mister Kaivos. You've never seen it because the Keledan stopped maintaining their armor when they ceased sending soldiers out to fight."

Teegan cringed. "So we must face real battle before we know the strength of our shields?"

"Yes. But you must also have faith you'll not be tested beyond what you can bear."

You'll not be tested beyond what you can bear. Connor wondered if that could be true. Tehpa's shield had collapsed under the weight of a single goblin knife. And he'd seen the hordes on Master Jairun's map table. He knew what waited for them on the other side of the peaks.

Master Jairun seemed to sense his fears. "This is why we train and teach you—to thicken your shields and temper your breastplates. We'll not send you out before you're ready."

Connor might have taken these words as a comfort, but he saw Quinton shoot the headmaster a worrisome glance.

37

A PAIR OF GOBLINS WADDLED PAST KARA, ONE wearing a fur it had definitely stolen from her stall. She recognized her own poor handiwork. Goblins loved to steal odds and ends, another method of tormenting their victims. She once saw a swamp goblin wearing just one muddy boot with its claws sticking out through the toe, proud to flaunt a human's possession even though the poor fit clearly caused it pain.

She eased back into the shadows at the outskirts of the market square. The threat of being recognized by someone who knew Liam frightened her more than being spotted by Nesat. If Liam heard she'd come to the hilltop, he'd rope her to a table post for the rest of winter.

Not that Liam had any cause to be angry. Had he not refused to take her with him when he set off to check the winter traps? She needed an escape from the cottage. But Keir had yet to return from his journey to see what the goblins were building east of Maidenwood Grove, and Liam was worried. It would be cruel for Kara to worry him more.

She waited until the goblins moved on, and then she crossed to the other end of the lodge, planning to use to the stable hand's door to check on old Wilibrond.

Trader's Knoll had changed. A layer of filth covered the pavers, dirt from the inner road and manure from passing horses and who knew what else. Her trading booth lay broken to pieces, a pile of wood scraps and torn canvas. She would have gone to it, but men sat in the muck nearby, squabbling over dice and drinking from stoneware jugs.

At the far end of the lodge, she ran into a new fence. Orcs guarded the only gate–three of them, grumbling to one another in their corruption of the Elder Tongue. She crept closer to get a better look. Their black pyranium armor absorbed the light, and their halberd shafts were as thick as war pikes. Did monsters like these hunt Keir each night? She hoped he'd kept to the inns as promised.

The nearest orc sniffed the air. Kara froze. The runes carved into its hide were tinted silver, either with dye or some trick of its metallic blood. She tried to picture the letters glowing as Liam had described, and an image formed in her mind, flashing to life and filling her vision.

The orc loomed over her, half-lit from behind by flames. The runes on its body burned like molten iron. The creature lifted a halberd to drive the spear point through her heart, while a dark form screeched in the sky above. She heard the beating of massive wings.

Burn.

The voice in Kara's head was not her own.

Yes, queensblood. Burn.

The orc still loomed over her with its fiery runes. The flames rose higher. She drew a sharp breath and willed the vision away.

Trader's Knoll surrounded her once again, and she fell back against the fence, heart racing. The orc–the real orc–growled and looked her way. Strong arms yanked her around the corner into the square. Hal. He put a finger to his bearded lips. "Do you remember the songs of your mother, child?"

"Hal? What are you doing here?"

"I would ask you the same, but there's no time." He hummed a familiar melody. "Do you remember the song? Your life may depend on it."

All Kara could manage was a nod.

"Then sing. And pray the beast has not seen too much already. I'm trying to block him myself, but his mind is powerful. Sing the song with me, child."

The Sleeper wakes by a meadow stream

On a path of gold 'neath the silver gleam

Of the stars up in the heavens.

How did she know this song?

Hal sang quietly as he guided her across the square. No one noticed them. All the people in the marketplace, even the men at their dice game, gawked up at the sky. She tried to look up too, but Hal stopped her.

"Eyes down. Sing, child. You must."

Child beckons. Follow me,

To the mountaintop by the crystal sea.

Field Mouse rides on Leopard's back.

Brown Bear strolls 'tween Cow and Calf.

Kara sang with him. She knew the words as if they were etched on her soul.

Wolf walks side by side with Boar.

Child laughs as Lion roars.

And the Sleeper wonders,

Where are all the dragons?

The melody was soft and sweet. A lullaby. Something clicked in Kara's mind. The mehma whose face she could not remember had sung the same lullaby to her every night. The image of the orc and the flames came flooding back, but the scene had changed. Rather than a halberd, the monster lifted a woman with platinum hair and flourishes of blue-gray speckles on her cheeks and nose. Kara saw her own tiny hands reaching. All the while, as the iron claws dug into the woman's arms, she held a trembling smile and sang.

All creatures flock to fire's ring,

where Lion bows, for Lamb is king.

Kara's knees buckled. "Mehma?"

Halas dragged her to her feet. "The song, child." He steered her to the cover of Charlotte's tattered awning. "Focus on the song and nothing else. Leave your past behind."

A shadow spread across the market. The townspeople ran for cover. Kara tried her best to obey, and the image of her mehma faded, leaving only the song and the old man–and the same beating of massive wings.

Lamb cries, Joy, goodwill, and peace!
Let battles end. Let all wars cease.
Banish dark with light divine.
Let fire dim. Let starlight shine.
Let thunder fade. Let storm clouds break.
Let Watchman rest.
Let the Sleeper wake.

The shadow passed. After another heartbeat, Hal let out a long breath. "Well done, child. Yes. Well done, indeed."

Kara blinked away tears. Everyone had fled inside, leaving the square empty. "How did you know?" She let Hal guide her through the gate and out to the trees on the knoll's southern face. "How did you know Mehma sang that lullaby to me as a child? I've never remembered her face until now."

"It is an old song, 'The Sleeper's Hope,' and an even older melody. Some parents in the north still teach it to their children." Hal moved at a quick pace down the trail. "The melody is unchanged from the ancient days–a tiny fragment of uncorrupted creation that began as the heartsong of the Dynapha, smallest among the Elder Folk. Its purity clouds a wyrm's ability to hear thoughts." He glanced up at the Impossible Peaks. "'The Sleeper's Hope' is as impenetrable to a dragon as the icy mists atop those mountains."

"A dragon." Kara said the word with awe and a touch of regret. A dragon had passed over their village, and she hadn't seen it. "You stopped me from looking."

"That particular breed is beautiful and terrible to look upon. Had you met the dragon's gaze, you would have succumbed, and no amount of song could have blocked him from seeing into–"

"My mind? My memory?" Kara halted. "What do you know of my past, Hal? What do you know of my mehma?"

"Not enough." He took her arm and got her moving again. "Come. We must get you home. And this time, you must stay there."

Hal waited with her at the cottage until Liam returned, and the two huddled together in the cottage's smaller chamber late into the night. Once they emerged, Liam told her little, except that he and Hal were worried about Keir.

Hal slept by their hearth, and in the morning, the men prepared to set out.

"Take me with you," Kara begged Liam. "Don't leave me here to worry for your safety."

"I can't."

"Why?"

"You know why, Shessa." Liam held her fingers, glancing down at the sleeves she'd drawn to her knuckles. "It's too risky."

She pulled away. "I've worked our market booth often this year. No one ever suspects a thing."

"The Trader's Knoll you speak of is gone, and its people are different. The world beyond our little wood is changing fast, thanks to Nesat. There are curfews now. The Highland Forest is crawling with barkhides and goblins. And worst of all, the town watchmen require journey writs after sunset, accounting for every person to pass their gates. We can't have them looking too closely."

"But, Liam–"

"I said, no!"

Hal placed a calming hand on them both. "We'll return in

a few days, Kara. Five at most. Liam will look for Keir. I must visit this castle–see the goblin crew's progress–then report my findings to those who are able to help you, if you'll let them."

"Help us?" Kara said. "And who'll help you? Who will look after an old collier wandering a winter forest crawling, as Liam says, with barkhides and goblins?"

Hal looked out the open door into the woods. "A friend, child. A very good friend."

38

"SHE'AM PO NABOLIOV . . ." TEEGAN'S EYES WERE CLOSED and her face lifted up, addressing her request to the Rescuer.

Connor wrung his hands. If the Rescuer answered by opening the Shar Razel, she'd be the last of his friends to pass the test. Dag had been the first, after a month of trying.

In the weeks since Master Jairun first introduced the students to the Shar Razel, winter had settled in. Ice covered the ridges surrounding Ras Telesar. The leaves fell from the oaks in the Forest of Believing, and the spruces were tipped with white.

Day after cold day, Master Jairun stood the five before the Iron Door. And day after cold day, the door remained shut. When the Rescuer finally unlocked it for Dag, the big miner broke down and cried.

The answer to Dag's prayer had been as the turning of a key for the others. Lee succeeded the same afternoon, and Tiran the next, to everyone's surprise but his. Now, on this third day, Teegan seemed likely to follow.

"*. . . kavah po mashteliov; doq po keshar felasiov.*"

She lowered her eyes to the door. There was no flash of light, no puff of scented smoke, only a quiet click. The Shar Razel cracked open. Teegan let out a stunned and grateful breath, and the others gathered around to hug and congratulate her. All except Connor. He had made his plea only moments before. The answer had been another devastating *No.*

"May those for whom the door opened go in this time?" Tiran asked, one arm wrapped around his twin. "Will you let us see what's on the other side?"

Master Jairun shook his head. "Not yet. As I've said, initiates go through as a class or not at all. In those times when an initiate has failed too long and too often, he or she has always chosen to leave the academy and let the rest continue with their training."

Tiran shot Connor a hard look, and Connor read the command in his eyes loud and clear. *You failed. Go home and let us move on.*

Connor hung a pace behind as they followed Master Jairun up the library stairs to their next lesson. The guardians had made a favorite of him and showed no desire to keep it a secret. *Here is your crook, Shepherd Boy, now go and lead your flock into battle.* They'd made him the class leader against his will. And now, in this one thing the guardians could not control, Connor was holding everyone back–this one, fundamental thing.

Faith.

Lee and Teegan paused to let him catch up. "The Rescuer will open the door for you in his own time," Lee said. "Perhaps tomorrow."

"And pay no attention to Tiran," Teegan added. "Do you want me to let Aethia preen her feathers over his pillow? He won't stop sneezing for days."

"No. Thank you."

They climbed a few more steps in silence before Lee made an obvious attempt to change the subject. "I bet the guardians have another secret meeting planned tonight. We're still going to listen in, right?"

The trio's first taste of sneaking about the fortress had been their last. Quinton's training left them no energy for late-night missions. But Lee had discovered a way around the exhaustion.

Using instruments borrowed from Master Belen and figures scratched in chalk on the stone beds beneath his mattress, the scribe had worked out the secret map chamber's precise location. Its windows were visible from the barracks balcony, and its lanterns had been lit on Sethrel, the night before Resteram, twice in a row. If the pattern held, they'd be lit again that very evening.

Connor nodded. In this, he would not fail his friends. "Yes. We're still on."

Lee turned and walked backward in front of him. "Perhaps this time the headmaster will bring his furry friend."

The word *friend* came out as a grunt as the scribe bumped into Dag's broad back. Master Jairun had stopped the troop at double doors carved from oak, birch, and cherry and inlaid with onyx. His eyes were on Lee. "What is this about a furry friend?"

"I . . . Uh . . ."

Teegan flicked the scribe's arm. "A feathered friend, Headmaster. We were just talking about Aethia, and how her preening makes Tiran sneeze."

Tiran frowned at her. "Only because she lets the bird preen over my things."

"*Fur and feathers.*" Master Jairun pushed the tri-wood doors open to let blue-green light spill across the threshold. "Perfect. For that is the topic of the next lesson."

The initiates filed into a long, curving chamber behind the library shelves. Wood and stone blended together on the walls, sculpted into a mural of animals. Wolves and bears, badgers and horses, walked together in forests or raced over golden plains while falcons and crows soared above. Panes of blue and green stained glass set among the trees made it seem as though the winter sun shone in through living branches.

"Beautiful." Teegan said.

"As all memorials should be, my dear."

Tiran scrunched his nose. "A memorial? To animals?"

"Not just any animals. They are the Havarra, the royalty of the animal kingdom. They were the first, meant to guide and keep the rest in partnership with man. The Havarra were sentient."

Connor watched the headmaster and the others walk on. After the day he'd been through, he hated to admit he didn't know what *sentient* meant. Dag seemed to read his mind as he lumbered past. "It means clever–as clever as you and me. The Havarra could talk."

39

"BUT THE HAVARRA ARE A MYTH." LEE HAD CAUGHT up to Master Jairun. "Children's stories. They were never mentioned in the Sacred Scrolls."

"And why should the scriptures mention the Havarra? The scriptures are *our* story–the story of mankind's romance with the Maker. The Havarra have a story of their own."

The headmaster took a seat on a curved stone bench below the depiction of a splendid black stallion leading a field of wild horses. A golden horn grew from the stallion's head like a crown. "The Maker awakened mankind from the dust and gave him dominion over the beasts and birds. But each species had its shepherds–the Havarra. Together they ruled Talania, and perhaps the other continents of Dastan, under the counsel and care of the Elder Folk."

Connor touched the flank of a gray wolf so lifelike he half expected to feel the softness of its fur. "The Elder Folk built Ras Telesar. Did they sculpt this memorial?"

"Yes, therefore . . ." Master Jairun drew out the word, nodding for him to finish the thought.

"Therefore . . . the talking animals vanished before the Elder Folk left for the Celestial Realm."

"A sound deduction, child. But they did not vanish so much as they were purged, the last great tragedy before the Elder Folk departed."

"They were killed by the dragons, then."

Master Jairun gave him a grave nod. "After Heleyor, lord of Ras Pyras turned traitor, he and his followers took dragon form, as we've discussed before. Half spirit, half flesh, the dragons spun their knowledge into the illusion of sorcery and offered it to the kings and queens of man. Mankind greedily accepted, betraying the Maker."

Dag gazed up at the kingly stallion. "But the Havarra didn't accept, did they?"

"No, they did not. The hearts of the Havarra remained pure. And so Heleyor and his minions hunted them near to extinction." Master Jairun planted his staff and pushed himself up to walk on through the narrow chamber. "Despairing, the remaining Elder Folk departed. Some say many Dynapha–the faeries–stayed behind, but that is only theory."

Lee elbowed Connor. "Did you hear that?"

Something in Master Jairun's story had set him off, but Connor couldn't tell which part. "Hear what?"

The scribe called out to Master Jairun. "You said near to extinction, as in not entirely gone."

"I did." Master Jairun came to another tri-wood door at the end of the gallery and waved them all through. "So now we come to the main point of the lesson."

A new chamber opened before them, carpeted with red silk rugs and lit by skylights. The initiates fanned out, admiring spears and swords encased in glass, and strange, polished saddles mounted on pedestals. Paintings of armored men and women lined the walls, standing side by side with huge bears and solemn wolves.

"Are these the kings and queens of the elder days?" Teegan asked. "With their Havarra companions?"

"No." Connor's arms and legs went numb. "They're not."

"How do you know?"

"He knows," Master Jairun said, "because he's found a painting of his grandfather."

A painting at the end of the hall matched the one over Tehpa's hearth. Connor could barely speak the words breaking from his mind. "These are lightraiders."

"The surviving Havarra are scattered." Master Jairun strolled up beside him. "They are hidden throughout Tanelethar. But once in a while, the Rescuer calls one out to fight. The men and women you see here are their lightraider companions. They are bear knights and wolf soldiers."

"What about lions?" Lee lowered one of his lenses, inspecting a saddle broad enough for a bear. "Were there any lion . . . er . . . lion warriors?"

"The white lions of the north were a magnificent house, yes—advisors to the oldest line of kings. Sadly, I don't believe any survived the dragons' purge."

Connor had yet to tear his gaze from the painting, absorbed in the eyes of the wolf, deep and golden, with all the restrained power of a gathering storm. "Where is *he*?"

The question seemed to startle Master Jairun. "Where is who?"

"The silver wolf who walked with Faelin."

"Ah." Master Jairun cleared his throat. "The wolf. I can honestly tell you I don't know where he's gone. Most of the Havarra companions died in battle beside their lightraiders, for all Havarra are fiercely loyal. But I'm fairly certain that was not Pedrig's fate."

Connor stared at the old man in surprise. "What did you call him?"

"Did Edwin never tell you the name of Faelin's companion? Ah. Well, a wolf's pack-given name is generally unpronounceable for us humans—a good bit of growling and rumbling." Master Jairun regarded the wolf in the painting. "But in the Common Tongue, this one chose to be called Pedrig."

40

CONNOR, TEEGAN, AND LEE SLIPPED INTO PLACE WELL before the guardians' weekly meeting. The three climbed down from the bulwark above to their new listening spot, the map chamber's roof.

"It's snowing." Teegan lifted a palm to the clouds. The flakes never reached her, evaporating in the rising vapors from the streams. She lowered her hand, looking disappointed, and laid it on the roof between her knees. "The stones are thick. How are we to hear what the guardians are saying?"

"Over here." Lee signaled for them to join him near a corner of the roof. "Last time, I noticed steps against the chamber's rear wall. Steep ones." He lifted a stone hatch from its frame and stood his chalk in the gap to keep it open. "Roof access. We can watch and listen from–"

A series of clinks and clangs echoed across the fortress, followed by a pained cry and a fading stream of grumbles.

"Master Belen again." Teegan looked toward the tower workshop. "He may be hurt. Should we go and help?"

"Too late." Lee flattened himself beside the hatch. "Someone's coming."

Yellow light grew in the dark space. The guardians had arrived.

The trio lay on their stomachs and peered down through the hatch.

Quinton lit a second lantern and hung it on a hook near the steps. "What news from Pedrig?"

Teegan whispered in Connor's ear. "Your patehpa's wolf."

He nodded. The pieces fit. Lee had spotted a creature with gray fur in the grotto, and a battled-hardened wolf would make the perfect messenger to run between Keledev and Tanelethar. The Assembly's order forbidding Keledan from crossing the barrier said nothing of the Havarra.

A light *crick* sounded from Lee's chalk, then another. A hairline crack spread through the white stick. Tiny flecks of dust fell into the chamber. "Uh oh," Lee whispered.

The chalk split. Connor shoved his fingers into the gap to stop the hatch from crashing down. He managed to pinch off most of the cry in his throat, but not all.

Master Jairun's voice rose from below. "I heard you up there."

"All o' Ras Telesar heard," Quinton added. "An' Mer Nimbar. An' Glimwick down in Ravencrest, I'll warrant."

Teegan and Lee pried up the stone as Connor inspected his throbbing fingers for broken bones. The three shared a look and eased forward to peer down into the room.

But none of the guardians were looking their way. Master Jairun shook his head at Belen, who had just arrived. "You're late again, Pavel. Did one of your contraptions go awry?"

Belen collapsed into a padded leather chair and removed a copper band and candle holder from his forehead, complete with a broken candle. "I tripped, if you must know. And then I had to make my way down in the dark." He accepted a copper mug from Quinton and took a sip. "You both know quiet movement was never my best skill."

The swordmaster frowned at him. "Stealth, Pavel. I told ya we're callin' it stealth from this class onward. A new start is a good time ta let a few o' the old traditions go." He turned to Master Jairun. "So, now that we're all here, I'll ask again. What news from the wolf?"

"None, I'm afraid." Master Jairun laid his hands on the

table. "I've heard nothing this week. He's overdue. But that is not so unusual considering all we've asked him and his friend to investigate–the powder, the hollow hills, the new castle."

Connor inched back from the hatch. Pedrig was late. Master Jairun had told him he didn't know where the wolf might be. So the headmaster hadn't lied. Teegan urgently poked his arm, and he pulled himself up to the edge again.

The guardians had asked the Rescuer for the map. Mists swirled along the glossy green surface. Connor could hardly see through the icy clouds topping the Celestial Peaks, but something–something big and dark–sailed low over the trees in their foothills.

Lee lowered one of his lenses and sucked in a breath. "A dragon."

Master Jairun gestured at the creature. "*That* was the main thrust of the last message we received."

"The dragon arrived last week, as we know." Quinton poured himself a cup from the copper kettle. "An' with Pedrig late or missin', I say we assume the worst. That beast raised hisself an army of dark creatures and barkhides in the borderlands, and now he's come to command them."

Master Jairun looked hard at the swordmaster. "One dragon building an army is not unusual, my friend. What concerns me is what he plans to do with that army. We've seen dark creatures as close as Mer Nimbar, remember? If the wyrms have uncovered a hollow hill with an unstable exit on our side of the barrier, then the mind of a dragon may steer it with terrible accuracy."

"And widen it," Belen added. "I've been studying all we know about the portals of old. The great wyrms possess the ability to grow them temporarily–sending whole platoons of orcs through in a single push. A strong wyrm may even have the power to pass through a hollow hill itself. Though I can't see how the Rescuer would allow it."

"A dragon in Keledev"–Quinton thumped his cup down–"leading an army of orcs an' goblins. The Assembly must hear o' this, Avner, whether they want to or not. An' it's high time we tell the initiates too."

"There's no need to tell them."

"And why not, pray tell?"

"Our pupils already know. Well, three of them do." He thrust his staff upward, knocking the stone hatch out of the way.

The guardians stared up at the trio.

Connor and Teegan dropped their faces into their hands.

Lee offered a withered wave. "Hello, sirs. Lovely night isn't it?"

41

BY THE HIGH ONE'S GRACE, RESTERAM FOLLOWED THE student's ill-fated snooping. Master Jairun thought it best for all concerned if the guardians waited until after morning worship to administer judgment. The initiates were to leave their clunkers at the barracks. Combat training had been cancelled, leaving Quinton plenty of voice to roar at the three when they met the guardians in the headmaster's chambers.

"Sneaking about the fortress? Eavesdropping? The lightraiders are a military order. We have rules. Structure. When you lot are meant to know something, yer superiors'll tell ya!"

It did not help Quinton's mood when Lee raised a sleeve to wipe spittle from his lenses.

"And yet," Master Jairun said, turning to the irate guardian, "a military order values initiative. Times are strange, Angus. Dark creatures have entered the land. Our faith in one another is shaken. They saw something out of place and sought a solution." His eyes shifted to the initiates. "Which does not justify their choices. But it does give cause for leniency."

Belen came up with the final punishment. "If these three have enough vigor left at day's end to go wandering about the fortress at night–a precarious pastime, I can tell you–then I'd say they have enough vigor left to clean it. After combat training. Before baths. One hallway per night."

"The others too," Quinton said with a growl. "A class of initiates lives and dies together. That is the lightraider way."

After the meeting, Connor and Lee sat in their favorite spot on the fourth wall, shrinking under the glares of both Tiran and Dag. Tiran crossed his arms upon learning of the new cleaning duties. "I'll think of you both fondly with each sweep of my broom. *And* my shessa. You can bet all three of you will feel my fondness when next we spar."

Dag looked more upset than Connor had ever seen him. "Why didn't you tell us?"

"We were going to." Connor met the miner's hurt gaze. "Honest. But we wanted to learn more first."

This seemed to quell Dag's anger but not Tiran's. "Seriously? That's all you have to say?" He stormed off, giving them no chance to reply.

Dag ambled off after him, and Connor turned to Lee. "Where is Teegan? Shouldn't she have been here to take the brunt of Tiran's ire?"

Lee let his feet dangle over the bulwark. "None of this was her idea, remember? And she took Master Quinton's scolding hard. I think she went off with Aethia to hunt." He looked through his lens down the glade's white road to the place where the steps descended the cliff to the switchbacks and the Forest of Believing. "Yes. There she is. She's been flying Aethia from the top of the stairs ever since the snows came to the forest."

To Connor, Teegan was little more than a smudge of dark green against the white gravel. He could not have hoped to see the falcon.

"The Forest of Believing," Lee said, twisting his ring. "Huh." He produced a piece of chalk from his satchel and drew a map on the parapet between them. "According to Master Jairun, dragons can steer the exit of an unstable portal."

"Yes . . ."

"And if a dragon can steer one through the barrier, we have to presume it can steer it anywhere in our land. So, my friend, why Dayspring? Why Mer Nimbar?"

To Connor's dismay, one of Lee's map labels read *Enarian Farm*. He swallowed. "What are you saying?"

Lee drew a circle at the farm. He then drew a circle near the label *Mer Nimbar*. "I don't think these are random. In our studies, Master Belen told us dragons sometimes look through the eyes of their dark creature servants. What if he saw where each group landed?"

"The dragon isn't just steering the portal." Connor grabbed the chalk from Lee's fingers. "He's dialing it in like a catapult." He drew an arrow through the two circles. It pointed north, straight at the third location Lee had labeled. Connor circled that one as well. "Ras Telesar. The dragon is steering the portal here. And if it misses again, the creatures will land—"

"In the Forest of Believing."

They stared across the glade toward the top of the stairs. No matter how he tried, Connor could no longer make out the dark green blur he'd seen before.

Lee lowered a lens in front of his eye, and then another. He gripped Connor's arm. "Teegan is gone."

42

A TERRIBLE SCREAM REACHED THE RAMPARTS FROM across the glade.

Connor dropped from the battlements, landing in a crouch on the balcony below. "I'm going after her. Raise the alarm."

"But you have no weapon."

"I have my sling. Get going!"

A shortcut through an empty chamber, two flights of broken steps, and a long leap brought Connor to the second level, where the maze stopped him. He ran back and forth on the battlements, searching for a path onward. He couldn't jump all the way down to the gate courtyard. Could he?

Another scream. Teegan appeared at the top of the steps. From the closer wall, he could see her dress was torn at the shoulder, her bare arm red with blood. A goblin scrambled onto the white road behind her, grasping at her heels.

"Teegan, look out!"

Even as Connor shouted, a white flash streaked from the heights and smashed into the goblin's helmet, knocking the creature off its feet.

Aethia let out a screech, wheeling upward for another pass, and for a moment, he thought the falcon had bought her mistress enough time to make the gate.

Then a ragged bolt of black and purple ripped the air between Teegan and the fortress. Black smoke drifted away, leaving a huge creature with skin the texture of iron ore standing on the road, blocking her path.

Teegan veered away, and the creature did not give chase. Perhaps it had not seen her. An arrow plinked off its helmet, and it turned to face the fortress, letting out a terrible roar.

Looking back, Connor saw Lee aim his longbow from the barrack's balcony, a snub-nosed practice arrow on the string. Dag stood beside him with Connor's leather-bound sparring staff, gripping it like a javelin.

The miner shouted down to him. "This is all we've got. Catch!" He hurled the staff, but put too much power into the throw. It sailed over Connor's head, out of reach.

Without considering the consequences, Connor leapt after it, out into the empty air above the courtyard. He caught the staff in midair and clung to it, with the black rectangular pool in the gate courtyard rushing up to meet him. *Dear Rescuer, let it be deep enough.*

He knew it wasn't. He'd seen Tiran fall in on the first day. The water had only come up to his waist.

Protect me if you will. I know you can. Let me live to serve you.

He splashed through the surface and slammed into the bottom.

Yet Connor felt no pain. He sensed a silvery glow all around him. Then the current took him, and darkness closed in.

Not until his head broke the water's surface, out in the glade's cold light, did Connor know for sure the fall hadn't killed him. The current had carried him through the culvert. On he went, fighting to keep his head above water, through the outer pool and into the River Gathering that flowed across the glade toward the cataracts.

On the road, the big creature swiped at Lee's practice arrows, bellowing in frustration. Jumbles of sticklike runes glowed orange on its legs, arms, and face. Farther down, near the head of the cataracts, not one but three armored goblins closed in on Teegan. Connor fixed his sights on the nearest and swept up a couple of stones from the riverbed, shoving them into his pouch.

The current picked up speed, driving him toward the falls.

After a long breath, he planted the tip of his staff in the rocks and pushed with all his might to launch himself out onto the bank. Momentum carried him across the frosted grass, sliding feetfirst into the goblin's legs.

The creature squealed and hit the ground. Its helmet rolled away. But it recovered fast and came after him.

For all his training and effort, Connor wound up in the position he feared most–on his back with a goblin on top, knife raised, just like Tehpa. The knife came stabbing down. Connor threw an arm across his face, praying in his heart for the Rescuer's help.

I live to serve you. I live by your grace.

A silver shield, strong and wide, deflected the blade, and it dug into the sod. Connor shoved the goblin off, seated a stone in his sling, and loosed at close range, earning an ugly *crack* from its brittleknit skull. The creature fell lifeless to the grass.

"Connor, help!"

He yanked the goblin's knife from the earth and spun around, stunned by what he saw. Armor, translucent and shimmering sea green, covered Teegan's entire form. She held off a relentless double attack with a glowing shield.

But her strength was fading.

The two remaining goblins sliced and hacked at the shield in a rasping, snarling frenzy, pressing her down the riverbank. Fighting for breathing room, Teegan punched one of her enemies in the face. A shower of sparks flew from her pale green gauntlet. The goblin reeled backward, and she shouted at Connor, "Weapon, please!"

"Right. Sorry!" Connor tossed her the knife, hilt first.

Teegan caught it and shoved the blade straight through her translucent shield into the nearer goblin's chest. The creature teetered toward Connor, who whacked it into the water with his staff. The river carried it screaming over the cataracts.

The goblin Teegan had punched recovered, shaking its head, and took one menacing step before a feathered shaft sprouted from its left eye. A joyous shout drifted down from the fortress. Lee had found some real arrows and put the features of his spectacles to use.

Connor nearly laughed out loud, glancing over his shoulder to call out his thanks, but found the fortress obscured by an orange-and-black creature, getting larger fast.

Resounding pain smashed through his body. Then he was airborne, flying along the stream bank. Connor crashed down beside Teegan. He'd forgotten about the orc.

The monster's chest heaved. Arrows protruded from its right arm and left leg, charred and smoking. Another arrow clanked off its helmet, and the runes carved into its skin flared. It faced the fortress, lifted a scimitar above its head, and roared.

Connor leaned to one side and shouted up at Lee. "You're just making it angry!"

The orc's attention focused again on Connor and Teegan. They raised their shields together, cringing as the creature swung its blade. But to Connor's surprise the scimitar bounced away. There'd been no power or strength behind the blow.

The orc toppled forward with two double-bladed axes embedded in the thick hide at its back. Connor recognized the weapons from his first night at the fortress and looked up.

Quinton waved from the gatekeeper's passage, an arm around Dag. A few yards away, across the outer pool, Master Jairun drew his sword from the body of a second orc.

Dag grinned wide. "You were right. Lee's arrows were making the creature angry, so Master Quinton and I sent his axes to simmer it down."

Tiran had gained a victory as well–two, in fact. A pair of goblins Connor had not noticed before lay dead at the end of the bridge, black blood leaking onto the grass.

Master Jairun surveyed the lawn-turned-battlefield. "Not since the days our beloved Blacksmith walked this glade have dark creatures fallen here. It is high time for real action."

43

MASTER JAIRUN LED THE FIVE STUDENTS AND THE other two guardians across the western lists to the long gray house. Connor had always known there must be treasures inside. Most doors at Ras Telesar were wood, but the doors of the gray house were stone, banded with iron, and twice as tall as Master Quinton.

After the battle, Master Jairun had treated Teegan's wounds, allowing Lee to pray over them with sacred words, a privilege Connor had still not been granted. And then the headmaster had brought the full company up to the lists. "This is the day you trade those leather-bound clunkers for bare steel."

When they reached the doors, Quinton tugged at a chain around his neck and lifted a huge quartz key from beneath his tunic. He slid it into the lock and pulled open the door. "Arms Day, m'lass an' lads–third best day behind Forge and The Rising. Toss yer clunkers in the bins on the left, then gather at the central table."

A bronze shield hung on the wall above the bins, depicting what Connor assumed to be lightraiders sparring on the lists. There were many such shields on the chamber walls–gold, silver, copper, and bronze, embossed with swordsmen, archers, and the like. Oaken racks stood between them, loaded with weapons.

"Welcome, young sir." Belen patted Connor on the back as they entered. "Welcome to the lightraider armory."

The students joined the guardians at a table near the center of the space. The weapons lying upon it matched those the students had chosen. Master Jairun lifted the ebony crook and Faelin's sword. "There is no better staff or sword I can offer you, Connor. May these serve you well, as the sword served your grandfather."

Belen called Lee forward next and gave him the same ash bow the scribe had used to shoot the lion weathervane. In place of a dagger, he offered two sheathes with six knives in total, each with two gold-tinted blades instead of a hilt or handle. "Together, these are *sikaria*, young sir. One alone is called a *sikari*, and using it requires both aim and speed. Wear them within quick reach of your fingers."

Teegan and Tiran were next. Instead of rope, the net Master Jairun gave Teegan was made of fine copper-colored mail, with weights shaped into deadly spikes. "And the shaft of this trident," the headmaster said as he held out the second weapon, "is white ironwood, wrapped in a double spiral of steel forged as a single piece with the tines."

She bowed her head as she stepped back with the gifts. "They're beautiful."

"The word is deadly, my dear. Take care in their use, especially when facing the Aladoth."

For Tiran, Master Jairun offered a choice of two swords–his original blade and a more ornate sword, a little shorter. "You may choose the weapon you brought with you, but your swordmaster and I agree it's too long and heavy for your arm." He twirled the shorter sword, offering it hilt first. "This one will meld better with your fighting style."

In a respectful tone, Tiran declined the new sword. He took his old one–his tehpa's–along with a jeweled dagger and a mahogany bow.

Dag came last, head low, shoulders sagging. There were no axes on the table, only a war hammer with a head of black steel. "I suppose I am built to carry the heaviest burdens, and so I must carry only one weapon."

"'Tis true, yer lot is ta carry the heavy burdens, lad." Quinton stepped between the miner and the table. "Yer stature and strength're great assets. But so are yer cleverness, the encouragement o' yer cookin', and the bindin' power o' yer loyalty." The swordmaster unstrapped the double sheath holding his crossed axes. "You may take the war hammer I chose for ya, if ya wish, and start a new legacy. But if you'll have 'em, I'd like ya to take these. You've earned 'em."

The five pupils went out to the lists to get the feel of their new arms, and Teegan claimed Connor as her sparring partner. He'd hardly gotten his bearings before she wrapped his crook with her net. The blue alloy weights interlocked, and she tore the shaft from his grasp, laughing.

Connor raised his hands before she could threaten him with the trident. "I concede."

"You didn't have to." She tossed the crook back to him. "You still had your sword and shield."

"Our shields don't work on the training field."

"But they work in real combat." She batted his crook playfully with her trident to goad him into another round. "I saw yours. Incredible."

The leading tone of her statement left Connor confused. He shrugged a shoulder and took a shot of his own, smacking the trident's shaft. "You had armor too."

"No, silly. I mean my shield and armor didn't appear until after I saw yours." Teegan took a step to her left, forcing him to turn and shift his grip. "You came flying from the river to save me in full silver armor. And when the goblin pinned you down, your arm came up with a huge shield covering you from chin to knees."

As quick as a thought, Teegan stepped in close and trapped his crook with her trident. "When I saw yours, I knew my armor was there too, just as strong. Connor, your faith bolstered mine. If not for you, I'd have been lost."

He freed his crook and backed away. Could his faith, so frail, have strengthened hers? What was it Master Quinton said? *This class must live and die together. That is the lightraider way.* "But my armor was plain. Patehpa wore blue armor covered in gold scrollwork. All the lightraiders in the memorial chamber paintings had such decorations. How can we ever live up to their legacy?"

"Patience." Master Jairun appeared nearby, though Connor had not heard the slightest hint of his approach. He waved for his pupils to gather around. "Our adornments are bought at a price. Every flourish on a lightraider's armor represents a victory for the High One's glory. Each leaf is a heart saved by the Rescuer from certain destruction." The headmaster looked them in the eye, one by one. "Have no fear. You'll earn your decorations soon–far too soon for my comfort."

The following morning, Quinton arrived at the barracks to find the door open and his initiates dressed for battle, new weapons polished to a shine. "Excellent. I see the sleepers're all awake. Follow me."

He led them to the library rather than the kitchen or the lists, up the winding stair to the Shar Razel, where he nodded to Connor. "Now is the time, Shepherd Boy. Make yer request."

Connor took a deep breath, bowed his head, and spoke the sacred verse, pleading with voice, mind, and heart for the Rescuer to open the door that he might pass through into the service of the kingdom. "*She'am po naboliov, kavah po mashteliov, doq po keshar felasiov.*"

The echo faded. Connor dared not open his eyes, but he heard the quiet click of a lock.

The Iron Door opened.

PART THREE

ACROSS THE MOUNTAINS

"How narrow is the gate and difficult the road that leads to life, and few find it."

Matthew 7:14

44

CONNOR STARED AT THE SHAR RAZEL—NOW CRACKED open, with the unknown waiting on the other side.

"See, my friend," Lee said at his shoulder in a quiet voice. "His timing. Not ours."

Quinton motioned to the group. "After you."

Connor stayed put. The Rescuer had opened the door for each of his classmates before him. He had no right to walk through first. But Teegan touched his hand. "Go ahead. We're with you. Lead on."

The iron's coolness seeped through his palm and into his arm as he pressed the door open. Beyond the threshold, a steep stair led them up into the outcropping chapel, where a hot spring bubbled, feeding an indoor garden, and a cloud hung forever in the ceiling arches.

Masters Jairun and Belen met them at the edge of the long, roiling pool. The headmaster raised his staff in salute. "Congratulations, lightraider cadets. You've found the *Nevethav*, the House of Nine."

"Seek, and you will find," Belen said in a ceremonial tone.

"Knock"—Quinton came up the steps behind them—"and the door will open."

Connor took note of the change. "You said cadets." They'd come to the mountains as potentials. And after passing their quest, they trained for weeks as initiates. But now the Rescuer had brought them through the Shar Razel in answer to their prayers. "So, we've . . ."

Master Jairun lowered his staff, grinning. "You've been officially inducted into the Lightraider Order."

Tiran scrunched his brow. "Shouldn't we take oaths or something?"

"You did. Your oath is to the Rescuer, Mister Yar. Nothing more is required. Cadet is your first rank. One day you'll graduate as knights in whatever sphere or discipline the Rescuer plans for you." He sat on the edge of the pool. "But let's not get ahead of ourselves. Please, gather round."

Belen and Quinton sat down on either side of him. The tinker gestured at the chapel, inviting the cadets to let their gazes wander. "Every member of the Lightraider Order began the cadet journey here. You might say this place represents our core."

Water channels, paths, and bridges moved in easy curves throughout the garden, passing among bushes, trees, and vines, some heavy with fruit.

"How do the trees and vines bear fruit inside?" Teegan asked.

Belen nodded toward the chapel's giant doors. "How could they bear fruit if left out in the cold?" With his finger he traced one steaming ribbon of water channel through a section of bushes until it poured out beneath a window of translucent colored stone. "The pool feeds them. The windows bring light in just the right colors."

Connor counted nine sections of fruit blending one into the other. Not all were in season, but he guessed they all produced in their time. "Who tends the garden?"

"You will, from now on," Master Jairun said. "When you're here, and also when you're not."

Tiran gave him a look of confusion, but the headmaster cut his question off with a wave. "Don't forget, Nevethav was once the crown jewel of Ras Telesar, the Hill of the Fountain. The Elder Folk built it around this pool, which they named *Telbeath*, the Fount of Life. In an act of worship, they planted a garden with nine fruit trees and vines to represent nine aspects of the High One's character."

"I've read of this," Lee said. "The Nine Strengths of the Lightraider Order. They're the same."

"Yes, yes. Good, Mister Lee. I was getting to that." Master Jairun pointed with his staff at onyx markers of various shapes and sizes all around the garden, each marked with a single word in the flowing script of the Elder Tongue. "Love, joy, peace, patience, kindness, goodness, faithfulness, gentleness, and self-control."

"So"–Dag eyed a tree of candle fruit as if he could taste the sweetness–"the Order adopted those nine as their core strengths because Ras Telesar is their home?"

"Oh, no, young sir." Belen shook his head, taking up the lesson for Master Jairun. "We adopted nothing. The Rescuer made these nine aspects our core strengths after his return, when he sent the Helper to guide us. Thanks to the Helper, all Keledan carry the Fount of Life within. The Fount of Life feeds the nine strengths, if we allow it. And these nine strengths are a key part of our rescue efforts across the barrier."

Quinton gave them each a stern, *I'm watching you* look. "Thus, you lot'll tend the fruit in the chapel whenever you're here at the fortress. That way you'll remember to tend the fruit here"–he thumped his chest with a fist–"when you're away, especially when walkin' the world beyond the peaks. Swords and axes're great. But love, kindness, and all the rest o' the Nine Strengths–they're the heart o' the lightraider way. Understand?"

They all nodded–even though Connor wasn't sure he'd grasped it all. He remembered what Tehpa said. *The Order became mystics, Connor, every one of them.* Here was Swordmaster Quinton, the biggest, roughest brute among the guardians, talking of love and kindness, seated on a fruit garden pool, while mists swirled overhead through every color of light. *Mystic* hardly covered it. But Connor had seen what the Rescuer had done during the attack.

Perhaps all the Keledan should be such mystics.

Tiran still looked skeptical. "I see brambleberries and candle fruit. One grows on the coast, the other on mountain slopes. How can they grow together beside the same pool?"

"This water is special, as if you hadn't guessed." Master Jairun walked to a pedestal and lifted a copper chalice. "Particularly here at the source. Telbeath has provided healing and nourishment since the dawn of time."

Master Jairun dipped the cup in the waters. "All cadets drink from the fount after passing through the Shar Razel, but be warned. The first draught often causes deep sleep, like a death and a reawakening. I'll place my hand upon your back and support you." He held the cup, still steaming, to Connor's lips. "Are you ready?"

Death and reawakening? Connor glanced at Lee and Teegan. The scribe was bending close to the pool, wiping mist from his lenses so he could examine the water. But Teegan saw his look and seemed to catch its meaning. She answered with an *I'm game if you are* shrug.

He gave her a slight nod and tipped the cup. Hot, invigorating water slid down his throat into his chest. At first, it lit his bruises on fire. But the fire quickly faded, and with it, the chamber's colored light. He could sense Master Jairun moving the cup away and easing him down. Before his shoulders touched the stones, Connor slipped into darkness.

45

THE DARKNESS BECAME A VOID, SWIRLING WITH glittering silver dust.

What is this?

He tried to reach out to touch the swirling dust, but he had no control over his limbs. His body, or perhaps only his mind, rushed forward.

The silver dust flew past, joined by earth and crumbling rocks. In a flash of purple lightning and black smoke, Connor entered a vast flat expanse—a plain of polished stone beneath a starry sky.

He was not alone. A knight in blue armor covered in gold scrollwork stood a distance away at the edge of a black well with his back to Connor, head lifted to the sky as if in supplication. Connor could not see his face. All the same, a rush of hope filled his gut.

Until the dragon came.

Huge and glistening black, the creature landed before the knight, cracking the polished stone under its talons, and spread wide its red-tipped wings. Smoke snaked around the knight's feet. Fire glowed in the dragon's throat.

Connor wanted to call out a warning to the knight, but he had no voice.

Ignoring the danger, the knight turned, proving Connor's hope and dread to be true. The face beneath the helm matched the face in the painting hanging over Tehpa's hearth—older, with a white, braided beard, but the same. Faelin Enarian. Connor's patehpa, lost before his birth.

The knight smiled at him, then faced the monster and raised a sword with a purple starlot in the hilt.

The dragon unleashed its fire. Flames swallowed the knight whole.

Connor woke with a shout. "No!"

Master Jairun held his shoulders. "Easy, my boy. Breathe."

"Where . . ." The scent of the bubbling spring answered the question for him. He'd never left the Nevethav. "I had a dream."

"More like a nightmare, lad." Quinton lifted Connor to his feet. "Ev'ry cadet sleeps after the first draught, but I've never seen one thrash about like a flounder on a ship deck."

"What does it mean?"

"Nothing. It doesn't mean a thing." Belen took hold of Quinton's cloak, pulling him away. "Help us with the others. They're coming round."

Teegan woke, followed by Lee and Tiran, each rubbing their eyes and groaning.

Dag snored away until Master Jairun broke a clay tube of fragrant powder under his nose. "Hartshorn and vinegar," the headmaster told Lee as Dag shot up, gagging, from his slumber. "The two mix when you crack the vial, releasing a potent vapor known to wake any patient."

All had dreamed vivid dreams. Not unusual, according to the guardians, especially upon the first drink from Telbeath. "But never an entire class," Belen said. "Then again, there's never been a class so small."

Sweat beaded on all their foreheads, and so they retreated to the library's cooler air. Master Jairun retrieved a parchment and pen and asked them to describe their visions.

Teegan spoke first. "I saw the giant everleaves of Sil Elamar, the wood of our ancestors. Mehma said her family lived among the great falcon squadrons and hunted alongside them from elamwood branches broader than a cottage and higher than the Assembly's tallest tower."

"I wish I could have shared your dream." Tiran sat at a desk with his chin in his hands. "In mine, I saw the ramparts outside—same as they always look. Arrows flew from my bow, though my fingers never drew the string. It might've been today's battle, except I saw more goblins and orcs. And my arrows slew them all."

Master Jairun recorded his every word, then looked across the chamber to Dag. "And you, Mister Kaivos. What did you see?"

"Meat."

The quill paused. "Could you . . . say that again?"

"I saw meat, Headmaster. A slab of cooked red meat as broad as my axe-head. And I smelled it. Glorious rosemary and thyme. But then it vanished. The moment I tried to take some, it dissolved into a wolf."

This gained Connor's full attention. "A wolf?"

"Or a bear. I'm not sure. Sorry." And he did look truly sorry, as if by not remembering, he'd let them all down. "I thought I saw a silver wolf—a sad wolf. But when I looked closer, the animal roared like a bear, and suddenly, the face looked bearish too, but stiff and cracked like painted wood."

Lee had written his dream down while the others recounted theirs. He walked the parchment over to Master Jairun, who raised an eyebrow as he read. "Very intriguing, my boy. You've made quite a description of the waterfall."

"It was the most beautiful I've ever seen. A beam of sunlight shimmered on the pool, and within the cascade, I saw Elder Tongue script, as clear as day." He pointed to the parchment with his feather and read from it aloud. "*Vynovu ya ke'Rumosh obligah. Aler mod credah, po ker paliond*. What do you think it means?"

"I don't know." The headmaster set Lee's parchment down beside his own. "I remember this verse, which speaks of his faithfulness when we commit our way and trust, but I cannot say what it means for your raid."

Tiran, who had laid his forehead on the desk, looked up. "Raid?"

“Yes. I believe these dreams are all related to a single raid. But before I say more, let me hear from Mister Enarian.” He poised his quill again. “Go ahead, my boy.”

Connor had no desire to return to his nightmare or ponder its meaning. “I’d rather forget what I saw, if it’s all the same to you, Headmaster.”

“It isn’t all the same. We need the full picture.” Master Jairun’s eyes bored into him. “Talk.”

Connor did his best. But even after the headmaster’s firm prompting, he couldn’t bring himself to speak of his patehpa swallowed by the flames. He described the void and the swirling silver powder and told them of the open plain of polished stone and the terrifying dragon. “He belched a stream of flame. That’s when I woke, frightened, still feeling its heat.”

“All right, lad. All right.” Quinton laid a hand on his back. “You’re here and safe now. No cadet should ever face a dragon, not even in a dream. Now, Headmaster”—he turned to Master Jairun, rubbing his hands together—“what were ya sayin’ about that raid?”

46

THE CADETS CROWDED INTO THE SMALL MAP CHAMBER with Masters Jairun and Quinton, while Belen went to fetch them all a bite to eat. "Things are moving quickly," he said as he hurried away. "Yes, quickly. And quickness requires sustenance."

Master Jairun spoke his prayer, and the living mountains and forests covered the table. Connor had not yet seen the map up close, nor in the light of day. He marveled at the snow falling from the clouds and at the water flowing in the lowland rivers.

"This map," Master Jairun said, "represents the last communication from our spy near Trader's Knoll. We should keep that well in mind. He commits his thoughts to parchment with quill and ink, and by the Rescuer's will, we're able to see his recollections in living form. But remember, this is one man's perspective–days old. We do not know the full story, nor how much the story has changed."

"A great deal, I should think." Quinton sat heavily in the chair next to the copper kettle. He picked it up, as if expecting it to be full and hot, then frowned and set it down again. "Much must've changed to bring orcs and goblins to the very gates of Ras Telesar."

"Indeed, my friend. Indeed." Master Jairun's gaze settled on Connor. "And so we come to the urgency of our decision. At least one aspect of the dreams the Rescuer sent your class is clear. The time to act is now."

"So, the guardians will violate the Assembly's ruling," Teegan said. "You'll go on a raid."

"The guardians? No, my dear. You and your fellow classmates had the dreams, not us. The Rescuer is sending you."

Lee removed his spectacles and blinked. "We're to raid the Dragon Lands without you?"

Quinton laughed. "Nobody said nothin' about goin' without us, lad. What he meant was–"

"That is precisely what I meant," Master Jairun said. "Our raiding days are long past."

"But Avner–"

"This is *their* time, Angus. Their calling. And they're not going alone. Our cadets have each other and the Rescuer. But we're staying here."

Tiran laid a hand on his sword hilt and lifted his chin. "Don't worry. We're not afraid."

"Good. Good." Master Jairun patted his shoulder. "But you're staying here too, Mister Yar."

Tiran froze. "What?"

"What?" Connor and Teegan echoed the question.

"But we need him," Lee said. "Tiran is our best swordsman."

"And an excellent bowman," Master Jairun said, "as the two dead goblins near our bridge would attest. If we believe the dream the Rescuer showed Tiran, they won't be the last to walk there. Tiran must remain here and help three old men defend the academy."

Tiran seethed, but neither he nor any of the others argued further.

Master Jairun directed their eyes to the map table. "Be comforted by this. You'll have a guide. A guardian. Our spy works as a collier near the town of Trader's Knoll and goes by Halas–Hal for short."

Lee scrutinized the living town on the map. "I see Hal in the forest below the knoll, giving this message to the wolf. Before you lost contact, you asked him to look into our goblin problem, correct?"

The headmaster pressed his lips together. "A tidbit you learned during your eavesdropping. But, yes. In my last message, I told him we believed a dragon had found a way to direct a hollow hill portal through the mountain barrier and asked him to discover what he could."

"This dragon." Quinton gestured at the miniature wyrm cutting circles through the clouds east of the giant tree grove. "We suspect he's buildin' a castle on a northern slope o' the peaks, perhaps to guard the hollow hill. But there's much we don' know. Find Hal. If anyone can lead ya to the portal, it'll be him."

"Then what?" Teegan was leaning on her trident. "How do we plug a hole in the fabric of creation?"

As she spoke, Master Belen backed through the door wearing his leather mitts and carrying a tray in each hand. Aromas both sweet and savory entered with him. "I believe I can answer that, young lady. The solution lies with the Leander Kings."

Dag widened his nostrils as the trays passed.

Belen paused. "What do you think, young sir? I halved and grilled long candle fruit from the chapel, sprinkled with basil and mint. Or you might like a fig caramelized with honey."

"Pavel," Master Jairun said and inclined his head toward the map. "You were saying?"

"Oh, yes." Belen let Dag claim one of each type of cooked fruit, then moved among the others with the trays. "Before the dragon conquest, the Leander Kings, ruling from the far north, used a mineral called shairosite to extend their influence deep into the Talanian continent–or so the stories tell us. According to legend, their philosophers used this powder to manipulate the hollow hill portals almost as well as the Elder Folk."

Teegan plucked up a caramelized fig. "The Leander Kings are long gone. How does this mineral of theirs help us? What did you call it? Sharo . . . Shiro . . ."

"Shairosite." Belen gave her a smile. "Better known as banishing powder. Not all the Leanders were especially adept in its use. In a few stories, the philosophers collapsed the portals by accident–with great fanfare, I might add. Mountains crumbling, valleys falling in upon themselves, and the like."

"So," Dag said, taking a bite of candle fruit and talking between chews, "we can use banishing powder to destroy the portal. But, how will we find some? What does it look like?"

"Hal began seeking evidence of a lost hollow hill and banishing powder in the Highland Forest soon after the goblins appeared in our land. We must trust the Rescuer to provide. As to the powder's appearance, the stories describe raw shairosite as pure—"

"Glittering silver." Connor fixed his gaze on the map table's dragon. "The dust I saw in my dream was banishing powder, right? I saw the portal's destruction."

"Just so." Belen set his trays down beside the map chamber's kettle and removed his mitts. "And this—of course—enraged the dragon. But there are other dangers besides an angry wyrm. A collapsing hollow hill is violent. It can create a new chasm or bring the castle down. And one other thing." He lifted a cloth from the kettle and held it before the cadets. "Do you remember our conversation about the hollow hills working like pinches in the fabric of creation?"

They all nodded, except for Tiran, who'd backed into the shadowed corner by the stairs from the roof. Connor sensed a need, but he didn't go to the boy. He wanted to understand the guardians' plan. He could comfort Tiran later.

Master Belen set the cloth flat on his palm and pinched a fold as he'd described. "I don't believe these portals may be truly destroyed. Rather, they are collapsed, an important distinction. Observe." He flattened the fold with two fingers, and another fold popped up not far away. He tried twice more, each time with the same result. "I believe the hollow will appear somewhere else. Do your best to discover where, or we may find ourselves fighting the same battle all over again."

"And if the banishing powder doesn't work?" Teegan asked. "Or if we can't find any? What then? How will we sever the dragon's connection to Keledev?"

Her question brought a troubled look to Master Jairun's face—sad, even. "I hope it doesn't come to that, my dear. The only other way to collapse a dragon-steered portal would be to kill the dragon itself, a challenge for which none of you are prepared."

47

THE CADETS HAD MUCH TO DO BEFORE THEIR DEPARTURE. The guardians brought them down to a room in the lower bulwark known as the outfitter's chamber.

"This is where ev'ry raid party chooses their supplies," Quinton said, holding a chaos of leather straps, pockets, and buckles up to Dag's shoulders. He tossed it aside, then reached for another hanging from a line of hooks. He stretched that one out and shook it into some semblance of order so the cadets could see. "The tinkers call these vests *manykits*. Kits for short. Lightraiders rarely have horses on the road, so this is how we lug our gear. The eberlast lining in the pockets'll keep yer essentials dry."

Connor found one the correct size, then struggled with the straps for some time before he got them sorted. Buckles at the chest and thighs kept the manykit in place. With ten pockets of varying sizes and several clips, he could carry way rations, bandages, a flint and steel, and the like without feeling overbalanced.

His scabbard went on over the kit, and then a cloak, which Teegan brought him. She placed it over his shoulders "Try this one. They're wool, lined with eberlast like the kit pockets. Master Quinton says it's a sort of gum made from a bush that grows in the Forest of Believing. This cloak will keep you bone-dry in the worst storm if you wear it right."

Tiran watched from the doorway. "What if you jump in a lake?"

"You mean the Passage Lakes," Teegan said. "I think that's different." She helped Connor fit a sheath to his back for his crook. She already wore a matching sheath for her trident. "I'm sorry you don't get to come this time, Brehna, but you heard the guardians. You're needed here."

Connor tried to think of something encouraging to add, but Lee spoke first, fiddling with the strap of his quiver. "Perhaps it's good you're staying behind, Tiran. I mean, what if the Rescuer doesn't think you're ready for a raid?"

The other four stared at him. Quinton too. Tiran let out an angry huff and walked out.

"That was not what yer friend needed to hear, lad," Quinton said. "Not from you."

They didn't see Tiran again until supper at the Hall of Manna. The guardians presented a feast they'd been saving for the day their initiates passed through the Shar Razel to become cadets—stone cups filled with cooked egg and cheese, pork loins smothered in a raisin sauce. Master Jairun tried to make it a celebration of their induction into the Order. But urgency kept the mood somber. Another goblin might land on their doorstep at any moment. And no one had heard news from Pedrig or Hal in days.

Tiran kept to himself at the table's end. When Belen brought out little crusted chocolate cakes for dessert, Connor took his and sat with him. "If it were up to me—"

"But it's not up to you, is it? My dream could've meant anything. I might shoot those arrows from our ramparts tomorrow, before you leave, or long after you return. It's not the Rescuer who's holding me back, Connor. It's the guardians."

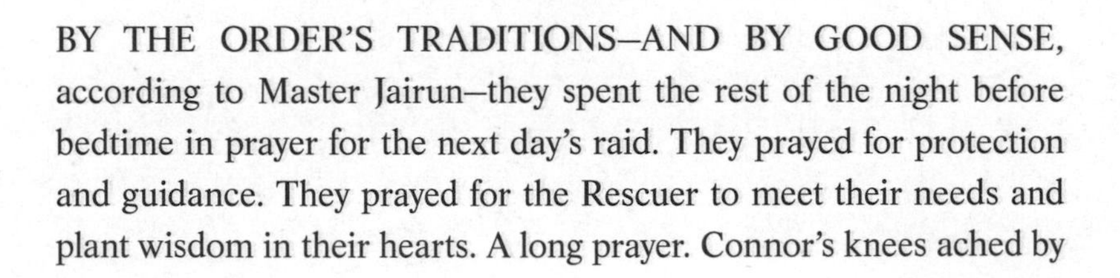

BY THE ORDER'S TRADITIONS—AND BY GOOD SENSE, according to Master Jairun—they spent the rest of the night before bedtime in prayer for the next day's raid. They prayed for protection and guidance. They prayed for the Rescuer to meet their needs and plant wisdom in their hearts. A long prayer. Connor's knees ached by the time Master Jairun uttered the final words.

"Vynovu, Rumosh. Se vy'enu."

Your ways, High One. Not mine.

As the guardians walked the cadets to their barracks. Connor hung close to the headmaster. "Is this part of knowing his will? A long prayer before a raid?"

"Of course. And it is a way to temper your Keledan armor for the coming fight. But, my dear boy, the prayer is not over. Tonight was the preamble. Henceforth, you'll be in continual prayer until the quest has ended. That is the lightraider way."

Sleep came quickly but did not last. A scuffing noise roused Connor, and he rolled over to find Tiran seated at the barrack's table, rubbing tallow into his boots by candlelight. What was he up to? After their conversation at supper, Connor could guess. "You look like you're readying those boots for a long snowy road instead of standing a wall. Did something change?"

The question earned him a dire look. "I'm following the raid party to the Passage Lakes, Shepherd Boy. Masters Quinton and Belen are staying behind to watch the fortress. Master Jairun wants me to help bring the horses home after you leave–unless you feel the mantle of raidleader gives you the right to overrule him."

Lee sat up in his bunk, scowling at Tiran. "Connor never claimed the raidleader mantle."

Dag sat up as well, a clear sign he'd never gone to sleep in the first place. "No, he didn't. But I hope he'll wear it. He's been our leader since the first night."

Tiran's eyes never left Connor. "Yes, the shepherd's in charge. Fine. So, what'll it be? May I accompany your greatness to the Passage Lakes and wave fondly as you step into the water?"

Every word felt like the stab of a dagger. Connor let his head fall to his pillow. "Do as you wish tomorrow. For now, though, snuff out that candle and let us all get some sleep. We've a long and dangerous road ahead."

48

LIAM AND KEIR WERE NEVER COMING HOME. KARA KNEW it in the deepest reaches of her heart. Hal too. They were all dead.

"We'll return in a few days," Hal had told her before he and Liam left. "Five at most."

They'd been gone six. And yesterday, a man she recognized from the market had nailed a parchment to a tree outside the cottage. Nesat had brought the curfew to Trader's Knoll. His noose had finally tightened all the way to her doorstep.

Kara dropped into the chair by the hearth and raised a waterskin to her lips. Empty. They were all empty. She checked out the window in the bedchamber. The woods outside were going dim. No sense in passing the night thirsty on top of everything else. She'd take the wheelbarrow, fill all the skins at once, and be back in the cottage in less than a tick, only a little past curfew.

In most seasons, the forest grew loud at sunset, a wanton riot of buzzing, chirping, and croaking. But not in winter. All of nature had gone silent with the cold, leaving only Kara and her squeaking, clacking wheelbarrow, loud enough to draw every goblin within a hundred leagues. By the time the trail brought her to the stream's edge, she feared she'd made a poor choice in coming out in the evening. Once she knelt with the first waterskin, she knew it.

Ice. The stream had frozen over. Kara hammered at the surface with her knife. *Thock. Thock.* So much noise. Finally, it yielded, but only enough to let a small trickle through. She'd have to scoop the water with one skin to fill another, a little at a time.

The cold and toilsome work stiffened her fingers, and she'd only filled one and a half skins before they were too frozen to go on. But, at the slow pace, one and a half skins had seemed to take forever. When she looked up, she found the bright moons on the rise over the Impossible Peaks. How long had she been out there? Far past Nesat's curfew, for certain.

A twig snapped. Kara ducked behind the barrow. "Who's there?"

A light rustling answered. Or was it a snicker?

She caught a gleam of yellow, but only for an instant. "Show yourself. Are you one of Nesat's creatures? You've no reason to bother me. I'm filling skins for my household. Curfew or not, a family must have water to drink, right?"

The trees and brambles stayed quiet. Perhaps she'd imagined it.

"Right. I'm going now. Don't try to stop me." Kara lifted the wheelbarrow's handles and pushed, letting the wheel begin its ugly squeaking. She found the trail. "Very well, then. Good night."

Two images wandered across her mind–one of a goblin sheathing its long knife and slinking away, and another of a bewildered winter hare watching this babbling madwoman trundle off with her wheelbarrow.

The rabbit-goblin was not Kara's only scare. On the walk home, she might have heard a dozen frightening noises over the barrow's racket. Or not. Every time she stopped and put her hand on her knife, the forest went silent.

The last of these mysterious sounds reached her ear as Kara came within a stone's throw of the cottage. She kept going, but so did the noise, a crashing and groaning. A silhouette formed on the eastern path between her and the door, too big to be a man, heading toward her with a stilted, lumbering gait. A squeal escaped her lips.

"Hush, Kara!" The voice, a harsh whisper, belonged to Hal.

"Help me carry him!" The collier's struggle brought him into the dim wash of the moons, supporting a young man, half conscious and bleeding from a head wound.

"Liam!" Kara ran to them. She placed her brehna's arm over her shoulders. His sleeve felt wet, and his feet dragged behind her. "Liam, speak to me!"

"I told you to stay home," Liam said, slurring his words. "You never listen."

They laid him on the cottage floor, and Kara ran to light a lamp. The moment the wick took the flame, she saw the blood covering her palms, her clothes. None of it was hers. Hal mumbled over Liam–the Elder Tongue, she thought. Kara grabbed rags from the cupboard and dropped to her knees beside them. "We must wrap his forehead and stop the bleeding."

"His head is not the worst of it, girl." The old man took one of the rags and pressed it against Liam's stomach, below his ribs. His voice bore a touch of finality. A touch of death.

"But you can save him, right?"

"I'll try. I've been trying, ever since I found him more than a league to the east. But much of the saving is no longer up to me."

She didn't know what he meant, and she didn't ask. "Liam, stay awake. Talk to me. Tell me what happened."

"Goblins. Keir."

"You saw Keir?"

Hal took her hand and pressed it to the rag covering Liam's wound. "He picked a fight with a pack of forest goblins, so I gather, while trying to rescue Keir from Krokwode's clutches."

Blood soaked through and seeped between her fingers. She watched her brehna wince and swallow. "He needs water. I have some in the barrow."

"Not right now. Let him be."

She frowned and tried to get up anyway.

Liam held her fast. "I wanted to save him, Shessa. There were too many. He's . . . Keir is . . ." His eyes closed. A tear fell down.

"He's what, Liam? Captured? Taken?" She couldn't give voice to the word fixed in her mind.

Hal intervened. "From what Liam told me, he tracked Keir to a barkhide camp and tried to drag him home. But Krokwode's infection is strong. Keir argued, drawing the attention of a goblin patrol."

"We were separated in the fight," Liam said. "I saw Keir go down. I charged, trying to reach him, but a black knife stopped me cold. In the next instant, I took a blow to the head and came to, bleeding, in the brush." Guilt hung heavy in his voice. "The goblins and Keir were gone."

"That's all behind you." Hal wiped the blood from his forehead with the other rag. "What lies ahead is more important. Remember what I told you before we left. You must trust the gift."

"What gift?" Kara asked.

Hal held up a hand to quiet her. "I know your mother taught you more than the song, boy. Remember." The word became a command. "Remember. The knowledge is there. Bring it to the surface. Understanding will follow. And understanding enables trust."

The old man bowed his head and began speaking the Elder Tongue again. Then he stopped and looked at the door. "Our time is up. I sense their evil. They're coming."

Kara saw nothing but a still door and a dark threshold. "Who, Hal? Who's coming?"

A roar broke the quiet, followed by two more.

"Orcs. They must have sniffed out the blood trail. They hate it when the goblins leave a job unfinished."

Hal grabbed the edges of their table. With unnatural strength for his age, he heaved it against the door and muttered to himself. "May the Maker forgive me. I waited too long."

Liam touched Kara's cheek with a trembling hand. "I have something for you. You must take it and run."

"I'm not leaving you."

"Yes, you are. For I'm leaving you, whether we like it or not." He pulled a chain from under his shirt. From the end hung a silver bear hugging a polar sapphire—a perfectly round, deep blue stone with a white star reflecting the lamplight from within. He pressed the bear and chain into her hand. "This was Mehma's. She'd want you to have it."

The door shuddered. There were snorts and huffs from the other side.

Still mumbling and muttering, Hal added their stools and firewood to the barricade and laid both hands on the table. A white glow passed through the whole pile. The creatures outside howled as if struck by arrows.

Liam pushed Kara away. "You . . . need to go."

"I won't."

"You must, Shessa. Please."

"On this point, your brother and I agree," Hal said, returning to them. "That barricade won't hold for long, or the orcs will find another way in. The iron ore clans aren't as clever as their quicksilver cousins, but they're not mindless, either." The door shuddered again. Another flash of white. More angry howls. "Well, they're not entirely mindless."

"Even if I wanted to go, how could I?" Kara asked. "The cottage has no other door, only a small round window in the bedchamber. I can't squeeze through in my winter furs. And if I did, the orcs would snatch me up."

"All good points." Hal took her arm and spoke the Elder Tongue again, but this time in a clear, strong voice.

Kara felt a surge of energy rush through her, not from his touch, but from deep inside, spreading out to her limbs.

Hal thrust his bearded chin at the back room. "You'll find the window wider than before, and perhaps lower to the ground. And the Rescuer will hide you from the orcs. Trust him."

She started to argue, but Liam cut her off. “Quickly, Kara. There’s no time.”

Hal smiled down on her brehna as if smiling down on his own sehna. “And I see you trust as well, don’t you, child?”

Liam gave him a pained nod. “I do.”

“Then tell him so. Speak the words with me.”

Before Kara could ask what the two of them meant, the red-hot blade of a halberd cut through the door. The wood around it burst into flames, and an instant later, the door split into fiery shards. A hideous gargoyle orc stuck its body through the gap and roared.

“Not yet, you foul corruptions!” A dagger flew from Hal’s hand and caught the creature in the throat. Molten metal flowed from the wound.

Kara stared in awe. “So they do carry flame inside.”

Hal pointed at the back room. “Get out now. There won’t be another chance.”

Two more orcs cast their comrade aside and breached the threshold. From under his cloak, Hal drew a stacked crossbow and fired two bolts in quick succession. He cranked the string for another volley. “Now, Kara!”

She looked to Liam, who gave her a peaceful nod and let his eyes close.

With no other choice, she fled.

49

MASTER JAIRUN GUIDED THE CADETS ON THE RIDE TO the Passage Lakes. Winter had closed the high pass, forcing them to take the long road south past Watchman's Gate to get around the massive Anvil Ridge. Frost slickened the trail, and the horses' careful steps slowed their column. Before they turned north again, up the Anamturas Valley, the sun had begun its descent toward the western horizon.

Connor looked up at the fireglass as they made the turn around the western tower. For Tehpa, this place had become a memorial after Faelin disappeared. *I rode to Watchman's Gate every week–like a pilgrim rides to a tomb.* Would he make that ride again if Connor didn't return?

He spurred his horse to ride next to Master Jairun. "Will he know?"

The headmaster did not need to ask of whom he spoke. "He will. I'll send a raven to Glimwick the moment Tiran and I return, and he'll send ravens to the Assembly and all your families. To do otherwise will only place a dagger in the hands of our detractors."

"But what will Glimwick tell them?"

"The truth, my boy. The Rescuer has ordered you across the barrier. Whether they believe this or not is up to them."

During the northward ride, the headmaster gave each raider a small flask to clip to their kits. "These are filled with water from Telbeath, the chapel fountain, to speed your healing when you are wounded."

"*When* we're wounded?" Lee asked, blinking at him through his spectacles. "I mean, wounds are not a foregone conclusion on every raid, are they?"

Master Jairun didn't answer and instead gave Dag a small leather bundle, tightly wrapped. "From Master Belen. Use this to bolster your friends when they need it most."

The miner's kit looked different than the others. For him, Quinton had chosen a vest with a padded steel harness. Spikes stuck up through Dag's cloak at the shoulders, not meant for intimidation–though they made him look formidable–but as pegs from which two big satchels hung to his hips. He would be the party's mule. Dag thanked the headmaster and slipped the bundle into one of the satchels.

Connor also received a gift–or a loan, at least. Master Jairun gave him the spyglass he'd used at Mer Nimbar. "I'd like it returned to me in one piece, Mister Enarian. It has . . . sentimental value."

By nightfall, the road brought them to the lowest of the Passage Lakes, marked by a fireglass tower. Lee saw the tower and its vale first and pointed, telling them all about it. "Small peaks and feathered waterfalls separate each lake from the next in two stair-step vales. Seven lakes in all. This one is Mount Charity Lake, at the bottom of the Eastern Vale."

But Connor saw only dark trees and water and slopes on every side. The quiet rush of the many distant falls Lee described took an act of faith to hear.

Dag reined his horse at the lakeshore and stared down at the water. "That looks cold."

"It is." Master Jairun came up behind him. "The Anamturas is not fed by a hot spring like the Gathering. Nothing shocks the flesh like icy runoff from the highest reaches of the Celestial Peaks. Once you are waist deep, you'll need to lean on the Helper to keep going."

"To keep going?" Dag said. "How much farther than waist deep must we go?"

"However far the Rescuer wills."

The miner dismounted. "Great." He hefted his satchels, adjusting the straps. "I'm going to sink like a millstone."

Behind them, Lee tightened his spectacles. Master Belen had added a delicate red lens before they left but hadn't told them its purpose, only that Lee would know how to use it when the time came. "I'll take care of you, Dag. My family walks with fishes, as Tehpa used to say."

"I might need looking after too," Connor said. "The Enarians aren't much used to water, unless sheep ponds count. But we'll be all right. Teegan is a strong swimmer. She and Tiran grew up . . ." He trailed off as he looked toward the twins. They'd stepped away from the party, speaking in hushed tones, and neither looked too pleased with the other. Aethia watched them from a nearby pine, head cocked as if trying to listen.

Whatever their argument, Master Jairun cut it short. "Come to the water's edge, children. No time to waste."

The four raiders lined up on the shore. Teegan beckoned for Tiran to stand with them and see them off, but he shook his head and stayed by the horses. Aethia wheeled over the lake, crying out with concern.

"Don't worry about your falcon, my dear," Master Jairun said. "The guardians will look after her." He waded out ahead, ankle deep, with his lantern spreading gold over the black surface. "Two final warnings. Take care in your search for the banishing powder. Few remain in Talania who know of its existence, and the dragons want to keep it that way. Any deposits will be well defended. Now, all of you, step into the water."

The raiders left the shore, cautiously at first, with Teegan holding Dag's elbow. Master Jairun backed up with them until his robes floated around him, then let them go on alone. "Well done. The first steps of any raid are a leap of faith, but the first steps of this *first* raid may be your hardest. When the water deepens, let go, or you may drown in the attempt to make the passage."

"Drown?" Dag asked.

Lee dove in and popped up again, arms gliding below the surface in steady rhythm. Water beaded on the red paste in his hair. He grinned. "Whew! Cold! So cold!"

Before Connor followed the others, Master Jairun spoke in his ear. "Never forget, this is the Rescuer's mission, Mister Enarian–not your own. A Havarra wolf like Pedrig is fiercely loyal, and so should you be. But be loyal to the Rescuer, not your own desires. Follow his command, and your raid is sure to succeed."

Connor gave him a last, questioning look, then forced his legs to carry him out into the freezing deep. At first, he held onto one of Dag's spikes, since the miner's boots stayed in contact with the lake silt far longer than his.

When Dag reached the place where his square chin skimmed the surface, he spoke with utter calm. "You might want to let go, now. I think this is the part where I drown. If I don't freeze to death first."

Lee swam between them and took their elbows. "It's all right. Kick your feet–like running, but slow and steady."

Connor tried, and it worked, but not well. He sputtered, fighting to keep from swallowing the whole lake.

Teegan took his other arm and swam around to catch Dag's. They formed a circle with the strong swimmers keeping the other two afloat. High above, Aethia still cried in bewilderment.

"It's f-fine, Aethia." Teegan's teeth were chattering. "I'll c-come back. I p-promise. Be good, and don't eat any p-p-paradragons while I'm gone." She looked at the others. "N-now what do we d-do?"

Connor would have shrugged if he could still feel his shoulders. "I'd thought we'd be stepping out of a hollow t-tree b-b-by now."

Between bobs below the surface, he saw Master Jairun, lantern held high. "Faith. Do you understand? A leap of faith, children. Let go!"

Let go.

In obedience, Connor pulled his arms from both Teegan and Lee and immediately sank. He grabbed them again and pulled himself up, coughing hard. "Nope. That's n-not right."

But Teegan nodded. "Y-yes. It is. I think it's n-not so much letting g-go of each other, but of our own strength. Stop s-s-swimming. L-let yourselves sink. On three. One, t-t-two, three!"

Their heads dropped beneath the surface, arms drifting. In the growing dark, Connor saw his companions fade. First Dag, then Lee, then Teegan. Whether they'd vanished into a portal or sunk to the bottom, he couldn't tell. Why hadn't he gone with them?

He heard a muted splash. A hand caught his wrist. Had he failed? Was Master Jairun trying to save him? The form blocked out the moonlight. He couldn't make out the face. And this nameless person didn't pull him upward, but drove him down, deeper and deeper. Where had the lake bottom gone?

The last of Connor's breath gave out, and he opened his mouth. Water flooded his throat.

50

THE WATER FILLING CONNOR'S NOSE AND MOUTH became air–cold, pure air scented with pine. One foot, then the other touched solid ground, crunching on frozen needles, but his balance didn't hold. Someone still gripped his arm, pushing him. Connor ducked to avoid banging his head on gnarled wood and pitched forward into a snow drift.

Tiran landed on top of him.

"Get off!" Connor shoved him aside. "Were you trying to drown me?" Frigid water dripped down Connor's face and neck. But when he recovered his feet and brushed off the snow, he found the rest of his clothes were dry.

Tiran was not. He freed himself from the snowbank and stood, dripping and shaking, soaked to the bone. The snow clung to his cloak and trousers as slush. No amount of brushing or sweeping did any good. Teegan tried, but her twin pushed her hands away. "Stop that. I'm fine."

The others had made it safely through the portal–a hollow in a broad and twisted bristlecone pine. Dag had taken up a watchful position, eyes on the forest, one axe at the ready. Lee, meanwhile, tilted his spectacles and emptied them of water, the only part of him to get wet.

When he finished, Lee walked around the bristlecone. "How amazing is the Maker's work." He touched the smooth bark at the apex of the gap in the trunk, and it began to close, knitting itself together from top to bottom. "Oops. I hope no one else wanted to come through."

But someone did. Aethia shot from the closing portal and knocked him off his feet. She spiraled up to a bristlecone branch and puffed up, looking terribly unhappy with whole experience. Below her, the last edges of the gap twisted together into a root that dug itself down through snow and earth.

Connor helped Lee up. "That's one loyal bird, Teegan. I wonder how deep she had to dive to chase you."

"And yet"–Lee eyed the falcon through his spectacles–"she's dry like the rest of us."

"Not all of us," Tiran said. "I'm freezing."

Teegan stepped in front of him. "And whose fault is that, Brehna?"

"I don't know, Shessa. Why don't you tell me?"

"You weren't supposed to come through."

"An interpretation made by the guardians. Yet here I am."

"Only because you held onto Connor. What would you have the Rescuer do? Cut him in half to prevent your disobedience?"

From the edge of the group, Dag mumbled something.

Teegan ignored him. "And another thing–"

The miner waved his axe at her. "Quiet, I said. Argue later. I saw movement in the woods downslope."

"How close?" Connor asked.

"Too close. Let's go."

Despite the urgency in Dag's voice, none moved until Connor unsheathed his crook and set off uphill.

"Wait," Tiran whispered. "Surely the Rescuer brought us to the barrier's northern slopes. Trader's Knoll will be below us. Shouldn't we go downhill?"

Lee paused. "Toward the movement Dag saw?"

"Could be townsfolk."

"Doubt it," Teegan said. "These are the lands of the dragons, where the monsters come out at night."

Her brehna would not give in. "We should at least try and find out."

"Enough!" Connor turned to glare at them. "There *are* monsters in these woods, so we must keep quiet." He pointed uphill with the crook, toward a patch of moonlit sky visible through the trees. "And we need to get our bearings, so I'm heading to higher ground. Follow me if you wish."

The moonlit forest felt dimmer here, oppressively so. The bright moons always traveled in the sky's southern half–southernmost in winter, lighting the slopes of the Celestial Peaks. The northern slopes remained trapped in shadow, even with the moons at their full height. The great peaks loomed above, bleak and imposing. Such a different view from one side to the other.

Just as Tiran regained some of his bluster and asked if Connor planned to climb back over the barrier, the slope leveled out.

Teegan squinted through the trees. "I see firelight. Or lanterns, perhaps. Lee?"

"It's a town." The scribe lowered a lens into place. "Yes. I see lanterns in a gatehouse . . . and in the second floor of an inn. That must be Trader's Knoll. I see no movement in the lights, but goblins and ore creatures don't favor the light, do they?"

They headed downslope again, toward the town, until Lee's sharp eyes found a road. They might have joined it, but Teegan signaled for them to crouch a few paces from the edge of the trees. She inclined her head to the northwest and tapped an ear, mouthing, *Listen* to Connor.

He heard the steady pound of marching.

Lee pointed up the road. Orcs. Only six, but the weight of iron ore twisted into supple flesh shook the ground. This close to the road, the creatures would see them for sure. But if they moved away, the orcs might hear.

Lee poked him, then touched his spectacles and directed Connor's gaze to the southeast.

He saw the shape of a narrow mound. A collier's mound. Hal's place. He made eye contact with Teegan, Dag, and Tiran and motioned for them to follow, staying low and silent.

Moments later, they broke into a clearing. Hal's hummock cottage looked exactly as it appeared on the living map. Connor pushed the door open and ushered the others inside, leaving Aethia perched atop the mound to keep watch.

"Halas?" Teegan whispered into the dark. "Hal? Are you home?"

There was no response.

Connor tried the lightraider motto. "The Rescuer is with us." A salt warrior spy or Havarra ally was supposed to reply *Always and forever.* But still no one answered.

"Nobody's here." Tiran lifted a piece of charwood from a pile beside the hearth. "I'm lighting a fire while I still have the use of my fingers."

"No," Lee said. "Someone will see."

Tiran picked up another log. "The Aladoth live here, Lee. They go about their lives much as the Keledan. Or did you think they huddle together in darkness every night in fear of orc patrols. What looks more suspicious, a hovel with a fire in the hearth or five people milling about and whispering in the black?"

Lee could not argue.

Nor could Connor. "I'll help," he said and knelt next to a dark doorway at the edge of the hearth to pick up the salt warrior's flint and steel.

As he lifted the tools to light the fire, he felt the tip of a blade at his neck and hot breath at his ear. "Strike that flint, thief, and I'll slit your throat before the spark lands."

51

CONNOR DROPPED THE FLINT AND STEEL AND STOOD, hands raised. His crook rested against the mantle, but he doubted his reach could outpace the blade at his throat.

Tiran drew his sword, while Teegan advanced, hand on the trident strapped to her back, but Connor settled them with a look. "We're not thieves. We're friends of Halas, who owns this cottage."

"Liar. I've never seen any of you before, and I knew Hal well. He was like . . . like a . . ." The girl's voice cracked.

Teegan seemed to take this as a sign of weakness and whipped the trident from its sheath.

The Aladoth girl extended her blade.

Connor snatched the crook from its place and spun away, planting the spike behind her ankle. With a flick and a push, he stole her balance. The girl hit her head against the mantle and crumpled. Eyes so blue they seemed almost indigo in the low light lolled back into her head.

"You didn't have to kill her," Lee said, rushing over.

"I wasn't trying to." Connor knelt next to the girl and felt the back of her head. Wherever he touched her hair, a coating of soot came away to reveal platinum. Strange. The soot had not come from her fall against the hearth. "No blood," he said, "though a bump is rising." He laid her head on the earthen floor. "Will she be all right?"

Lee placed an ear near her mouth, then nodded. "She'll wake. But I doubt she'll be happy with you when she does."

"I'm still cold," Tiran said. "If anyone cares."

While her soaked twin built the fire, Teegan helped Lee bind the girl using twine from Hal's charwood stacks.

Dag set his satchels down across the room and stretched. "Did you hear what she said, Connor?"

"About slitting my throat?"

"No. About Hal. She spoke of him in the past, like he's–"

"I heard. But let's not draw any hasty conclusions. Hopefully, she'll tell us more when she wakes up. In the meantime, we need to search this place."

"All right." Dag lifted an upturned bowl from a shelf and peered underneath. "What are we looking for?"

"Maps. Notes." Connor scanned their surroundings. "Anything to tell us what happened here, or where we might find the banishing powder."

Lee and Teegan found a straw bed in the next room, a sort of workshop and bedchamber. They carried the girl in there to let her rest more comfortably, but they'd only been gone a few moments when Teegan called out to the others. "Come in here. You need to see this."

Tiran rubbed his hands over the fire, lifting his chin to Connor and Dag. "You two go if you want. I'm not leaving this spot until I dry out."

Teegan struck an oil lantern and cast the orange circle of its flame over framed char drawings hanging on the wall. "What do you make of them? Hal's work?"

Each sketch seemed to tell a small story. A woman walked into a seamstress shop wearing an expression that said no amount of gold could buy what her heart desired. An innkeep swept the pavers in front of his lodge, eyes fixed on the upper window of a tall house, as if he feared the shadow watching from inside. A nasty creature with horned wings and a wicked sneer stared straight out of the hide canvas from the market square, making Connor want to look away. "Is that a granog?"

"I think so." Teegan moved the light to the centermost picture, framed with polished driftwood. "I was more interested in this one. Look familiar?"

The artist had sketched their Aladoth captive. Connor glanced at her, still on the bed. He couldn't deny the resemblance. "Hal drew her portrait."

"Or she drew her own and gave it to him. Look at her. She's pretty, right?"

He shifted his feet. "If you say so."

"I know so. Now look at the drawing–the hardness in the lips, the deep set of the eyes. This is how she views herself."

"Perhaps."

"I'm right. Trust me."

Intending to study the sketch closer, Connor lifted it from the wall and found a niche concealed behind it. "Teegan."

"I see it." She reached inside and drew out two items–an unadorned dagger with a hilt of leather and steel, and a key. She let the key dangle from its chain. "I'd say this is important."

"Put it down. Now."

Connor spun to see the girl sitting up in the bed, the twine lying on the floor at her feet. She held a sling with a stone in the pocket, ready to fly. His sling. "How did you–" She must have taken it from his belt while she held the knife to his throat. "Now who's the thief?"

"Still you. Put down Hal's things before I scream and bring an orc patrol down on us all."

"They'll kill you too."

"You're the bandits. I'm just an innocent trader."

"Doubt it." Tiran appeared at the door with his dagger raised, holding it by the tip. "If you try, it'll be a short scream, I assure you."

Lee stepped between them. "Let's all calm down, shall we? I'm Lee Trang. This is Connor Enarian. And you are?"

"Waiting for your friends to put down Hal's things."

Teegan nodded and complied.

So did Connor. “Happy?”

“No.” But she set the sling and stone on the mattress anyway.

Connor let out a breath. “Thanks. Why don’t we start again? Perhaps you could tell us how you know Hal.”

“You first. Where did you come from?”

A tricky question. Teegan widened her eyes at Connor.

“We’re from the south,” he said. “Due south. The same place as Hal. Now it’s your turn, Miss . . .”

“Kara. Kara Orso. And there are no lands due south of the Highland Forest, only the peaks.”

Connor bit his lower lip, holding back, but a voice inside told him to trust her. “Think . . . beyond the peaks.” He fended off a swat from Teegan.

Kara picked up the sling again. “You’re from Keledev across the barrier. You’re lightraiders–knights of the Southern Overlord.”

“Overlord.” Lee let out an awkward chuckle. “I’ve only read that one in the oldest of our texts. But he goes by many names. I prefer the Maker.”

Dag thumbed the edge of his axe. “I like Our Beloved Blacksmith.”

“King of the Forge,” Tiran said.

Teegan smiled at her twin. “Or Lord of the Fountain.”

“Most commonly, we call him the Rescuer.” Connor held out an open palm, making a pointed look at his sling. “Hal served him. And if you spent as much time with him as you say, you’ll know this to be true.”

Kara stared Connor down for a long moment, then placed the sling into his hand. She lowered her gaze. “I do know it. I knew it last night.”

Connor sank to a knee before her, fearing the answer to his next question. “Will you tell us where Hal has gone?”

Kara dropped her face into her hands. “He’s dead. They’re all dead.”

52

THROUGH HER TEARS, KARA RECOUNTED HER brehna Keir's disappearance and Hal's return with the older one, Liam, stabbed and beaten. She told them of Hal's magic—a powerful magic she'd never seen before—and how he'd helped her escape before orcs overran the cottage. No longer caring for her own life, she'd crept back in daylight and found the place burned to cinders. "Liam, Keir, Hal. Everyone I love is gone. What am I to do?"

Connor had no idea how to console her. She might be acting. She had, after all, demonstrated skill as a pickpocket—not the most honest trade. But Tanelethar was a different world, with a deceived morality. Perhaps the people here considered petty thievery an honorable profession. He looked to Teegan for help.

She shrugged, a clear *I don't know what to do with her any more than you do.*

"No way." Lee paced the room. "There's no way a couple of orcs took down a lightraider guardian."

"Guardians aren't immortal," Tiran said, "not in terms of the first death."

"But she didn't see him die. She found no bodies."

Tiran shrugged. "Fine. We don't know for certain what's become of Hal. Dead? Captured? Either way, the fact that he's not here is troubling. We're not likely to find him. We should search for the wolf."

Dag smacked him in the chest, darting a glance at the girl.

But she'd heard. "Wolf?" she said, wiping her eyes. "What do you know about a wolf?"

Tiran pushed Dag's hand away and crossed the room, pointing at her with his dagger. "What do *you* know about a wolf?"

"I heard a snarl once when I came to visit. I ran into this room and saw Hal sharing a meal with a gray creature. The creature fled, but I'd swear by the nine dragons it was a wolf."

Lee bristled at her oath. "We'd rather you didn't swear by any dragons, if you don't mind."

She locked him with her gaze, as if he'd committed some high crime. "Try challenging such an oath in the Bristlecone Lodge, and see how it goes for you. Even better, if you truly want a fight, swear by your Blacksmith."

"We don't do that either," Connor said, trying to regain her focus. "Hal was meant to be our guide. And if not him, the wolf. We don't know what's become of them, but alive or dead, they're not here now. We'll need your help in their stead."

"Why should I help a pack of Keledan knights?"

"Because the dark creatures who killed your family and burned your home are on the brink of doing the same to ours. We're here to stop them."

The raiders had all gathered behind him, and Kara searched their faces one at a time until her gaze settled once more on Connor. "Fine. I'll grant you a little trust. But I won't guarantee my help. Let's start with that key. I've seen it before. It unlocks Hal's woodshed outside."

Teegan laid a hand on her hip. "You expect us to believe Hal keeps the key to his woodshed hidden in the wall behind a drawing?"

"Usually he keeps it around his neck. I don't know why he left it hidden. But I'll tell you something else. That's no mere woodshed. It's built like a fortress."

Connor and Lee exchanged a knowing look, and both spoke at the same time. "An armory."

They all snuck out to the structure with a shuttered lantern. While the twins kept watch for orcs, Connor turned the key and hauled open the door.

"Nope," Dag said. "It's a woodshed."

Wood and charwood were stacked as high as the miner's head. Aethia clucked softly from the top of the mound, in what might have been a falcony laugh. Connor shot the bird a frown, then nodded to Lee and Dag. "Let's move these stacks. This can't be all there is."

Kara held the lantern, keeping it shuttered. "Perhaps the logs themselves are the weapons. In the stories I've heard, you Keledan marauders are witless barbarians who conk young women on the head and drag them home as wives and concubines."

"I didn't conk you on the head." Connor set an armload of charwood on a growing pile beside the shed. "I tripped you, after you held a knife to my throat. And I won't be dragging you home to be my wife."

Teegan threw a glance over her shoulder. "No, he certainly won't."

"I think there's a false wall." Lee came out from between the dwindling stacks in the shed. "I've found another keyhole, but it's much smaller than the first."

"Then force it," Tiran said. "We can't spend all night searching for another key."

Lee hurried toward the cottage. "We won't have to." He returned a moment later with the dagger Teegan had pulled from the niche. He toyed with the hilt, twisting the pommel. "Must be some kind of–" With a quiet *shink,* the cross guard slid apart to release the blade. Lee pulled the blade away, leaving a grooved metal key sticking out of the hilt.

"Well don't just stand there," Dag said, claiming the lantern from Kara. "Let's try it."

The key fit perfectly. Lee gave the hilt a turn and pushed open a small section of wall. He ducked through with Dag right on his heels.

"We'll be as quick as we can," Connor told the twins, then nodded to Kara. "You coming?"

Inside, Lee and Dag had found stacks of woodland gear, maps, travel writs, and a stash of weapons–enough to outfit two or three raid parties. Dag lifted an oak bow and quiver and showed them to Connor. "For Tiran. He left his behind."

At the very back, Kara pulled open the top drawer of a chest and gasped. "Over here. Bring the light."

The chest held coins of copper, silver, gold, each kind in its own leather pouch. Kara opened the next drawer, and the next. All were the same. "Petas. Beoks. Halfins." She picked up a large gold coin. "This is a double claw. There must be a fortune in here, currency from every region of Tanelethar. But Hal lived like a pauper."

Connor plucked the gold double claw from her fingers and dropped it into its pouch. "Because this money doesn't belong to Hal. It belongs to the Rescuer."

Lee began picking through the pouches, making stacks on top of the chest. "We'll need some coin to survive–southern currency only. Twenty coppers and ten silver petas each should keep us fed. Perhaps five or six gold halfins for the party just in case."

Kara stopped him as he picked up the halfins. "No gold. You'll make us a target for bandits, even if you never use them. The sharpest eyes will spot them every time you open your pouch.

"Us?" Connor looked at her. "So, you'll come along and act as our guide in Hal's absence?"

"Guides need to be paid."

"We'll give you a fair wage."

"Make it more than fair. I can always run to the granog regent and ask if he'll pay more."

53

CONNOR HERDED HIS FLOCK INTO THE COTTAGE AS soon as possible, with the wood stacks in place and the shed locked up. He didn't like being out in the open or having Hal's small armory unlocked and exposed, but all those travel writs, maps, coins, and weapons gave him a sense of peace. The Assembly may have ended excursions into Tanelethar, but the Rescuer had clearly continued his work here. Through Hal, he'd built an outpost, a sanctuary at the edge of enemy territory, ready to outfit or restore knights on their way to and from the battle.

From Hal's supplies they'd taken hunter's writs, a manykit vest for Tiran, and extra rations. Lee had questioned the salted meat, sniffing the bags. "It's not goblin or anything, right?" Dag had snatched the bag from his hands and bopped him on the head with it.

But they'd been unable to find a map of Highland Forest. A search of the cottage turned up nothing either.

Connor lifted a silver peta from a coin pouch and held it up to examine the script and the crescent moon stamped into its face. He turned the coin over, and it slipped from his fingers, rolled along the table, and bounced against a small peg at the corner, falling flat. Connor tried to wiggle the peg, but it didn't move. "I wonder what this is for."

Tiran, who had returned to drying himself out by the fire, shrugged. "Looks like Hal didn't pound it all the way down. It's poor carpentry, is all."

"Poor carpentry?" Teegan asked. "From the same man who built the armory out there? With a secret door and all those beautiful chests and shelves?"

The secret door. "I have an idea." Connor moved the coin pouches to the floor, enlisting Lee and Teegan to help him. Once they'd cleared the table, he gave the others a look that said, *Watch this*, set the heel of his palm on the peg, and pushed down. It failed to move, leaving a deep impression in his flesh. "Ow," he said, shaking out his hand.

Teegan rolled her eyes and shoved him aside. "When will you boys learn? Brute force isn't the only option." She blew on her thumb and forefinger, rubbed them together, and twisted the peg. The table's central plank popped up.

Lee lifted it high. "And there's the missing map."

ALL SPREAD OUT, THE MAP PARCHMENT–BACKED WITH leather–took up much of the table and offered a detailed survey of the entire Highland Forest region.

Lee studied the markings with two lenses over his right eye and the lantern in hand. "The ink is less faded in some places." He traced a finger east to a castle on the mountain slopes and tapped a dragon perched on its highest tower. "The ink here is brand new. I'll bet this is where we'll find the hollow hill."

"A good start," Tiran said. "But we need the shairosite before we go anywhere near the dragon or its portal. And I see no mine symbol or lettering saying 'Dig here.' How do we find it?"

Lee lifted his nose from the parchment. "I suppose we follow our dreams."

"Yes." Teegan said. "Yes, of course. Otherwise, what were they for? What did we all see?"

"I saw a wolf," Dag said, slowly raising a hand.

Tiran laid a hand on his forearm to push it down. "You saw a bear."

"I saw both. I think."

"Bear. Wolf." Connor shook his head. "Doesn't matter. We need a place, not a beast."

Teegan leaned over the map. "I saw a place. Sil Elamar, the village of my ancestors. But I don't see it here. Kara, do you know of Sil Elamar?"

Kara had said little after their return from the woodshed. She sat apart, toying with some jewel hanging about her neck. She looked up at the mention of her name. "I'm sorry. What?"

"Sil Elamar," Teegan said again. "The village. Do you know it?"

"Sounds like the Elder Tongue. Perhaps the name has changed. Can you describe the town?"

Teegan closed her eyes and breathed in, as if she could smell the wood. "Sil Elamar is a grove of giant trees in the deepest valley. I saw it in my dream, but before that, I saw it in my mehma's stories. The elamwoods rise high and spread their canopies wide with domes of everleaves at many levels. They are like maidenhair trees, except so tall and broad you can build a house on every branch."

"You speak of Maidenwood Grove." Kara came to the map and tapped a drawing of trees about ten leagues from Trader's Knoll. "This place is a curse in my heart. Maidenwood Grove is where Keir went on his way to see what the goblins were building."

Lee had continued studying the map, and the farther he bent over the table, the more he tilted the light. Connor noticed too late. "Lee!"

The clay oil well dropped from the lantern and shattered on the table, sending flaming oil across the parchment. Teegan grabbed a blanket and smothered the fire, but when she pulled it away, the damage was done. Oil and charring obscured a whole section of the map. She threw the blanket aside and flopped down in her chair. "Lee, did you have to—"

"Oh, that's brilliant!" The scribe snatched up the map, and the others exchanged a look as he carried it to the hearth.

Tiran spread his hands. "Are you trying to finish the job?"

"The lantern's broken, and I need the light." Lee held the map precariously close to the fire. "Yes. It's as I thought. The burning parchment brought out ink markings not visible before."

The others joined him, and he showed them flowing script at the edge of the blackened portion–runes of the Elder Tongue. Lee read them out loud. "*The Meadow* . . ." He shook his head. "I can't make out the rest. But it's clear Hal made hidden markings on this map."

"How secretive," Tiran said. "And how do we see these markings? Burn the whole thing?"

Lee ignored him, looking to Connor instead. "Remember when Master Belen added the lens to my spectacles? He said I'd know when to use it." He flipped the red lens down over his right eye and grinned. "Yes. Oh, yes!"

The scribe returned the map to the table, spreading it out, while Teegan struck a small candle lantern from their supplies. Lee's eye followed the light wherever it went. "There are secret notations everywhere. Your cottage, Kara. A goblin tunnel underneath Trader's Knoll. Pedrig's hollow tree, which looks to be the place we arrived. I wish you could all see this."

"I think we can." Connor had noticed a bronze map glass on the worktable in the other room, with lion's-foot supports and a red-tinted lens. He fetched it and set it on the map, centered over the markings at the edge of the scorch mark. Flowing script hovered in the lens above the parchment. Connor completed Lee's reading from before. "*The Meadow* . . . *Beneath*." He raised his eyes to the others. "I'm not sure what it means. But next to the words, Hal's drawn a waterfall and a letter S in the common hand."

Lee let out a short laugh. "Shairosite."

54

CONNOR ROUSED THE RAID PARTY BEFORE SUNRISE. They'd set a rotating watch through the night.

While the others took a breakfast of porridge and salted meat by the fire, Teegan pulled him aside, next to the front room's eastern window. "Are you sure about this?"

Outside, he could just make out Aethia–a white bird on a snowy branch in the predawn gray. If he went through with the new plan, he wouldn't have the benefit of a falcon scout, but Lee and his spectacles were a fair substitute. "We don't know how long we have before the dragon can send an army through the portal, or pass through itself. Splitting up is our best chance. You, Dag, and Tiran take the map and head to Maidenwood Grove. Lee, Kara, and I will look for the waterfall and the shairosite."

"And we meet near the dragon's stronghold, at the cave marked in hidden ink on Hal's map. You've promised to be there in two days, three at the most." She didn't sound convinced.

"Is there something wrong with that part of the plan?"

Teegan turned, resting against the sill, and watched Kara. "Perhaps I should go with you and this Aladoth girl. You and I can find the falls. Send Lee with Dag and Tiran."

"The falls were in Lee's vision. He must go. Besides, if we're dividing the party in two, you should be the other leader. Tell me I'm wrong."

She opened her mouth as if to do so, but snapped it shut again and looked away.

"What? There's something else you want to say, so say it."

She lowered her voice. "Last night, during my watch. Kara got up and paced around near the back door—as if building up the courage to run off and betray us."

Connor glanced at the Aladoth girl. She sat close to Dag, by the hearth, staring down at the jeweled pendant hanging around her neck the way she had the night before. "But did she?"

"No."

Kara looked their way, and they averted their eyes. "Then for now, we trust her. Her actions on the road will tell us all we need to know."

Teegan pushed away from the windowsill. "Her actions on the road may get both of you killed."

The parties left the hummock cottage at dawn, intending to stick together for the first four leagues of the journey. Connor went over to Kara while the others strapped on their kits and weapons. "Still going with us?"

She gave him a brief nod. "I suppose I'll feel safe enough traveling with lightraider knights."

"Good. And we can pay you up front."

"You already have." Kara flashed a gold halfin. "I took five from the drawer while your friend stacked his coins."

"Only five?"

"You'll have to take my word for it. Try and search me, and you'll learn how fast your fortunes here can change."

Connor raised his hands in surrender. "Fair terms. Fair price."

The air thickened the moment they stepped into the woods, pressing in on body and soul to remind Connor they'd left the safety of Hal's small sanctuary. Aethia seemed to feel it too. She launched from Teegan's arm and shot above the trees. Teegan called out to her in a hushed voice, but Tiran shook his head. "Let her go. She'll serve us better as scout than passenger."

In the first half tick, they passed Trader's Knoll. Kara stopped to look up at the gatehouse.

Connor left the trail and stepped up beside her. "Change your mind already?" He followed her gaze. On the road into town, a short, fungus-formed goblin swatted a passing Aladoth with a stick. The girl bowed her head and walked on, as if the Maker had created men to walk in subservience to the dragons' soulless corruptions.

"Trader's Knoll wasn't always this way," Kara said. "Liam brought us south to get away from those creatures and the grip of dragon talons. But I suppose we always knew they'd spread their infection here. And look how quickly we've accepted them."

"Their infection will spread even farther south if we don't stop them."

"As you've said before, but how could the dragons invade your land through the barrier? You Keledan have always been protected in your perfect little kingdom."

A cough from Teegan halted Connor's response. He inclined his head toward the trail. "Come on. Show us the way eastward. We've a lot of ground to cover."

Kara proved useful, leading them overland from game trail to game trail. She confessed that her elder brehna had not let her roam much in the last season, but she'd walked leagues and leagues through this forest. Swam in its lakes. "I don't prefer to be around people. The woods are my closest friend."

The party walked three leagues before noon in the cover of the trees. But they could not avoid the region's main routes forever. Kara brought them up an embankment to a gravel highway, well-rutted from wagon travel. "This is the Southland Road. The land is broken, here, and the ravines in the woods are treacherous for the next league or so. We'll have to stay on the road or risk missing the fork where we plan to part ways."

"Some guide," Teegan said. "We can follow roads on our own.

Since when is a half-day's work worth five gold pieces?"

Kara answered her with a glare and walked on.

Lee, Dag, and Tiran followed her, but Connor held Teegan back. "Why are you being so hard on her?"

"Someone must, before she gets you and Lee alone and charms you into the hands of a granog."

"Teegs, that's–"

"Don't *Teegs* me. You're not Tiran. And you don't have a brehna's right to ignore whatever I say. Why are you so quick to give this girl your trust? She hasn't earned it. Look at where we are, Connor. This isn't Keledev."

He'd not heard such a tone in her voice since the road to Ravencrest on the night they'd met, that tone reserved for little children and very old men. And Connor began to think that under all the encouragement, all the support for him as the class leader, part of her had never stopped seeing him as a child to be steered and reared–the huntress leading the guileless farm boy.

"I'm not a fool, all right? I'm keeping a sharp eye on Kara. But think of this, *Teegs*. Perhaps it's *we* who need to earn *her* trust if we don't want her to betray us." Connor left her there, mouth slightly agape, and strode off after the others.

The Southland Road, which Kara said ran east and west across the region, never seemed to move in those precise directions. Rather, it bent and wound through the foothills and ravines. More than a tick of travel brought no sign of the fork. The sloped valleys all looked the same. Pines. Rocks. Snow.

While the highway curved along the northern edge of one of these valleys, a caravan of merchant wagons appeared at the coming bend. The lead driver looked hard at the group. "You travel well-armed, friends. Is the road so dangerous?"

Words failed Connor. Was it a crime here for people to travel armed?

Kara saved him. "If you haven't brought your wares to Trader's

Knoll in recent months, you may find the place much changed."

Before Connor could protest, she drew Faelin's sword from his scabbard and held it out to the man. "A caravan like yours should travel protected. We have a sword to spare, for a price. Six halfins. A bargain for such a fine weapon. Look at the jewel, the workmanship."

The merchant snorted and pulled his fur cloak aside, showing her a triplet of daggers on his hip. "If I'd known you were hagglers, I'd have kept my mouth shut. Keep your cheap sword and its glass jewel, girl, and I'll keep my gold." He drove on.

Connor gritted his teeth while Kara held his patehpa's sword up to every driver in the caravan. "Six? Five, then!"

The moment, they'd all passed, he lowered his voice below the grind and squeak of their wagon wheels. "That was my patehpa's. Give it back, and never touch it again."

Kara shoved the sword into his chest. "Don't freeze up, and I won't have to. If you can't talk to the local merchants, what will you do when we meet a granog?"

From behind her, Teegan shot him a look that said, *I told you, this is not Keledev.*

From then on, their road never seemed to escape the valley. It curved and straightened, shallowed and steepened, but always climbed, bending south, until the rock walls on either side closed in and grew sheer.

Aethia, well above them, let out a cry.

Teegan shielded her eyes to look up at her. "Something's coming. She's trying to warn us."

"So now you speak the language of birds?" Kara said. "The merchants came from the same direction. Why did your falcon say nothing about them?"

"The merchants were human."

Among the boulders and rock walls, Connor saw no way off the road. But he remembered their first morning at Ras Telesar, when he saw no path down to the lower courtyard. He steered his party close to the rocks. “Call her, Teegan. Quietly as you can.”

She frowned at him, but he cocked his head and frowned right back. She might think him guileless, but he was still the raidleader. He mouthed the words. *Call her.*

Without releasing him from her glare, Teegan gave a low whistle. Connor looked skyward and saw the falcon sweep down to vanish behind the clifftop. A moment later, she reappeared ten paces ahead, shooting out from the wall, and circled wide to land on Teegan’s arm.

“There!” Connor ran toward the spot. “Hurry!”

They found an east-facing crevice, starting at eye level and barely wide enough for Dag, but broadening as it rose toward the cliff top. The miner cupped his hands together and propelled the others up while Connor kept watch on the bend. Moments later, Dag touched his shoulder. “You next.”

“You go. I’ll follow.” Connor dropped to his hands and knees and grunted as Dag used his shoulders as a foot stool. With help from Lee and Tiran, the miner clambered up, then turned and beckoned. Connor took a running start and jumped, planting a foot on the rock face to gain more height. Just like the boulders of his pasture. He caught Dag’s hand, and the miner pulled him into the crevice.

The sound of marching came from the road. Heavy footfalls.

The others had reached the clifftop by the time Connor and Dag arrived. Tiran lay flat on his belly, peeking over the edge. “Orcs,” he whispered. “More than twenty.” He looked to Teegan, then Kara. “You were right. She set us up.”

Kara tried to answer, but Connor silenced the argument until they’d all retreated into the trees. “She couldn’t have known,” he said.

“Couldn’t she?” Teegan crossed her arms. “We don’t know how often or how regularly the dark creatures travel this road. She may know their habits.”

“Well, I don’t believe she did.”

"Excuse me." Kara pulled him away from Teegan. "Do you mind if I speak for myself?"

She didn't get the chance. Lee, who'd dug the map from Dag's satchel, had wandered off toward a short hill. He came running back. "You'll all want to come with me, I think. Teegan, especially."

The hilltop gave a commanding view of highlands to the east and north. Connor allowed Lee to direct his spyglass, then smiled. "Incredible." He held it steady and moved aside. "Teegan, you should have a look."

The moment she put her eye to the lens, she seemed to forget her anger. "Sil Elamar. The giant trees of my ancestors. They must be leagues away, but they're so big I feel I could reach out and touch the everleaves. For the first time, they're real to me. And soon I'll walk among them."

"Not so fast." Lee tipped the spyglass down. "Look what stands in our way."

55

CAMPS, MORE THAN CONNOR CARED TO COUNT, dotted the pine-covered hills and troughs between the party and Maidenwood Grove like so many herds of sheep.

He twisted the spyglass tubes to sharpen the view, looking closer. Some camps used long white tents like those the Stonyvale clerics would set up each year for the Forge celebration. Others had stretched a patchwork of wool and leather between trees. Each camp boasted a dozen or more men and women. He passed the glass to Kara. "Where did they all come from?"

She peered through the lens. "Krokwode could empty every town in the southlands and not recruit so many. They must be marching them in from the north. But why?"

"Why is not important," Teegan said. "We need to decide how to get past them."

"We split now." Connor took the spyglass from Kara and collapsed the tube. "Lee, Kara, and I can skirt the western edge of the camps, heading north before we turn east again toward the shairosite. But the road to Maidenwood Grove runs through the heart of those barkhides. There will be goblins or–"

"Or the oaksquid himself," Lee said. "And if the wood troll challenges you, the journey writs we found may not matter." He smoothed the map over the ground and studied it under his red lens, then tapped a spot south and east of their hill. "Here." He set the red map glass over the same place to show them one of Hal's hidden markings. "Will this work, Teegan?"

She nodded. "From what I remember of my mehma's stories, I think so."

PARTING COMPANY IN THE FACE OF THE BARKHIDE camps gave Connor no comfort, but he stuck to his plan. He gave Teegan the map, the spyglass, and the red map glass. When she asked why he didn't need the map, Lee–beside him–touched his own temple and said, "It's all up here."

Connor hoped that was true. They divided up what supplies they could–rations, bandages, balms–to lighten Dag's satchels, but Connor and Lee's kits could only take so much. "We'll find whatever else we need on the road," he said, and they made their goodbyes.

They'd only walked a few paces apart when Teegan hurried back to him and startled him with a hug. "I'm sorry we fought, but I do hope you'll be careful." She pressed her cheek against his and whispered, "*Watch* Kara."

Connor pulled himself back to arm's length. "You know I will."

The high ridge afforded Connor's party a view of the main road north, climbing out of a valley to their northeast. Kara pointed it out as they walked. "The next town on that road is Ashbarrow, and if Hal's map is accurate, your waterfall lies somewhere in the woods due east of it, though I know of no rivers there."

"Perhaps it's part of a stream," he said. "A small cataract."

But Lee shook his head. "I know what I saw. The waterfall is big. And beautiful."

"Whatever you say." Kara ducked a dormant vine instead of brushing it aside.

Connor quickstepped around a tree to catch up and walk beside her. "I'm sorry about Teegan. She's just cautious."

"She doesn't want me getting too close to you. I get it. A girl has to protect her own."

"No. That's not what I . . . What?"

Kara gave him a nose-wrinkled grin. "You should see your face. But don't tell me about Teegan. I'd rather know about you." They continued on, and she slipped between a pair of saplings, fur coat ghosting past without brushing so much as a flake of snow from their delicate branches. "How did you make your leap from the road? Some feat of lightraider sorcery?"

"There is no lightraider sorcery, only gifts from the Rescuer. But I learned to leap through boredom, jumping against the boulders in our family pasture to pass the time."

"A pasture. So I take it you were a shepherd before you were a knight."

Lee leaned out to look at her from the other side of Connor, frowning beneath his spectacles. "You couldn't tell from the crook? What about you? I heard you speak of hunting, or was that only your brehnan's work."

The mention of Kara's brehnan slowed her steps. "Yes. Liam and Keir, mostly, until the mocktree and Nesat and all the trouble."

Connor flared his eyes at the scribe for bringing up her sorrows. "Forgive us, Kara. We didn't mean to–"

"It's all right. They're gone. I'll have to get used to it."

Soon–too soon–they came within sight of the barkhide camps, where the westernmost tents stood on both sides of the road. The troll's recruits had stopped a wagon, inspecting the driver's wares.

Kara clutched the jewel at her neck. "They'll take what they want. Liam told me this is how it goes in the north when a mocktree musters an army. His barkhides grow drunk with power and find fault with every journey writ."

Connor gave her arm a gentle touch to keep her moving. "Then I'm glad we have you to guide us around such dangers. What can you tell us of wood trolls?"

She bit her lip as if he'd asked a difficult question. Didn't she know her own land? "Wood trolls are brought to life by dragon sorcery," she said. "They recruit armies to serve a dragon's purpose, though I've heard the barkhides of two trolls may fight each other."

Connor waited. "Is that all?"

"They're . . . corky fellows?"

Perhaps the Aladoth didn't learn about these creatures–just endured them. Connor hopped up on a fallen log, holding his arms out for balance. "Lee. Tell her."

"Wood troll. Oaksquid. Known in the uplands as a mocktree. They travel on their roots like tentacled sea creatures–can also use them as whips. Mocktrees prey on the disaffected, promising power but making them mindless drones." Lee screwed up his face in disgust. "And they spread this mind infection by filling the air with spores from their rotting innards."

Connor hopped down at the log's end and pulled a green rag from his kit. He tossed it to Kara and tugged at a similar rag tied about his neck. "If we see one, put this over your mouth and nose. For the spores."

Kara shook her head. "What spores? Mocktrees use song sorcery."

"The song is part of it," Lee said. "But according to our studies, mocktrees are–"

"Studies." Kara stepped ahead of them and paused in a narrow space between two large boulders, blocking the way. She pointed a finger at Lee but directed her glare at Connor. "Does all your knowledge come from books? What sort of knights are you? Have you never faced these creatures before?"

"We've faced goblins," Lee told her. "And an orc. Two orcs, if you count Master Jairun's–"

Connor kicked the scribe's heel to quiet him. "We're cadets, Kara." From the cast of her brow, he saw she didn't know that word. "It means we're still in training."

56

KARA TROMPED DOWNHILL THROUGH THE SNOW. "I should go to Nesat right now."

"Nesat?" Connor hurried after her.

"The granog." She spoke as if the question exposed him as a complete idiot. "I should turn you in—all of you. I said to myself, 'Kara, if you're turning traitor against the dragons, at least you'll be with a pack of legendary magic knights who can protect you.' But you're not knights. You're . . ." She looked back at them both, teeth clenched. "I don't know what you are."

"Cadets," Lee offered. "Think of it like a knight-to-be. A book-knight."

He wasn't helping. Connor caught up to her. "We *are* in the Lightraider Order. And we never said we were full knights."

"You didn't say you weren't. You let me think it. And that makes you a liar."

Was she right? She'd called them knights at the cottage, and he hadn't corrected her. Even so, how could she think it? "Look at us, Kara. We're a bit young to be seasoned warriors?"

She flung her arms at him. "Again, you show your ignorance. In Tanelethar, we have fighters and sorcerers who train from birth. Children of the Scarlet Moon have claimed rule over whole cantons before their fourteenth birthdays."

She kept tromping onward, downhill, and Connor feared she might get too close to the road. "Please, stop," he called after her. "I'm sorry."

"You will be. Just wait until—"

Her threat ended in a sharp cry as a short creature in armor too large for its body sprang from a grouping of pines and knocked Kara to the ground. It dragged her several paces by the hair, then held its long knife to her throat to stop her from kicking. "Just wait until what, my dear? Wait until what? What, what?"

Connor's heart stopped. A goblin. Where had he come from?

Lee's hand went to his bow, but Connor signaled him to let it be. He gave his thigh a subtle pat, then advanced one step at a time, crook poised like a walking stick. "Leave her alone. We've troubled no one here."

"Trouble, young shaggycap? Oh, you mean trouble. Trouble. Yes. We saw you sneaking."

By the look in Kara's eyes, Connor might as well have been the one holding the knife to her throat. To her, his falsehood had done this, making her likely to feel alone and lean on her own strength for escape. If she tried, the goblin would slit her throat.

"Sneaking. Sneaking," the goblin went on. It wore a scarf around its neck, on top of its armor, and human boots with the toes cut out for its claws. The creature pinched its eyes half closed. "We see less in the day. See less. See less. But we saw you on the ridge with the sun behind. Foolish shaggycap. Sneaking in the woods, but sneaking poorly. Poorly. Poorly." It bent its knobby head straight down to leer at Kara. "Now, now, little slenderstalk, I think you'll be the first to paint the snow."

At Connor's signal, Lee's hand flew from his hip. A double-bladed sikari entered the goblin's forehead beneath its ridiculous helm. It fell over, jerking one booted foot, then lay still.

Lee scanned the woods. "It said we, Connor."

"I know." He kicked the body toward the scribe so he could recover the sikari. "More will come."

When Connor tried to help Kara up, she shoved him away and stood up on her own. "Oh? Is that what your studies tell you?"

"Yes. But in this, I also have experience." Connor remembered Tehpa's eyes, tinted yellow by the goblin infection. He remembered his words too. "They hunt in packs."

57

THE SPYGLASS CONFIRMED TEEGAN'S FEARS ABOUT the most direct route to Maidenwood Grove. Too many camps. Too much risk.

A plateau of sparse pines and ash formed the last quarter league of the western approach. From the plateau's eastern cliff, a series of wooden ramps and platforms climbed into the treetop village. The elamwoods' giant trunks dropped out of sight into the valley below—a wondrous sight. But as much as she loved seeing ancient Sil Elamar still alive as a bustling town, everything else she saw through the spyglass filled her heart with dread. "We'll never make it through. The trees are too thin for cover, and the camps are everywhere. Plus, the barkhides are checking writs and hassling travelers at the gate of that wooden road."

Tiran, lying flat beside her, raised his chin from his forearms. "I could have told you as much without the glass."

"Perhaps. But you're not seeing everything." Teegan settled her lens on a cluster of tents and cooking fires. Goblins hobbled and shuffled among the humans. Two of the fungal creatures tilted their heads with quick movements, enthralled while a young man drew a flaming brand from a fire and pressed it against his own neck. He clenched his teeth but made no visible cry. She winced and lowered the glass, unable to look any longer. "The barkhides are hurting themselves."

"I read about this," Dag said. "The guardian Master Carthia spent weeks hiding near the camps at Sil Belomar and rescued many victims of the mocktree Tegbat, called Oakwither. The recruits burn their skin to make it rough, like bark–thus, barkhides–and they drive stakes through their arms to make weapons, just as the mocktrees do."

Tiran had taken the glass to look for himself. "Except a troll's arm is formed of dragon-corrupted wood. A stake will do it little harm. Without treatment those barkhides will lose their limbs or die." He rose to his knees. "We should find this Krokwode and kill him, before he does any more damage–release these Aladoth from its hold."

"That's not how it works," Teegan said. "Didn't you listen to our lessons? Killing a dark creature does nothing to restore its victims. That requires medicine and counsel. And our counsel falls on deaf ears if the patient doesn't recognize the authority of its author, the Rescuer."

"Why do you think Master Carthia spent so long in Sil Belomar?" Dag added. "He needed time to show the barkhides the Rescuer's love. Once he destroyed the troll, a dragon came, forcing him to flee with those he'd rescued. Many who failed to listen were left behind."

They backed down the plateau's western slope into the thicker pines and huddled around the map, while Aethia looked on from the branches above. Teegan held the red glass over the parchment. "Look here. Hal drew a gully to the south in his hidden ink. It merges with the valley below Maidenwood Grove, where a stream feeds their giant roots." The red lens did more than make the gully visible. It gave it depth and dimension. Teegan could see it rise with the higher terrain to the south, then fall sharply into the elamwood valley.

"You know something about the valley, don't you," Dag said. "You meant to go there all along."

Tiran answered for her. "Our mehma told us the Rapha made a home in that valley to care for the elamwoods. They carved steps into the tree trunks so they could commune with the town above. But the Rapha are long gone, Teegs."

"The steps aren't, any more than Vy Asterlas was gone from Dayspring Forest. And if the lower route to Maidenwood Grove is just as forgotten, I'll wager it's unguarded."

Hal proved a skilled mapmaker, and the three had no trouble finding the gully entrance. Though barely wide enough for Dag, and thick with brush and pines, the gully offered plenty of cover. But good cover meant slow going. When they pushed out through heavy thickets near the valley's southern end, the day was mostly spent, and the sheer western wall blocked the late sun.

Dag swept dead leaves from his cloak and loosened its clasp. "At least it's warmer down here."

"A trick of the steep terrain," Teegan said. "And this stream, perhaps. I think it's warm like the Gathering." Most streams they'd seen since Trader's Knoll were crusted with ice, or completely frozen over. But the stream running down the center of this valley had no ice at all.

A stone path appeared from under the dark soil, and then a low wall grew beside it, and another to hem in the stream. Looking north, Teegan saw torches flaring to life high in the elamwoods. "We're almost there. This must be the start of the irrigation system the Rapha built. Mehma said there were many plazas and chapels among the water channels–bridges formed from the giant roots. You'll see."

But they could see little in the failing light. And the closer they came to the great elamwood trunks, the less the valley looked like a place any Rapha might love.

Broken water channels had flooded the paths and courtyards, turning them into a mire of mud and black water. Crumbling statues overcome by yellow-green moss lingered among the willows and ferns like grave markers. And soon, the same moss covered every stone.

Aethia seemed ill at ease. She flitted among dead pines and ash dripping with goat's beard, refusing to stay at any perch too long.

"Well this is cheery," Dag said.

Teegan found a huge, brittle leaf lying on the wall beside the path. "This is an everleaf. Or was. But Mehma told me they never fall." She looked up at the village, closer now but still far above them. "This mire is making the trees sick. Sil Elamar is dying."

"The mire doesn't concern me." Tiran bent to examine a gray trail of dead moss. "Not as much as this." He tore up a fistful, and the strands turned to powder in his fingers. Ahead, more ribbons of gray crossed one another and climbed the wall like snail trails, except far wider. "The moss turns to ash wherever they go." He drew his sword. "I don't like it."

Dag and Teegan drew their weapons as well.

"We best keep moving," Teegan said and quickened the pace. But they couldn't keep at it for long. Within sight of the root bridges her mehma's stories described, a toppled section of wall had let the mire overrun the path. If Teegan looked closely, she could see the mossy stone reappearing twenty paces or more away–gray trails and all. She tested the mud's depth with the shaft of her trident. "The stone is solid underneath. I think we can wade across."

As if in argument, Aethia swooped down and squawked at her.

"What is it, girl?"

The falcon perched among the goat's beard of a bare pine and squawked again.

"Quiet your bird," Tiran grumbled. "She'll bring some evil down upon us."

Teegan thought she saw the mire moving–perhaps a trick of the darkness, perhaps not. Then she heard a splash. "Her squawking doesn't matter. I think *some evil* is already here."

Moaning came next–like mournful wounded animals.

Tiran bent an ear toward the mire. "Woe . . . is me."

"What did you say?"

"I hear it in their groans. Listen." He mimicked the sorrowful cries. "*Woe is me.*"

With a splat, a drop landed on Teegan's boot and sizzled. The scent of vinegar and bad cheese filled her nostrils. Not good. "Quick," she said to Tiran. "Strike a lantern."

He drew their largest from one of Dag's satchels and struck the flame, then held it out over the mire.

As if offended by the light, a slug as big as a fox and covered in wriggling mud whiskers, reared up from the slime and screeched with rage.

58

MORE SLUGS ANSWERED THE FIRST WITH PIERCING screeches, all rearing up from the mire.

"What are these things?" Tiran shouted, eyes wild.

In the glow of the lantern, Teegan saw the source of the sizzling and the foul smell. Spots of greenish-brown slime had struck her cloak and boot, sending up vapors and bleaching the leather and wool gray. What might such a substance do to unprotected flesh? She leveled her trident. "Arms! Destroy them!"

Dag swung an axe. The blade passed through his target as through a stream of water. The slug fell into the mire in two pieces. A second later, it rose up again, whole. Its strange whisker appendages rippled forward and flung a barrage of caustic mud. The miner's glowing shield dissolved them all.

All but one.

A drop of slime flew past Dag's shield and struck Tiran in the neck. He let out a cry and wiped the mud away with his sleeve, leaving behind a growing blister. "Their bodies are poison, and we can't kill them. We'll never survive this."

The slugs closed in, echoing him with their moans. *Woe is me. Woe is me.*

Teegan stabbed one with her trident. The creature recoiled for only a moment, then kept coming. She stabbed it again with the same result. "We never studied these. What are they?"

"Mudslingers." Dag chopped his foe in half once more. "Talin wrote of them in his chronicles. He called them muks, for short, and warned that you should never let them touch you."

Teegan stabbed at two slugs in quick succession. "Yes. I think we figured that last bit out."

With each passing moment, the slugs closed in, and the cadets drew tighter into their defensive formation. Caustic mud burned their clothing and dissolved against their shields. Tiran dropped his sword and clutched the lantern to his chest, cowering between the other two. "I can't do this. I shouldn't have come."

Each time he spoke, the creatures replied with their mournful chorus. *Woe is me. Woe is me.*

"Woe is me," Dag said out loud.

Teegan shot a glance at the miner. "Not you too." The muks had infected Tiran, and he'd stopped fighting. If they'd infected Dag as well, the party was done for. "Dag?"

The miner fended off mud barrages while digging through a satchel. "Ha!" he said and drew out a leather bundle. "Tiran, open this. Hurry."

While Dag returned to the defense with axe and shield, Tiran untied the twine. He held up two small tins and several balls of white powder wrapped in cooking parchment. "Spices?"

A slug pushed through Teegan's trident and thrust itself against her shield, wailing as its liquid body popped and sizzled. "Use your words, Dag. What are they for?"

Dag plucked a white packet from Tiran's hands. "Master Jairun told me to use them to bolster my friends when they need it most. I thought he wanted me to cook for you." He hurled the packet down, and it burst upon the muk attacking his shield in a puff of white dust. The slug let out a hideous shriek and shriveled into a dry husk. "But in *Talin's Chronicles,* I read that these things hate salt."

He smashed another packet down on the creature attacking Teegan, and it shriveled too. She grabbed a packet of her own and threw it sidelong at a pair of slugs coming at her flank. One shriveled immediately. The cloud of white drifted over the other slug and coated every slimy whisker. The wriggling appendages retracted into its body, and it sank down into the mire but soon floated to the surface as dry and dead as its friends.

Woe is me. Woe is me.

The others gave up the fight, moaning as they fled, but Teegan had no intention of being ambushed later. "Get them, Dag!"

No slug could outpace the big miner's arm. Covered in white, they convulsed and contracted, squealing and sizzling as they withered.

With no other threats in sight, Teegan lowered her shield arm. "I'd rather not go through that again."

"I can't believe we survived." Tiran sat on the path with the lantern and Dag's spices. "But the mire is probably filled with them. We'll never make it to the town."

Teegan knelt to examine her twin. "You're shaking, and this blister is horrid. Dag, have we anything to treat it?"

After rummaging through his satchels, Dag managed to find a jar of poplar balm. "This might help. I think. Lee's the one studying to be a renewer."

The balm's soothing scent and coolness and a sip from a Telbeath flask returned life to Tiran's eyes. But his fretting continued. Teegan doubted even Lee could help. Her brehna needed counsel from one who knew the Sacred Scrolls better than any cadet. "What else can we do?"

Dag picked up the lantern and set it on the wall beside them, then laid one big hand on Tiran's shoulder and the other on hers. "We pray for him. And while we're at it, I get the feeling we should pray for the others too."

59

A BLACK ARROW SKIMMED THE PINE BOUGHS ABOVE Connor's head as his party fled through a shallow trough between two ridges.

"I guess we should be thankful," Lee said.

Connor ducked another arrow. "For what?"

"Eyes opened by dragon sorcery have poor aim."

"You're babbling again, Book-Knight," Kara said, then looked to Connor. "Why don't you kill these things, as you did the first?"

"I hope to, but it's not the goblins I'm worried about."

The goblins behind them seemed a different sort than those the cadets had fought at Ras Telesar, and not merely because of their greener flesh or the shingles of fungus on their arms, marking them as forest goblins. The creatures at Ras Telesar had worn armor clearly built to suit them. And as strange as it seemed, they'd been more disciplined.

The goblins pursuing Connor and the others now hopped through the trees in no discernable formation and wore ill-fitting, incomplete armor–a gauntlet here, a greave there. One wore a human's hooded fur coat, hem dragging through the snow and brush as it ran. But the goblins had proved to be scouts, ranging for a more dangerous threat.

"Halt!" a distant voice shouted. "In the name of Krokwode and Lord Vorax, master of these highlands!"

Connor urged them onward. "Don't stop. We're not prepared

to face an Aladoth patrol." He pointed uphill with the ram's horn curve of his crook. "Head for those rocks."

The rocks, some as large as wagons, offered temporary cover, and Connor readied a stone in his sling as he turned and crouched behind them. He loosed it at a goblin with no helm and dropped the creature in its tracks. Lee fired two arrows in quick succession, taking both his targets in their throats above their sagging breastplates. That left only the fur-coat lover, well behind its cousins, but still far ahead of the Aladoth.

Lee nocked an arrow, then lowered his bow an inch. "You want the last one, Goblin Slayer?"

"No. He's all yours."

The scribe gave him a shrug that said, *Just thought I'd ask*, and let the arrow fly. The goblin fell headlong to the snow, covered by the fur coat except for one twitching hand, gripping its long knife.

Connor didn't wait to see if the creature got up. "We've bought some time and distance. Keep moving."

"Why run?" Kara asked once they'd picked their way through the rocks. "You're trained well enough to fight goblins. Are you afraid you'll be defeated by barkhides?"

"No." The quickness of his own response surprised Connor—and the truth of it. He didn't fear Krokwode's recruits, at least not in the way Kara thought. "I'm not afraid of defeat. Barkhides fight with abandon for their master. I'm afraid Lee and I may be forced to kill them."

When they cleared the rocks, Connor turned west, farther uphill, thinking to distance his party from the camps, but Kara stopped him. "Not that way. We'll be trapped."

"No. We'll be trapped if we head east, closer to the road." Connor looked to Lee, his walking map, and received an affirming nod.

But Kara wouldn't give in. "Wrong, Book-Knight. Did you hire me to be your guide or not?"

The approaching shouts of the barkhides left no time for argument. "Fine," Connor said. "Lead on."

She took them northeast, downhill, into denser forest. While Kara ghosted through the spruce and bristlecone, Connor and Lee fought every branch.

The scribe pushed a pine bough away after it smacked him in the spectacles. "So, when you stormed downhill toward the road before, you weren't threatening to turn us in to the camps."

"No–at least, not truly. I told you before, the foothills in this region are broken. There are many ravines."

The three emerged from the brush, and Kara threw out an arm to stop Connor from taking another step. Pebbles dislodged by the shuffling of his feet skipped away into a deep gorge.

Lee peered over the edge. "This wasn't on Hal's map."

"Which is why you needed a guide," Kara told him. "The road bridge is more than a quarter league south, but I know another way across. Give me a bit to find it. I haven't been this way in months."

More shouting. Connor spotted figures in winter furs among the trees not far behind.

One looked their way and pointed. "Kara, we don't have a bit."

"There. Follow me." She crawled over the edge of the gorge.

About a man's height below the ledge, a trail sloped downward to a fallen tree wedged between the ravine walls. "It must be thirty paces long," Lee said.

"Forty. Come on." Kara walked across as if walking any other trail, though the tree bowed as she passed the middle.

Lee stepped onto the log after her, then stepped off again. "You go, Connor. I prefer my bridges to be at least as wide as I am."

A burn-scarred man appeared above them, sneering through his overgrown beard. "Firth, Hollis, over here! I've found them!" He leveled a sword. "Stay where you are."

Connor slung a rock to force him back. "Go, Lee! Hurry up!"

The scribe teetered only once along the way, causing the tree to bounce. Connor raced after him under the cover of his arrows. Nearing the tree's end, he drew his sword. He set one foot on the steep ravine wall and extended his crook up to Kara. "Hold this and aid my balance."

"Are you mad?" Kara asked, seeming to sense his plan. "You'll fall."

"I'm well aware, thank you. Just hold the crook."

A fletched bolt skimmed off the rocks at Kara's feet. One of the barkhides had a crossbow. Lee shot back, splitting a pinecone an inch from his head.

Connor leaned out as far as he dared and swung his blade again and again. On his third chop, he heard a sickening *crack*. The tree gave and his body dropped.

60

"STAIRS." DAG HUGGED THE AGE-OLD ELAMWOOD WITH one shoulder. "Ever since Mer Nimbar, we've dealt with stairs. Up stairs. Down stairs. Mountain stairs, castle stairs." His foot slipped, and he let out a frustrated grunt, clawing the bark to hold on and nearly dropping the lantern. "Stairs as slick as wagon grease. When will it end?"

The slickness, Teegan agreed, was the worst of it. But nothing about this ancient elamwood stairway gave her comfort. For all the wisdom Mehma granted them in her stories, the Rapha of Sil Elamar had cut the steps too far apart—for her, anyway. And halfway up the giant tree, her legs and back ached.

The steps had all the hallmarks of Elder Folk craft—so perfect in their even spacing and seamless in the way they merged with the tree, as if all elamwoods grew with a long spiral stair around their trunks. But time and neglect had worn many steps so narrow that only the heel or toe of a boot fit them. And the moss, though it thinned as they climbed, did make them as slick as wagon grease, just as Dag said.

"I'm in constant worry of a fall," Tiran said. "Your hallowed Sil Elamar Rapha might have considered a rail, wouldn't you say, Shessa?"

"If they did, it has long since rotted away. Now hush. Conserve your strength for the climb."

Even the falcon despised the staircase. She landed on a step above them, squawked her displeasure at the moss and flew higher to find a better perch.

Dag watched her go. "I guess she'll meet us in town."

Nearly a tick later, an escape from the steps required Dag to saw through a wooden bolt with his hunting knife. They'd come to a hatch in a wide platform in the lowest branches of their tree. Underneath, its planks and beams were overgrown with mildew and colonies of tiny spiders. Once Dag cut the bolt, the door still wouldn't budge. He braced his shoulders against it and heaved. The groaning hinges told Teegan it had not been opened in years.

Up top, Dag brushed the spiders from his cloak. He watched them skitter up a rope-and-plank ramp to the grove's high wooden thoroughfare and caught his breath. "Well, that's a sight."

Teegan followed his gaze, struggling to find her voice. Stairs, ramps, and bridges joined the high thoroughfare to the treetop town's many levels. She watched a horse and cart roll by and laughed in amazement. "Sil Elamar. The Eternal Forest. Imagine this village in the elder days, when the faeries darted among the branches, spreading blue-white light on the terraces. They cared for the everleaves with song, playing music so soft you only heard it in your heart."

"Leave the stories in the past," Tiran said. "And let's get on with this. Someone may have seen our arrival. The watch will come and hand us straight to the granogs."

"No one saw." Teegan followed Dag's spiders up the ramp. "Quit worrying."

Since when had Tiran ever been a worrier? She wished Hal had been there to guide and advise them, to help her heal her twin. What could she say? She let him catch up and wrapped an arm about his shoulders. "The Rescuer has us in his hand, Brehna. Have faith. But I agree, we should move quickly to discover what he sent us here to find."

"And how do we do that?"

She had no idea, but Dag saved her from the need to confess this.

"We go in there." The miner had fixed his gaze on a three-tiered inn engulfing the lower branches of an elamwood at the town's center. "Do you see it? Above the door. It's the angry bear from my dream."

61

SKILLED HANDS HAD CARVED THE BEAR FROM THE stub of a minor branch jutting out above the inn's door. But Teegan decided the bear had always been there in the slopes and flats of the broken branch. The artist's knife had liberated the beast inside the tree, and paint had given him vigor. But the paint had faded, the wood had cracked, and the bear's fierce anger had waned to sadness.

Dag watched the patrons pass in and out below the sculpture. "They don't even look at him,"

"Neither should you," Teegan told him. "Act like you walk these planks every day of your life."

But she struggled to follow her own advice and keep her eyes from roaming. How wonderful it would be if the houses of Sil Tymest could be like these, high up in the canopy. The Bear's Head Inn wrapped around the huge trunk in three levels, each one narrower than the last. The builders had carved the main hall deep into the trunk. She wondered if they'd have time to get a look at the rooms above.

"Teegs." Tiran touched her elbow. "The climb took its toll on our legs, and the blister on my neck is throbbing. We should find somewhere to sit if we can."

The curfew had packed the town. And by the looks of it, many had come to the Bear's Head for supper or a bed. She searched for an open table, and before she could find one, Dag wandered off. She and Tiran hurried after him, dodging the patrons in his wake, and caught up with him at a long serving counter with stone slabs of breads and cheeses.

"Are you really this hungry?" Tiran asked.

"I was following my nose." Dag lifted his chin toward a pair of young women farther along the table–siblings, Teegan thought, by the sameness in their button noses and slight cheekbones. The two carried a huge broiled cow's flank too large for its stoneware serving platter. "Cooked red meat as broad as my axe-head, just as I saw in my dream." His gaze tracked the platter. "We should buy it."

Teegan heard hope in his voice. "Sorry, Dag. I think that flank is spoken for."

The servers elbowed and pardoned their way through the crowded hall, wobbling to and fro and dribbling juice from the platter. The cadets followed at a distance until the servers set their burden at a table packed with men and women in furs and leather–hunters, Teegan thought. A burly fellow at the table's head with long brown hair and an equally long brown beard flipped one gold halfin to each server, then flipped another to the nearest. "For your father. Tell him to keep the cider coming."

The cadets slipped into an alcove close to the hunters. Tiran conjured up a horrible false laugh and slapped Dag's shoulder, bending his head between the miner and Teegan. "Laugh, you two, unless you want to be caught. We couldn't look more like lightraiders if we had our beloved Blacksmith's hammer inscribed on our foreheads."

To Teegan's eye, not many in the place looked joyful. Most seemed intent on just getting through their meal.

But Dag took her brehna's words to heart and let out a resounding guffaw, slapping Tiran on the back in return. "Better?"

Tiran's reply came out as a wheeze. "Yes . . ."

Whether out of courtesy or sheer discomfort from the boys' antics, the Aladoth seated in the alcove pushed their plates away and relinquished its small table. Teegan took the stool closest to the hunters. "Sit. Both of you. And let's have no more pageantry, or we truly will be caught."

Spurred by a pair of silver coins, the girl who'd taken the extra gold coin from the bearded hunter brought the cadets three bowls of stew. She offered mugs of two different kinds of cider. Teegan took both to be brambleberry, but the darker mix smelled more pungent. She wrinkled her nose.

The girl set down three wooden mugs of the lighter juice. "I take it you've not had aged cider before. In that case, drink the fresh. The aged will sour your stomach." A burst of raucous cheering drew her eyes to the hunters. She pursed her lips. "And it makes you act the fool."

Despite this apparent disapproval, she brought her trays to the hunters next and replaced their empty mugs with the darker cider. And she seemed pleased enough to take their coin in return.

Tiran sniffed his mug and stared down into the pink foam. "It's cloudy. Something's wrong with it."

Dag took a sip and swished it around. "Tastes all right. Fresh brambleberry juice. Hot. With cloves and cinnamon. They've added milk, that's all. Must be the tradition here."

"Milk?" Tiran asked. "In cider?"

Dag swallowed. "Goat's milk, if I'm not mistaken."

"Where would they keep goats in a treetop village?"

"Same place they keep the cows, I imagine."

"*Boys.*" Teegan kicked them both under the table. "Keep quiet."

With her companions sufficiently hushed, she blocked out the crowd's buzzing and listened to the hunters. Ivano, the bearded man, seemed to know few of those at his table well, other than the two seated closest to him–a bald man with chains dragging his earlobes to his shoulders, and a black man with hair dyed green. From what Teegan heard, the rest had been lured to the table by the promise of a free meal.

"Tell us what has you spending your gold so freely, Ivano," one guest demanded. "The barkhides have picked the winter woods clean, leaving us to starve. We'd be grateful to share in your fortune."

"Which is why I'm paying, friend. But I can only afford to feed this many for one night. Tomorrow, I'll reap my secret harvest and be gone, retiring to some sleepy fishing village on the Western Sea."

Ivano's secrecy only tantalized his guests. The more they ate and drank, the more they pestered him.

"I'll wager he's found a den of gahracubs."

"No. It's the lost egg of Threskos."

"Even better. He's found a rumblefoot's horde."

Ivano deflected every question with flattery and long stories. Only once did his armor fail him, and the gap was not his own but his friend's. The bald man said the spread of too many barkhides had shrunken the good hunting ground to the foothills southeast of the grove. For this indiscretion, Ivano punched him in the ribs.

All her listening and the goat's milk cider robbed Teegan of her appetite. She pushed her half-finished bowl of stew to Dag and whispered what she'd learned.

Dag ladled the soup into his mouth. "I'll give you one guess as to what, or who, he's hiding."

She knew. They all did. The Rescuer had revealed it all to them in Dag's dream.

"But *southeast of the grove* is not enough," Tiran said. "We could spend days scouring those woods. Ivano will get to his prize first. We'll have to wait and follow him."

Teegan nodded, sitting back again, and froze with her chin lowered.

Ivano's eyes bored into her. "Hello, lass. Did no one teach you eavesdropping is poor manners?"

A loud murmur swept through the hall, stealing his gaze.

A granog–the first Teegan had seen apart from the books of Ras Telesar or Kara's sketch–tucked his wings close and ducked through the door beneath the bear's head. Mud and the damp of melted snow soiled the hem of his black velvet cloak.

Two scarred men and a woman pushed in behind him. Barkhides. The woman had blood on her tunic. She shouted over the noise. "Traitors and murderers!"

That quieted the crowd.

"Poachers slaughtered four goblins near the road to Ashbarrow. Our people saw two young men and a young woman. For this reason, the high regent, his lordship Nesat, has graced Maidenwood Grove with his presence. He'll pay well for information."

Two young men and young woman. Teegan inched her stool away from Ivano and leaned close to the boys. From the quickness of Tiran's breathing, she guessed he'd come to the same conclusion that she had. The other party had run into trouble.

Dag spoke their thoughts out loud. "Connor."

62

CONNOR PEELED BACK THE WOOL BLANKET COVERING the window—what passed for a curtain at the Golden Calf, the smaller of two inns in Ashbarrow. He watched the cobblestones below the inn's dilapidated yellow sign. "Still no one."

"And there won't be, unless you keep showing yourself at the window. Sytol would never sell me to the granogs."

"How can you be sure?"

Kara didn't answer, and Connor and Lee exchanged a glance. Lee repeated Connor's question. "Kara, how can you be sure?"

"Sytol has known me since childhood. When my brehnan and I came south, she found us on the road, starved near to death, and cared for us. Even though . . ."

"Even though . . . what?" Connor asked.

Again, she didn't answer. Connor returned his gaze to the cobblestones outside. He held his breath as a hooded figure shuffled into the lamplight spilling from the inn's open door. But the figure shuffled on. Connor let the curtain fall into place. "I never thanked you for saving me."

"You'll pay for it later with another gold coin. I know you're good for it."

The tree bridge had given way under the hacking of Connor's sword and the weight of his foot. Without its support he might have fallen into the gorge, but Kara faithfully held her end of the crook. She pulled with all her might, while Connor dug his boots into the steep wall and climbed. The two had clambered over the edge with Lee's arrows to protect them from the barkhide's crossbow.

Forced to cross well east at the road bridge, the barkhides lost them, and Connor's party made it safely to Ashbarrow. Under the cover of darkness, they climbed over its stone wall, and Kara brought them to the Golden Calf's rear door. She had waited to announce herself until the inn's matron Sytol brought out her kitchen leavings for the night.

Sytol had welcomed her with a warm embrace.

Now Kara sat cross-legged on the rug near the room's small hearth. She looked to Lee, who'd taken a place at the table to clean the sikari he'd thrown at the goblin. "Tell me, Lee. Your dagger and your arrows found their marks with the goblins in the woods, yet after you fired many at the ravine, not one man fell. Why?"

"Sikari."

"What?"

"It's not a dagger." Lee showed her the double-bladed knife. "It's a sikari. And I can't get this goblin blood off the spine. I need a water basin and some rags. I'll be back." He walked out.

"Sorry," Connor said. "He does that." He shed his kit and scabbard, hung both over his crook, and leaned the whole of it against the mantle. "Lee spared the Aladoth because that's the lightraider way."

"But why? Why kill one enemy and spare another?"

"Goblins are soulless corruptions. The Aladoth are not. Do you know the meaning of *Aladoth* in the Elder Tongue?"

"Everyone knows. Our dragon-loving ancestors chose the name. It means many peoples of one birth, unified under dragon rule."

Unified under dragon rule. Connor cringed at the thought. "Not quite. But dragon loyalists did choose the name. They chose ours too, as a jibe against our faith. Aladoth means the many who are born once. Keledan means the Twiceborn. The name was meant to shame our beloved Blacksmith's rebels, but they wore it joyfully."

"Why twiceborn?" Kara patted the rug, inviting him to sit beside her. "How can anyone have two births?"

"One physical and one spiritual." He lifted two bowls of soup from a tray and brought one to her. "But if there are two births, there are also two deaths. To be spared the latter, you must accept the gift of the former. Thus, lightraider knights"–she stopped him with a frown, and Connor bent his head in submission–"*and* lightraider cadets are forbidden to kill Aladoth. To usher anyone toward the second death brings us great sorrow."

"I see. And who is worthy of this second birth gift?"

Lee trundled in, burdened with a washbasin and rags, and his footing failed him. Water sloshed from the basin, dousing Kara.

An instant later, Connor's mouth dropped open.

Lee seemed equally stunned, too stunned to apologize.

Strands of wet hair fell over Kara's face. Sooty drops hung from her chin and fingers. But it was not her soaked state or even the indignant fury in her eyes that shocked the boys.

Lee handed her a rag. She ripped it from his grasp and wiped her face.

At Hal's place, Connor had noticed a platinum tint to her hair, but nothing more. Now, washed of most of its soot, it shined in the hearth light with glints of blue.

And her face. She had wiped away the black streaks, leaving behind spiral flourishes of silver-blue freckles. He swallowed hard. "You're . . . royalty."

"Queensblood," Lee said, finally regaining his voice.

A dry laugh escaped Kara's lips. She dipped the rag again and continued to wash, uncovering more flourishes on her forehead and the backs of her hands. "They don't call it queensblood anymore, Book-Knight. Not here. There are new words. The blue pox is one, and it condemns me as an illegitimate child of the fool-kings who fought the dragons."

"Is that what happened to your parents?" Connor asked.

"Your mehma?"

"It's why they came for her, and why Liam brought us south, where the marks are rarely looked for." She wiped away another sooty drop that might have been a tear. "When a queensblood appears, always in the far north, our days are numbered. Someone always sees. Someone always talks. It is a miracle Mehma lived long enough to bear three children. She hid the curse well, for both of us."

A pox. A curse. Connor hated hearing such things said about the beauty the High One had given. But he dared not challenge her words about her own blood.

Lee, who seemed to have forgotten about cleaning his sikari, lifted a bowl of soup from Sytol's tray and sat on the rug before Kara like a child before a Resteram storyteller. "I trained as a scribe for our Assembly. I've read the thickest tomes about the northern nobles. They all say the dragons utterly destroyed the royal lines, even the Leanders, who first capitulated."

"Lee . . ." Connor held out a hand to quiet him.

But the scribe kept talking, quickening his words. "You must know something of your birth. Where are your parents from? Your grandparents? Do you remember your grandmother?"

"Lee," Connor said again. "Stop."

Kara touched Connor's knee. "It's all right. My parents worked the ice farms on the shores of Val Glasa, north of Emen Yan. I know nothing of my mamehma." She lifted the jeweled pendant from beneath her tunic and held it out to the end of its chain for them to see. A silver bear hugged a polar sapphire as deep blue as the sea. Wherever Connor moved, the white star moved within the round stone to follow him.

After that, each went to their own small corner. When Kara had finished washing, Lee poured some of the water into his empty soup bowl and set about cleaning his blade. Connor rested his head against the wall beside the window, intending to check the street every once in a while, but he nodded off.

The lamp had burned out and the fire had dimmed by the time Connor woke again. Lee quietly snored, spectacles off and head resting on the table. Outside, the lamplight no longer spilled from the inn's doorway. Sytol must have closed up for the night.

Kara had taken the bed. She stirred, restless. Cold, perhaps. The blanket had fallen. Connor rose to cover her, but when he approached, she rolled over, eyes open.

He knelt to lift the blanket for her. "Sorry to wake you. I thought you might be cold. I'll leave you be."

"Wait." She shifted, pulling the blanket up about her shoulders. "Come and sit."

Connor obeyed. He rested a shoulder against the bedpost, close enough to speak without waking Lee. "Trouble sleeping?"

"Can I trust you with my secret?"

"You know you can, no matter what happens."

"Do I? I trusted you were lightraider knights, and look what happened."

He stifled a laugh. "You mean how we saved you from a goblin's knife, and–"

"And what?"

And what? Why had he kept silent when she called him knight? He knew a small part of him wanted to impress her, as she'd impressed him by catching him off guard. But there was a larger reason. "I never meant to deceive you. I didn't correct you when you called me lightraider knight because that's what I'm training for–what I aspire to be."

"So, you want to be like Hal."

She didn't say it as a slight. Whatever she'd been through with the old salt warrior, she clearly cared for him.

Kara drew a small wooden frame carved with swirls and stars from under her blanket. "I wasn't ready to show you before. I took this from the worktable. It's a sketch I drew for him." She passed the frame to Connor. “This is old Hal, my friend.”

The dim hearth played tricks with the face in the sketch. Connor brought the picture closer to his eyes. No. It was no trick of the light. He bolted to his feet, bumping into a shelf.

Lee woke with a start. “What is it? Orcs? The night watch?”

Connor ran to the fire. He stoked the flames to life and looked once again at the sketch. The face held more wrinkles. The beard was longer and braided. But Kara had captured the eyes. The same eyes had looked down at Connor from the painting over Tehpa’s hearth his whole life. He felt the blood drain from his face. “This man’s name isn’t Hal. It’s Faelin Enarian.”

PART FOUR

THE LOYALTY OF WOLVES

"If anyone comes to me and does not hate his own father and mother, wife and children, brothers and sisters–yes, and even his own life–he cannot be my disciple."

Luke 14:26

63

STOOLS AND CHAIRS SQUEAKED BACK FROM THE tables all around Teegan and the two boys. Plenty of Bear's Head patrons seemed happy to profit from Nesat's request for information, whether they knew something or not–or perhaps they wanted to show their loyalty. They crowded around the barkhides, pushing and shoving one another.

"This is the larger village," Tiran said. "Why does this Nesat make his base at Trader's Knoll?"

Dag stacked the stew bowls. "The knoll offers good ground for orc tunnels, I expect. That, and granogs hate heights."

Tiran gave him a flat look. "Granogs have wings. They can fly."

"Doesn't mean they like it. According to Mistress Ravenel, in *The Sigil of Selmor,* when dragons corrupt the Maker's creation, it often causes such paradoxes."

"How many books in that library did you read?"

"As many as they'd let me. You should give it a go."

Teegan snapped her fingers. "Hush, boys." Ivano was muttering to his two friends, and she wanted to hear.

The hunter glowered after his guests, who'd left his feast to crowd around the barkhides with the rest. "Rats on a ship berthed in a tree. They'd sell their own grandmothers for a loaf of bread."

The man with the green hair bent close to his ear. "What if our treasure is part of this plot? Nesat will blame us."

"Not if we bring him the creature's head. He'll still pay, perhaps even more."

Two hunters from their table had gained an audience with the woman in the bloodied shirt. Ivano flicked the bald man's ear chain. "Codrin, go find out what our dinner guests are saying."

Codrin rose from his stool and cracked his knuckles. "Gladly."

"We need to leave," Dag said. "The granog is looking for a young woman and two young men. That describes us as much as it describes the other raid party."

The girl who'd brought the stew glanced toward their table while chewing the scarred ear of a barkhide. Teegan reached for her trident, keeping her hand low and out of sight. "Gather your things. We're leaving."

But a man with the stern look of a town watchman had stepped into the doorway. As the cadets watched, he blocked the path of a young couple. He crossed his arms and sent them back into the hall.

Tiran shook his head. "We won't get past him without a fight."

"Upstairs, then," Teegan said. "There'll be windows within reach of a branch. We can climb down and mix with the townsfolk as if we were never here." A wave of shoving and jostling passed through the sea of patrons. One poor fellow crashed into a table and sent a half-filled stew bowl flying into the face of a girl. The man sitting beside her jumped up, shaking his fists. Things were unraveling. If this turned into a brawl, Nesat might crack down. "You two head for the stairs. Now."

"What about Ivano?" Tiran asked. "If we lose him now, we may never find him again."

"Let me take care of that. I'll meet you upstairs."

The staircase wound around the trunk in harmony with the main hall and the guest floor above. Teegan watched the two boys make their way to the bottom step unchallenged, then turned her attention to Ivano. She drew her hunting knife and concealed it in her sleeve, slipping between the mob of patrons as best she could.

Her path took her within inches of a barkhide, and she saw he'd chopped off two fingers on each hand, leaving the thumbs and the middle and forefingers. The remains gave his muscled arms the look of knobby branches ending in twigs.

Ivano turned, and Teegan matched his motion, the way she'd taught Connor. A heartbeat later, she had what she needed.

As she climbed the stairs, the crowd's roar dropped to a murmur, then silence. Something had changed. Teegan backed up a few steps until she could see a small portion of the hall. She stifled a scream. Ivano's bald companion landed at the base of the steps with blood flowing from a slash across his neck.

Talons clicked on wood in steady rhythm, coming closer. A gravelly voice with an air that proclaimed it to be an order above the species of man said, "Anyone else wish to interfere with my purpose here? No?"

A second body fell on the first.

"And would anyone else care to offer me another child's tale about a Havarra conspiracy?"

She heard no response beyond the timid squeaking of a stool or two.

"Good. Now, one of you knows *something*. Speak in an orderly fashion and be rewarded."

A shadow fell over the bald man's body. Teegan retreated up the steps, slow and quiet, and heard the gravelly voice again.

"Check the rooms. Bring me anyone you find."

She reached the top and raced along the upper passage. "They're coming."

The few open doors revealed rooms like wooden caves dug into the tree. The only windows were in the passage wall—round hatches, open to let the air and the village torchlight in. Teegan pointed at one of these. "Go, Dag!"

He tried to climb through with his satchels and axes but

shook his head. "I'm too big. You'll have to hand my gear through."

"Then let's get to it." Tiran pulled a satchel from the miner's shoulder.

Without his burdens, Dag just fit. The twins passed him his gear, and with footsteps approaching in the passage, they clambered out after him.

Teegan yanked the hatch shut and signaled the others to press their backs to the wall between the windows.

The footsteps paused. The window's hatch flew open.

Aethia chose that moment to flutter down from the everleaves and perch on a narrow branch across from her mistress's hiding place, chuffing and chortling at them.

Teegan tried to shoo her away and received an indignant squawk for her efforts.

"Well, aren't you a pretty lit'le birdy?" A burn-scarred hand reached through the window. "Have ya somethin' ta say, pretty bird?" If the barkhide leaned farther out, she'd see the cadets for sure.

Under her breath, Teegan uttered a sacred verse. "*Men adveranesh liberaheni. Alerov anamesh recrethanah.*" *Rescue me. I hide in you.*

She heard the creaking of a door inside, perhaps a guest peeking out of a room. The scarred hand disappeared. The footsteps resumed. "You, there. Come out here."

Teegan motioned the boys toward a branch that offered a quick climb down to one of Maidenwood Grove's high walkways. "Hurry!"

"We're out," Tiran said once they were down and looking across the gap at the Bear's Head. "But the watch will guard the town gates. We're still trapped in these trees. And we've lost Ivano."

"No, we haven't." With a low whistle, Teegan called Aethia to her arm. She showed the others a tuft of fur, then held it close to the falcon's eye. "I cut this from Ivano's cloak. Find him, Aethia. Hunt him down."

64

AETHIA WEAVED HER WAY UPWARD THROUGH walkways, branches, and houses until she'd climbed above the elamwood canopy. She circled on the air, searching.

"If Ivano is still inside," Dag said, "how will she see him?"

Teegan kept her gaze on the bird. "Falcons are patient hunters. When he steps into the open, she'll tell us." As if cued by this statement, Aethia gave a cry.

With Aethia to guide them, the cadets tracked Ivano and his green-haired friend to the east end of town. They watched from a high walkway as the two entered a wrapping terrace laden with crates and barrels.

"Where's the bald one?" Dag asked.

Teegan had no intention of troubling her brehna further by describing what she'd seen from the staircase. The mudslinger's blister seemed to feed on such fears. "He won't be coming. Let's leave it at that." Lagging a pace behind Tiran, she ran a subtle finger across her throat, and Dag seemed to take her meaning. He didn't mention it again.

On the terrace below, Ivano and his friend disappeared around the elamwood trunk. Teegan waited for them to reappear. There were no other walkways, no place farther east for them to go, and watchmen guarded the town's eastern ramp. But the hunters never reappeared.

Aethia let out a cry and wheeled farther out, over the ramp and the eastern ridge. Tiran lifted his chin toward the bird. "Where's she going?"

Aethia never lost focus. It was not in her nature. Teegan could think of only one other explanation. “Ivano has a smuggler’s route. We have to get down there.”

On the terrace, behind the barrels and crates, they discovered a hatch much like the one they’d used to enter town. And underneath, a set of Rapha steps was carved into the elamwood’s trunk. But the hunters had not climbed all the way down to the swamp. A rope-and-plank bridge joined the Rapha steps to the wooden structure beneath the town’s eastern ramp. And within that structure, the smugglers had laid down longer planks to make a passable road. Teegan set off across the bridge. “Hurry. They’ll be far ahead of us by now.”

By the time the cadets reached the woods, Aethia’s white form was little more than a tiny star shooting across the night sky. But the falcon knew her business well. She circled back to find her mistress, who gave her the signal to continue the hunt.

There were no barkhide camps on this side. Goblin and orc patrols were a risk, but Teegan had heard Ivano and his friend plotting to bring Nesat their captive’s head. She couldn’t allow that. “Faster.” She pushed their pace to a jog, praying the Rescuer would hide their noise from the enemy.

Aethia’s circles between the cadets and her quarry grew tighter and tighter, until she dove into the trees.

Teegan halted the boys at a copse of pines. “We’re close. Ivano is a hundred paces ahead. Perhaps less. I think they’ve stopped.”

Dag peered into the forest. “She’s not . . . attacking them, is she?”

“No. Ivano is wearing beaver. With such large prey, she waits for me to do the killing.” She led them onward, picking her steps carefully now and motioning for the boys to do the same. “I suppose it’s a good thing he’s not wearing rabbit.”

At thirty paces, they gained sight of the hunters and fanned out to flank them with Teegan taking the middle. At twenty, she came within earshot.

"Is he not more valuable alive?" the green-haired man said. "If we take him north tonight, the granog will never know. We can make our fortune with the traveling fairs."

"Don't be a fool, Nicu. Nesat is out for blood. You saw what he did to Codrin. If he learns we took a Havarra from these woods now, we're dead men. No. We cut our losses. He'll pay a hefty price for the head, and we'll earn some good will."

"But he's Havarra."

A Havarra wolf. The Rescuer had led them to the hunters, and the hunters had led them to Pedrig.

Teegan watched through the branches of a spruce. Ivano and his friend argued in a small clearing, unremarkable except for a pile of dead brush at the far edge, dusted with snow. The green-haired man–Nicu, if she'd heard right–stood defiant between Ivano and the brush pile.

Ivano's grip tightened about the shaft of a short spear. "I know he's Havarra. It's what made him so valuable before, but now it makes him a danger to us."

"Then turn him over alive."

"And let him explain how we caught him? With a poacher's trap? Think, Nicu. The Havarra talk. It's the whole point of them."

The pile of dead brush behind Nicu shuddered. Twigs and branches slid away, from the muzzle of a silver wolf. The wolf lifted his head an inch, fixed his golden eyes on Nicu, and growled. "Fear not, child of Eido. If your friend wants to test his spear, let him do so, and we shall see how it goes for him."

As if to add weight to his threat, the wolf tried to stand, shaking the brush free. He was so much larger than any wolf Teegan had seen in Sil Tymest. Were he to stand on two legs, he might be taller than her Tehpa. But he could not even stand on four. A vicious toothed vise held one of his rear legs in its jaws, caked with blood and puss. His forelegs refused to hold him, and he collapsed, letting out a weak and frustrated groan.

Barely five paces to Ivano's left, Dag leaned into the moonlight from behind a bristlecone, axe at the ready. Teegan held up a closed fist, signaling him to hold. They had to do this right or risk killing one or both Aladoth. The miner gave the hunters a dark look but nodded and retreated into the shadows.

In the clearing, Ivano moved to sidestep his companion, but Nicu laid a hand on his chest. "This is murder. The Havarra are not dragon aberrations. They are an ancient people, among those the Eidolar are not permitted to harm. Would you have me enter the afterlife with this wolf's blood on my head?"

Ivano shoved him to the ground and pointed the spear at his throat. "I'll have you enter the afterlife tonight if you keep this up."

With one hunter off his feet, Teegan saw her moment. She stepped into the clearing with her trident drawn, shouting at the top of her lungs. "Poachers! Hunting after curfew! Seize them!"

Dag and Tiran took the cue and stepped out of hiding. "Take them! Seize them!"

Nicu took one look at Dag, jumped to his feet and fled.

Ivano shouted after him. "Stop, you coward!" But the smaller man kept running, lurching and tripping through the brush, until he vanished into the dark.

Teegan pushed Ivano to do the same. "If you were clever, you'd run with your friend instead of facing arrest for poaching."

"Nice try, girl." Ivano drew a sword and held it and his short spear out to his sides, low and poised for a fight. "You are no more a watchman or a barkhide than I am golmog. This wolf is mine. And I won't let three children take it from me."

"This wolf has suffered enough at your hands. Leave him be and go in peace. We don't want to hurt you."

"You don't want–" A disbelieving laugh shook Ivano's chest. "The granog is looking for a young woman and two young men. Hurt me? Little girl, I'm going to kill these two, and take their heads to Nesat along with the wolf's. But I'll let you live and claim you as part of my reward." He took a threatening step. "What do you think, Little Red? Want to be my wife?"

"Stay away from her!" Tiran charged between them with his swords.

Ivano met his blade with an upward swing. Tiran toppled sideways, overpowered. He smacked his head into a tree and fell bleeding and motionless to the snow. The hunter moved in to finish him off.

"Don't!" Teegan cried and shoved the trident at his shoulder to stop him.

Ivano wheeled his blade and caught her tines. "Good, Little Red. I like your spirit. We'll make an excellent match."

She tried to wrench his sword away with the trident, but Ivano was too strong, forcing her to drop her net and commit both hands to the struggle. At the edge of her vision, she saw Dag raise an axe. "Don't kill him," she said, breathing hard. "Disarm him."

"I know." Dag swung at the hunter's spear.

With the flourish of a practiced fighter, Ivano whipped his weapon from the axe's path and thrust it at Dag's chest. A ghostly breastplate deflected the tip.

Dag swung again with a backhand. And again, Ivano swept the spear out of the blade's path and thrust out with its point. Dag's breastplate took the blow full-on and sent a wave of shock up Ivano's arm.

The hunter yanked his sword free of Teegan's lock and retreated, looking from one to the other. "Sorcery."

"The Rescuer," Teegan said. "Yield to him now, and be spared."

"So, you're Keledan. We haven't seen your kind here for a generation."

"Two generations." Dag lowered his axe and straightened. "But we've returned, and there's no need to fight us. You've no love for the dragons. The Rescuer can save you from their oppression. Trust him."

In answer, Ivano lunged at them with both spear and sword.

While Dag fended off the spear, Teegan tried again with her trident. She hoped to off-balance him, not skewer him, but accomplished neither. Ivano ducked Dag's axe, dodged her trident, and knocked the shaft out of her hands with his swing. If not for the trident's steel bands, he would have chopped it in two. And with his next swing, he aimed to sever her head.

An axe broke the blade. A flash of white the size of Dag's armored fist sent Ivano stumbling backward.

But he did not fall.

Tiran, on his feet again, caught him from behind and sliced Ivano's hand with a dagger. The spear fell to the ground. He pulled the hunter's head back by his long brown hair and pressed the dagger's tip up under his bearded chin. "Now who's the pretty little girl?"

Tiran blinked against the blood trickling from the wound on his forehead, eyes blazing with fury. She reached for him. "Stay calm, Tiran. You're hurt. Not thinking straight. Let Dag and I handle him from here." In a single move, she snatched up her net and slung at the remains of Ivano's sword. The weights locked over the hilt. She jerked it from his grasp. "He's disarmed, Tiran. See? Job done. Let him go. Let him run."

"I can't." The blister on Tiran's neck pulsated as he spoke. "What if he doubles back to kill us? What if his friend returns?" The dagger's tip bit into Ivano's skin. A trickle of blood ran down the blade. "What if they kill Dag and me, and you're left alone with this monster?"

"He's not a monster," Dag said, "not an orc or golmog. He's Aladoth."

"He's a killer. You heard. You saw. He–"

With a mighty shout, Ivano arched his body and threw Tiran off his feet. The two rolled and grappled in the snow, coming to a stop with Ivano smothering Tiran.

Dag hauled Ivano off, and the hunter flopped over into a snow-filled ditch. His body convulsed and went still, eyes staring sightless at the night sky with Tiran's dagger buried in his chest to the hilt.

"I . . . I didn't mean to." Tiran sat up, staring at the blood on his hands. "He was so strong, I–" Without warning, he scrambled into the ditch and yanked the dagger from Ivano's chest. Blood spilled out, soaking the poacher's tunic, and Tiran covered the wound with his hands. "No. You can't. You have to wake up. Please, wake up!"

Dag pulled him away, but Tiran thrashed until he'd freed himself and covered the wound again, sobbing. "I didn't mean to. I'm sorry. I'm sorry."

"Leave him be, son of autumn." The wolf had managed to stand. Hc shook thc brush free of his fur. "What's done is done. Some hurts you can never take back."

65

CONNOR PASSED THE NIGHT'S FOUR WATCHES IN FITS and starts, plagued with visions of Faelin engulfed in dragon fire.

He'd been suspicious ever since he'd learned the messenger Pedrig was the same wolf who'd walked with his patehpa years ago. But he'd refused to accept that Halas and Faelin were one and the same. Why had Faelin let his family believe he'd died in Tanelethar?

Or perhaps Tehpa had known the truth and kept it from Connor.

These thoughts tormented him for a league of slow, hard travel as sporadic barkhide camps pushed his party north. The farther they diverged from their planned route to the waterfall, the more the chance of knowing a living patehpa—of saving him from the dragon in his dream—slipped away.

Not until the party came to a seemingly endless field of rocky hills, could they turn west again. After more than two ticks of this painful terrain, Connor planted his crook in frustration. "How much farther to the falls, Lee?"

"Hard to say. We dropped off the north edge of the map, so I don't know. Three, perhaps four leagues? Assuming we can veer south again soon."

"Our road has grown too long. Forget the falls. The moment we're clear of the barkhide camps, we head straight for the meeting point above the castle."

Kara sat down on a boulder and crossed her arms, tugging her sleeves to her knuckles. Using the cold hearth's ashes she'd remade her disguise. Soot darkened her air. Streaks of char hid her gray-blue freckles. "I thought you needed the banishing powder."

"We do. And we'll get it. Just not yet. We should free Faelin first, then regroup. If we wait, we may never get the chance."

Lee set his gaze on his hands, twisting his ring. "What if he isn't there? I mean, I want to believe he survived the orc attack too, but–"

"I saw him, all right? Faelin was the knight in my dream, and I–" Connor clenched his teeth, then forced himself to give voice to the image he dreaded so much. "I saw him roasted by the dragon, Lee–swallowed in flame. I didn't know what it meant before, but now I do. The Rescuer wants me to save him."

The scribe was quiet for a moment. "You can't know that for certain."

Connor grabbed his tunic at the shoulder and jerked him close. "I do know. Finally, I *know* what happened to my patehpa. He was here the whole time, and now he's been captured. I'm meant to save him."

Lee remained calm, hands hanging at his side. "Connor, we can't enter the dragon's stronghold without the shairosite. We may only get one chance."

"I don't care about the shairosite." Connor released him and strode on. "You coming, Kara?"

"As long as you're still paying."

Something bounced off Connor's shoulder. A pebble? He kept walking and felt another–harder. It stung. He spun around and glared at Lee.

The scribe glared right back at him. "You don't get to make this choice, Connor, raidleader or not. This is not your mission. It's the Rescuer's. And he sent us to destroy that portal." He held up another pebble. "I'll keep throwing these–until you make the right choice or come over here and fight me for leadership of this party. Which will it be?"

Connor stormed up to him, steaming.

Lee dropped the pebble and laid a gentle hand on his arm. "You want to save Faelin. You want to have a grandfather like most of us. I understand. I want that for you too, my friend. But ask yourself, is what you're trying to do the Rescuer's will or yours?"

They believed they could discern the Rescuer's will. Imagine believing a man can know his creator's mind. Tehpa's scornful words from the road to Watchman's Gate returned to him. But Connor had learned so much since then. The Rescuer had spoken his will into his word. And the guardians and the Shar Razel had taught Connor that discerning how the Rescuer wanted him to live that word was a matter of faith and prayer, not arrogance as Tehpa thought.

Had Master Jairun foreseen this moment? Of course he had. He knew about Faelin.

Never forget, this is the Rescuer's mission, Mister Enarian—not your own.

A Havarra wolf like Pedrig is fiercely loyal, and so should you be.

Patehpa's wolf. Would Pedrig be loyal to Faelin or to the Rescuer first? In his heart, Connor knew the answer.

Lee gave his arm a firm squeeze. "Trust the Rescuer, my friend."

Connor nodded. "His path. Not mine."

A few paces away, Kara had taken a seat on a boulder again. "Should we get on with this? Or are you planning to make camp on these horrid rocks?"

The woods returned after two more leagues, and they held no sign of barkhide camps. The party veered south until Lee spotted a narrow lake he recognized from his memory of the map. Not long after, he showed them an overgrown trail. "Faelin drew this path in hidden ink. We're close. Very close. But the exact location was—"

"Burned beyond reading by a careless oaf with an oil lantern?" Connor asked.

"I was going to say obscured." Lee pushed ahead onto the

trail, scanning the brush and muttering to himself. "The meadow beneath. The meadow beneath. Beneath what?"

To Connor's surprise, Kara echoed him. "The meadow beneath. The meadow . . . beneath." She began to hum.

Connor recognized the tune. He heard the words in his head.

The Sleeper wakes by a meadow stream,

On a path of gold 'neath the silver gleam

Of the stars up in the heavens.

The meadow beneath. The words from the map were there in the song. But where had a girl from the far north of Tanelethar heard "The Sleeper's Hope"? He sang the next few measures.

Child beckons. Follow me,

To the mountaintop by the crystal sea.

She stared at him. "You know Hal's song."

"Faelin," Connor told her. "His name is Faelin."

"Whatever. Did he sing it to your tehpa? Did your tehpa sing it to you?"

He let out a dry laugh. "Tehpa doesn't sing. But all Keledan know 'The Sleeper's Hope.' It's part of every festival–a song about the hope of our Blacksmith."

"I know the words," she said, lowering her chin to give him an incredulous look. "There's no mention of a blacksmith."

"And yet, he's there. Our Blacksmith is the Rescuer. And the Rescuer is the Child."

"And the Lamb." Lee returned to them along the trail. "Those loyal to the High One first sang 'The Sleeper's Hope' during the dragon scourge, many years before our Blacksmith led the rebellion. The melody is as old as time. The song prevents–"

"A dragon from seeing into your mind. *Hal* told me." Kara glanced at Connor as she said the name. "He helped me remember the words."

Connor narrowed his eyes. "Helped you remember? Then where did you learn it?"

Kara told them about the memories of her mehma and the lullaby she sang, even as the orcs took her away. She held her bear pendant, looking down at it. "There's so much about her I don't know. Where did she learn song sorcery?"

Lee cringed. "Don't call it song sorcery."

"Then what should I call it?"

"Call it pure. Call it the High One's holiness. Sorcery is a vile mockery of his power, twisting the abilities he gave the Elder Folk when he created them."

"Song sorcery," Connor said, shifting his gaze south.

Lee punched him in the arm. "Hey. You know better."

But Connor hushed him with a warning hand. "Listen." The song was faint at first. Then the forest erupted in a deep undulating tone. Quinton had mimicked the sound in his lessons about wood trolls. "The mocktree. Masks!"

66

SIX GOBLINS MATERIALIZED AMONG THE PINES. FIVE had their long knives drawn. The sixth brought a short bow to bear and loosed an arrow that skipped off Connor's shield.

Lee answered with a sikari, and his throw drove the blade deep into the goblin's bow arm. The goblin howled and dropped the weapon.

Despite Connor's warning, Kara's cloth still hung loose about her neck. "Kara! Mask!"

She gave him a frightened nod and pulled it into place, staring into the distance past the goblins.

Krokwode.

Twice Connor's height, the oaksquid glided through the undergrowth on tentacle roots. Branches swayed like a tree in the wind, some pierced with spikes, one holding an axe in three twig fingers. Tiny orange eyes blazed within two large and uneven black holes–small candles in dark windows. Much faster than its goblin servants, the troll brushed one out of the way with a root and charged. Its throaty song echoed in Connor's ears.

A deep voice resonated within the changing tones, throbbing in his chest. *The boooy can ruuule. A priiize, he is. Powerrr is yourrrs. Powerrr. Controlll.*

Power. Control. These were the keys to the wood troll's infection, it's pathway to the mind and heart. The cloth over Connor's mouth and nose would block the spores flowing from the web of rot within its yawning mouth. His training–his reliance on the Sacred Scrolls–would block the song's attack.

This boooy can ruuule. Ruuule with the girrrl. A kiiing. A queen. Powerrr. Controlll.

But what a strange attack it seemed.

A root whipped out and wrapped Connor's crook, trying to rip it from his hands. He cut it free with Faelin's sword. Another came at his head. He sliced that one too, retreating until he bumped into his friends.

The three stood back-to-back, surrounded.

Lee slashed and stabbed with two sikari. A goblin fell. Then another, dropped by Kara's hunting knife. As if surprised by her willingness to fight, the troll roared. It caught her ankle with a root and dragged her off her feet.

"Connor, help!"

He chopped the root away. Where was Kara's armor?

Of course. She had none.

The troll held its distance with an axe high, clasped in three twiglike fingers. Roots snapped at Kara like whips, while the goblins hacked at the cadets' shields. Two goblins fell back with sikaria in their throats. Connor parried a slash from another and shoved his sword through its chest. It dropped to its knees, and he felt a sudden reprieve. No more knives. Had they killed all the goblins?

The troll gave him no chance to count. A root encircled Kara's waist. Others caught her wrists and ankles, threatening to tear her apart.

The cadets rushed the creature's flanks. The axe swung down at Connor. A spiked branch came at Lee's neck. Shields flashed. Connor drew his crook from its sheath and drove it into bark-like hide.

The creature howled. Thick yellow ooze flowed from the wound. The troll released Kara and backed away beyond the crook's reach to resume its evil song. A thick cloud of spores spewed forth.

This boooy can ruuule. Ruuule with the girrrl. A royaaal pairrr. Powerrr. Controlll. The draguuun knooows.

Kara's mask had been torn away. Connor pulled her to her feet. "Your tunic, Kara." He and Lee stepped in front of her, weapons out. "Pull it over your nose and mouth and hold it there."

The song grew louder.

A royaaal pairrr. The draguuun knooows. The boooy will learrrn. He muuust learrrn.

A sikari snuffed out one of the strange candle eyes. Lee followed it with a shouted verse. "*Se vi streg, sod va premat, dar vo Anamesh ke'Rumosh noshah.*"

Not might. Nor power. By his spirit.

Connor echoed the verse–wise counsel from the Sacred Scrolls to fend off the infectious song. "*Se vi streg, sod va premat, dar vo Anamesh ke'Rumosh noshah.*"

Enraged, the troll came at them again. A flurry of roots whipped the air.

Lee advanced, making good use of his last two sikaria to clear a path. Connor took two long steps behind him, caught a flailing branch with his crook, and let it lift him high over his friend. He let go, and with all his might, plunged his sword down into the creature's throat. It toppled to the brush, rancid yellow sap bubbling from its open maw.

"That's disgusting," Kara said, pulling the tunic away from her mouth.

Connor didn't answer. Something nagged at his mind. He couldn't account for all the goblins. He turned from the mocktree and saw the goblin bowman who'd fired the first arrow running at Lee with the scribe's own sikari. Lee, kneeling to remove one of his blades from a carcass, was oblivious.

"Lee!" Desperately, Connor jerked at his sword hilt to draw it from the troll's throat. It moved an inch. He jerked again. Another inch. "Lee, look out!"

The sword came free. Connor swung. The goblin's head rolled into the trees.

Lee sat back to his haunches, stunned. He and the others stared as the headless corpse dropped beside him. The fungal creature still held the sikari in its grasp. The arm flopped out, as if offering the blade's return.

Connor might have retched, but a root from the mocktree, still wriggling and perhaps seeking vengeance, gave him no chance to do so. He tripped, dropping the sword in surprise, and fell. His shoulders crashed into the forest blanket of twigs and dead pine needles. But the blanket gave way, and Connor kept on falling–and falling–through dank, empty air.

67

AFTER LEAGUES OF MARCHING, TEEGAN STOPPED HER party for a break. She cupped her hands and had Dag pour a few sips from the Telbeath flask for Pedrig. How strange she felt, watching the dignified Havarra lap the healing water from her palms. But Pedrig did not seem to care about such appearances.

Once finished, he tilted his head back, and Teegan squeezed her fists over his open mouth as he'd taught her to do the night before—so as not to waste a single drop. "Your leg looks better," she said. "I noticed you limping less over the last tick or so."

The wolf lowered his muzzle, ears rotating forward. "The pain is less, daughter of autumn. This is true. And Havarra mend quickly. But I'm not as young as I once was. The poachers' wound may stay with me until I lie down for good." His tail sagged a bit, and when he took a step, it sagged even more. But he padded on without complaint as he had all day, leading them on some invisible trail only his golden eyes could see.

They'd covered Ivano's body with dirt and stones in the ditch where he lay with his broken sword for a headstone, then spent the night in gloom and the near-freezing cold. None wanted to camp near the corpse, so Pedrig led them eastward to a rock overhang that would shield them from the wind. A fire, he warned, might be seen from a great distance. But when the cadets began to shiver, he took pity. He commanded them to build a fire circle and fill it with wood, then prayed to the Rescuer in some wolfish version of the Elder Tongue. Flames sprang up as dark green as the pines, tipped with the blue-white of moonlit snow. The sparks were like rising snowflakes.

In the quiet crackling of this fire, Pedrig spoke encouragement to Tiran. Teegan did not understand all the ancient words, for they were not meant for her ears, but she picked up some. *Lilies. Birds. His gift of peace. A tree planted by the water. A table among my enemies.* When he finished, the mudslinger's blister had all but vanished. She doubted Tiran's other wounds–the one on his head and the one left in his spirit after killing Ivano–would heal as fast.

When they woke the next morning, her twin looked shrunken, swallowed by his own cloak. And now, leagues later on the way to the place they'd promised to meet Connor, the gash on his head refused to stop bleeding. He trudged along behind, dabbing it with a bloodied rag.

Teegan moved to the front next to Pedrig and kept her voice low. "Once you show us the dragon's castle, you and Tiran should make for the hollow tree and return to Ras Telesar. He needs a renewer's hand–Master Jairun's hand. And I daresay, you do as well."

"He needs time, daughter of autumn. And prayer. Yours. Mine. His own." The wolf's ears fell back. "I fear he'll carry his burden long, and his spirit will not let his flesh fully heal until he lays it down at the Fountain. As for me"–he regarded her with something on the edge of a snarl–"I am not yours to command. I'll not return to Keledev until I learn whether Faelin is alive or dead. My loyalty lies with him. Even more, my loyalty lies with the Rescuer and his mission here. If your brehna wants to make for the hollow tree, he must walk alone. And that, I do not advise."

The wolf's path turned southeast to a saddle in the northern branch of a massive spur supporting the Celestial Peaks. The higher the party climbed, the more snow fell. When the trees thinned, the wind picked up, and Aethia struggled to hold her perch on Teegan's arm. She raised her cloak to offer the bird a little shelter.

"Perfect," Tiran muttered from his place at the column's rear. "Perhaps we'll be too frozen for the dragon's fire to roast us."

Teegan watched him for a moment, then shook her head. "He's not supposed to be here, you know. His vision at Telbeath was clear. The Rescuer did not want him to come. Tiran was hurt, I think. Angry. And so, he disobeyed."

Pedrig stole a glance at Tiran. A thoughtful growl rumbled deep beneath the white fur of his chest. "The muk's infection made his challenge harder. The Rescuer wanted to spare him this painful trail. Too often we forget the Rescuer's commands are his beneficent gift rather than chains about our necks."

"But he's suffered so much. Shouldn't we find a way to send him home?"

"You cannot spare the time. And if you think the Creator did not know Tiran would disobey, then you have much to learn. Our Maker works all things together for our good." A gust blew snow in their faces, becoming a gale. Pedrig bent his head against it and flattened his ears. "All things!"

The rush and howl of the wind ended all conversation until the party had descended past the saddle. Pedrig shook the snow free of his fur after the gale diminished. "Too bad. I was hoping the storm would stay with us."

"Why would you hope for a storm?" Tiran asked.

"Snow harries ore creatures. It spoils their sight and thickens their molten blood."

"And are there many orcs guarding the castle? Isn't a dragon enough?"

An impatient growl escaped the wolf's throat. "Where there are dragons, there are orcs, son of autumn. The orcs at Trader's Knoll and Maidenwood Grove are outlying colonies. This castle and the surrounding ridges are their hive, and the hive is already stirred."

"This castle," Teegan said. "Do you mean to say we're close?"

In answer, Pedrig hobbled to the edge of their trail and looked out over a canted mountain vale.

As the cadets joined him, a low cloud drifted north, parting as it went. A gray-and-black fortress materialized on a field of white far below. Swarms of goblins scurried up and down scaffolding to complete the outer walls and watchtowers.

Pedrig lolled his head to one side to look at Teegan, ears up. "Didn't you sense it, child of autumn? The oppression. The darkness of a dragon's presence. Couldn't you smell it? We're not close. We're already here."

68

THE WONDERING STRUCK CONNOR HARDEST. WHEN will I hit? What will I hit? He couldn't make sense of what he saw above him—a cold white sun in a sky of dark blue gems. He'd been here before. Not the gems, but the fall, as if the Rescuer had wanted to prepare him. A prayer flowed through him. *Dar oveh, Rumoshtesh, e'darmaz hal ensecral'eni, onoresh, ke'Arosh, dofesh vyk rumah.*

A shield. My glory. You lift my head.

He saw the glow of his armor an instant before he hit.

Armor or not, the impact hurt like an icy club against his back and neck.

Water closed about Connor's face. He came to himself and flailed to roll his body over, kicking as Lee and Teegan had shown him at the Passage Lakes. "Lee!"

"I'm here." The scribe sounded distant, muted by the rush of falls pouring into the pond. "You fell a long way. Kara and I need time to get down there. Well done, though."

"Well done?" Connor reached for the shore, but the grass looked strange, fine needles and blades of green crystal too sharp to grab. Crystal. Like the blue sky above. He sputtered, kicking against the deep, and searched for a safe place to drag himself a shore. "For what? Falling?"

"No, silly. For finding the meadow beneath."

His foot found purchase, a rock shelf under the surface. Connor swept his arms until he'd gained his balance and crawled out onto a wide spot of smooth, yellow stone, but he sliced his hand on a cluster of green blades in the effort. He sat up, dripping and bleeding, and whispered to the Rescuer. "Thank you."

The meadow beneath.

Sunlight streamed in through many holes in the blue crystal ceiling, though none were as wide as the hole directly above the pool. Wherever the rays fell, the green crystals carpeting the cavern floor grew up in high groves like pines. More pools besides Connor's reflected the ceiling's dark blue, but his was by far the largest, and with good reason.

White water gushed down from a fissure in the cavern wall, pounding the main pool ever deeper and wider, and sending a sparkling mist through the shafts of light. Connor cupped his hands to his mouth. "Lee! Do you see this? It's your waterfall! Are you there?" His own breath stung his hand. He winced and frowned at the deep cuts in his palm.

The bandages in his kit remained dry–a small miracle brought by the eberlast lining. Lee had the salves and balms, and would know the best one, but the cuts were deep, and Connor didn't feel like bleeding to death while waiting for the scribe to find a way down. He wrapped his hand, then tied the dressing off and tore with his teeth. "Lee! What's happening up there?"

"I have no idea. I'm down here." Lee walked out with Kara from behind a set of candle-like formations near the cavern wall. He gestured over his shoulder with Connor's crook. "We found a cave entrance in the hillside. Steep, I'll admit, but much safer and far less soggy than your route. And keep it down, will you? The oaksquid and its goblin friends might not have been the only dark creatures about. Remember what Master Jairun said about the banishing powder."

Connor did remember. *Any deposits will be well defended.* But a cautious walk through the crystal meadow along the few stretches and patches of smooth yellow stone revealed no enemies. It revealed no banishing powder either.

"This cavern is beautiful." Kara touched a red bud on a bulbus, dark green formation she'd decided was a crystal holly. "But perhaps it's the wrong place."

"Keep searching." Lee examined a vein of blue and gold under his colored lenses. "The map says the shairosite is here." He glanced at the torrent pouring into the pool. "And that's the waterfall from my dream, I'm sure of it."

Neither argued, and for more than a tick, they searched.

Holly bushes. Glistening pink and blue spheres, which Kara declared to be flowers. Candle pillars and crystal pine groves. Faelin's Meadow Beneath held many wonders, but none were silver veins of shairosite.

Kara gave up first, then Connor. He joined her on the yellow patch of shore where he'd dragged himself from the pool. "It's no use. But there's no point in leaving–not tonight. We won't find a safer shelter than this, which I suppose is why it's marked in hidden ink on the map."

"S for safe," Kara said.

"Or secret, or shelter. Faelin might have meant anything with the letter he drew beside the falls."

After the mention of his patehpa, Kara watched Connor for a time. "You miss him?"

"I never knew him." Connor drew his knees to his chin. "I suppose I miss the thought of him. Since before I can remember I've wished to know the knight above our hearth, to hear his stories over a pot of Mehma's brambleberry cider. Now I wonder. Is he the hero I imagined?"

They filled their empty waterskins at the falls and returned to the same spot to eat their way rations. Kara chuckled to herself.

"What is it you find so amusing?"

She tapped their patch of yellow stone and nodded at the stretches they'd walked in their searching–like natural paths and stepping stones on a crystalized green. "The sleeper wakes by a meadow stream, on a golden path, beneath the silver gleam." She tilted her head back, prompting Connor to look up through the hole in the ceiling.

The sun had gone, and the first tiny lights of evening twinkled in a darkening sky. "This is a pool, Kara, not a stream. And I'm not the sleeper."

Lee raised his lantern from the other side of the pool. "But I'll bet you saw stars after you hit the water."

Connor laughed at the jest.

Kara didn't. "But if you're not the sleeper, who is?"

"All Keledan."

She crinkled her nose. "Truly? And when the Child wakes the Keledan, will you walk with him to the mountaintop where the Lamb King waits? Are all Keledan so pure–so holy–that they're worthy of such an honor?"

He saw a flicker of hardness in her eyes, baiting a trap, and he willingly walked in. "You know we aren't, because I deceived you when I let you believe we were lightraider knights."

Kara gave him a slight nod.

Connor lowered his gaze. Was he ready for this? Was she? He took a breath, finding the words. "*Mi koth pachatend po koth ma ke'onor Rumosh fyr plumatend.*"

"You know I don't speak the Elder Tongue."

"It's a verse from our Sacred Scrolls. It means we've all fallen short. None of us measures up to the High One's glory and holiness, not one–not since the Leander Kings and their nobles betrayed him and sold their loyalty to Ras Pyras for a taste of Heleyor's sorcery."

Kara sat back on her elbows, clearly unimpressed. "If even the Keledan aren't worthy, then what is the point of your traditions?"

Belen had only begun the cadets' classes in speaking to Aladoth about the Rescuer. Connor wished he'd learned more before the raid. "I–" Another verse came unbidden to his mind. "*Mi Rumosh ke zavol ne avahend, mod benod aroshkef gevend, lut vykef fi mod credam sedrengiond dar beath elam cresiond."*

So great a love. His only son. Believe in him and never perish.

"That was a mouthful."

"Truly. But it's worth it. That verse is all about the High One's great love and his son's sacrifice. Do you know the story of the Blacksmith who became the Fountain and then the Mountain?"

"Liam told me the tale once or twice. A children's story, meant to explain the Impossible Peaks. The Southern Overlord, who grew up as a blacksmith in the Gray Mountains, led the Keledan rebels in a losing fight, until an army of dragons trapped them at a temple, which–"

"Ras Telesar," Connor said. "The dragons trapped them in the hilltop sanctuary of Ras Telesar. And now it's our academy."

"Do you want to tell it?"

"You're doing fine. Keep going."

She frowned but continued. "To save his army, your Blacksmith made himself into a wall of water–the Fountain. And the dragons spent all their fire to vanquish him. Days later, before they could rekindle their flames, he rose from the dead, bringing with him the Celestial Peaks and the Storm Mists to protect the Keledan forever."

Kara told the story well enough to give Connor hope that she might see more. "Good," he said. "The Blacksmith is the High One's son–the same High One whom the Leander Kings and their nobles betrayed. That's important. Are you following?"

She hit him with a blank stare.

He tried a different approach. "Think of it this way. The High One, the wealthiest of kings, sent his prince to live among the very peasants who'd betrayed him. Most rejected the prince, until finally the dragons hunted him down and killed him. But the prince was pure–holy and perfect. His sacrifice atoned for the peasants' betrayal. His resurrection restored to the king those who accepted him. That was the king's plan all along."

Kara raised an eyebrow. "And to reward his followers, he built a giant mountain barrier to hem you in?"

"He set us apart as his own. But he did more than build the barrier. He became a bridge between us and the Maker, which is his right, because he and the Maker are one."

At this, she crossed her eyes.

Connor laughed. "You'll get it. The Child and the Lamb King, the Blacksmith and the Creator. The Maker and the Rescuer. They're all one. All divine. With his divine sacrifice the Child made worthy those who could not be worthy. And the Keledan will sing with the Lamb on the mountaintop when all the dragons are no more."

Kara pushed herself to her feet and wiped her hands on her cloak, looking about the cavern. "Lamb kings and fountains. A world without dragons." She made a short jump to another patch of yellow stone. "A bedtime story. No good king who loves his son would send him to die for a bunch of peasant betrayers. And how can the king and the prince be one and the same?"

Light played on her cloak, a rippling reflection from the pool. Connor glanced up at the opening in the ceiling and saw Phanos shining down. "The moon," he said, mostly to himself.

"What about the moon?"

"Do you see her on the water? Phanos is up there, but also down here." He nodded at the ripples of white on her cloak. "You can't see the Phanos from over there, yet you stand in her light because she's also here, on the water. So it was with the . . ." Connor let his voice trail off, entranced by the silver sparkles glittering in the moon's reflection on the water.

Silver sparkles.

He bent closer. "Lee, bring the lantern. Quick."

Lee hurried over and held the light above the water. The extra light pushed past the surface, down into the deep pool. More silver sparkles glittered back.

The scribe caught his breath. "Banishing powder. The bottom is covered in shairosite."

69

PEDRIG BROUGHT THE CADETS TO THE CAVE FAELIN HAD drawn on his map in hidden ink, overlooking the dragon's stronghold. "We found this den when we came to check the goblins' progress. It is natural, not orc- or goblin-made, and well clear of the tunnels and patrols I've observed."

"So, we're safe here." Dag let his two big satchels drop to the dirt with a hefty *thump*.

The other three merely looked at him.

"Safe, son of spring?" Pedrig let out a growl. "We are far from safe. Be on your guard. This close to the stronghold, the stench of the dragon's evil is so pervasive, it obscures all others. I'll not smell an orc or goblin coming." He padded away toward the entrance. "Come, daughter of autumn. We must use our time here wisely. We'll examine the stronghold for weaknesses."

Teegan found Aethia a rock shelf where she could rest, then lay on a ledge next to Pedrig, close enough to feel the heat of his side. She propped herself up on her elbows with Master Jairun's spy glass. "Why do you call me daughter of autumn and Dag son of spring?"

"These are the seasons of your births, are they not?"

She didn't know the day of Dag's birth, but the wolf had spoken correctly of her. "How could you know this?"

"Each season has its own scent, and to those who are not its parents, every wolf cub is known by its season until it comes of age. You cadets are young. To call you by your given names feels strange. I'm sorry if this offends you."

"No. Not at all." She said no more about it and lifted the spyglass to her eye to examine the dragon's stronghold. Shaped as a diamond within a diamond, the fortress took up much of the valley. The sloped bulwarks defended an inner keep topped with a dome and four spires. Broad towers at the midpoint of each side and two at the barbican gate to the north offered commanding views over the vale. "Is Vorax expecting an invasion?"

"The dragons are ever fearful of the future, for they cannot see its pages. While he whom they betrayed authored every word." Pedrig, who needed no aid for his vision, directed Teegan's glass with his gaze. "Look to the south. See how Vorax drives his fungal corruptions in their labor?"

The outer wall and the two southernmost towers remained unfinished, draped in scaffolding and swarmed by goblin workers. Teegan watched their frenzied work for a time, then moved the spyglass north again. "In their hurry, they've left bits of scaffolding against the finished walls, taking only the ramps. We might gain entrance there when the others come."

"Mmm. Agreed. Let us hope they come soon."

A thought occurred to Teegan, and she leaned on an elbow to face him. "But are you able to climb scaffolding without the ramps?"

His wolfish lips curled back. "Do you mean because I have no thumbs?"

"No. Your limp. It's . . ." She bit her lip. Teegan had thought Pedrig seemed less prone to offense than humans, but perhaps she'd been wrong. "I didn't mean–"

Pedrig shook with what she took as a laugh–a series of grumbles trapped in his chest. "Forgive me, child of autumn. I could not resist. Do not trouble yourself. A Havarra wolf can climb well, even one who is lame."

Grand pyranium doors formed the diamond keep's entire northern tip, so black as to absorb the light. If the diamond were a dragon's head, they would open like its jaws, with great teeth down the middle. Goblin craftsmen worked from swinging platforms, etching runes into the metal with fire and acid. They were paler than the cave goblins Teegan had fought at the academy–a little taller too, with feathery white hair. “Are those frost goblins?”

“They work more efficiently in winter. By now, all the cave goblins who started this fortress are tucked away in the hive underground.” The wolf moved her glass up a few degrees with his muzzle. “All except that one.”

The lens settled on a cave goblin absolutely drowning in furs, perched on the roof near the keep’s dome. It waved a blood-red cane about, screaming at the workers.

“That one endures the cold against its nature for only one reason,” Pedrig said. “It’s been chosen as Vorax’s eyes, a surrogate mind to direct the work while the dragon bends its whole spirit into growing and steering the portal.”

Tiran appeared behind them at the cave’s mouth. “Then we should kill this goblin and slow the dragon’s work. I’ll wager I can make the shot from here, given our height. They’d never know from whence the arrow came.”

“Don’t be rash, Brehna,” Teegan said. “Wait for Connor.”

“Yes, Shessa. Wait for the shepherd boy. Everything depends upon the shepherd boy.”

Ears back, Pedrig pressed himself up and growled. “Rrrrest, son of autumn. Eat to build your strength. Prrray. These are your wisest actions now. Battle will come soon enough.”

Tiran shook his head and walked into the cave.

Teegan sighed, watching him go. “I thought his failure with Ivano would teach him humility.”

“It may, child of autumn. Every failure presents two trails to the hunter. One leads to nourishment, the other to a rotting corpse. Your brehna still stands at the fork, sniffing the air. We must help him choose wisely.”

She settled to her elbows and lifted the spyglass again. Where was that goblin foreman? There. She found him still on the rooftop, shouting and waving his red cane. How absurd he looked in those furs. But she supposed cave fungus did not fare well in a winter storm. She smiled at the thought, until the goblin ceased its shouting and snapped its yellow eyes her way.

She lowered the glass. "Pedrig? The cave goblin. He can't see us from there, can he?"

Pedrig grunted. "Not possible. Your spyglass does not work in both directions. And a cave goblin's vision is poor in the day–even worse with the snow's glare."

She pushed herself away from the edge, anyway. "I've seen enough."

One tick passed, then two, then three, into the first watch. The others didn't come. Tiran moved often to the cave's mouth to look out. "They should be here by now."

Teegan did not disagree, but she said nothing and set her mind on sharpening the tines of her trident.

Dag built a fire using dry wood they'd collected on the way. He melted snow in a pot and added way rations and spices to make a stew much like the one he'd made at Mer Nimbar. He fanned its aroma toward Tiran. "Come and ease your hunger. Master Belen says a full belly grants patience. Connor and Lee aren't due till tomorrow."

"No," Tiran said. "They were due today."

"But we gave them until tomorrow. They had the longer road."

"Guided by an Aladoth thief almost certain to betray them." Tiran looked to his twin. "Right, Teegs?"

She kept running her sharpening stone over her tines, refusing to acknowledge him. But she could not deny she'd harbored the same concern. Kara could not be trusted.

The snow and wind returned with evening, driving all four deep into the cave. Pedrig made them smother the fire and took the first watch. He curled up a short distance away and laid his muzzle across his paws, but his eyes remained keen, ears twitching.

Teegan nodded off, then started. Had she slept? The light had changed. The wind had calmed. As her mind cleared, she saw Tiran, restless and shifting on the hard floor. He grumbled to himself. "Late. Too late. For all we know, they're dead. And the dragon's portal grows. If he wins, what was it for?"

He went on, stirring, grumbling, until finally, he slapped the earthen floor and stood. He girded his sword and stormed past the wolf.

Teegan sat up. "Tiran, wait."

"I'm done waiting. Come with me or don't, but I *will* find a way to close the portal. Otherwise, I killed a man for nothing." He left the cave.

Pedrig limped after him. "You stay, child of autumn. I'll go. I need to work out the stiffness of my leg, and your kin needs an older and firmer bark than yours." His tail, bristling, passed out of sight beyond the cave's mouth.

Teegan hugged her knees to her chest, waiting and listening. Without the wind to hide them, she heard the echoing shouts of the cave goblin driving his laborers in the vale, and the deeper rumble of orc voices–many orc voices. The night had brought them out in force.

But she heard nothing of Pedrig or Tiran, not for a long while.

"Tiran?" Teegan crept toward the mouth. How far could they have gone? "Tiran, are you there?"

She never made it through the opening. Orcs poured in, a dozen or more, all with halberds leveled. They pinned her against the cave wall far from her trident.

"Dag! Orcs! Dag, wake up!"

No use. The miner's greatest asset and worst fault was a slumber impervious to noise. They surrounded him before he came to.

The orc leader, marked by a red dragon emblazoned on his armor, relaxed his halberd and bent near to Teegan's face. He rocked his gargoyle head one way, then the other, and let out an ear-crushing roar.

70

KARA KNELT AT THE WATER'S EDGE. "BANISHING powder. I don't believe it. See how it glitters?"

"Beautiful," Connor said.

Lee nodded. "Quite beautiful."

"And worth a fortune." Kara pulled off her boots and let her cloak fall from her shoulders. "I'm going down. You brought pouches to carry it, yes? Give them to me."

When Connor hesitated, she folded her arms. "You still don't trust me? There must be barrels of powder down there. Plenty to go around."

Lee pulled the lantern back, stealing its gold light from the water. "Shairosite is not treasure. It's dangerous. We'll take only what we need." He dug into a pocket of his kit and brought out two leather pouches. "Our guardians gave us these two for the job. Fill them to bursting."

Connor didn't like the way she looked at the silver dust. "Lee will go down with you. He's an excellent swimmer."

"Oh, Connor, be brave." Kara took one of the pouches from Lee. "It's a pool, as calm as a quiet breath. If one of you must dive with me, let it be you."

"She's right, my friend," Lee said, oblivious to Connor's signals. "What better place to practice swimming than a little pool? It's far better than where I learned, in the waves and currents of Lin Kelan." He tossed the second pouch at Connor's chest. "Don't count on my help unless you're drowning. I'd rather not get water in my spectacles."

After barely giving him a chance to shed his cloak and sword, Kara took his hand. "Deep breath. Kick straight to the bottom."

Kara punched through the surface like a spear, but Connor hit it like a sheep thrown at a pond. The impact stripped his poorly tied dressing away, and he watched a thin stream of blood float through the moonlight toward the dark of an underwater cave. Perhaps tunnels connected the cavern's many pools. The idea might lure Lee in for a swim as well, spectacles or not.

But, for the moment, the scribe watched from the shore, a dull figure with a lantern behind rippling glass. Kara tugged Connor's hand to gain his attention. They'd reached the bottom. She kicked to hold their position, caught in the moon's rays. Platinum hair hung suspended about her, washed clean of soot. Her flourishes of blue-gray freckles had returned to her cheeks and nose, and more adorned her bare ankles and the tops of her feet like little jewels. What a horrible land this was to make her hide such gifts.

Kara shook her pouch, already full. Connor nodded and ran his own through the shairosite silt. Job done. She released him to tie his strings, planted her feet, and launched for the surface, sending up clouds of silvery dust.

Connor's floundering battle to get his feet underneath him turned him to face the underwater cave. He blinked against the cold water and the cloud of silt. The darkness moved.

A shape took form. A leviathan snout. Rows of teeth. Red eyes.

Connor's feet found solid ground, and he shot for the surface, gasping for air the moment he broke through. An arrow flew into the pool.

"Get out!" Lee shouted. "It's a rattlefish!"

A river troll–the largest and most dangerous troll kind.

Connor felt Kara's hands at his wrists, hauling him onto the shore. The rattlefish snapped and missed, but a finned tail sailed past and sliced his calf through his trousers. He let out a yelp as she pulled him up. "It got me!"

"How bad?" Lee asked.

Connor tried the leg. "Not bad enough to make me stick around." He made a grab for his weapons, but a tempest of waves and spray sent him stumbling back with only the sword. The troll landed on webbed reptilian feet near the crook and scabbard, balanced on a long scaly tail.

The creature stood as tall as the mocktree despite the hunch of its broad shoulders. One muscled arm hung closer to the floor's crystal blades than the other. It bared rows of teeth and flared the spiked fins running down its back. The red eyes gleamed.

They had only the moonlight shining down through the ceiling to see by. Lee had dropped his lantern when he took up his bow, snuffing out the flame. He let another arrow fly and hit his mark, but it skipped away, deflected by armored scales. The troll, little troubled by the attack, picked up Connor's crook and swung it in a broad arc to force Connor back onto the green crystals. He felt them crunch under his boots.

Boots. Kara. Her feet were still bare.

Connor risked a glance away from the danger and found her on a patch of yellow stone, hunting knife out, one foot bleeding. Her boots were with his cloak under the troll. He could no more fetch them for her than fetch his crook from the creature's three-fingered grasp. He shoved the banishing powder into the top pocket of his kit and dug out his sling from another. He threw the sling at Kara's feet. "Break the crystals with your knife. Use them as missiles."

The red eyes traced down Connor's neck to the pouch of banishing powder. A forked gray tongue flicked out, and a hiss and rattle erupted from the troll's chest, making the gills at its neck quiver. Song sorcery. Connor heard whispers within the rhythmic sound.

A thief like usss. Yesss. Yesss. But did you think you can sssteal from usss, Twiceborn?

The troll knew they were Keledan. Connor detected a sneer.

Yesss, Keledan. I tasssted your homeland on your blood. I ssshall tassste more sssoon.

“Hey, fish!” Lee fired again, only to see another arrow deflected. But he gained the troll’s attention. “Yeah, you. There’s three of us. You’re outnumbered. Drop the crook and dive back into your hole, and we’ll forget this ever happened.”

The troll only glowered at him. But Connor heard a strange reply within the its song.

Three of usss. Yesss. Three of usss.

The troll lifted its eyes to the crystal ceiling, pounded its chest, and let out a pulsating screech.

Lee and Kara covered their ears. Connor gutted through it and charged. Black claws clinked off his sword with a metallic ring. The crook came at his head. Where were Lee and Kara? “A little help, please!”

“Sorry!” the scribe shouted. “Busy!”

Looking past the troll, Connor saw a horned creature near the candle pillars at the far end of the cavern. A rotund black belly dotted with gray fungal boils stuck out beneath its leather breastplate. A golmog, with one of Lee’s arrows already buried in its leg. A second golmog with pinkish-red stripes lumbered out from behind the first, heading for Lee with a curved sword.

Lee drove an arrow into its throat. The creature slowed but didn’t fall. The scribe fired again. “Your troll called in a pair of golmogs!”

“He’s not my troll!”

Three of usss.

“Yeah,” Connor said. “I get it now. We have three. You have three.” He stabbed at its throat.

The troll knocked the thrust aside, wielding the crook as a crude club. But it made more practiced use of its long iron claws. They sparked off Connor’s shield.

Tassste your blood, Twiceborn.

A sharp green crystal smacked a golmog between the eyes. Kara slung another and hit it again. Watery gray fluid dripped from the wounds, but the creature didn't fall. With its cousin, it barred the way to the cave behind the pillars.

"Lee, we need another way out of here."

"Sure." The scribe fired an arrow. "Got a rope?"

Connor pressed the troll, goading him into a swing with the crook. He knocked it away and stabbed. Faelin's sword penetrated the armor. The creature shrieked and staggered back, leaving a black smear on the blade. Was it enough? The guardians had warned them about the formidability of river trolls. And with two golmogs keeping his friends busy, Connor would rather find a way out. There'd been more to Lee's dream. What was it? "You saw a sacred verse in the falls, right?"

"Right."

The troll came at him again. Its claws dug deep into his shield, leaving fading streaks of silver. The attack pressed him toward the falls, closer to Kara then Lee. He yelled at the scribe. "What was the verse?"

Lee fired again, leaving only one arrow in his quiver. "*Vynovu ya ke'Rumosh obligah . . .*"

"Yes. That's it." Connor finished the rest. "*Alermod credah, po ker paliond.*"

Commit your way. Trust in him, and he will do this.

Commit your way. "There's a tunnel behind the falls! That's our way out. Take Kara and go!"

"One moment." Lee spent his last arrow on the closest golmog, matching his first shot to the neck. The creature fell face first into a crystal holly. "That'll do," he said, grabbing Kara's hand, and they leapt through the falls together.

Connor hopped backward through the deluge onto a slippery tunnel floor, while a clawed hand swiped at him. It jolted his shield, knocking him to a knee, and he punched through the wall of water with his sword to keep the creature at bay.

Lee and Kara stood another twenty paces down the tunnel, lit by a blue orb hovering over Lee—a gift granted by the Rescuer to a prayer the scribe must have uttered. Connor knew it well. *Mo pednesh Logosovu pyrlas, po mo vynesh e'las. For my feet, your word is a lamp, and for my way, the light.*

The orb's glow gave Connor a surge of hope. But Kara looked fearful. She clutched at Lee's sleeve, eyes roving. Her knife moved back and forth, unsure of its target. Lee held her still and readied himself to throw a sikari.

"Don't," Connor said, returning his attention to the waterfall and the creature. "The tunnel's too narrow. If you hit me, I'm done for. Go find better ground where we can ambush this thing."

"I can't. We're not in a tunnel—not the kind we thought."

The falls split like curtains over a toothy snout and a hunched back. The troll screeched and rushed Connor's shield. Silver-white light flashed. Connor stumbled back a pace but kept his feet and countered with a thrust. The troll dodged—wary. Faelin's blade had taught it respect.

"Use your words, Lee. What are you saying?"

"Remember what Belen taught us? This is a portal, Connor. We're in a hollow hill."

The crystal cavern. The shairosite. Connor should have guessed. The troll rushed him again, crook held high. Connor stooped under the protection of his shield to absorb the strike. "Where does it lead?"

"We've no way to tell. We've run into the part of the map I burned."

71

CONNOR SCORED ANOTHER STAB TO THE TROLL'S abdomen and a slice across its calf to avenge the burning cut it had given him at the pool. But he needed to do more than score points. He had to get Lee and Kara out of there.

A hard blow knocked him back three more paces, and he heard a chortling gurgle.

Tassste your blood, young prinsss.

Prince?

"Make a choice!" Lee shouted. "Do we stand here in the dark or go through?"

The portal might send anywhere—perhaps to the frozen wastelands on the bottom of the world. But this place was no better. Beyond his foe, Connor saw the remaining golmog pushing through the falls.

He made his choice. "Take her in. I'll follow. I promise."

He might have promised too much. Iron claws flew at him. More heavy blows. The troll's fury made retreat impossible. If Connor turned and fled, he'd feel the spike of his own crook in his spine. If he backed into the void, off-balanced and disoriented by the portal, he might not see the claws coming before they tore out his throat.

Sssoon, Twiceborn. A prinssslymeal, and my firssst lightraider in yearsss.

"Hate to disappoint you." Connor ducked a sweep of the crook. "But I'm just a cadet."

Master Quinton had taught them a verse to gain breathing room—separation from a dark creature in the heat of battle. What was it?

Help me remember. Show me how to call for your aid.

The words came to his lips, quiet at first, then strong. "*Ye'Rumosh cedah. Heleyor opostah, po menov rethrediond.*"

Submit. Resist. He will flee.

The crook's point came stabbing at his neck. Connor parried and raised his shield to block a downward swipe from the claws. They stuck fast.

The shield pulsated, holding the claws. The red eyes flared, confused. The troll jerked its arm, almost yanking him off his feet. Connor leaned into the pull and slashed at its neck. His blade sliced through the scales, and the troll staggered free of his hold.

A quiet voice in his mind said, *Now.*

Connor turned to run, but he slipped and fell.

His pouch of shairosite burst open on the floor. Fine silver powder wafted up on the breeze from the waterfall and drifted into the void. A cloud of black pushed out like a billowing fog, crackling with purple lightning, and then the portal sucked it back in.

The creature came at him. In desperation, Connor swept up the remains of the pouch and powder and hurled them into the eyes of his enemy. The troll hid its face and shrieked in anger. Silver dust clung to its wet scales and gathered in the black blood around its wounds.

With so much shairosite on the air, the portal became a brewing storm. Lightning flashed within swirls of black fog. Connor half crawled and half ran down the passage and dove through.

His body slammed into hard, dry stone in a new passage, lit by the blue orb following Lee.

The scribe dragged him away from the turbulent void. "It's collapsing, Connor. We've got to—"

A screech drowned out his words. The troll lunged through and froze, suspended in the storm. Its angry cry dwindled to a whine, then nothing. But its mouth remained open, tongue curled. Lightning arced around and through its body. Behind the black fog, a wall of smooth stone flashed in and out of existence.

The tunnel shook, and with a rending *crack*, the ceiling split, dropping rocks and dust. Connor and Kara turned to flee, but Lee held them back. "Wait. It's calming."

The shaking stopped. The smooth wall flickered out of view for good. The lightning ceased, and the void sucked the black fog into a flat, lightless face. The river troll dropped to the floor in flopping pieces.

They all looked at each other.

"What of the golmogs?" Lee asked.

"You killed one." Connor walked a pace at a time toward the troll—cautious. He wanted his crook back. "They were linked to the troll. I'm sure of it. Either the portal or this creature's death severed the other golmog's connection. He won't follow."

The arm holding Connor's crook was still connected to the head and most of the torso. He crouched near the troll with his sword ready. The red eyes were open but sightless. "Yeah," Connor said, gingerly pulling his crook from the creature's grasp, "this thing is good and dead."

The portal crackled.

A roaring golmog barreled through the void and crashed into Connor's shield. The impact knocked him flat on his back. But before he could recover his sword, the golmog dropped dead onto its troll companion with a pair of sikaria protruding from its head between the horns.

Connor sat up and looked back at Lee. "Nice throw. Any guesses as to where we are?"

72

ON LEE'S URGING, THE THREE WALKED A GOOD distance down the passage before tending their wounds.

The scribe sat Kara against the wall and placed his Telbeath flask into her hands for a sip. Her eyes traveled, never seeming to focus, and the cadets exchanged a worried glance.

Lee rubbed a balm into her cuts, wrapped her feet with eberlast cut from the lining of his cloak, and bound the wrappings with bandages. "These shoes won't impress any cobblers, but they'll keep your toes warm and dry until we find you some boots."

Kara squinted at his work. "I'm sure they're beautiful. If only I could see them." She felt his arms, then the chest pockets of his kit. "A light would do me some good. Do you happen to have a candle in there?"

"But we have a—"

Connor stopped his friend with a touch. The problem had finally dawned on him. Kara couldn't see the orb of light sent by the Rescuer. And without it, in the cave's present darkness, she couldn't see anything at all.

"A candle," Connor said, nodding to Lee. They both had small holders clipped to their kits. "Yes. We can light a candle for you. We both will." How foolish he'd been. Kara didn't know the Rescuer, didn't trust him. So how could he expect her to see the orb? Like the water reflecting the moon in the cavern, they would have to shine the light for her.

Connor dug out two candles and struck the flames, placing each in a holder, and set them close to Lee to aid his work treating the wound on his calf. No longer needed, the orb winked out of existence.

The scribe wiped away the filthy gray slime on Connor's leg, which eased the throbbing, but then he scrunched his brow. "Hmm."

"Something wrong?"

"No. Quite the opposite. Rattlefish slime is known to poison the blood and reinforce its song sorcery, enhancing the victim's lust for wealth, but I see no evidence of infection here."

Master Jairun had told them each lightraider was prone to certain dark creature infections and resistant to others. "Perhaps we've discovered one of my immunities."

Lee finished the dressing and straightened, stretching his back. "That would explain your success in holding him off. But take care with your words. We may be resistant to a dark creature's sorcery, but not one of us is immune."

They helped Kara up, and she tried her makeshift boots, walking in a circle around them and limping only a little on her cut foot. "Why did the portal trap the troll? Was it lightraider magic?"

"If you mean to ask if it was a gift from the Rescuer," Connor said, "then yes, I think so. The banishing powder trapped the troll, and—" He stopped and patted the empty chest pocket of his kit. "The banishing powder. I lost mine."

"Mine too," Kara said. "I dropped the pouch when I pulled you from the pool." She glanced into the tunnel's darkness, toward the dead creatures. "But, what's to stop us from going back?"

Lee blanched. "Nothing but the smell, I suppose. That troll came apart with the stench of rotting fish. It'll only get worse."

He wasn't wrong. The troll's stink thickened the air near the portal, and the golmog, leaking clear gray fluid, added a certain musk of its own. "Are we ready?" Connor asked, trying not to breathe.

The others nodded. All three raised their blades, just in case, and stepped through.

There was no waterfall and no passage. They emerged from the void in a cavern, much smaller than the underground meadow, though the same blue crystals covered its ceiling. A crevice in the far wall looked out over a black forest choked with fog. Pale green lights flashed within the mist.

A much closer light flickered to life outside their cave and remained steady. It drew nearer, becoming a figure in a ragged cloak, holding forth a lantern. The apparition glided through the crevice and tilted its hooded head, staring at them with empty sockets in a drawn face.

"Back," Lee said. "Back! Into the portal!"

Neither Kara nor Connor needed his prompting. They ran into the void, and Connor took care not to trip over the dead troll or the golmog.

But he needn't have worried. The troll and the golmog were gone.

They'd come through into yet another version of the blue crystal cavern. The roof of this one had more slope to it, with a low flat opening near the floor. Swallowing, Connor crept forward, gravel crunching under his boots, and lowered himself to a knee to peer through the gap. He saw a great lake reflecting the two bright moons, with islands joined by shimmering bridges of light.

No dark creatures attacked this time—a small consolation. "I destabilized the hollow hill," Connor said as Lee came up beside him. "By throwing the powder onto the troll and leading it into the portal, I dislodged the hollow hill from its destinations. We could be anywhere."

He hoped the scribe would argue, assure him what he said was not possible. But Lee only nodded, eyes wide behind his spectacles. "You're right."

"I'd rather I wasn't."

"Still think our escape was a gift from your Rescuer?" Kara asked.

Lee knelt to look out through the gap. "I saw this place on the living map table. Fantasia Shieling. Hundreds of leagues from our goal. Hundreds, Connor. What are we to do?"

"We keep trying." Connor returned to the void. "If it's dislodged, perhaps it's trying to stabilize itself. The two sides may be hopping from hollow hill to hollow hill, but they might soon settle and return to the waterfall cavern."

"Or," said Lee, "the first portal has moved on, leaving us at another.

And this one may return us to the cave with the hooded ghoul. Are we willing to risk such a danger?"

"Do you have a better suggestion, other than walking a few hundred leagues south to the meeting point and hoping our friends are still alive and Keledev is still free when we get there?"

Neither Kara nor Lee gave an answer. Connor took a step toward the black. "All right, then. Let's go."

Lee caught the collar of his tunic. "Wait, my friend. We should pray first."

To Connor's surprise, Kara agreed before he did. She shrugged. "It can't hurt. If your Rescuer did this to help you defeat the rattlefish and the golmogs, can't he return us to the cavern?"

During their struggles at the Shar Razel, Master Jairun had advised the cadets against the pitfalls of a *well-why-not* attitude of prayer, but Connor said nothing about it now. Kara was opening up to belief. Whatever their circumstance, that was one step forward, right? They joined hands and knelt in the cave's gravel. Connor and Lee, each in turn, acknowledged the High One's sovereignty over their path—their very existence. They recognized their failure in not calling on him sooner and asked for his intervention in completing their mission.

While the words *Your ways, High One, not mine* were still falling from the cadets' lips, Kara pulled them both to their feet. She looked up at the blue gems in the ceiling. "And we wouldn't mind if there were no more creatures to attack us when we got back. Thanks." With that, she squeezed their hands. "Deep breath." And they all stepped into the void together.

An instant later, black fog swirled and billowed outward from their party, leaving them standing in a field of snow. No cavern. No portal. Just the snow and the moons. Connor lifted his eyes to the huge Celestial Peaks, hugging his shoulders against the cold. "Well. We're in the southlands again. But where?"

"Does it matter?" Kara sat in the snow. "We're not in the cavern. We can't get you any more banishing powder. I should've. . ." Her voice faded.

Connor glanced down at her. "You should have what?"

She stayed quiet for a moment, then shook her head. "I should've stayed at Hal's place, that's all."

"Faelin. His name is Faelin."

"Whatever."

"She's right about the powder," Lee said, placing his cloak about Kara's shoulders. "We'll never collapse the portal now. The Rescuer is letting us fail." He sat down in the snow beside her. "But why? What did we do wrong?"

Connor had the same question. He looked up at the stars. *We asked for your help. Is this your answer? How can we save my patehpa now?*

The longer he stared, the more the stars seemed to move. They quivered and whirled, growing larger, and descended on the field of snow like star beetles, not far away. "Lee?" Connor asked, unable to tear his eyes away. "Are you seeing this?"

Music. The lights sang a lilting tune with the smoothness of a hundred flutes. Drawn by the sound, the three waded through the deep snow.

"Dynapha," Lee said. "The Rescuer sent faeries to help us."

The lights seemed to acknowledge them and floated toward the party, and as they approached, Connor sensed human forms, held aloft on iridescent butterfly wings.

One of them alighted on Lee's finger. He jerked his hand away. "Ow! It stung me!"

Insects. The creatures had human-like faces and long hair, but they had six limbs, not four, and stingers that shined white. More swept in and landed on the scribe. "Pine sprites," he said in a failing voice, and collapsed unconscious against Kara.

"Lee?" Kara lowered him to the ground.

Connor swung both sword and crook to defend his party, but the big weapons were no use against darting sprites. They swarmed in and hit him with more stings than he could count. He toppled face first into the snow.

73

AWAKE, SLEEPER.

Connor groaned and rolled onto his side. Another early morning at the academy. The straw in his mattress had parted again, leaving him to lie on the hard slab. He'd let Tiran answer the barracks door for once. Let him deal with Swordmaster Quinton.

Awake, Sleeper.

The voice didn't sound like Quinton's. It was soft and close, without the incessant pounding.

"Tehpa?"

Awake, Sleeper.

No. Similar, but not Tehpa. This voice was lighter. Older.

"Connor, wake up. Come back to us."

Us? He groaned again, unwilling to open his eyes. *Leave me alone.*

"He took more stings than Kara and I combined. So much poison."

"I'm surprised it didn't kill him."

"Are you? I'm not. If I may boast, he has my blood. The blood of a lightraider."

Faelin.

Connor's eyes popped open, but a haze made everything gray. He tried sitting up and crashed to the floor again. "Ohh. Where am I?"

"He's awake . . . Sort of."

Connor's throat felt as dry as parchment. "Lee?"

Two sets of hands lifted him and rested his shoulders against cold stone. Blurry faces resolved into Lee and Kara. "Talk to me," the scribe said, supporting Connor's wrist and patting the top of his hand. "Can you feel this? Say something."

"It's . . . only you."

Lee let the hand fall. "Yes, my friend. It's only me."

"I thought I heard my patehpa."

The older voice from before let out a laugh. "You did, child. You did, indeed."

Lee and Kara parted, and Connor saw a door made of iron bars. In the cell across from them, an older man sat with his back against the wall. He looked like the man in Kara's sketch—like the man in the hearth painting. "Faelin. You're alive."

"For now." A smile lifted the beard. "I'm glad you're awake, child. Those stings might've kept Belen down for days. You've only been here a few ticks."

"What is this place?"

"The northwest tower of Vorax's stronghold. I'd say a swarm of blue pine sprites stumbled upon you in the vale and handed you to the dragon's orcs."

"And the orcs took everything," Kara said, backing into the corner. She sank down and lifted an arm to show him the empty space at her belt. She'd lost her money pouch. Connor felt his chest and sides. His kit was gone. Their captors had taken everything but their waterskins. Kara laid her head back and stared at the ceiling. "Your Rescuer has a strange and unsatisfying way of answering prayers."

He knew what this meant to her—without the soot and char to mask her blood. She'd faithfully acted as their guide, and they'd paid her with a death sentence. "Kara, I'm sorry."

"Don't blame yourself. This death was destined for me since the curse of my birth, but I thought I'd have a little comfort from your gold before it found me." She let out a slow breath. "At least those evil bugs only stung me once. You were stung—"

"Fifty times or more," Lee said. "There were so many sprites."

Faelin sat forward, dragging the chains clasped to his wrists across the floor. "There always are. And now we must deal with the poison. Tell me, Connor. What is your heart's desire?"

"I want to be free, of course. To get us home. To sit by the fire and sip cider with my patehpa as I should have done since boyhood." He felt the bite in his voice but didn't care. "I want to forget Tanelethar ever existed."

"No one would begrudge you this—least of all me. But what *should* you desire?"

"Should? What does should have to do with desire?" Just asking the question made his head and limbs hurt all the more. Connor closed his eyes against the pain.

He heard Faelin's chains clinking. "Do you see his suffering, Lee? Sprite poison is both vicious and insidious. It hurts most as we purge it from our spirits. Speak the verses I taught you. Correct him as I corrected you. It's the only way to help him."

Lee took Connor's hand again and laid his own on the back of Connor's neck. "Listen close, my friend, despite your pain. This is a big one. *Hal kashav yi shurnovu–se ca ke'ysofo, dar ke'sofo–po ke'thilsom ratav penah, okeb drachel hal ke'lama. Na hal se dunsev, dar kevash ke'Rumosh belnah.*"

Pay attention. Walk with the wise. Understand his will.

The pain subsided. Connor let out a breath. "I should desire to do the Rescuer's work. I should desire to finish the quest." He opened his eyes and met Faelin's gaze. "But how? We're prisoners. And we've lost everything–our weapons, the banishing powder, our team."

A new voice joined them. "Not your whole team."

"Teegan?" With help from Lee, Connor rose and staggered to the door. Thanks to the curve of the tower passage, when he pressed his face against the iron, he could see Teegan in the next cell over. He flashed a pained grin. “I’m glad to see you.”

“And I, you,” she said and seemed to try her best to return his smile.

Dag’s big hand thrust out beside her, fingers waggling in greeting. “I’m glad to see you, as well. Though I wish we’d met at the cave. Orcs caught us by surprise last night. Aethia managed to dodge them, but not us.”

The other cells within Connor’s vision stood empty. “What of Tiran?”

Teegan moved away from the bars. “He and Pedrig left the cave before we were captured. We’ve no idea if they’re alive or dead.”

“My child,” Faelin said, rattling his chains with a calming gesture. “He’s alive. And so is my wolfish friend. I’m sure of it.”

“If my brehna and Pedrig are alive, then why haven’t they come for us?”

“All in the Rescuer’s time. If it helps to pass the ticks, I suggest you pray. All of you.”

Kara gave Faelin a long, hard look. “Lot of good that did us before.” She returned her gaze to the ceiling and tilted her waterskin for a drink.

Lee jumped up. “Stop, Kara!”

The waterskin hung frozen at her mouth. “Why?”

“Your lips. They’re glistening. Wonderful!”

What had gotten into him? “Lee,” Connor said. “I don’t think this is the time for–”

The scribe hushed him and lowered a lens to examine Kara’s face. “Yes. Truly wonderful.” He gently took the waterskin from her fingers and corked it, then brandished it for Connor as if showing him a crown of pure gold. “Banishing powder. We still have some.”

74

"BANISHING POWDER." LEE TOOK CONNOR'S WATERSKIN and set it beside his and Kara's. "The underground stream carries it from some higher vein, and we filled our skins at the falls."

Dag told them it meant the shairosite acted more like salt than silver. "In Huckleheim we boil water to extract such powders. But with only three small waterskins, you won't get much–a thimbleful, perhaps."

With his shackled wrists resting in his lap, palms open toward heaven, Faelin smiled. "Our Blacksmith can make much from a thimble."

They combined Connor's belt with Lee's as a rope to knock a torch from the passage wall. It held its flame, and Lee managed to hook it and drag it to the cell. "If Vorax is here, why don't we feel him attacking our minds? Isn't that what dragons do"–he wiggled the torch to make the flame jump–"when they're not roasting people for sport?"

"Vorax's mind," Faelin said, "is bent on widening and directing his portal. But every now and again, I hear his thoughts probing. I've been keeping him at bay for all of us."

Connor watched him closely, trying to detect his pupils drifting or some other sign of diverted attention. "You're singing the song, aren't you? Even as you speak with us?"

"In time, you'll learn to do the same, to shield thoughts in battle. Until then, I suggest you flee from any fight with an unburdened dragon." Faelin dumped a moldy piece of bread from a tin plate and rolled it across the passage. "Use that to distill the powder."

Lee removed his boots to balance the plate between them, set the torch beneath, and poured the water a few drops at a time. As it boiled away, it left behind a silver crust. "It's working."

But the work was slow. While he waited, Connor chatted with Teegan and Dag through the wall, catching up on all that had happened.

But Kara took no part in the storytelling. She paced, agitated, and finally settled her forehead against the bars, glowering at Faelin. "Why are you still here? Tell me truly."

The hardness of her question struck Connor. His patehpa merely raised a wrist, showing her the chains.

Kara snorted. "I don't believe for an instant those chains can hold you. At my cottage, you flung a table like a strongman. With a word, you stretched a window into a door. Can't you break those shackles? Can't you make the bars bend to your command?"

"My child, you've seen and heard so much. Now, you're being willfully blind. What a shame."

She slammed her hands against the bars. "I get it. The all-powerful Rescuer did those things for you. He saved me from the orcs." Tears came into her eyes. "Then why couldn't he save my brehnan too?"

"The Rescuer did save Liam. I'm not certain of Keir's story, but Liam knew the High One's love. I saw the light in his eyes, even as life faded."

"Love doesn't watch someone die–not when it has the power to save them." Kara wheeled on Connor, directing her anger at him. "Do you hear me? That's how I know your story is a lie. If your High King had such great love for his son, why would he send him to die in a storm of dragon fire?" She walked to the back, wiping her eyes.

Faelin spoke softly in the quiet that followed. "Please try to understand, Kara. It was not a lesser love that sent a son to die. It was the greatest love of all."

She laid a hand against the wall, head down, and Connor wondered if he should go to her. But in that moment, something white sailed past the bars. He heard Teegan give a delighted cry.

75

CONNOR STRAINED AGAINST THE BARS TO SEE AETHIA check her flight in the tower passage and return to land on Teegan's arm. "Where'd she come from?"

"Doesn't matter," Teegan said, easing the falcon into her cell. "She's here."

Dag appeared beside her at their door. "It does matter. If the orcs or goblins saw her, they may come running. Lee hasn't finished distilling the powder."

"Wrong," Lee said. "I have."

The scribe pulled on his boots and offered Connor a wool stocking weighed down by a clump at the toe. "I scraped the powder into my sock for safekeeping."

"It's more than a thimbleful for sure." Connor held it up to his eyes but kept his nose well back. "About a half pouch, I'd say. But will it be enough?"

"If it isn't, we may have to kill the dragon," Faelin said. "His mind is steering it, widening it. If we remove his influence, a small amount of powder may do the job."

Kara lifted her head with a harsh laugh. "Aren't you forgetting something? We're still locked in a tower, and your Blacksmith hasn't seen fit to break these locks."

Faelin stood to his full height, until his chains went taut, and cracked his neck from side to side. "Have faith, child."

Three orcs came trundling down the passage. As Dag surmised, they must have spotted the falcon flying into the tower. They grumbled in their perverted Elder Tongue, gargoyle faces bobbing before the bars, searching each cell. None seemed to spot Aethia, hidden behind Dag's large form.

But the one gawking at Connor and Lee saw the plate and the smoking torch at their feet. Its runes flared, and it opened its mouth for a roar.

An arrow passed clean through its ugly head before it could utter a sound.

The orc fell. And as its two companions turned to face a threat Connor couldn't see, Faelin spoke a sacred verse. Light flashed. The orcs reeled. One crashed into the bars, and Connor wrapped an arm around its neck, gritting his teeth against the heat from its runes. The other went down, dragged to the floor by a wolf's powerful jaws. Pedrig, teeth glowing with pine-green Havarra armor, backed away a moment later and spat out sizzling molten blood.

The last orc struggled against Connor's hold, clawing at his arm. Only by Connor's Keledan armor was he spared terrible wounds.

Tiran shoved his sword through the creature's side and nodded for Connor to let it drop. "These three saw Aethia from the ramparts. More may come. We should leave."

Teegan appeared at her bars with Aethia on her arm. "We'd love to. Did you bring us a key, Brehna?"

"Do I have to think of everything, Shessa?"

"Well, you might have thought of that."

"I did. But your dumb bird rushed the plan."

Faelin stood at the front of his cell scratching Pedrig's ears through the bars—a gesture Connor doubted the wolf would accept from anyone else. His shackles lay open on the floor. Wolf and lightraider bowed their heads and spoke the Elder Tongue in unison. "*Ond shelendni esanthi mi ke'hosala yi declah po yi ke'orba restefel bi kazon, ke'oprala ya liberend.*"

Release for the captives. Sight for the blind. Freedom for the oppressed.

The doors of every cell swung open.

Faelin's eyes twinkled at Connor. "His timing. Not ours."

"What about our weapons?" Lee asked. "They took them."

"But not far." Dag shouldered his way past Tiran and led the group toward the tower stairs. "When they brought us in, they dumped our weapons in the first cell."

The door stood open. Their kits and arms were there. Faelin secured a dagger and crossbow to his belt. "Take only what you need for battle. If we survive, the Rescuer will provide the rest."

"If?" Lee asked.

"To live is him, child. To die is gain."

Lee nodded, though he looked no more encouraged than before, staring down into an empty quiver.

Tiran unshouldered his own. "Use mine. I'll stick with a sword."

They found three Telbeath flasks among the scattered gear. Connor took a long draught, and turned to pass it on. "Kara, you should–"

She wasn't there.

He looked around. "Where's Kara?"

None of them had seen her since the short fight with the orcs. Connor shoved Faelin's sword into his belt and ran with his crook along the curving passage. He expected to find orcs and goblins pinning her in the cell. Instead, he found her alone, facing the back. She'd pushed the bars closed again.

Faelin strode up beside him. "Kara, come out of there."

"I won't. It's safer in here. Don't you see?"

"No, it isn't," Connor said. "The orcs may hurt you in their rage if they find you alone. And destroying the portal may bring this entire stronghold down. Please, come with us."

She shook her head. "If I die in this fight, I'll feel the second death you spoke of. I'm Aladoth, Connor. I do not have the twiceborn gift of the Keledan."

He didn't know how to respond.

Faelin answered her for him. "That is up to you, Kara. The Keledan are not a race but a people—a family with one loving father. The Scrolls say, *Dar yi koth vyk mod nabolend, ya koth vyk aler numod credend, ke'priveg yo hal tafa bo Rumosh lod gevend.* To all who receive him, he gives the right to become his children." He pushed open the door. "The choice to accept this gift is yours."

"Orcs!" Tiran appeared at the passage curve with Dag. "We heard them on the stairs, likely coming to see what happened to the others. If they sound the alarm, dark creatures will flood this tower. We'll never get out."

"Come, child," Faelin said. "It's now or never."

For a moment she stood there, unmoving. But then she turned and gave him her hand. He passed it to Connor. "Good. Now, Tiran, did you see another way out from the stairwell?"

"One floor down, an archway opens to the battlements. It's how we got in."

Three orcs met their party on the steps. Aethia clawed at their heads, and Dag and Tiran fought them until the others reached the archway to the battlements. Once the rest were through, the two boys lured the orcs into the open and dove clear. Faelin and Lee pelted them with bolts and arrows.

All eight crouched low to escape the eyes of the goblins and orcs in the valley. Teegan nodded toward the scaffolding and the laboring goblins to the south. "They're sure to notice us soon. We must keep moving. Where's the portal?"

Faelin pulled a smoldering bolt from an orc's eye and used it to point to the four pyranium spires around the high dome, beset with pulleys and chains. "That is a dragon gate. The workings open the dome so the dragon may leave and enter his throne room at will. Vorax's throne will be directly beneath. The portal will be near him. But we need a way in."

"There," Connor said, looking toward a wing joining a corner of the inner diamond to the outer bulwarks. The gravel walkway on top served as a bridge, and the shadowed archway at its end promised access to the interior. "I'd say that's our best chance."

The stronghold's great size left them two hundred paces or more to run, with the whole course in view of the laboring frost goblins. The party had not yet reached the bridge when screeches and shrieks erupted from the scaffolding. Workers swarmed the ramparts, wielding hammers and knives.

"So much for surprise." Dag sprinted ahead with a twirl of his axes. "Now it's a foot race."

Faelin and Lee arced their shots over the lumbering miner and dropped four goblins, log-jamming the walkway with bodies to slow the incoming tide. But goblins make for poor dams. Their cousins ran over them and kicked them from the wall. The fastest creatures reached the bridge before Dag.

The miner hit the leaders at full stride and swinging hard. But some took to the wall itself, crawling around him with their sticky fungal hands.

When the rest of the party were on the bridge, Faelin called out to him. "Your job is done! Fall back. Pedrig, help him!"

The wolf uttered a prayer and let out an echoing bark. A sphere the same pine color as his armor hurtled over Dag into the goblins and burst into flame. The creatures within its reach unraveled into boiling lichen.

"Well done!" Dag said, retreating. "I never—"

A black arrow sank into his shoulder.

He fell into Faelin's and Tiran's arms, breath coming in ragged gasps. "They had tools . . . not bows. Where . . . did that come from?"

Connor pressed his body against the parapets and looked below. Orcs flooded the courtyard between the keep and the outer wall—more orcs than he could count.

76

MISSILES FROM THE NORTH AND SOUTH, FAR LARGER than goblin arrows, sailed past the lightraiders. Tiran and Lee bolstered Dag between them, giving all their attention to their shields, while Faelin and Pedrig dealt with the frost goblins attacking from the ramparts. Some crawled past them along the side and leapt over the parapets to bar their way. With crook and trident, Connor and Teegan sent them flying to the courtyards below.

Connor hooked the neck of the last creature in their path and thrust him from the wall, then rushed into the long archway. He found a closed pyranium door, too heavy to break down. He tried pulling on its ring. "It's locked. We're trapped."

Faelin fired another bolt. "Are you sure? Try again."

By now, he knew better than to question the old warrior. Connor gave the ring another tug, sensing dim white sparks at the edges. The door swung open. Faelin caught his eye as he ushered the raid party inside. "How often must he answer before you give him all your trust?"

Teegan came through last. She whispered to her falcon, and Aethia launched into the air. Then she slammed the door closed and dropped the bar. "I don't want her in here with a dragon. We'll find her in the woods when this is over."

The passage they'd found ran the diamond's perimeter–an archer's loop with arrowslits letting in the winter sun. Lee and Tiran sat Dag against the wall between the shafts of light. He fought them, eyes burning. "Let me out there. I'll kill them all."

"Stop, Dag," Lee said. "I can't deal with the arrow if you won't be still."

Kara and Teegan rushed to help, while Faelin stared out through an arrowslit. "Orc poison. The rage is setting in. Do you know what the Scrolls say of human wrath and futility?"

Lee opened his mouth to reply, but Faelin waved his answer away. "Tell it to your wounded friend. Let the verses soothe his spirit. Pedrig will guide you."

With the wolf and the others helping Dag, Connor had his first moment alone with Faelin. He could hold his questions in no longer. "Why, Patehpa. Why did you do it?"

"Why did I do what, child?"

A cry from Dag interrupted them, as Lee snapped the arrow shaft. Connor winced. Not only did he hate to hear Dag suffer, but the noise might bring the inner keep's guards down upon them. "Why did you let us all think you were dead? Why do that to Tehpa. Why do it to me? Master Jairun must've spoken of my birth in his letters."

Creatures pounded against the pyranium door. Missiles clicked off the stones around the arrowslit. "Does he blame me?" Faelin asked. "Edwin, I mean."

"He doesn't even know you're alive."

This earned Connor a quiet laugh. "Yes, boy. He does."

He knew. Tehpa knew. Connor felt the wind knocked out of him as sure as if an orc had jabbed him with the butt of its halberd. "But he told me he thought you were dead."

"For a time, he did. Until Avner settled an arrangement with a few key leaders in the Assembly. And when Edwin married Mara, he told them both. She tempers him, makes him less rash."

"And me? Why couldn't I know?"

Faelin inclined his head, looking Connor straight in the eye. "You are young, and my work here must remain secret. There are still some from Keledev who enter Tanelethar and might betray me to the dragons. Not all who are born there choose the gift. You know this."

"The ships," Connor said.

Faelin nodded.

Looking past his patehpa's shoulder, Connor watched his friends help Dag up. Lee had bandaged the wound and strapped the miner's arm to his chest. Dag could stand, and perhaps wield an axe, but Connor doubted he'd survive another charge into a horde of goblins.

Scouting along the archer's loop, Tiran found an intersecting tunnel. He signaled the others, waiting for them to catch up. "A passage. Short, only ten paces or so. Two orcs guard the other end. I think it leads to the throne room."

"If so," Pedrig said, "there'll be more orcs inside. Or golmogs." He let out a low wolf chuckle. "Or both."

"And a dragon," Lee added. "Don't forget the dragon."

"He hasn't, I can assure you." Faelin knelt, gathering them close to him. "The creature you are about to face walks the boundary between flesh and spirit. This particular variety is a gaze dragon, able to cripple a man with its stare. It is not a thing a human may face alone and live. So, hold to one another and the Rescuer in heart, mind, and soul. Can you do that?"

Connor glanced around to meet the eyes of his worn and battered companions. They all gave him nods, even Kara, and he spoke on their behalf. "We can."

"Good. Now, all together, the Rescuer is with us."

They cadets and Pedrig replied in unison, "Always and forever." And then they crept into the passage.

77

TIRAN AND CONNOR SNUCK UP TO THE ORC GUARDS, rammed their swords through their backs, and dragged them into the passage. With their path clear, the party hurried to the throne room, and Connor almost pitched over the edge of a walkway four paces wide. He caught a column to stop his fall.

Three stories of columned walkways ran the perimeter of a vast chamber. Above these, for three more stories at least, were smooth white walls etched with a thousand golden runes. And below, in the chamber floor, a black well.

The party spread out along the walkway, taking cover in twos behind wide columns. Connor stayed close to Kara as Faelin had commanded, unable to take his eyes from the vortex. The emptiness roiled with the same black fog and arcs of purple he'd seen before. The goblin builders had constructed a stepped circle leading down to the void, but ten paces of bare soil separated the bottom step from the edge of the black. Room to grow. The void pushed ever outward, reaching for this boundary, almost large enough for the dragon.

"Is it asleep?" Kara whispered.

Faelin had warned them not to look the dragon in the eye, or anywhere near its head, but Connor risked a glance. A pyranium bed cushioned with gold silk hung beneath the dragon gate in the chamber's southern half. And on it lay curled a dragon as black as the void beneath.

Wings tipped with red stirred, and smoke curled from its

nostrils. Connor heard a smooth and pleasing voice in his head. *Welcome young king. Welcome to you and your father's father. He is proud. Your royal line will make a handsome coupling with a queensblood.*

"No," he said to Kara. "The dragon's awake. And confused."

Connor knew his ancestry. The Enarians had always been shepherds. Both trolls had suffered the same delusion of Connor's royal heritage, and now the dragon. Walking with Kara beside him, a queensblood, must have befuddled their senses. He hummed *The Sleeper's Hope* to keep Vorax out.

Tiran widened his eyes at Connor from three columns away. "Throw the powder. Do it now, and let's be done."

But Faelin held out a warning hand. "Patience. One puff of flame, and the powder's gone. From this height, the dragon has too much time to react. The shairosite will never make it to the void."

The colonnades were not empty. Orcs with halberds stood in many archways, guarding all entrances to the chamber. None of them moved. "They must see us," Lee said. "What are they waiting for?"

"They wait for me, fisher-scribe!" a sniveling creature called to them from a platform beneath the dragon's hanging throne. "They wait for me. For me!"

The goblin, robed in green leather, held a red jasper cane like a scepter, as if he himself were controlling the void. "For me. For me! The orcs wait for my orders. Did you think we did not smell your Keledan filth–your *filth*–from the mountainside? Did you think our keen eyes could not see you coming? Did you? Did you? We let you in. Gave you comfort in our tower. Permitted you an audience here out of respect for royal–"

"Silence, fungus!" Pedrig barked, ears flat and tail bristling. "Go back to your cave. This fight is beyond you."

"You do not command me, Havarra abomination. Abominable wolf. I am Malid, chieftain of the Highland clans and servant of

Lord Vorax the Unquenchable. I am his eyes, his ears, his great and wondrous nos–"

An arrow pierced the goblin's head. It teetered for a moment, then tumbled down the well steps and rolled into the void.

Tiran returned Lee's bow and shrugged. "I had to. I feared his prattling would never cease."

Faelin raised his voice. "You want to speak to us, Vorax? Then rouse yourself and speak."

The portal storm settled to a low simmer. The red-tipped wings unfurled, and the tail slid away from the dragon's great head.

"That's done it." Faelin abandoned his column and pushed Connor into a run. "Move!"

The party split into fours, making for the staircases. The orcs guarding the archways left their posts to chase them.

The first orc to challenge Connor met him on the steps, thrusting upward with its halberd. Connor parried with his crook, and with a counterthrust, he knocked it back into its comrade. The two orcs lost their footing and fell, smashing into the chamber floor. He raced on, but as he prepared to engage another pair, he felt the air heating up.

Faelin shouted behind him. "Beware the dragon!"

The warning had not been for Connor. Ducking a halberd and looking back, he saw a stream of fire rush over Lee and Dag, who'd been separated from Teegan and Tiran on the second level. They rolled out of the way behind two columns, shields glowing hot, while the orcs attacking them howled and crumpled into heaps of smoldering rock.

"Lee!" Connor shouted. "Are you all right?"

"Yes!" The scribe waved his bow with a whoop of relief. "My first dragon–"

The ledge beneath him crumbled, and he and Dag fell amid a cascade of blackened rubble.

Connor tried to go to them, but Kara caught his shoulder. Fire split the air between him and his friends. He ducked behind his shield, feeling the heat from the edge of the stream.

Teegan and Tiran were closer and rushed to help, while the others drew Vorax's attention. Connor and Kara made for the last set of stairs to the chamber floor with Faelin and Pedrig. Faelin fired a bolt on the run, but the dragon knocked the missile away with its tail.

Below, Connor saw the twins pull Lee and Dag from the rubble. Both were bleeding and limping. Orcs came at them from the lowest arches. Hampered by the effort of keeping their friends upright, Teegan and Tiran fought the creatures in a losing retreat, out into the open.

Another orc came at Connor. He rushed the oncoming halberd with his shield and snapped it in two, then shoved his sword through the orc's neck. As the creature fell, Connor saw his four friends on the well steps, hard-pressed by the orcs. Tentacles of black smoke reached from the simmering void. One by one, they ensnared Teegan, Tiran, Lee, and Dag and dragged them into the vortex. In a ripple of purple flashes, they were gone.

Vorax's laughter shook the air. "You brought a pack of children and a dying dog, old man. Did you really think they'd be a match for me?"

The song in Connor's mind had ceased. He heard the dragon's voice in its place. *Do not worry for your friends, young prince. I sent them home to their academy–straight into its thickest bulwark.*

"Don't listen, Connor," Faelin said, as if hearing the same thoughts. "A dragon feeds its sorcery with lies."

Serve me, boy. You need not die like your friends. Your ancestors bowed to Ras Pyras. Bow as well, and you and the queensblood can rule here together. As my tribute, I'll send this old man home to his boy.

Connor turned his back to the column, fighting for breath. His friends–the entire class of initiates meant to restore the Lightraider Order–were dead. What had it all been for?

Kara grasped Connor's arm. "What's happening? I don't understand."

Yes, young prince. Too much death. Too much waste. But you can stop it. Serve me. Swear allegiance to my master and the Red Throne.

Connor stepped out to face the dragon but kept his eyes from meeting its gaze. "No! My allegiance is to the High One and his Rescuer!"

"Then die in your allegiance." The dragon rose from its bed on massive wings. "It is time for me to end this."

Heat burned the air ahead of the flames. Connor spun back to the column and wrapped his arms around Kara. *Protect her with your shield. Protect us both.*

She screamed, though he barely heard it over the fire's rush. His shield glowed all around him as it had when he first hit the water at Ras Telesar and again at the crystal meadow. He felt like a roast in one of Belen's great ovens.

The flames ended. Kara looked up at him, unsinged. And then Connor heard a great, disheartening groan.

The huge doors of the keep–six stories of pyranium–opened to the light of day.

An army of orcs marched in.

78

"TRUST HIM, CONNOR," FAELIN CALLED TO HIM. "THE Rescuer is with us!"

With the rhythmic stomp of the orcs approaching, Connor tucked his sword into his belt and pulled out the old sock of banishing powder. He hefted it in his hand. "Do we have enough?"

Still pressed at his front, Kara gave him a resigned smile. "With this, we do." From a fold of her tunic, she produced a full pouch. "I never dropped mine. With the troll and golmogs dead, I thought you could return to the cavern and get more. Who would be the wiser? This stuff is more valuable than gold."

"And when we were captured?"

"I thought I'd use it to buy my way out of trouble. Even in our cell, I told myself this bag of priceless powder could save me. But that was always a lie, wasn't it?" Kara let out a quiet laugh, meeting his eye, then placed the pouch in his hand and bolted from his side.

"Kara!"

The dragon's head cranked her way, and Connor felt heat on the air.

Emerging from his hiding place, Pedrig barked at the vile creature. "Look to me, you worthless, traitorous wyrm!" He ran, limping in the opposite direction of the youth. "Look to me!"

The dragon roared, turning from the girl to the wolf. "Lame Havarra dog. Die!"

With the dragon's attention divided, Connor raced up the middle to the well and dumped the sock and the pouch into the void.

The silver powder swirled into glowing lines, sparking and crackling.

At the edge of his vision, he saw Pedrig slide on all fours into an archway, dodging the worst of the dragon's fire. His pine-green armor absorbed the rest. Across the chamber Kara reached the stairway leading up through the colonnades to the gears of the dragon gate and hid beneath the steps.

Curls of black fog spat high from the well, and the lightning within boiled to a new fury. The castle shook, knocking Connor from his feet.

"Banishing powder," the dragon growled. "What have you done, boy?"

The void retracted, and the well fractured and split. Fragments of gold runes rained down amid a terrible rending of stone and metal. The orcs stopped their advance, gargoyle eyes fighting to see upward into broadening daylight as a fissure ran across the ceiling. When it reached the jawlike pyranium doors, their hinges snapped. They toppled over and silenced the howling orcs under their crushing weight.

Great hunks of stone from the walls and roof followed. Connor ducked beneath his shield, feeling it vibrate under the impacts. He couldn't see Kara through the dust and debris. "Save her," he whispered.

When the quake passed, two of the chains supporting the dragon's throne had broken free, leaving it to hang awkwardly under the partially open dome. Dust hung in the daylight streaming down through the shattered roof. Faelin had run to Connor in the chaos, and the two crouched together behind a pile of plaster and stone.

The dragon landed on the well's boundary, breaking the steps with its talons, and bent its great head low over the void. Tremors, almost imperceptible, still troubled the ground, and lines of glittering shairosite powder spiraled in the black. But the dragon's will seemed to hold the portal in check.

"Old man. Lightraider who was. Neither you nor your son's son can overpower my spirit with any craft from the crust of this world. Your quest is ended. A failure. And soon I will wreak a long-deserved havoc on the lands of your despot king."

Much of the northern quarter of the diamond had caved in, burying the orc army. The guards lay under broken columns and crumbled walkways. Not one moved. Connor saw Kara peeking out from her stairwell shelter, but he could find no sign of Pedrig.

"I watched your mother scream, boy. I felt my teeth bite into your father through the mind of the goblin you killed. Yes, boy. All I do is by design. I drew those mindless toadstools into the void to be my scouts, and I saw your people. The Keledan are weak, cowering within their borders. There are no watchmen at the gate."

"You're wrong," Faelin said. "The Rescuer has restored the Order. In him, the lightraiders will stand."

A blast of flame hit their pile of rubble. Connor winced against the searing heat. His shield flickered.

The dragon laughed. "Did you not hear me? Did you not see? I sent the new hope of your Lightraider Order to their deaths. Such waste. Like your ewe, boy. Remember the cuts, the suffering? Dear Shepherd, prepare. My armies are coming for your flock."

A black tail swung their way. Faelin grabbed Connor's tunic and pulled him away as the dragon obliterated their shelter. The force of the blow knocked them apart and sent them sliding into the debris. Connor scrambled for cover behind a fallen wedge of ceiling. "Patehpa?"

"I'm here, Connor." Faelin had found a ruined column a few paces away.

"And me." Kara caught his eye and directed his gaze up to the broken dragon gate and its tattered system of gears and chains. It took Connor only a moment to work out the plan she had in mind. They could do this.

He hummed the song. Kara and Faelin hummed too.

"Silence!" Vorax swept his tail across the rubble but only succeeded in sending a few stones flying over their heads. "Heresy! Tyranny!"

More than shut him out, the song seemed to pain him.

The Sleeper wakes by a meadow stream,

On a path of gold 'neath the silver gleam

Of the stars up in the heavens.

The gears that parted the dragon gate dome also raised and lowered the throne, which now swung by its last two chains. If Connor and Kara could get up the stairs to the main crank, they might bring the throne down on Vorax's back. They could knock him into the unstable portal. But would a storm filled with banishing powder kill the dragon as it had killed the troll?

Child beckons. Follow me,

To the mountaintop by the crystal sea.

Field Mouse rides on Leopard's back.

Brown Bear strolls 'tween Cow and Calf.

Faelin seemed to read the looks that passed between the other two. With a sad smile, he nodded his understanding.

Connor scrunched his brow at his patehpa. Why the sadness? Then he saw the flaw in the plan. One of them had to keep the dragon distracted while the others went up the stairs–a long and deadly confrontation.

Faelin crawled through the rubble, working his way toward an open patch of chamber floor near the well. The song hung between them as he went.

Wolf walks side by side with Boar.

Child laughs as Lion roars.

And the Sleeper wonders, Where are all the dragons?

"Stop!" Connor shouted. "We'll find another way. We came here to rescue you!"

"I don't need rescuing. My eternity awaits, child." Faelin

walked into the open on the descending steps of the well and pointed at Kara. "Don't you see? The Rescuer brought you here to rescue her, not me. Kara was your mission all along!"

The dragon attacked.

Connor ran to Kara, and together they took the steps two at a time.

Faelin sang in a bright and booming voice.

All creatures flock to fire's ring,

Where Lion bows, for Lamb is king.

Lamb cries, Joy, goodwill, and peace!

Let battles end. Let all wars cease.

Talons came at him from both sides and sparked off a sphere of deep blue light etched with gold. Faelin walked the rim of the void, taking each blow. Looking on as he ran, Connor saw the knight from his dream, armor blazing, stepping between him and the dragon.

But the image wasn't quite the same. Connor felt for the blade tucked in his belt and touched the purple starlot in its hilt—the token of a lightraider. The knight marching to face the dragon needed his weapon, a weapon kept safe for him across two generations.

"Patehpa!" Connor hurled the sword down from the stairs.

Faelin caught it, raised his eyes to absorb the dragon's crippling gaze, and kept singing.

Banish dark with light divine.

Let fire dim. Let starlight shine.

Let thunder fade. Let storm clouds break.

A stream of flame blazed over the storm. The lightraider's shield held firm under the onslaught.

Connor reached the crank ahead of Kara and found it locked in place by a monstrous hook and peg designed for a golmog's hands. He shoved his spike under the hook and hung from the crook's shaft, hoping to lever it free. "Help me, Kara!"

They pulled with their collective weight. The hook moved a

hair's breadth, then another. Connor prayed. *Only with you can we succeed.*

Instead of moving, the hook fractured and broke free. The crank spun wild, screaming, and the dragon's throne crashed down onto its back, tangling its wings with the chains.

Faelin leapt across the storm. From the other side of the well, a beacon of pine green and silver shot into the air–Pedrig in his full Havarra armor, teeth bared.

Above the dragon's rage and the clatter of the chains, Connor heard his patehpa whisper the last words of the song.

Let Watchman rest.

Let the Sleeper wake.

Wolf and wolf soldier fell upon the beast together. Pedrig locked his jaws into the dragon's burning throat, while Faelin plunged a sword into its flank. All three vanished into the roiling storm.

79

WITH A BLINDING FLASH AND A CLAP OF THUNDER, THE portal closed. Silence descended on the dragon's keep, except for a chain falling to the bare soil at the well's center.

Connor and Kara held each other in the quiet, until he heard the creak and whine of protesting metal above. One half of the dragon gate dome–the half almost straight above them–broke free of its housing and dropped.

Kara yanked Connor close to the broken plaster as the pyranium dome smashed through their platform on its way to the floor. The quaking returned. The whole place was coming down.

Drawn by the falling dome, a chain whizzed past on its way up through a pulley on one of the dragon gate's four spires. With a great leap, they both caught it and sailed up together.

"Get ready," Connor said, watching daylight approach. "Now!" They jumped free and rolled across the shaking roof.

Once they had their feet again, they ran, dodging the cracks opening before them. Swaying platforms meant for goblin laborers gave them a path down to a walkway atop the eastern wing, and from there, they made it to the outer bulwark and the steps to the valley floor.

They encountered only one dark creature in their flight–a frost goblin on the bulwark, bald with feathered white fungus for eyebrows. It looked as surprised to see two humans as it was to be caught in a quake. Connor leveled the spike of his crook without breaking stride, and the creature threw itself from the wall.

Not until Connor and Kara had climbed the ridge slope to a rock outcropping did they stop to look back. The stronghold–every wall and tower–caved into the orc and goblin tunnels beneath it.

As the shaking settled, a white falcon fluttered to the ground at Connor's feet, chuffing in concern. Connor watched her for a time, searching for her mistress, then fell to his knees and wept.

They were gone. His friends. Pedrig. The patehpa he'd waited his whole life to know.

Kara dropped beside him and pressed her cheek, wet with tears, against his temple. "I see it now."

He fought to gain control of his voice. "What do you see?"

"You loved your patehpa so much. You suffered. The dragon took your friends and taunted you with their death. You had only Faelin in that moment, but you let him sacrifice himself to save me. You gave him up out of love for another."

Connor nodded, but he wasn't sure he understood.

Kara smiled through her tears. "Don't you get it? You're a boy who gave up his patehpa, like the king who gave up his sehna. I understand now. I believe the Blacksmith's story." She moved to his front and lifted his chin. "I'm ready to accept his gift."

Connor saw the life in her eyes. A new life. Had Kara been the mission the whole time, just as Faelin said? On their knees in the snow, shivering but joyful, they bent their heads together and spoke a prayer the guardians had taught Connor and his friends. As they finished, a pine sapling sprang up into a broad bristlecone tree. A portal, glowing with the gold of a lantern, opened in its knotted trunk. Connor shook his head. "So, Belen was right."

"How so?"

"He told us that when a portal is destroyed, another pops up somewhere else, like when you squash a wrinkle in a blanket. I think the Rescuer made the best of this one."

They walked together to the opening, but Kara hesitated. "Where will it take us?"

"Home," he said. "A hollow tree will take us home."

EPILOGUE

GOLD DISSOLVED TO SOFT GREEN, AND THE COLD GAVE way to warmth up to Connor's knees. Aethia passed over him and Kara to fly off into a forest of spruce and oaks, lightly dusted with snow. "This is not Lake Charity," he said, helping Kara to the shore of a small pool. "Nor any of the Passage Lakes. But the trees look familiar."

They both stepped with dry feet onto the grass. The air here was cool, but not frigid, far warmer than any mountain air deserved to be in winter. Looking higher, past the trees, Connor saw a high rock wall with switchbacks leading to a staircase. "This is the Forest of Believing. The hollow tree brought us to Ras Telesar."

"Your academy?"

"We're on its grounds. There's a glade at the top of those stairs, and . . ." His voice faltered as his eyes fell on a sword jammed into the soil not far up the path. A purple jewel glinted from the pommel. Connor ran to the spot and pulled it up. "Faelin's sword, Kara. It's my patehpa's sword!" He scanned the trees. "Patehpa? Faelin!"

"He's not here, son of winter." The words were sad–a labored growl. Pedrig hobbled out from the shadow of a spruce. "I searched the forest to be sure, but I've lost his scent. My friend–your grandfather–has moved on."

Connor felt the tears welling up again, but the wolf lifted his sagging tail and shifted his ears forward. "Be at peace. For I am. Faelin has gone to *Elamhavar,* the house of eternal joy, which is hope to us all. Our master prepared a table for him even as he fought the beast within the storm."

Pedrig laid a paw on the blade in Connor's hands. "He willed that you should have this, else it would not have come through the portal. This sword is now a dragonslayer and will have a place of honor within the Order. As it's bearer, you must give it a name."

They said little more, until they came to an oak near the sheer wall to the north and found Aethia hopping from branch to branch, chuffing at a squirrel hole. Something inside answered with an exasperated chirp.

Kara peeked into the hole and laughed. "That's no squirrel, Aethia. And he's only a half morsel. Are you sure you want him?"

She moved aside to let Connor look, and an orange face peered out at him. The creature chirped again and spun in a circle–a tailless orange paradragon. Connor scooped him out and held him in his palm, stroking his head. "So, Aethia didn't eat you on the day when we rode to Mer Nimbar. She only got your tail. Quite a trick. The two of you had us fooled."

The paradragon chirped at Aethia, who chuffed back, then stopped and cocked her head. She let out a cry and launched skyward.

Pedrig lifted his black nose to the breeze and sniffed. "Can it be?"

"Connor!"

Connor's knees nearly buckled at the voice. Teegan waved to him from high among the switchbacks and held out her other arm for her bird. Aethia bent her feathered head to nuzzle her mistress's nose then flew off again to soar over the forest.

"Aethia is happy to be back in her favorite hunting ground," Connor told the paradragon, returning it to the hole in the oak. "I'd advise you to stay in there for a while."

Teegan met them on the switchbacks. Connor told her of the dragon and Faelin, then hugged her tight. "Vorax told us you were dead."

"You shouldn't have believed him," she said with a shrug. "Dragons are liars. We landed on the front lawn like drops of rain."

"And how is Tiran? And Lee and Dag?"

"Bruised and broken, but Master Jairun is seeing to them. They'll mend."

Pedrig allowed Teegan a kneeling hug, which he soon most surely regretted. Teegan buried her face in his fur and squeezed until he let out a quiet yelp. He coughed and growled. "Please forgive my outburst, daughter of autumn, but I did just battle a dragon." He paused to look down the trail past Connor. "As did we all."

Kara had stepped a pace back from the others, eyes downcast, tugging her sleeves to her knuckles.

Connor met Teegan's expectant gaze and told her what she must have surmised already, but it felt good to say it out loud. "Kara accepted the Rescuer's gift, Teegan. She is Keledan now."

A heartbeat passed in silence. Then Teegan clapped her hands and hugged Kara as she'd hugged Connor and the wolf. "Welcome to Keledev. Home of the Twiceborn. In the Common Tongue, we call it the Liberated Land because the Rescuer set us free."

The force of her greeting caused Kara's sleeves to shift and expose the flourishes of blue-gray freckles on her hands. With an embarrassed smile, she tugged the sleeves into place again and brushed her platinum hair down over her cheeks.

Connor tried to explain, but Teegan stopped him. "I have freckles too," she said, sliding her arm into Kara's and leading her past Connor and the wolf, on up the switchbacks. "Mine are not as dangerous, I know. But there are days I don't like them–not at all–and days I love them. Whether I like them or not from day to day, I know I never have to hide them. And guess what? Here in the Liberated Land, you never have to hide yours either."

At the barracks, the cadets nursed their wounds and recounted all they'd seen to the guardians, including a fourth–Dame Silvana, who'd come to help protect Ras Telesar while they were gone.

The diminutive Silvana paced before the cadets, stroking a long gray braid bound with leather. "Shoddy work, that's what you lot are. Shoddy work, indeed. The result of disorganized instruction." She made a *tsk* sound, frowning down at Lee and Dag, who lay recovering in their beds. "The Rescuer might as well have sent the village cats on a raid. I suppose I'll have to stay and sort you out." Her hard gaze shifted to the other three guardians, huddled together in the corner. "And I'll sort you lot out as well."

The guardians had slain more than a dozen orcs and goblins during the cadets' absence. And not long before Teegan and the others returned, a strange item had come through. A red jasper cane topped with a jade ball and collared with diamonds had sprouted from a parapet on the lowest ramparts. When they heard this, the cadets insisted there might be a rotting cave goblin inside, still clutching the cane. But none wanted to crack the wall open and find out.

In the following days, Connor spent many a tick with Lee and Dag, bringing them meals and sitting with them in the barracks—Lee especially, because he'd broken his leg. But Teegan proved the scribe's most attentive nurse. In the evenings, the two sat on the balcony, while Aethia flew over the glade. They played at spotting the first stars of night or naming the constellations. Lee often twisted the cobalt ring about his finger, but if he told Teegan its story, Connor didn't hear.

On those evenings, rather than disturb them, Connor walked the ramparts with Kara. Forge was almost upon them, and he wanted to share with her the festival's many traditions.

"This is how the Great Rescue began," he told her on one of their early walks. "With the humble birth of a blacksmith's child at home in his tiny forge."

Kara lifted her eyes to the uppermost wall, where Tiran pushed a cart of lanterns, helping Belen and Quinton hang them from the battlements. "And what of those?"

Tiran occasionally dabbed his forehead with his rag, speaking in earnest to the guardians, and Connor suspected they were discussing topics far deeper than festival illuminations. "Those lanterns represent the Miracle of Candles. On the night of our Blacksmith's birth, every standing candle in his mountain village took flame of its own accord. Wax and wick together declared the arrival of a king, because the villagers were blind to his coming."

They watched Belen lean precariously over a parapet, with Quinton holding the hood of his robe. "So," Kara said, "on the night of his birth, the Rescuer brought light to the world."

"And the Order continues that work. This is why we want the Assembly's blessing to rebuild and send raids across the barrier again." His words disturbed her, Connor could tell. But he didn't press her until they turned back toward the barracks. "Kara, something's troubling you. I can feel it."

"It's nothing."

"Something is never nothing. And Keledan are supposed to be truthful, if you hadn't heard. Let me help if I can."

She slowed on a stairway, then stopped to face him from the step below. "I want to be a lightraider, Connor. I want to go on raids with you, back into Tanelethar. But I'm not sure my reason is the right one."

"What reason is that?"

"The trolls and the dragon, I heard them in my mind. And the things they said . . ." She looked away.

Connor's throat went dry. He knew what they'd said. A royal pair. A king and queen. What an offense that must have been to Kara, to presume he'd claim her as a bride. He scratched the back of his neck. "I wouldn't concern yourself. As my patehpa said, dragons feed on lies. And trolls echo their deceit. Whatever they said about you and me–"

"You and me?" She wrinkled her nose. "They said nothing about just you and me. They said if I betrayed your raid party and served the dragons, they'd let me live despite my queensblood. But more than that, they promised to take me to my brehna. Connor"–

her voice trembled—"all three of them said Keir is still alive."

With a little urging, Connor convinced her to share this news with the guardians, as well as her desire to join the Order. Master Jairun asked for her patience while they sought the Rescuer's guidance, and Kara agreed. In the meantime, she'd stay at the academy.

Not long after, Connor's parents arrived from Stonyvale. Tehpa seemed to expect the news of Faelin's passing, and so his tears were few. And with Mehma there to keep the peace, he and Connor exchanged no harsh words. Connor saw Tehpa's frustrations with the Order in a new light now, and he saw how hard it must be for him to let his son join their ranks. With some prodding from Mehma, he promised he'd remember this epiphany the next time an argument between them boiled over.

On the night before the Forge, known as the Kindling, the whole company gathered in Salar Peroth for a supper of roast lamb. Afterward, they sipped brambleberry cider by the hall's great hearth, while the guardians and Pedrig told stories of Faelin's battles and victories.

"I'll not return to the fight without him," Pedrig said, muzzle resting on his paws. "It's time I retire." He raised his head and looked to Connor's parents, ears forward. "Perhaps I'll go to Stonyvale with you and spend my days on the Enarian farm. I could help with the sheep." As with the wolf in the painting, Connor couldn't tell if the curl of his lip was a snarl or a smile. The others laughed.

When the fire burned down, the merrymakers left in twos and threes, until only Connor, Tehpa, and Master Jairun remained. They doused the coals with the last of their cider and walked out among the thousand lanterns hanging from the battlements.

Tehpa had gifted Connor a leather-bound book of empty parchments with a quill and ink, a symbol of his blessing for Connor's future at the academy. Connor had a gift to give as well—or at least, something borrowed to return. He unshouldered a long cloth bundle tied with a leather strap.

Tehpa peeled back the cloth and turned the exposed blade to reflect the many lights. "Faelin's sword."

"The scabbard is gone. I'm sorry. I lost it in the cavern where we faced the river troll."

Tehpa made no reply, caught in some memory.

Connor cleared his throat and went on. "I named it *Revornosh*, meaning Truthsayer, because Patehpa used it to extinguish the dragon's lies. Now that he's gone, I thought it only right you should have it again."

"No, boy." Tehpa retied the cloth and returned the bundle. "You should keep it. If you insist on staying in the fight, I want you to have Revornosh at your side. I wish these battles were over for our family—for all Keledan. But I sense from your headmaster they are not."

Master Jairun nodded, leaning on his staff. "You sense rightly. Our long sleep, forsaking our commission, has brought us to a dangerous threshold. From what the cadets have told me, I believe the dragons are preparing for a greater offensive than one portal could enable. And we still don't know what allowed Vorax to steer it through the barrier in the first place."

"So, what are we to do?" Connor asked, slinging the wrapped sword across his back. "We have four guardians and five, perhaps six cadets. If an army comes through the barrier, we'll be overrun."

Master Jairun looked out over the lantern-lit battlements, and to Connor it seemed his gray eyes looked far past Mer Nimbar to the forests and plains beyond. "Lightraider Academy must grow, my boy, and grow quickly. And we must train the villages and towns for defense. Tomorrow Keledev celebrates the Forge. The day after, we'll begin the hard work of stirring them from their slumber. The Keledan must prepare for war."

ACKNOWLEDGMENTS

GLORY TO GOD! WITHOUT HIS HAND OF PROVIDENCE, this story would never have made it to such a wonderful publisher as Enclave. I am so grateful to Him for opening this door and to many of His servants for helping me pass through it. I may be the writer, but I'm part of a large team.

Steve Laube and Enclave are amazing. Steve's strong leadership and personal touch have made me feel like a part of the family. Also amazing is my agent Harvey Klinger, who helped me bring this project to them.

There would not be a Lightraider world without its creator, Dick Wulf. There will never be enough words to express my appreciation to him for passing the torch and trusting me to carry the ministry tools he developed forward to a new generation.

I am not alone in the development of this world. Stewards like Joe Revesz, Rich Sezov kept it alive, kept the vintage game boxes moving out into the world, and are still contributing their talents and creativity to the game. It was Joe who put me in touch with Dick and suggested the novels to me in the first place. And Rich (among many other things) gets credit for suggesting the Rescuer as an alternative to the original OverLord of Many Names. Also, Seth, Gavin, Ashton, James, Rachel, and Katie as my Lightraider team became the original testers for many of the places and concepts of the expanded world.

Pastor James R. Brown has been a blessing, contributing his

knowledge of the Word, his storytelling and game creation talents, and his voice of wisdom when it all seems too much to bear. He is an incredible creative sounding board. Likewise, our Lightraider communications director John Carroll has been a creative advisor and a peace-giving shoulder to cry on.

Dr. Gary Huckabay is the original theological advisor on this project, and continues to advise on Lightraider games and adventures, most notably writing the real-world applications for our Scripture memory cards. Many of those applications informed my use of the same verses in this book. It is Dr. Huckabay who envisioned the decay of the dark creatures and the shadowed reaches of Tanelethar, noting that our Enemy cannot create and only corrupts.

Finally, I need to thank my wife Cindy, who encouraged me to write these stories and keeps me going day by day. You are my life and love.

AUTHOR'S NOTE

THE WEIGHT OF EXPANDING A BELOVED GAME WORLD into a series of novels is no small thing. I won't deny that I dreamed of taking the task on for years. I also won't deny that I didn't fully understand the responsibility until it finally happened.

One big thing I learned the moment I started is that growing the world from its game roots requires adaptability and change. I'll acknowledge some of the changes here, but I'll provide detail about them on our lightraider website listed below.

The bigger changes include: Lightraider Academy in place of DragonRaid, the nature and form of dark creatures, the Rescuer in place of the OverLord of Many Names, and shifting people and place names from English to an imaginary language.

I know there are many other questions, and you can look to the website for answers, but I want to take this short space to address two important and connected concepts: the allegory of the Lightraider world, and Sacred Verses (formerly WordRunes).

In any fiction, the line between allegory and the literal may shift and blur. Do the Keledan represent the Church? Yes, but don't take the allegory too far. If you seek a perfect allegorical match between every aspect of a fictional world and ours, you'll wind up writing non-fiction with changed names. Lightraider stories are meant to engage and teach, and strict allegory would destroy their ability to do so. One area where this is particularly noticeable are the sacred verses.

Scripture used in the Lightraider world has fictional (allegorical) effects that represent real-world applications, like bringing light to a character's path. However, if our game characters and novel heroes are to learn and grow, those real-world Scripture applications must also apply in the fictional world. Do you see the conundrum? So, again, don't get too bogged down in allegory.

Quoting Scripture directly in an imaginary realm with its own history presents another problem. It breaks down the immersive reader experience. In a game designed to teach Scripture memory and application, this is unavoidable. In a novel, we have the opportunity to work around it. This is why I developed the Elder Tongue. I didn't feel comfortable altering Scripture to suit the world and presenting inaccurate verses in English. The Rescuer is a representation of Christ, but he is not Christ. The Sacred Scrolls of Keledev are a representation of God's Word, but they are not the Word. Thus, sacred verses spoken in the Elder Tongue only *allude* to the real Word through the characters' summaries and partial translations. With this device, I'm also presenting you with a challenge. Try to recognize the real verses represented in the story, and look them up to see the true translation. Please read the verses around them as well to better understand the context and meaning.

As a final thought on allegory and Scripture in *Wolf Soldier*, I'd like to draw your attention to the cornerstone and three pillars of Lightraider stories. The cornerstone is the Word. The three pillars are presenting the Gospel, nurturing the fruit of the Spirit, and tempering the armor of God. I hope you noticed all four in this story. And that's about all the room I have for explanations. If you want to learn more, or if you're new to the Lightraider world and you want to know about our games and learning tools, I hope you'll visit us www.lightraiders.com.

ABOUT THE AUTHOR

AS A FORMER FIGHTER PILOT, STEALTH PILOT, AND tactical deception officer, James R. Hannibal is no stranger to secrets and adventure. He is the award-winning author of thrillers, mysteries, and fantasies for adults and children, and he is the developer of Lightraider Academy games. As a pastor's kid in Colorado Springs, he guinea-pigged every youth discipleship program of the 1980s, but the one that engaged him and shaped him most as a Christ-follower and Kingdom warrior was *DragonRaid*, by Dick Wulf—the genesis of the Lightraider world.